THE
House of
STONE
& IVY

A Regency Romance

THE
House of
STONE
& IVY

ANITA STANSFIELD

Covenant

Covenant Communications, Inc.

Published by Covenant Communications, Inc.
American Fork, Utah

Printed in the United States of America
First Printing: January 2019

25 24 23 22 21 20 19   10 9 8 7 6 5 4 3 2 1

ISBN 978-1-52440-856-5

Chapter One

THE FRIENDLY STRANGER

Lancashire, England —1808

HENRIETTA WOOD HURRIEDLY TIDIED THE tiny room in which she lived. Given that it could barely be classified as habitable, she felt an obsessive need to keep it as clean and orderly as possible, as if doing so might somehow compensate for the leaky ceiling, the cracked and peeling wallpaper, and the continual film of dust that came from a source she could not identify; cleaning the dust away every day helped her feel some measure of dignity despite her squalid surroundings.

Despite sleeping later than she should have, Hennie still felt tired; but then, she always felt tired. Using the small, hazy mirror in her room, she did the best she could to wind up her dark-blonde hair and pin it properly into place. She tied her bleached and starched apron around the waist of the drab, gray dress she was required to wear and hurried down the first flight of stairs from the floor that housed the employees of the inn, to the floor where every room was fine and lovely to accommodate traveling guests who paid good money to rent comfortable rooms. She rushed down the next flight of stairs to the ground floor, where meals and drinks were served to what seemed a never-ending crowd. The inn was a popular local gathering place for the villagers, as well as a reputable home away from home for travelers.

Hennie quickly got to work before Mr. Grenville—her employer and sole owner of the inn—had a chance to even notice that she had arrived a few minutes late. He was a strict timekeeper and had high expectations of his employees. The guests who ate, drank, and slept at his establishment respected him and were consistently treated kindly. Hennie only wished he might be half as kind to those who worked for him, those who made it possible for his inn to be so highly respected. But Grenville was well-known among his employees for his critical, demeaning comments and snide threats that he generally spoke quietly enough that they could never be overheard by the guests. But nearly two years of working for this brute with his dual personality had worn down Hennie's spirit in ways she could never measure. She could only do her best to focus on her gratitude for having employment, when work was not easy to find in the present climate, and she had no family or friends to rely on. She often wondered what it might be like to go home each day after work to people who loved her and cared about the difficulties of her life. To cope with the tedium of her work, Hennie often fantasized about telling a father or brother about how unfairly Mr. Grenville treated her, and how they might become so incensed they would threaten Grenville into behaving more appropriately. But such fantasies never lasted more than a few minutes before the reality of life surrounded her once again like a heavy fog. The serving of drinks and meals never ended. If she took even a few minutes to escape to the privy at the back of the inn, or to try and keep her stomach full by eating a little here and there, a minute at a time throughout the day, she would often be met with Grenville's critical glare or some quietly spoken threat about her need to stay on her toes and keep busy or she'd be out on the streets. Hennie had experienced life on the streets—sleeping in the open air, trying to stay warm, begging for food—and the very thought of it triggered deep alarm in every fiber of her body and spirit, so much so that she sometimes wondered what lengths she would go to just to survive—just to never have to face such unspeakable circumstances ever again.

Days eased into weeks, which merged into months. Summer turned to autumn, which inevitably ushered the cold of winter into the air. Hennie loved the beauty of falling snow when she could watch it through windows that protected her from the freezing temperatures. But she could never watch it fall without recalling the times she'd had no choice but to just try and stay warm enough to survive when she'd had no shelter to protect her from the cold. This fear kept her motivated to do everything required by her deplorable employer, even though she hated every minute.

Hennie's days were long, and she was given only half a day off in the week in which to take care of personal errands and launder her dirty clothes. Beyond that, the only time she had to herself was on Sundays when she attended church. She delighted in the respite of this favorite time of the week, but she always had to hurry back to the bustling inn, since Grenville himself had no respect for the Sabbath—even though every other business in the village was closed on Sundays. Grenville only considered this to be an advantage for him, since there were always people who wanted to eat and drink and rent rooms, and if other establishments were closed, all the better for him. Hennie understood that sometimes people had no choice but to travel on Sundays and they certainly *did* need rooms to sleep in and food to eat. She enjoyed serving and cleaning up after such travelers, feeling as if she were contributing to their genuine needs. What Hennie hated were the local men who came to the inn seven days a week to drink until their speech was slurred and they could barely stagger out when the inn finally closed for the night. Most of these men came here to avoid spending time with wives and children, and because of the way they spoke so disrespectfully of the women and children who were at home doing chores and tasks these men should have been doing, Hennie had no respect for them whatsoever. The worst part of having to serve them was the way they treated her. The more inebriated they became, the more they believed they had a right to inappropriately harass and persecute the women serving them. Hennie understood that many of the women who worked for Grenville actually enjoyed such unsavory attention, and some even encouraged it. Hennie had nothing in common with these women and generally avoided any interaction with them beyond the polite exchanges necessary for working together. But she often wondered if they *really* enjoyed having their bottoms slapped or pinched by drunk men, or if they'd just become so accustomed to it that they'd stopped caring. Hennie *hated* it! And every time it happened, she had to bite her tongue and swallow her temper, knowing that if one of the customers complained to Grenville about her being *uncooperative* in the way she served these despicable men their ongoing flow of liquor, she would be let go immediately without question. Hennie not only had to endure the straying hands of such men, but there was also the inevitability that the drunker they became, the more apt they were to speak crude vulgarities, most often aimed at the women serving their drinks. Each night after the inn was closed and Hennie's work was finally done, she'd return to her shabby little room and desperately wish that she could just soak in a hot bath to somehow cleanse away the disgusting speech and behavior she was exposed to daily. But a bath was a luxury she didn't have access to, and the best she could do was use the limited amount of soap and water available to sponge away the dirt and sweat of a long day. During her minimal time off once a week, she would wash her hair while she was laundering her clothes; that was the time she felt the cleanest and the most refreshed, until she inevitably had to return to work. Then she would feel contaminated all over again.

As winter finally began to recede and signs of spring were poking their way up out of the ground and bursting through the seemingly dead trees and shrubberies, Hennie felt especially depressed about the circumstances of her life. In the past, spring had represented relief from trying to survive the cold of winter, and subsequently she had found hope in the physical evidence of the world erupting with new life. But Hennie had no time to appreciate the beauty of spring, except during her quick walk to church and back on Sunday, and even then, she was always mindful of the time and felt the need to hurry. Instead of finding any joy whatsoever in the wonders of spring, Hennie's thoughts became preoccupied with the inevitable reality that each day would pass the same as the last, making up the months and seasons that would follow one after the other, with no hope of a better life.

Following a stretch of some fairly warm days, a deluge of cold rain poured down relentlessly. Despite having to strategically place a basin, two bowls, and a pot on the floor of her room to catch the water dripping from the ceiling, Hennie loved the rain—mostly because business was always slower at the inn. Such rain discouraged the horde of regular customers from venturing out of their homes to drink and socialize. Grenville hated the rain for that reason, but Hennie loved it. She enjoyed being able to work at a slower pace, without having demands thrown at her continually. And fewer drunk men meant fewer occasions of having to fend off their revolting remarks and gestures.

During a brief lull, Hennie was suddenly surprised to realize that for the time being there was absolutely nothing to be done. Every customer had been served and they all appeared content. The women she worked with appeared equally surprised, as they gathered in a little huddle to chatter and giggle, overtly excluding Hennie. But that was fine; Hennie had no desire to share the kind of social interaction that took place among such women. She was well aware that some of them had resorted to the most unseemly occupation of taking men up to their rooms. Grenville was nothing but pleased with such atrocities, since it brought more men to his inn who were seeking the opportunity to drink too much and engage in deplorable behaviors, most of them having wives and children at home. The entire matter sickened Hennie to the point that she had to force herself to avoid even thinking about what she observed, and that also meant avoiding any interaction with the rest of *Grenville's girls,* as he liked to call the women who worked for him.

Grenville appeared displeased with the way his *girls* were doing nothing productive, but it was evident he couldn't find anything to scold them about when every customer was clearly cared for and everything was tidy. Just then, the door swung open as a man entered, huddled beneath his coat and hat, seemingly shoved inside by a gust of wind, and bringing a hefty portion of rain in with him as it dripped off him into a puddle on the floor even after the door had closed behind him. Grenville didn't mind the water that would have to be cleaned up; he simply appeared delighted to have another customer. Hennie didn't wait for any of the other girls to volunteer to help the newcomer. She would far rather be busy than idle, forced to listen to their shallow and sometimes crude conversation.

"Let me help you," Hennie said to the new customer as she stepped forward and took his dripping hat while he eased out of his wet coat and she took that too, hanging both on nearby hooks that were well used on such nights.

"Thank you," the man said with a voice that was pitched a little high but had a slight gravelly texture.

"What can I do for you?" Hennie asked as the man pushed his hands through his damp, dark hair to get it out of his face. Clearly his hat had not done very well at keeping his head dry. "Something to drink? A meal? Are you in need of lodging for the night?"

"All of that," the man replied.

Hennie barely glanced at him as she motioned with her arm toward a nearby table. "Make yourself comfortable," Hennie said, and the man sat down with a sigh that implied relief at being someplace warm and dry after much exhaustion. He wasn't a local customer; therefore, she assumed he'd been traveling. His wanting a room supported that theory. As he was seated, Hennie noticed he was thin and not quite as tall as she was, which made him somewhat short for a man. His face seemed kind, but he mostly kept it turned away, which implied some degree of shyness.

"Thank you," the man said, and Hennie was glad to serve a customer who was kind and polite.

"We have shepherd's pie or venison stew tonight," Hennie said. "Which would you prefer?"

"The pie sounds grand," the man said while he avoided looking at her.

"And to drink?" Hennie asked.

"Ale is fine," the man said. "Something light to wash down my meal is all I need."

"Very good," Hennie said and hurried to the kitchen, refreshed by this traveler who had come in out of the rain. It only took her a couple of minutes to dish up a helping of shepherd's pie—which she knew from experience to be very delicious and a specialty of the inn—and to fill a tankard with ale. She set both on the table in front of her new customer, along with a fork. Steam rose off the food, which had been kept hot in one of the ovens, and the stranger leaned his somewhat frail-looking face into the warmth while he inhaled the aroma and smiled.

"Thank you," the man said and smiled, even though he still didn't look up.

"I'll arrange for a room so you can have some privacy and rest as soon as you're done eating."

"Thank you," the man said again and glanced toward Hennie for only a second. He looked vaguely familiar, but not enough for her to place him in her memory; he was probably someone who had passed through here before, but she'd likely been too busy to pay much attention.

"Glad to help," Hennie said and left the man to enjoy his meal. She spoke with Grenville about the customer wanting a room—which was the established procedure. Grenville went to the table where the man was eating to personally collect money for the room and the meal. Hennie hated her employer's constant attitude of greed and the way he didn't trust anyone except himself to handle the intake of money. But at the same time, she was glad to not have to ask the customers to pay; something in her simply didn't want to have to handle Grenville's money. Beyond the money he paid her each week for her wages, she had no interest in his obsession with keeping track of every penny that was owed to him.

Hennie kept an eye on the man eating his shepherd's pie as if it were something heavenly and miraculous. She also kept an eye on a couple of other customers who were her responsibility. But they were all content and undemanding, and she had the unusual sensation of feeling mildly bored. When the man had finished his meal, Hennie approached him and asked if he would like more or if she could interest him in some apple cobbler. He smiled shyly and declined anything more to eat, so she took the key to his room out of her pocket and handed it to him. "I can show you to your room, then," she said, motioning for him to follow her after she'd retrieved his coat and hat from the hooks near the door. "The innkeeper will have lit the fire by now, so hopefully you'll be able to warm up and feel comfortable."

"You're very kind," the man said as he followed Hennie up the stairs.

Hennie didn't reply, but she secretly savored his kind gratitude, and she wondered why such niceties were so rare in her life.

With the stairs and hallway lit by sconces hanging on the walls, Hennie led the way to the second door on the right and waited for him to turn the key in the lock while she followed the usual protocol and said, "I'll just make certain everything is in order and leave you to enjoy your privacy and get some rest."

"Thank you," the man said again as the door to the room opened to reveal a fire burning vibrantly; combined with the two lamps that had been lit, the room was warm and inviting. Hennie allowed herself only a moment of feeling some envy over being able to spend the night in such a room, in contrast to her dark and leaky room with a very tiny fireplace that was incapable of producing more than the barest minimum of heat.

Hennie hung up the man's coat and hat on a rack near the fireplace, saying, "These should be plenty dry by morning." She nodded toward the washstand.

"You'll find clean water and linens there." She turned to look at him and asked, "Is there anything else I can get for you?"

"I'm certain I have everything I need, except . . ." He hesitated, seeming nervous, which prompted Hennie to feel the same. This man had been kind and respectful, but she was standing in a room with a bed, and he was standing between her and the door. Did he expect something more from her, something that she would never willingly give? It was far from the first time she'd felt a momentary panic in such a situation, and she'd always managed to get out of the room—but there were many instances when that hadn't necessarily been easy.

"Except?" she asked when he hesitated, while she moved toward the door, glad to be able to easily move past this man who turned to keep looking at her as she stood in the doorway.

"I need to talk to you," the man said in a whisper.

His nervousness increased, and Hennie instinctively felt safe with this man. She whispered in return as she asked, "Are you in some kind of trouble? Do you need—"

"No," he said emphatically, and his shyness was no longer evident. "Hennie," he added, and she took in a sharp breath to hear him use her name. How could he possibly know her name? "It's me, Hennie," he whispered even more emphatically, with a complete absence of that gravelly quality in his voice. "It's Lottie."

Hennie took another sharp breath while she squinted and looked more closely at this man, certain her eyes were deceiving her—or that she'd surely heard him wrong. This made no sense whatsoever; she simply couldn't connect in her mind what she was seeing and hearing and have it make any sense.

"I know it's strange, Hennie. But look at me. It's Lottie. I cut off my hair. I'm pretending to be a man. But it's me. Just look at my face . . . listen to my voice . . . and you'll know it's me."

It took Hennie another minute to do as she'd been told and allow the information to settle. And then she knew. She knew beyond any doubt that this was the best and truest friend she'd ever had in her whole life. She was so thrilled to see her that she temporarily banished every possible question over why her friend was in disguise—and how she had managed to find Hennie after nearly two years of separation.

"Oh, Lottie!" Hennie muttered on a quivering exhale as she threw her arms around her friend and absorbed the tight, familiar embrace that Lottie returned. Oh, she'd missed this woman so much!

Once she'd embraced Lottie long enough to be convinced that this was real, and to breathe in some tiny degree of the friendship she'd been starved of for so long, Hennie stepped back and took Lottie's shoulders in her hands, looking her up and down while she attempted to accept what she was seeing. "What on earth are you—"

"It will take some time to explain," Lottie said quietly, reminding Hennie that the door was open, and she would indeed be expected to appear back downstairs right away. "I know you have work to do. Come back here when your work is finished; make certain no one sees you. Then we'll talk, and I'll tell you everything."

"Hopefully I can be done early," Hennie said, glad that it was a slow night. She could barely restrain her curiosity over this strange situation—but even more, she desperately wanted to just be with her friend every possible minute.

Hennie forced herself away from Lottie's comfortable friendship—even if her appearance right now was completely foreign. She hurried downstairs and made herself busy cleaning up after guests who had finished their meal and left. The other girls were still chattering, but Hennie was glad to have been the first to accomplish the necessary task. Perhaps Grenville would notice her zeal in attending to the work more promptly than the others and let her leave a little earlier after he closed the inn for the night and the mandatory cleaning was completed in preparation for the following day.

With that in mind, Hennie began cleaning tables and chairs that were not currently in use—even those that had already been cleaned once they'd been vacated. Keeping busy made it easier to not appear anxious and tense while her mind ran wild with the knowledge that her only true friend was upstairs this very moment, and she couldn't begin to imagine what circumstances Lottie might have found herself in that would have necessitated her pretending to be a man. It seemed a miracle that business at the inn had been slow when Lottie had arrived, and that Hennie had been the one to help her. She felt certain that Lottie would have found a way to alert Hennie to her presence at the inn either way, but as it was, Hennie had been the one to take Lottie to her room, and nothing at all would appear suspicious to Grenville—who was suspicious about everything.

When closing time came and Grenville had gotten the last reluctant customers out the door, locking it securely afterward, Hennie felt pleased to hear him scold the other girls for sitting around and cackling—as he put it—most of the evening. He offered a rare expression of appreciation to Hennie for her hard work, which had left most of the necessary cleaning for the night already done. Miraculously, he told her that she was welcome to go ahead and leave and the others could finish up.

"Thank you," Hennie said and got nothing in return but a nod, although she knew Grenville well enough to know that a gracious nod was about the best she could ever expect from him. She accepted it with a grateful heart and went up the stairs, but instead of going up the next flight of stairs to her cold and leaky room, Hennie made certain the hallway was empty and no one was coming up the stairs behind her before she knocked quietly on the door to Lottie's room. It came open so fast that Hennie knew Lottie had been waiting anxiously for Hennie's return. In the time it took for Lottie to open the door wide enough for Hennie to come in, and then close it again, Hennie could see that Lottie was wearing a man's nightshirt, stockings, and a terribly old and worn dressing gown for warmth. Hennie had to take in Lottie's appearance all over again, with her dark hair cut short in a masculine style. But it was still her dear Lottie, and they embraced once more, needing no words to express how glad they were to be together again.

"How long has it been?" Hennie asked, easing away and sitting down in one of the two comfortable chairs near the fire. The question seemed pointless when she knew the answer; she'd counted the months in her head over and over. But perhaps she needed Lottie to verify that her perception was accurate. Their separation had felt like it had been much, much longer.

"Forever," Lottie chuckled, sitting in the other chair and curling her feet up beneath her in a way that was completely feminine. Here, out of the public eye, she moved and behaved like the same old Lottie, which made Hennie realize how carefully Lottie had taken on the mannerisms and conduct of a man while she had been in public. More seriously she added, "Two years next month. That's the last time we saw each other. You needed to leave that wretched place, and I believed that I needed to stay."

"So that Toby could find you," Hennie stated, recalling the anguish of their good-byes, and her concerns for Lottie at the time, knowing that she'd fallen in love with a man who was in reality a rogue and a cad. But Lottie had been unable to see anything except her love for him, and Hennie had been unable to convince her friend to leave with her. Those concerns came back to Hennie as she asked a question that—however obvious the answer might be—needed to be asked. "And did he?"

"Clearly he didn't," Lottie said with a matter-of-factness that made it evident she had put Toby behind her; Hennie was glad for that. "It didn't take long for me to realize he *wasn't* coming back, and then I heard rumors of his dalliance with another woman. So I packed up and left, wishing I had gone with you."

"But you knew where I would be," Hennie said, unable to avoid a literal shudder that started at her neck and moved all the way down to her toes as she allowed herself to recall for just a moment the deplorable place where she and Lottie had endured years of something akin to slavery. Hennie had been barely eleven years old when her mother's death and the absence of any other relatives had landed her in an orphanage that was cold and bleak and horrible in every way. Lottie was ten at the time and had been at the orphanage for nearly as long as she could remember; she had only some vague memories of another life. The place had been little more than a mausoleum for the living that barely kept children alive—except when it didn't. Lottie had lost more than one of her orphanage friends due to unknown illnesses before Hennie had arrived, and by some miraculous means, Lottie had been put in charge of the newcomer, which meant their beds were next to each other. And since the beds were placed very close together to fit as many as possible into the rooms, they were able to reach across the narrow gap and hold hands when they felt alone or afraid. They'd quickly taken on the habit of falling asleep holding hands, and they were always glad to not be alone when one or the other of them woke up from a bad dream or felt the need to cry in the darkness, missing their deceased loved ones, and experiencing all the fears related to being sentenced to live in such dreadful conditions.

It had been standard procedure for every orphan to move on to a workhouse once they reached a certain age. Since Hennie was a little older than Lottie, she was set to be moved, knowing that Lottie would be left behind. But Lottie had gone to the headmaster and begged to not be separated from Hennie, promising to work hard and always be good if they could only be kept together. The old miser had taken mercy upon Lottie's pleading, and the two of them were moved to the workhouse together and were once again given beds next to each other. Being able to converse in whispers through the darkness and occasionally reach out to just hold each other's hands was likely the only thing that kept them sane in a place where they endured a whole new kind of horror. All they could do was work, eat, and sleep—although the food was despicable and the opportunity for sleep was never sufficient. But they had each other, and they always fell asleep holding hands. Their friendship had saved their lives; they both knew it. They'd talked about it hundreds of times. And they'd often whispered in the dark of their plans to break away from that horrible place when they were old enough, and they'd promised each other they would never allow themselves to fall into any kind of unsavory means to support themselves, since they were well aware of many other young women who had left the workhouse out of desperation, only to end up living on the streets or selling themselves to merely survive. Both Lottie and Hennie felt a deep compassion for such desperation, but they were determined to find a better way. They prayed together every night and genuinely believed God would guide them to a better life if they each did their best to work hard and never compromise their belief that their value in God's eyes surely had to be far more than the slave labor they were enduring simply to remain alive, if only barely. Most of the people in the workhouse eventually descended into a condition where their eyes became hollow and empty, as if their spirits no longer resided within their bodies; they'd lost all hope and had no vision of any possibility of a better life. Hennie and Lottie both believed they had helped each other hold on to the fragile hope that so many others had lost.

Hennie and Lottie were grateful to at least be able to work side by side, and as a way of keeping themselves distracted from the long, tedious hours of work and the horrible conditions in which they lived, they filled their time with conversation that focused on dreams for the future—dreams that were sometimes fantastical and even ridiculous. But imagining themselves as countesses or ladies-in-waiting helped them laugh and reach mentally beyond the prison in which they existed. They agreed at a fairly young age—from their limited exposure to people they encountered on their opportunities to leave the workhouse for their brief allotted weekly break—that one of the things greatly dividing the classes was their manner of speech. Therefore, they both paid close attention to the way people spoke, and every day, they practiced speaking to each other in a more refined way than those with whom they lived and worked. Not wanting to bring attention to their efforts, knowing it might even bring ridicule down upon them, they were careful to only speak that way to each other. But with the passing years, they were able to speak naturally in a more refined manner that gave the illusion they were more educated than they actually were.

Despite the horrors of the workhouse, Hennie and her precious friend had agreed they would hold on and not leave too soon, before they were capable of finding employment elsewhere. Once Hennie turned eighteen, she began talking with Lottie about their plan for leaving. They'd been blessed with an amiable kinship with one of the workhouse employees who was helping them—through brief snippets of conversation—to be more prepared to face the world outside. This woman had told them of an inn located in a village that was about a day's walk from the workhouse, and she knew the owner, and he had agreed to hire Hennie and Lottie as long as they "could clean themselves up and not bring any of that workhouse filth with them." That had been Hennie's first exposure to Grenville's attitude, although she couldn't really blame him. No customer at an inn would want to be served by employees who carried with them any tiny bit of evidence of the lack of hygiene and cleanliness of a workhouse—which was the very reason many people were never able to leave the workhouse and find better employment. But thanks to the miracle of this friend from the outside world, she had arranged for Lottie and Hennie to spend a few nights at her home, where she would help them get cleaned up. And she had already acquired suitable clothing for them that would suffice until they could start acquiring wages. In return for this clothing, Hennie and Lottie would spend those few days doing some work for this kind woman—some extra cleaning and repairs in her tiny home that she'd been unable to do herself, given a worsening arthritic condition. Hennie considered the arrangement nothing less than a miracle, and she thanked God every day for the hope she had of finding a way out of the workhouse.

Lottie's romance with Toby—another resident of the workhouse—began to complicate the situation. When Toby left suddenly, promising that he would come back for Lottie, Hennie had felt deeply concerned that Lottie had been led to believe in something that was hollow and meaningless and would only end up hurting her. For the sake of their friendship, Hennie had been willing to delay her plan to leave the workhouse, but she wondered how long Lottie would want to remain there and keep waiting, while every day felt to Hennie as if she were living in hell and the devil himself were holding them captive.

The situation worsened when one of the overseers took an overt—and completely inappropriate—interest in Hennie. When it became evident his advances were growing more and more impossible to avoid, Hennie knew that if she didn't leave, the worst would happen. She knew it had happened to other women in the workhouse, and the very idea made her feel literally sick if she allowed herself to think about it too long. Lottie had insisted that Hennie needed to leave and carry through with the established plan. Lottie knew where she could find Hennie, and as soon as Toby came back for her, they too would follow through with the same plan.

It will probably only be a few weeks, Lottie had insisted as she'd practically shoved Hennie out the door in the middle of the night. *You need to go! You're not safe here! Go!*

Hennie had run as fast and far as she could until she had collapsed on the ground and sobbed, heaving painfully. This had not been the plan; they should have been together. Being without Lottie had felt like having one of her limbs amputated. But the cold night air quickly brought Hennie to her senses, and she followed the directions she'd memorized to find the home of this friend who was willing to help her. She was deeply grateful to be received there with kindness, and to be given a warm place to sleep, even though that was only a blanket on a wood floor in front of the fireplace. It was all this woman had to offer, but it came from her heart, and Hennie was not one to overlook the power of such blessings and miracles. She'd fallen asleep praying for Lottie, and during the following days as she went through the process of shaking the workhouse off of herself, she prayed silently for Lottie every time she thought of her—which was practically all the time.

Less than a week after leaving the workhouse, Hennie had acquired work at the inn, and she'd settled into the tiny room with the leaky roof. But the situation was far better than anything she'd experienced since her mother's death, and she was grateful. Even though the work was far from ideal and she felt very much alone, she knew how much worse her circumstances could be. The most difficult aspect of her situation was Lottie's absence, and simply not knowing what had happened to her after weeks had passed—and then months. Hennie had written a letter to the woman who had helped her, and weeks later she finally received a letter from the landlord of this woman's tiny home, informing Hennie that the woman had died. Hennie not only felt sorrow over the death of one of the only people who had ever shown her any kindness at all since she'd lost her mother, but she felt deeply concerned for Lottie, knowing that their friend's death meant there was no plan in place to help Lottie escape the fate of the workhouse. Still, she held on to the hope that Lottie knew where to find her, and if Lottie could only get here, Hennie would help her clean away all evidence of the workhouse so that she would be fit for suitable employment. But Lottie didn't come.

Using a false name, Hennie wrote to the workhouse inquiring as to Lottie's welfare. In reply she received a terse notice that the woman called Lottie had left the workhouse months earlier. In the time since, Hennie had worried day and night about her friend, wondering what awful fate might have befallen her that had kept her from coming to this place where they were supposed to be working together. She had finally concluded that Lottie was probably dead. She didn't know if that was truly the only logical explanation for her absence, or if it was the only way Hennie could move forward with her life and not lose her mind.

Now a miracle had happened, and her precious Lottie had come back to her—but under circumstances that were entirely bizarre. Hennie wanted to hear every detail of what had happened in her friend's life since they'd last seen each other—most especially her reasons for living in disguise. But most of all, Hennie just wanted to bask in the pleasure of Lottie's presence and savor the deep relief she felt in simply knowing her friend was alive and well. Just being in the same room with her offered more hope and joy than Hennie had felt since the day she'd lost her mother and it had soon become evident that she was thereafter destined for misery.

Chapter Two

SEEKING EMPLOYMENT

"TELL ME EVERYTHING," HENNIE SAID to Lottie as she stood up to scoot her chair closer so she could hold her friend's hand, a sensation familiar and deeply comforting. "I need to know. I've wondered and worried myself sick."

"I'm sorry about that," Lottie said. "Everything just worked out so strangely . . . as you can see." She motioned toward her short-cropped hair and laughed softly, but there was something dark in Lottie's eyes that let Hennie know she had endured something horrible during the time they'd been separated—even more horrible than the unspeakable conditions of the orphanage and the workhouse. "When I finally realized that Toby was *not* coming back, I wanted nothing more than to find you as quickly as possible and tell you that you'd been right, and that I should have left with you. But my timing was terrible." She chuckled, but Hennie could tell it was more an effort to cover deep discomfort than an expression of any kind of humor. "Our friend had died, so . . ."

When she hesitated, Hennie said, "I wrote to her and received a reply from her landlord, so I knew she had died—which made me worry all the more about you."

"Well . . . yes . . . she had died . . . which meant I'd already left the workhouse and I had nowhere to go. I slept on the ground near her house that first night; thankfully it was summer. The next morning, I just started walking; I was hungry and thirsty, and I had no sense of direction. It turns out that I'd been walking in the *opposite* direction of where you were, and after a long time, I ended up in a completely different village, looking far more horrible than when I'd left the workhouse. Despite repeated attempts to find work, it became obvious that no one wanted to hire me or help me, and . . ." Lottie looked down, then turned her face away and Hennie heard her sniffle.

"What happened, Lottie?" Hennie whispered with compassion. "You can tell me anything." As Hennie made the offer, it occurred to her that what her friend needed to share might be the very thing Hennie had most feared would happen. It took only a minute for Lottie to prove her right.

"I was so desperate," Lottie cried, wiping a sleeve over her face while she continued to look away. "I was starving . . . and tired . . . and . . . I broke my promise to you, Hennie—and my promise to God. I did what we vowed we would never do."

With her confession spoken, Lottie dissolved into sobbing, turning to bury her face against Hennie's shoulder while she wept uncontrollably. Hennie wept with her, knowing within herself that Lottie's fate could have easily been her own. It had only been a difference in timing and the kindness of a friend that had made it possible for Hennie to escape Lottie's desperation. Hennie knew what many people did not: the hopelessness and despair that could drive a human being to do whatever it took just to stay alive. She felt no judgment or disgust toward Lottie; in truth, she felt quite the opposite. A warmth came over Hennie as she held her friend close and shared her grief. When Lottie had exhausted her tears, it was easy for Hennie to say, "I'm so terribly sorry you had to go through that, my dear sweet friend. But I completely understand the reasons; you would have died of starvation out on the streets. Your desperation is understandable. And I know, Lottie," Hennie shifted in her chair so she could look her friend in the eye, "I don't know how I know, but deep inside I know that God understands too. He will forgive you if He hasn't already. Obviously, you've found a way to move beyond that, and—"

"Oh, I have!" Lottie insisted fervidly. "The very day I acquired some decent clothes and enough money to get away from that dreadful place, I did. I'd heard of work being available at a great manor house only an hour's walk from town, so I went there looking my very best with the hope of finding employment."

"And did you?" Hennie asked, filled with excitement over the very idea. She knew that in many cases, working in such a place provided much better security than jobs such as Hennie's current employment.

"Eventually," Lottie said, and Hennie recalled that her friend was disguised as a man. She'd quickly become accustomed to Lottie's new appearance and had almost forgotten about it. "It turned out they weren't in need of any female employees. All of the positions for maids and kitchen or laundry work were filled. However, they were looking for help in the stables—but such jobs were only given to men. It was actually the assistant to the housekeeper I spoke to—a Miss Atkins—who came up with the idea for me to return in disguise and speak to the stable master, once I had assured her that I could handle the work. After what I've been through, I could do almost *anything.*" Lottie sighed. "It was a blessing indeed that no one else had actually seen me that day. Most of the servants had gone on a picnic since the family they cared for were away for a few days, and Miss Atkins had chosen to stay in. Lucky for me she did. So . . ." Lottie drew in a deep breath that implied she was coming to the dramatic conclusion of her bizarre story. "So, I went back to the village to a secondhand shop and discreetly acquired some men's clothes that were just a little too large, which helps disguise that I'm not shaped like a man. I cut my hair, figured out a way to wrap my chest to flatten it, and I went back to speak to the stable master, praying very hard that my efforts would prove fruitful—and they did. Mr. Parsons is a fair man. I've managed to fit in fairly well, all things considered. I mostly wash the horses and brush them to keep them healthy and looking beautiful; they are remarkable creatures." Lottie smiled and let out a dreamy sigh, which was the first sign of real happiness Hennie might have ever seen from her friend. "I love caring for them. Sometimes they need to be led around the stable yard for exercise. At first, I was nervous about that, since I'd lied about actually having experience with horses. But I quickly figured things out. Every one of the horses there is well-trained and quite magnificent. The worst part of my job is having to muck out the stalls in the stable, but it's not so bad—compared to the work we had to do in the past." Lottie took hold of Hennie's hands and her eyes sparkled as she added, "And here's the best part: I don't have to work every waking minute. I have a daily shift of about ten hours, and an entire day off every week to take care of my personal matters. I'm given my own room in the servants' quarters, so I have complete privacy, and the servants eat in the kitchen at the big house—delicious and plentiful meals unlike anything I've ever had. I'm given time to attend church on Sundays, even though I must do some work before and after because the animals still need to be cared for. But . . . oh, Hennie! I never imagined such luxury and security as part of making a living for myself. Beyond being given everything I need to live, I'm also earning a fair wage so that I can purchase clothes and other things for myself. I've even been able to buy some books! Can you imagine? I actually *own* books!"

"It almost sounds too good to be true," Hennie said, hating the way she felt skeptical; but then, life had taught her a great deal of skepticism. Some questions came to mind, the most prominent being, "But . . . if you're pretending to be a man, how do you manage with all the matters of being a woman? What about your monthlies and—"

"I've been able to figure out all of that, and as I said, I'm given my own room. It's very small but warm and dry. And Miss Atkins—who is the only one there who knows the truth—has become a friend, and she helps me when I need it."

Hennie took all of this in through a stretch of contemplative silence, until Lottie interrupted her thoughts by saying, "I've come to take you back with me, Hennie. Mr. Parsons needs more help, and I told him I had a friend that I knew to be a good worker. He let me use a horse and gave me a few days to come and get you." Lottie added proudly, "He said if my friend was as hard a worker as I've proven to be, allowing me the time off would be more than worth it. So here I am."

Hennie let that sink in, then gasped. "You're saying . . . you want *me* to do what *you* have done? To disguise myself as man? To live as a man?"

"Yes, Hennie—so that you can get away from this dreadful place! I know it's a far cry above what you've had to endure in the past, but don't think I didn't notice the way the innkeeper is watching your every move, and you can't tell me that the majority of those women working for him aren't doing a great deal more than serving in the dining room. How long do you think it might be until he expects the same of you?"

Lottie's question cut Hennie to the core. It was a reality she had chosen to ignore because she didn't want to think about it. But she'd seen the evidence of how Grenville seemed to expect that after a woman had been in his employment long enough to become completely dependent upon him, he began raising his expectations of their services. Hennie had secretly been prepared to just run away from here if he put such demands on her. But she'd been terrified about setting out on her own all over again. And the reality was that her wages weren't enough to make it possible to put money away. Grenville provided her a cold, leaky room in which to sleep and three meals a day, but her actual wages were pathetic. She knew it and she hated it, but she'd felt stuck—once again—and not certain what to do. She also knew that a part of her had been afraid to leave here, because she'd known that if Lottie was still alive, this was the only place where she would have known how to find her. And now Lottie *had* found her; she was here and safe—even happy—but what she was proposing seemed preposterous and even frightening.

"What if you get caught at this?" Hennie asked. "Would they not see this as dishonesty? As misrepresenting yourself? If I do the same thing, would I not be at risk for the same?"

"It's been going smoothly for more than a year, Hennie. There's no reason to think we would *ever* get caught."

"So . . . you intend to . . . what? Live out the rest of your life pretending to be a man?"

"If it gives me a good life, yes," Lottie said.

Hennie stood up and began to pace, as if that might allow her to think more clearly. "I don't know if I could do it, Lottie. Perhaps I'm not as good an actor as you are. Maybe I—"

"Listen to me." Lottie stood as well and stopped Hennie's pacing by taking hold of both her hands. "Do you want to stay here in this situation, or do you want a better life and more security? Wouldn't you like to work in a place that's safe? Where you don't constantly feel some kind of threat hanging over you?"

"I would!" Hennie declared. "But what about the threat of being discovered?"

"We won't be! I promise! But even if we *were* found out, I sincerely believe there's a chance that our hard work would have proven itself and they would let us stay on anyway. The worst possibility is that we would be let go, but we would have enough wages saved up to be able to go elsewhere and find other work. I already have more money saved than I ever imagined having. And we need to be together, Hennie. I've missed you so very much! And I hope you've missed me."

"Oh, I have!" Hennie insisted. "I've missed you terribly! You know we're closer than most sisters; we have been since the day we met."

"Then come back with me!" Lottie pleaded.

Hennie felt a little weak at the overwhelming nature of Lottie's idea. She moved back to her chair and tried to breathe normally. Lottie sat as well, remaining quiet as if she knew Hennie needed time to consider all that Lottie had proposed.

A troubling question occurred to Hennie and she looked up at her friend. "Why did you not contact me before now? You knew where I was!" She couldn't help sounding mildly angry, a result of so much time passing while she'd worried and wondered and endured so much loneliness. "Could you not have written? Something? Anything to let me know you were alive and well?"

Lottie hung her head, and Hennie heard her sniffle. "I wish I had a good answer to that question, Hennie. I knew you would ask, and I've dreaded having to try and explain." She looked up with tears trickling down her face. "The only thing I can say is that . . . I felt ashamed. For a very long time, I just felt like . . . what I'd resorted to in order to survive would make you so disappointed in me. There were times when I thought that I should have chosen death over such a choice. If I'd done that, my place with God would have been more sure, and I never would have had to face you with the truth . . . that I'd broken my promise to you, and to God."

"Oh, Lottie," Hennie said, leaning forward to take her hand, "God surely understands, and so do I. How could you not have known that?"

"I *do* know it," Lottie said. "At least I do now; it just took me some time. I think that when I was finally able to gain some self-respect and dignity by doing respectable work for an honest wage, I could look back and recognize how desperate I truly had been, and that my situation had not been of my own making. Despite having made some less-than-ideal choices—specifically, believing that a man would keep his promises to me when he was in fact a ruthless cad—I had always tried to do the right thing." Lottie sighed deeply and wiped her face with her sleeve. "It's taken some time for me to sort everything out and come to terms with it, but I'm doing better. I've started so many letters to you but just couldn't bring myself to finish them; and the more time that passed, the guiltier I felt for not having contacted you sooner. I'm so sorry for that, Hennie. So very sorry. I hope you can forgive me. When Mr. Parsons said he needed more good help, I heard myself telling him I had a friend before I even realized what I was doing. It felt as if God had pushed me past my own silly reasons for holding back . . . so, here I am."

Following a tense minute of silence while Hennie again tried to take all of this in, it was easy for her to say, "Of course I forgive you. It's going to take some time for me to get used to all of this, but . . . I understand, Lottie; really, I do. And I'm so glad to know you've found a life for yourself that's giving you some satisfaction—that you're safe and well. But . . ."

"But?" Lottie leaned toward Hennie. "Please don't tell me you're going to stay here in this wretched place, Hennie, not when there is an opportunity so much better than this. We don't have to stay there indefinitely. Even a year or two, perhaps, and then we could move on, find a place where we can reclaim ourselves as women—respectable women—and acquire even better employment. Please don't say no, Hennie. Now that we're together again, how could I ever leave here without you? How could I ever go about my daily business wondering if you're all right? Please don't say no."

"I need to think about it," Hennie said, unable to dismiss the obvious list of good reasons Lottie had given her for why this would be a beneficial choice for her—at least in taking the next step, a step that would get her away from Grenville and her leaky room in the attic.

"Yes, you need to think about it," Lottie said. "I'm certain everything I've told you is overwhelming, and what I'm asking of you is the same. Sleep on it, and we'll talk in the morning."

Hennie nodded, and they shared as tight a hug as possible while they both remained sitting. They held hands and talked of many things that had taken place during their time apart, until they both became too sleepy to even think clearly.

Hennie considered it a luxury to not have to go up the stairs to her cold, wet room that night. No one would notice or care that she didn't. Instead she spent the night in the warm, comfortable bed in the room Lottie had rented for the night. Its size felt enormous compared to the tiny beds they had shared in the orphanage and the workhouse, but they still fell asleep holding hands as they'd done literally thousands of times through the years they'd shared. Hennie felt luxuriously comfortable and deeply comforted by the friendship that had come back to her. She fell asleep silently praying and considering the finer details of what Lottie was asking her to do. She could never explain why she knew that heeding Lottie's advice was the right thing to do, but she *did* know; she *absolutely* knew. In her mind—and with a close examination of her feelings—Hennie considered the difference of making a decision based on fear and desperation, in contrast to feeling peaceful and confident according the practicality of Lottie's proposal. And she knew that her heart and mind were in the right place. By the time Lottie was fully awake, Hennie was ready to tell her she would be leaving this place with her friend today, and she was ready to test the idea of living her life as a man. In her mind she tallied all the evidence throughout her lifetime of how men always seemed to have an advantage over women. And while she had no intention of allowing this deception to go on any longer than necessary, she felt a distinct curiosity to engage in what seemed an experiment of life, and to see how it might play out.

Lottie was beyond thrilled that Hennie agreed with her plan, and that they would leave the inn together. Hennie sneaked out of Lottie's room, making certain she wasn't seen. By the time she ate her usual breakfast with a few of the other girls, she had packed up what little she owned. Before the inn was open to any customers, Hennie summoned all her courage and told Grenville she was leaving and she needed the wages she had earned that he'd not yet paid her. He scowled and grumbled and told her she was a fool to leave such marvelous employment, but he gave her the measly amount of money he owed her, and Hennie walked out of the inn for the last time.

According to the plan she and Lottie had devised, Lottie—in her male persona—would eat breakfast at the inn before she left to meet Hennie at a *different* inn on the other end of town. There they would undertake to transform Hennie into a man by all outward appearances. Lottie had brought with her everything they would need. Now all Hennie needed was to hold on to her courage and try and come up with some sense of adventure. Lottie had always been far more adventurous in nature, but Hennie felt confident that following her friend's example was the right thing to do. She could only pray that her instincts were not pulling her in the wrong direction.

Hennie looked at herself in the barely sufficient mirror that Lottie had to tip upward then downward in order for Hennie to see her entire reflection, but even then, the glass was aging and what she saw was distorted, which made it even more difficult to accept that she was actually looking at herself. On her feet were dark boots, a style typically worn by the men who worked with horses—according to Lottie. Lottie had found all the clothes at a secondhand store, knowing the two women were nearly the same size, except that Hennie was just a little taller and her feet were slightly bigger. Hennie could get her feet into Lottie's shoes, but they were tight, so Lottie knew that if she tried on boots and they felt a little too big, they would be just right for Hennie. And they were. Hennie also wore dark breeches that were just a little too large for her, as was the dingy white shirt. Dark braces went over her shoulders to hold up the breeches, and the overall effect certainly did well at hiding her feminine curves, especially since she'd wrapped a scarf tightly around her chest beneath the shirt to help disguise the fact that she was a woman. Thankfully, being much smaller than the average woman in that regard made the concealment easier, and the constricting sensation of the tight scarf didn't feel terribly uncomfortable. She felt certain she would grow accustomed to it without too much trouble. She didn't feel as confident about becoming accustomed to the change that had been necessary for her hair. Hennie's hair was long and thick, and she'd always found it a soothing ritual to brush it through at night and weave it into a long braid, which she would be able to hurriedly twist up and pin into place in the mornings so that she could appear presentable for work. Looking at how short Lottie's hair now was—barely touching the top of her collar where it hung down the back of her neck—Hennie recalled how long it had once been. Hennie's hair felt like a part of her identity, something that was hers and only hers in a world where she'd never had anything of value to call her own. Lottie had been compassionate regarding her hesitation and suggested a compromise.

"Plaits have mostly gone out of style," Lottie had said, holding the scissors in front of Hennie's face, "but there are still men who wear them; one of the men I work with in the stables as plaited hair. We don't have to cut yours as short as mine. I've got something you can use to tie your hair back; you'll still be able to look like a man, and not have to cut it all off."

Hennie agreed with her logic but had to close her eyes when Lottie began cutting. Now, with her shorter hair tied back in a way she'd seen many men wear their hair, Hennie looked at her reflection and tried to see herself as a man. Were her features not still feminine? Thinking back now to serving Lottie dinner the previous evening when she'd not known her identity, she couldn't deny that she'd assessed this *man* as being short and skinny, and having facial features that were somewhat soft. But some men were like that. Not all men were tall and strapping and brimming over with masculinity. Lottie had pulled this off for quite some time now; surely Hennie could follow her example and do the same. But it would certainly take some getting used to.

Lottie went down to the dining room of the inn where they would be staying that night and came back with some lunch for both of them. While they ate, Lottie talked about all she'd learned while studying the way men generally behaved, so she could fit in more comfortably. After they'd eaten, Lottie showed Hennie how to walk differently, sit differently, and even how to just stand differently. She couldn't deny that Lottie was somewhat of a genius for having figured all of this out. Hennie had never paid any attention to such things, but Lottie had become brilliantly skilled at ascertaining the differences in how men and women behaved and presented themselves, and even how they generally thought and perceived any given situation. Lottie told her that any interaction with other people required her to converse as a man would converse. They were like stage actors playing a very serious role, and unless they were in the privacy of their own rooms where they were certain no one would see or overhear them, they *always* had to behave like men in every respect.

Throughout the remainder of the day—sharing supper in their room as well—Lottie had Hennie practice many things over and over. Hennie knew that Lottie was feeling frustrated with the way that Hennie was not picking up all this as easily as Lottie had, but her friend was patient and kind, and before they went to bed, Lottie declared, "You're going to do just fine. I think it's best if you come across as shy, so you don't talk much at all. I'll tell the others we work with that you have to get to know people before you open up, which will give you some time to get more used to all this."

"I think I can do that," Hennie said, liking the idea but still feeling nervous. However, as she settled into bed for the night, the reality of no longer having to live under Grenville's watchful eye—and his leaky roof—warmed her with a sense of freedom she had rarely, if ever, felt in her life. If living life as a man would give her that, then she was all for it. Surely, she could do this!

Hennie slept well despite her nervous excitement about embarking on a new life. Once again Lottie went downstairs to get their meal, since they didn't want anyone to notice she'd arrived at the inn the previous day with a woman, and she was now sharing meals in the dining room with what appeared to be a man. Even though they would be traveling some distance from here to the place of their employment, they didn't want to tempt any suspicion toward them in any way.

After sharing a hearty meal, which Hennie had to force herself to finish—her appetite being diminished by nervousness—Hennie carefully packed the spare set of clothing Lottie had gotten for her into a traveling bag, which Hennie had also acquired, similar to the one she carried for herself. Beyond a hairbrush, which she packed, Hennie found nothing in her personal belongings worth taking along. Everything else was burned in the fireplace, including all her women's clothes—since she would want people here at the inn to believe she'd taken her belongings with her. And she also burned the hair Lottie had cut off so that no sign of Hennie's transformation was left behind.

After one final, lengthy gaze in the mirror at her new self, Hennie donned a man's coat and hat, and put the strap of her traveling bag over her head so that the strap went diagonally across her body and the bag hung over her hip, which would make it possible to keep the bag secure, and she would still be able to ride a horse.

Hennie left the inn discreetly a few minutes before Lottie did, and they met down the street at a livery where Lottie had left the horse Mr. Parsons had allowed Lottie to take for a few days so she could bring back what he was expecting to be a good and honest worker. He was also expecting that worker to be a man. Hennie knew she could sincerely be the former, and she forced herself to focus on that, fighting every few minutes to quell her growing nervousness over the situation. Her anxiety shifted to the reality of actually riding a horse—something Hennie had never done but had always wanted to do. But Lottie told her what to do and helped her mount, and it only took a moment for Hennie to be inspired by Lottie's confidence in that regard.

Since Lottie had acquired some bread and cheese, and she had a large flask of water, they set out in the direction toward this grand manor house in the country, which Lottie spoke of as if it were something akin to heaven. After all her years in the orphanage and then the workhouse, Hennie could understand Lottie's enthusiasm. She only wished she could share Lottie's confidence that their living in disguise would not bring different kinds of problems into their lives eventually. But Lottie insisted they needed to live in the present and not concern themselves for the future, since it was entirely out of their control—at least for the time being. As they rode together on the same horse, with Lottie controlling the reins, they talked everything through—some things repeatedly—until Hennie had to just stop talking about the same things again and again and force herself to set her mind to this new way of life. She was holding on to the promise she'd insisted they make to each other, that after some time had passed and they'd been able to put away some money, they would make a new plan and find a way to live a more honest existence—as the women God had created them to be. Lottie agreed to Hennie's terms, and Hennie tried to enjoy the scenery as they rode. The colors of spring were popping up in the form of many varieties of wildflowers in the meadows they passed, and the trees were showing green buds. Thankfully the rain had moved on and they were able to enjoy the perfect temperature of a clear sky and the spring sun.

A thought occurred to Hennie, and she asked, "How did you learn to ride a horse? I know for a fact that you'd never been on one—at least you hadn't the last time I saw you, because I'd never been on one either. We talked about that more than once."

"I confess that I had to tell a few little lies to get the job," Lottie said.

"*Little* lies?" Hennie echoed and laughed. "You mean like letting them believe you're a man? Little? Like that?"

Lottie laughed. "I concede that's no small deception. But I also had to tell Parsons I had some experience with horses, and I did a great deal of praying that despite my deceptions I would be helped in being able to figure out what I needed to do and be able to do it well. I started out doing the lowliest job in the stable—which is mucking out the stalls—but I didn't mind at all; it's by far much easier than the dreadful, tedious work we've had to do in the past. At first my muscles ached from doing labor I wasn't accustomed to, but that settled quickly enough. And I just kept a keen eye on everything else going on around me so that I could learn and do other tasks when I was asked to do them. It turns out that the horses and I get along fairly well." She chuckled at the implication that these animals had become her friends. "The first time I needed to ride one of them to take it to the local blacksmith, I was certainly unnerved, but I covered my anxiety and managed rather well. I don't especially enjoy riding as much as I thought I might, but I do enjoy caring for the horses. They're magnificent animals, and I love keeping them cleaned, and groomed, and fed." She sighed contentedly, indicating she found joy and fulfillment in her work, something that Hennie had certainly never observed in her friend—or felt within herself for that matter—and she couldn't deny that good things for Lottie had come out of this strange situation. Hennie hoped the same would be true for herself.

They stopped to stretch their legs and eat some of the food they'd brought along. Hennie could already feel her back end rebelling from the fact that she'd never before ridden a horse, let alone for so many hours. But she'd survived backbreaking labor; she could surely do this. When they were ready to move on, with the hope of arriving at the manor before sunset, Lottie insisted that Hennie needed to take over the reins, and Lottie would sit behind her. "You're going to have to be able to ride a horse to do this job," Lottie said, "which means knowing how to control one. I'm going to teach you, which will make it a whole lot easier for you than it was for me." In response to Hennie's hesitation, Lottie said, "Come along. It's simple. The animal is very well-trained—as are all the horses on the estate."

Hennie mounted in the way Lottie had showed her earlier, and she eased forward in the saddle to allow room for Lottie to sit behind her. Thankfully it was a large saddle and they were both fairly small—especially in contrast to the men who generally used it. Hennie was pleased to quickly realize Lottie had been right. It wasn't that difficult to learn how to use the reins to control the horse, and she laughed as they eased onto the road and continued their journey. Lottie had said she didn't necessarily like to ride, but Hennie already felt something free and perhaps powerful in doing so. She laughed out loud as they galloped for a short way, then slowed down to a comfortable pace that would not tire out the horse with the distance they had yet to cover.

"Well, I think you've got that mastered," Lottie said with a little laugh. "It seems you're a natural."

"Perhaps I'll be able to get away with this charade after all," Hennie said.

"Of course you will!" Lottie said with confidence.

They rode a long while in silence, which allowed Hennie to not only take in the beauty of the day and the countryside through which they were riding, but to also try and make herself more mentally prepared for this secret adventure she was about to embark upon with her dearest friend. In some ways she felt as if they were just little girls playing make-believe—something they'd never had the opportunity to do when they *were* little girls. They'd never actually been allowed to *play* at all. It had been all chores and lessons at the orphanage, and the workhouse had been nothing but work almost every possible moment. Perhaps seeing this endeavor as some kind of game they had never been able to play as children could help Hennie find some enjoyment in the deception, rather than feeling nervous or anxious. She talked the idea through with Lottie, and they both agreed lightheartedly that it was a very good attitude to assume.

A thought occurred to Hennie, and she asked, "Are you living under a false name? I just realized I can't be known as Henrietta! And Hennie certainly doesn't sound at all masculine! What on earth will I do about—"

"I've already thought this through," Lottie said. "Did you think I wouldn't take care of every detail? And I wouldn't let us arrive there without making certain you're fully prepared. When I first spoke to Mr. Parsons about getting a job and he asked my name, I *hadn't* thought that through, and I was taken off guard. But I was glad for a memory that came to mind in that very moment. When I'd first come to the orphanage—and you know I was very young—one of the mistresses there sometimes called me Lot, and she told me that it was the name of a man in the Bible who had been the only good man in a city of many wicked people, and he'd fled the city before God destroyed it. So, I told Parsons my name was Lot. When he asked for a surname, I told him the truth—that I don't have one, that I was raised in an orphanage and no one ever knew how or from whom I'd landed there."

Hennie knew that was true. Her friend had been left as a very young child in a crate previously used to transport potatoes, with only a ragged blanket and a little note that simply said: *Lottie.* It was a sad story at best. At least Hennie had some good memories of her early childhood—a loving mother and a safe and comfortable life with her. Hennie's mother had worked hard as a maid, so the other servants of the household had helped watch over Hennie, and she had been well loved and cared for. It was only upon her mother's untimely death that the tyrannical master of the house had wanted nothing to do with an orphaned child, regardless of how many of the servants had offered to care for her, pointing out that she was old enough to do certain tasks and earn her keep. But the master had wanted nothing to do with *the problem;* that's what Hennie had been labeled by this man she'd barely even seen a few times throughout her life. *The problem.* And so, she'd been shipped off, with nothing but a spare change of clothes, to the orphanage where Lottie had been living for almost as long as she could remember.

"Parsons had no problem with me simply being called *Lot,* so that's who I've become. I quickly realized that if I went by a name that had no resemblance to my own, I might give myself away more easily by not responding to my name when I'm called. But it only took a day or two for me to become accustomed to Lot because it's only an abbreviation of my real name."

"Very well, *Lot,*" Hennie said in a comical tone, and they both laughed. "But what shall I be known by? You told me you had it all figured out. I'm waiting for the final touches of my new identity, and I suspect we don't have very much time left before I'll be living this new life."

"Right you are," Lottie said. "So, it didn't take much thought to realize that Hennie sounds very much like Henry, but if you prefer, I think you should just introduce yourself as Hen—short for Henry. Then you're simply using an abbreviation of your own name—just as I am. What do you think?"

Hennie thought about it for a long minute. "Well . . ." she drawled, "I'm not certain about being called after a female chicken; the other men . . ." She stopped and laughed.

"What's funny?" Lottie asked.

"The *other* men," Hennie repeated. "We're not men at all, but we'll be working with *the other men.*"

"Yes, I suppose that's funny," Lottie said. "Ironic at the very least."

"So . . ." Hennie went on, "I wouldn't be surprised if I get teased over having a name like *Hen,* but I confess that I prefer it over any other possibility. So Hen it is."

"Hen it is," Lottie repeated, then added, "and to give you fair warning, *the other men* have teased me about a great many things. I'm the *scrawny* one—short and skinny, along with other similar comments. I just ignore them, laugh it off. When I laugh *with* them, they tend to pay less attention to the fact that I'm the scrawny one."

"And now you're bringing your scrawny friend to work there also," Hennie said, not liking the prospect of *that.*

"At least you're a little taller than I am," Lottie said. "But the important thing is that once they all realized I work hard and do my fair share—sometimes more than my fair share—and that I'm honest and decent, they've come to respect me, even though I remain a bit shy so as to not interact with the others any more than necessary. But I've looked for opportunities to help the others with *their* assigned tasks, and without a word spoken, it's helped me gain more respect and appreciation from them. I think any one of them would defend their scrawny workmate in any given situation. It's all well and good, my friend. You mustn't worry."

"I'm trying very hard not to," Hennie declared with feigned confidence. "Lot!"

"You just remember everything we've talked about and you'll be fine," Lottie said. "Hen!"

They both laughed at the use of the new versions of their names, although Hennie felt like her laughter was more a way of trying to conceal her growing anxiousness as the sun eased toward the western horizon, indicating that it was late afternoon. At least the position of the sun gave her some sense of direction. Until she'd realized they were riding toward the lowering sun, she'd been all turned around and had had no idea they were riding west. West meant they were getting closer to the sea, and she liked that idea. Her early years had been spent not far from the sea, and sometimes on her mother's day off, they had walked to the sea and shared a picnic and had taken off their shoes and stockings to wade in the waves. She found herself imagining the possibility of sharing such an experience with Lottie, and she hoped this grand manor house to which they were heading might be close enough to the sea for just such an adventure. All things considered, she felt as prepared as she could possibly be, and she actually felt some hope that this experience might bring good things into her life.

Chapter Three

A NEW HOME

Hennie and Lottie stopped to eat the remainder of the bread and cheese they'd brought with them. Hennie wished they had more because neither of them felt satisfied. But Lottie assured Hennie that once they arrived they would be given a good supper, and Lottie spoke of the food available for the servants as if it were a daily royal feast. Of course, after becoming accustomed to workhouse meals, Hennie could understand how Lottie would feel that way. The food at Grenville's inn had been fairly good—good enough to attract regular customers—and Hennie had always enjoyed it and had never gone hungry while she'd worked there, even if she'd always more or less been eating on the run. But Lottie talked of a great variety of remarkable meals and desserts at the magical manor house, which was their destination, since the servants were generally given the same food—or something similar—to what was prepared for the family they all worked for.

During the final stretch of the journey, Hennie rehearsed once again to her friend all that she needed to know to be prepared to face this *adventure*, as Lottie kept calling it. Hennie couldn't deny feeling some anxiety, but now that they'd come this far—and she'd become more accustomed to the idea of living outwardly as a man—she felt more anxious to just get there and face the initial introductions and settling in, so that she could relax into a new way of life, however strange it might be.

As the sun eased closer to the western horizon, its light became blinding since they were riding directly toward it. Hennie wished she could take in the view of her surroundings and familiarize herself with them, especially since Lottie had said they were now on the land owned by the family she worked for. Guiding the horse around a bend in the road, they moved into a wooded area, and the sun was now at their left, mostly blocked by thick clusters of trees. The road curved again as they came out of the trees, but instead of the sun shining in Hennie's eyes, making it impossible to see, its light spilled brilliantly over the enormous manor house and its surrounding gardens that were nothing less than magnificent. The beautiful stables and corrals were visible as well from this perspective, peeking out from one corner of the manor house. Hennie knew well enough that the size of everything in her view was much more massive than it appeared from this distance. In fact, she knew the view all too well, which seized her with a sudden panic.

"Oh, this cannot be happening!" Hennie exclaimed and slid down from the horse, resisting the urge to just run back the way they'd come. "This has got to be some kind of colossal mistake! Surely God would not do this to me!"

"What on earth are you babbling about?" Lottie demanded after she'd also dismounted, quickly securing the reins to a nearby tree.

Hennie couldn't think where to even begin to answer Lottie's question. Her mind was whirling with chaos as a myriad of memories—many beautiful and precious, others too difficult to endure—clashed with the reality that by some nonsensical twist of fate, Lottie had brought her back to the home of her childhood.

Suddenly weak from the onslaught of too many emotions to handle, Hennie dropped to the ground and just sat there, staring at the glory of Ivy Manor, shining like some kind of fairy-tale castle in the glow of the setting sun, its towers and chimneys and turrets all reaching toward the sky, the cream-colored stone from which they'd been built gleaming in a way that made Hennie realize her memories had not been distorted by time; in fact it was all more beautiful and magnificent than she'd remembered—if such a thing were possible.

"What is it?" Lottie asked, and Hennie realized her friend was sitting beside her, a gentle hand on her arm.

"This is the place, Lottie," Hennie murmured. "This is where I lived until my mother died."

"No!" Lottie said on a huff of breath that could have blown out the flame of a large lamp. "It can't be!"

"I'm afraid it is," Hennie said, overcome with a strange weakness.

"That is *far* too great a coincidence to be—"

"You and I have always agreed that we don't believe in coincidence." Hennie forced her eyes from the view and looked sternly at her friend. "We always told each other that even the horrors we were living in had purpose and meaning, and it was up to us to find that meaning. We always knew that—if nothing else—our being there had brought us together, and our friendship was worth the price we had to pay."

"Yes," Lottie drawled, "but . . ." She motioned with her hand as if to cue Hennie to finish the sentence.

"But . . . if I don't believe in coincidence . . . why do I fear that returning here is all wrong—impossible." She turned again to look at Ivy Manor. She knew from her childhood that the house had actually been called something different in generations past, that its name had been far more formal and somehow connected to the conquering ways of the man who had been responsible for building it—an ancestor to the family who now lived in the house and oversaw the surrounding estate. But at some point, the conquests of this man had come to be seen as barbaric, even shameful, and as if to denounce him and his ways, the house had simply been renamed *Ivy Manor*—because it was surrounded by lush, soft ivy that flourished so much it had to be carefully tended by the gardeners to keep it from completely overtaking the house and gardens. As it was, the ivy covered most of one side of the house, barely trimmed away from the doors and windows, and flowing down onto the lawn like a dark green blanket. Hennie loved the ivy, she loved the house, and she'd loved the people here—most of them, anyway. She also loved most of her memories here, but not all of them; some of her memories were too painful to even allow into her conscious mind. If they showed even the slightest appearance, she shoved them back into the darkness and slammed the mental door that kept them locked away.

"Fear?" Lottie said, startling Hennie from her deep contemplation of everything good she remembered about Ivy Manor. She'd only been the daughter of a servant woman, but she'd been well-fed and well-clothed; she'd been loved and looked after, even educated—until her mother's death had left her with no connection to this place, and she'd been sent away the very afternoon her mother's casket had been lowered into the ground. The lord of the manor at the time was a man she'd rarely even gotten a glimpse of; no child of a servant would have been allowed anywhere near him. But she'd known from the way the servants had spoken of him that he was a harsh and gruff man, a condition that had only worsened following the death of his wife, who had been a kind and gentle woman, one who had brought out the best in him. Apparently, he couldn't be bothered with the eleven-year-old daughter of a dead servant woman—even though Hennie had never lived anywhere else. The housekeeper had told Hennie she'd pleaded with the Lord of the manor to allow Hennie to stay on, that she was old enough to earn her keep, and she would be watched over by the women in the household who had all helped care for her the whole of her young life. But he would not be swayed, and Hennie had been sent away to the orphanage where she'd met Lottie. Every day of her miserable existence that had followed, Hennie had wondered what her life might have been like if this man had simply allowed her to stay. Even *earning her keep* would have never been as difficult as what had been required of her at the orphanage—and certainly a far cry from the horrors of the workhouse. She would have been safe and warm and fed. The *only* good thing that had come out of being sent away was her friendship with Lottie. She'd consoled herself countless times with the belief that if Hennie hadn't come into Lottie's life, Lottie would have likely succumbed—as many did—to the hopelessness and despair of such an existence, and she might very well not even be alive today. Hennie knew this in her heart because she felt certain that she herself would have given in to the temptation to just starve herself to death or allow illness to overtake her instead of fighting to survive. They had helped each other in that battle; they had survived together. And now Hennie was overcome to the point of hardly being able to move, or even think clearly. Lottie had somehow been strangely guided to find gainful employment—however odd the situation might be—in the very place where Hennie's life had begun, a place where she had once belonged and been happy. It *couldn't* be coincidence! It just *couldn't*!

"Hennie?" she heard Lottie say, even though it sounded far away. "Did you hear what I said?"

"Fear," Hennie repeated back. "Yes, I heard you." She looked again at Lottie. "It can't be coincidence; it's far too . . . impossible. Of all the manor houses in this county alone, that you would find work here . . . that you would bring me back here . . ." Hennie sighed so deeply that she realized she was finding it difficult to breathe. "But yes . . . I'm terrified." She took hold of Lottie's hands and squeezed them tightly. "I grew up here, Lottie. I knew these people! What if someone recognizes me? I shared meals with the servants, and some of them helped watch out for me. I've doubled in age since I was taken away from here, but have I changed enough to not be recognized? What will become of us if our ruse is discovered?" She sighed with a distinct quiver. "Yes, Lottie. I'm afraid."

"We'll be fine," Lottie insisted with a confidence that Hennie longed to share. "People won't recognize you because their mind will be set on remembering you as a girl, and if I've learned anything through this experience, it's that people see what you want them to see. I may be seen as a scrawny man with a high voice and features that might be less than typically masculine, but I'm still seen as a man. That's what people expect to see, and it will be the same for you. So what if someone says that you seem familiar? No one has seen you since you were eleven, and you're twice that age now; that's in essence another lifetime. Just laugh and pass it off without any fuss. If you don't give it any attention, no one will be the wiser; no one will pay it any mind. People resemble other people without any relationship at all." Lottie squeezed Hennie's hands. "Everything will be all right." She sighed, then chuckled before she added, "Maybe there's a reason you were supposed to come back here. Maybe it's destiny."

Hennie could only make a scoffing sound that was meant to discredit the possibility, but something deep inside couldn't quite dismiss it. Perhaps she simply felt terrified over what such a potential destiny might require of her.

As soon as Hennie had been allowed a few more minutes to become accustomed to what she now knew about their destination, Lottie insisted that they move on so they would have time to settle in and have a decent supper before the established bedtime for the stable servants.

Hennie's nervousness increased as they came closer to Ivy Manor and its enormity became more evident. In truth it was even bigger than she had remembered—and in her memory it had been impossibly enormous, like a castle growing up out of the lush, green ivy and the magnificent gardens that surrounded it.

The two women dismounted the horse and took a moment to collect themselves before Lottie led the horse by the reins into the open main doorway to the stables, and Hennie walked beside her. A handful of men all dressed similarly to their own attire were busy at various tasks and looked up to see who was there. A few of them just glanced and returned to their work, but there were a couple who set their work aside to take notice of Lottie and Hennie.

"Well, look who's back!" a stout man with thinning blond hair declared, setting his fists on his hips. "It's the scrawny one!" He laughed, but his teasing didn't seem at all demeaning; more accurately, it held a note of friendly affection. "I was hoping you wouldn't get lost."

"It's good to see you too," Lottie said lightly, with a subtle gruffness to her voice that Hennie knew to be an effort to sound more masculine. Until now she'd forgotten that when she'd believed Lottie was a man that first night she'd appeared in the dining room of the inn, she'd heard the same gruff quality.

"And this is the friend you went to find?" the man said, eying Hennie with a mild skepticism that seemed more teasing than actually skeptical. "Almost as scrawny as you."

"Why do you think we're friends?" Lottie said, completely at ease. "We had to stick up for each other in the orphanage and the workhouse, or we'd not have survived."

"Fair point," the man said and stepped forward to take the reins of the horse. "Let me see to the animal. You must be worn out from the travel."

"Thank you," Lottie said, then turned to Hennie as she added, "This is Mickey." She chuckled and surprised Hennie by lightly slugging Mickey in the shoulder. "He's been pretty good to me, all things considered. Mickey, this is Henry; although I usually just call him Hen."

"That's easy enough to remember," Mickey said, not making any teasing remarks about the name being the same as a female chicken. Hennie suspected that was a likely possibility among the other stable hands. "A pleasure to meet you, Hen."

"And you," Hennie said and realized she'd made no effort to alter her voice. She knew it was slightly deep for a woman anyway, but now that she'd spoken even those two words, it was too late to try and modify her voice without drawing attention to the fact that she was doing so. In a way, she was relieved. She didn't want to try and keep track of when she needed to speak differently. Lottie was a better actress than she was, and Hennie had no desire to make this any more difficult than necessary.

As Mickey took the horse down the long aisle between what seemed two endless rows of stalls, Lottie turned toward the other man who had stopped working when they'd come in. He was tall, broad-shouldered, and middle-aged. He had a commanding presence that was not lessened by the fact that he had almost no hair on the top of his head. If anything, his baldness made him appear perhaps more imposing. He came straight to the point and said, "So, Hen, your friend here tells me you're a hard worker, which is why I trusted him enough to give him the time and means to go and find you. I hope my trust won't be misplaced."

"This is Mr. Parsons," Lottie said. "The stable master."

"I answer to no one but the Lord of the manor," Mr. Parsons said, not in a way that sounded arrogant or cruel, but as a matter of fact. But Hennie had to discipline herself to not shudder visibly at the mention of this tyrannical man who had sent her off to the doom of an orphanage. "It's up to me to keep his stables in pristine condition, and his horses strong and clean and healthy. It'll be your job to do whatever I ask of you to make that happen. You'll be treated fairly and with respect as long as you prove yourself willing to do the work, and worthy of the respect."

"So Lot has told me," Hennie said, glad she remembered to use the male version of her friend's name. "He's spoken very highly of you, and I'm grateful that you're willing to give me a chance. I don't know much about horses, but I know how to work hard, and I can learn just about anything."

"Then we should get along just fine," Mr. Parsons said with a kind smile, extending his hand. Hennie shook it firmly, putting all her strength into executing a firm grip that might exude some measure of masculinity. Her new employer smiled more broadly, as if the handshake had pleased him, just as it seemed to have sealed the agreement that had just been spoken between them.

"The two of you have had a long journey," Parsons added. "Lot can help you get settled in. I spoke with Mrs. Reeves, and she's had a room cleaned and prepared for you, Hen, a few doors down from yours, Lot, I believe. She said she'd leave the door open so you'd know which one." Hennie was deeply taken by the reality of having a room to herself—especially one that was warm and dry. But the mention of Mrs. Reeves quickened her heart and made it difficult to concentrate. How well she remembered the kind housekeeper! And she wondered how she would keep herself from just hugging the woman when she saw her again. But she would have to maintain her distance and her disguise. Still, it was comforting to think of the dear Mrs. Reeves having been in charge of preparing Hennie's new room.

Hennie forced herself to stop reminiscing and pay attention to Parsons as he added, "I've also spoken to Mrs. Helton. Even though supper finished up a short while ago, she's keeping food warm for the two of you, since I suspected you would arrive tonight." Parsons motioned them out of the stables with his arms. "So, get yourselves settled in and fed. There'll be work aplenty to be done right after breakfast." He looked directly at Lottie and added, "I'll be expecting you to train your friend and let him know the rules we follow around here."

"Of course," Lottie said with that gruff voice Hennie would have to get used to.

Lottie led the way out of the stables and toward a side door of the big house that was not too far of a walk from the stables and the carriage house. Hennie followed Lottie but wouldn't have needed to. She knew the way to the entrance most commonly used by the servants. She felt both deeply comforted and distinctly nervous. But she focused on taking all of this on, one moment at a time.

"How are you doing so far?" Lottie asked just before they reached the door.

"Fine, I think," Hennie said. "I knew Mrs. Reeves—and Mrs. Helton. They both helped look after me."

"How remarkably strange," Lottie commented thoughtfully.

"It feels wonderful to think of being in their care—if that makes sense."

"It does."

"But at the same time, I'm a bit nervous. I hope I can cover my real feelings when I see them, especially if they recognize me in any way."

"You'll do just fine," Lottie insisted, and they went inside and started up the back stairs to the servants' quarters. Ironically, the upper part of this wing of the house reminded Hennie of the stables. The hallway was much like the long aisle between the long rows of stalls for the horses. In this case, the aisle was lined on both sides by a great many doors, all of which led into tiny bedrooms, each with a number painted on the door so that no one would mistakenly enter the wrong room. There were bathing rooms and water closets at the end of the hall; this Hennie knew without Lottie telling her. Even though they were in the men's quarters—a thought that was somewhat disconcerting—Hennie knew that the floor below this one had an identical version of rooms for the women, which was where she had lived with her mother. How well she remembered the tiny room they had shared, and how the extra bed in which she'd slept had barely fit between the other furniture, but that had made it possible to reach out in the night and actually touch her mother, and always know she was there. Until she wasn't. But Hennie slammed the mental door on her painful memories and chose to focus on the good ones. Now that she was actually here in Ivy Manor, her nervousness was covered by a distinct blanket of comfort. It was as if she'd come home; even though her mother wasn't here, and no one could know who she really was, she'd returned to a place that had made her early childhood years safe and secure and filled with pleasant memories. Whatever miracles might be at work, Hennie was ready and willing to take them in.

They found the open door just a few doors down from Lottie's room, and Hennie actually laughed when she stepped into her new room, noting the cozy quilt and pillow on the bed, the large window with curtains presently tied back and made from fabric that was not worn and rotting. The walls were painted a pale green without a single crack or flaw. The room had only a narrow bed, a little table with a lamp next to the bed, a small bureau with a few drawers, a washstand, and a narrow wardrobe where she could hang some clothes. But it was clean, and bright, and more than adequate. Compared to every place Hennie had lived since she'd left here, it was practically idyllic.

"Do you like it?" Lottie asked in a tone that made it clear she already knew the answer.

"Oh, it's heavenly!" Hennie declared, a slight quiver in her voice bringing her to the awareness of how deeply she was touched by the opportunity to live in a situation that did indeed almost seem celestial in contrast to the hellish circumstances both she and Lottie had survived.

"Leave your bag and you can unpack it later," Lottie said, even though they both knew it would take Hennie about three minutes to unpack the bag and put her minimal belongings away. In time, Hennie imagined being able to use her wages to acquire more personal possessions—even if that meant purchasing a wider variety of men's clothing. But she thought about being able to buy books. Oh, to own books! And with needing to work fewer hours, she would have more time to read. That too seemed heavenly!

Lottie motioned Hennie out of the room; Hennie tossed her bag on the bed before they left the room and closed the door. Each of them took advantage of the privies at the far end of the hall to freshen up before going downstairs to the enormous kitchen and adjacent pantries and dining hall where the servants ate. Hennie felt as if she'd come home, so much so that she wouldn't have been surprised to see her mother standing at one of the sinks scrubbing a pot while she chatted with cook, or perhaps seated in the dining hall while she took a break from her work and enjoyed a cup of tea with some of the other maids. Lottie mentioned something about how it would become easier to find her way around such an enormous house in time, but Hennie just whispered back, "I already know my way around."

Lottie looked momentarily confused, then enlightenment dawned as she obviously remembered their earlier conversation—that Hennie was returning to the home of her childhood. "So you do." Lottie laughed softly and shook her head in amazement.

Lottie introduced Hennie to Mrs. Helton—and Hennie pretended to have never met her before. The plump, tall woman had a few more wrinkles in her face, and a little more gray hair mixed into the dark, but beyond that she looked almost exactly as Hennie remembered, and it took great self-restraint to not just throw herself into this woman's arms and declare, *It's me! It's me! I'm your little Hennie! I'm the one you tried to take under your wing when my mother died! I'm back! I'm all right!* Words tumbled silently through Hennie's mind, while her voice uttered simply, "It's such a pleasure to meet you, Mrs. Helton. I hear you're one of the best cooks in the county and working here is well worth it if only to be able to eat your delicious meals."

"Well, aren't you a kind one, Mr. . . . . I didn't catch the name."

"Henry," Hennie said, knowing Lottie hadn't spoken a name. "But my friends call me Hen; I know it's a bit strange, but names often can be, don't you think?"

"That's for certain," Mrs. Helton said, without so much as a flicker of recognition in her eyes. Perhaps Hennie had changed a great deal in eleven years, or perhaps it was as Lottie had said, and no one would even think of any resemblance when they were seeing Hennie as a man. Perhaps it was both. Either way, Hennie felt relieved. And as Lottie and Hennie sat down to enjoy the delicious—even extravagant—meal Mrs. Helton put before them, that sensation of being in some kind of heavenly realm increased.

Mrs. Helton left them to enjoy their meal, and Hennie found it tempting to talk to Lottie about her feelings and impressions, but she knew it was mandatory—and they had agreed upon it without exception—that unless they were in the privacy of one of their bedrooms, they would always remain in character as men. They simply couldn't risk ever having even the slightest incongruity overheard or observed. Hennie appreciated how Lottie struck up conversation as Lot speaking to Hen, and she found it surprisingly easy to follow along and partici-pate—although she had to fight back the temptation more than once to giggle over their ridiculous names.

They stopped talking when a well-curved, plain woman with brown hair entered the room. Hennie guessed her to be about ten years older than herself. She wore a kind smile and was wiping her hands on the full-length apron that covered her dark-gray dress.

"Ah," Lottie said and stood up. Hennie did as well, reminding herself that a decent man of any class would rise when someone of the female persuasion entered the room. Oh, the things she would have to get used to! "I was hoping to see you tonight, my friend."

"And I you," the woman said, and they exchanged a nod and a smile. "I'd heard you'd arrived with your friend." She turned toward Hennie. "I've heard so very much about you."

Hennie also nodded but didn't know what to say when she had no idea who this woman might be. Lottie saved her by making a proper introduction. "This is my dear friend, Hen."

"Short for Henry," the woman said with a smile.

"That's right," Hennie said.

"Hen," Lottie went on, "this is Miss Atkins, an assistant to the housekeeper and also a dear friend. I've told you how we met the first day I came here looking for work."

"Oh, of course," Hennie said and tried to recall the details. There was so much information she'd had to take in and memorize the last couple of days. Lottie winked at Hennie and offered a conspiratorial smile toward Miss Atkins just before the latter leaned toward Hennie and whispered, "Your secret shall never pass through my lips, on pain of death."

Before Hennie could respond, Miss Atkins was on her way out of the room, saying, "I'm going to get myself a cup of tea and sit with you, if you don't mind of course."

"It would be a pleasure," Lottie said before Hennie and Lottie sat back down and returned to their meal.

Hennie looked directly at Lottie as she put a forkful of boiled potatoes into her mouth. While Hennie was chewing, Lottie mouthed more than spoke. "She's the only one who knows the truth; she's helped me a great deal. We'll talk more about that later."

Hennie nodded before she self-consciously glanced around to be certain they were alone, but then Lottie wouldn't have said what she did without already knowing that to be the case—and she'd spoken far too quietly for even Hennie to have understood without watching her lips move.

Miss Atkins returned quickly and took a seat, setting a cup of tea on the table in front of her, which she stirred nonchalantly while it cooled. She spoke comfortably with Lottie about how good it was to have *him* back, keeping up the ruse perfectly. Miss Atkins also spoke with Hennie, treating her every bit like a man while she asked *him* questions about life before coming here that were easy for Hennie to answer honestly without treading into territory where discrepancies might arise. Hennie liked Miss Atkins very much and enjoyed their visit almost as much as she enjoyed her meal. Hennie went to personally thank Mrs. Helton for the lovely supper, and the older woman smiled with pleasure in response to Hennie's gratitude and compliments. Oh, how Hennie had missed her!

Hennie went with Lottie to the room she'd been using for more than a year now, where they could talk privately and without pretense. Lottie locked the door, which she declared was an important habit, since she certainly didn't want anyone to walk in on her at any time and perhaps discover her secret. Hennie made a mental note to always lock the door to *her* room.

"People are polite and always knock," Lottie said, "but we must take every precaution."

"Of course," Hennie said while she admired more than a dozen books Lottie had lined up across the top of her small bureau. "Oh, they're lovely!"

"I've read them all at least twice," Lottie said with pride. "When you're able to purchase books, you should buy different titles so we can trade."

"What an excellent idea," Hennie said.

While Lottie unpacked the bag she'd taken on her brief journey, she spoke of her excellent friendship with Miss Atkins, and the kind and generous assistance this woman had consistently offered during the time Lottie had lived and worked here. Hennie asked about the woman's given name, or if they must always refer to her as *Miss Atkins*. Lottie explained that Miss Atkins didn't know her given name, since she too had been raised in an orphanage and the headmistress there had simply called her *Miss*. It was the only name she'd ever known, and she had not felt compelled to ever come up with anything different. Her own years in an orphanage had given her great empathy for Lottie's plight—and subsequently Hennie's. Miss Atkins explained that she had been saved when a wealthy man had come to the orphanage looking for some young servants. She had been chosen as one of them, taken to his home, scrubbed clean, put into decent clothes, and put to work. After the passing of a few years, a visitor to that home—a fine lady—had taken notice of Miss Atkins and had been very convincing about allowing the girl to come with her and be trained for a better position in a household, since she had detected great potential in the girl. This woman had been very kind to Miss Atkins and had put her under her housekeeper's care to be trained in the ways of properly managing a large household. At the death of Miss Atkins's benefactor, she'd had to leave that house, but because of the skills she'd acquired, she'd been able to find the position she still had today as an assistant to the housekeeper, with many important responsibilities—and also enough respect and privilege to be able to help Lottie with personal matters to help her avoid any unnecessary suspicion. Miss Atkins had been eager to help Lottie's friend as well, and Lottie felt certain the three of them would all become very good friends.

Hennie noticed as Lottie put away her things that she had a variety of men's clothes—most of them suitable for working, but also a suit fine enough to wear to church, and two different coats—one for rain and one for cold weather— and also a few pairs of boots. Despite the stark absence of anything feminine in the room, Hennie loved seeing evidence that Lottie had been able to purchase things for herself with money she had earned. It was a luxury that she doubted anyone could truly appreciate unless they'd come from a similar background. Lottie walked with Hennie to her own room to make certain she had everything she needed, and to see if she had any questions about her new surroundings. With the lamp on the bedside table lit and diffusing a warm glow over the room, Hennie felt safe and comfortable and adequately prepared to get through her first night back at Ivy Manor. Lottie promised to come and get her for breakfast and told her what time to be ready. In addition to a clock on Hennie's bedside table that would always make Hennie aware of the time, Lottie told her that a manservant always went up and down the hall knocking on doors to wake the staff, giving them sufficient time to get cleaned up and dressed, and to each have their turn in the privy.

Hennie and Lottie shared a tight embrace, filled with more hope than they'd ever shared in all the previous years of their lives as friends. The ironies were still difficult for Hennie to comprehend, but her gratitude for all that was good about this situation was impossible to ignore. After Lottie left, Hennie knelt beside her new bed to pray according to her lifelong habit, which had been taught to her by her mother. How clearly she remembered the two of them kneeling side by side in a room very similar to this one, with the very minimal floor space available being consumed by an extra bed. Hennie's eyes became moist with memories of her mother, and for a moment she had a strange but pleasant thought that perhaps her mother had guided her back to this place. She believed in angels, and it wasn't the first time she'd wondered if her mother had guided her or helped keep her safe—in spite of the many horrors she'd endured. But in the moment—if only for a moment—the sensation felt somehow more real than it ever had. Perhaps it was her surroundings, perhaps it was being back here in the home they'd shared, and perhaps those things had only stirred her imagination. Whatever it was, Hennie crawled into her new bed, between clean sheets and beneath a warm quilt, sighing on the wave of a little laugh to realize she'd forgotten what a truly comfortable bed felt like.

"Thank you, God," Hennie whispered aloud, even though she'd just finished expressing her appreciation in prayer. She just didn't want there to be any doubt about her gratitude. She could only hope and pray that both she and Lottie could successfully keep up their ruse long enough to save a significant amount of money—at least enough to go elsewhere and be able to start over with good employment in a situation where they could actually live as their genuine selves. But that was too far into the future to worry about now. For now, Hennie just basked in all that was presently good and drifted to sleep feeling safer and more content than she had since her mother's death.

Chapter Four

THE MISSING HEIR

HENNIE WAS ALREADY AWAKE—BUT ONLY for a few minutes—before she heard the knock on her door that Lottie had warned her about. She felt more enthusiasm than anxiety as she began her first day as a man working at Ivy Manor. Everything went smoothly in getting ready for the day, even though Hennie still felt so out of place with her reflection in the mirror as she adjusted her clothes and tied her much shorter hair back in a plait.

At breakfast she was introduced to many other servants, most of whom hadn't worked here when she'd been a child, and she could only hope to learn their names in a reasonable amount of time. She knew the servants ate in shifts because the dining hall wasn't large enough to accommodate them all at once; and with certain jobs, someone always had to be available, so breaks from work had to be alternated. Everyone was kind, even though Hennie received a few odd glances; but Hennie had already adjusted to being seen as one of the scrawny stable hands, and she felt more than ready to get to work—especially after eating such a hearty and delicious breakfast.

Hennie walked with Lottie and a few other stable hands out to the stables to begin the day's chores. With Lottie's guidance and training, Hennie quickly learned how to feed the horses and give them fresh water, which she thoroughly enjoyed. Carrying the heavy buckets of food and water wasn't much different from carrying buckets of water and sacks of food into the kitchen at the inn. Hennie was strong and healthy, and the work didn't feel like any kind of strain.

After the magnificent horses were all fed, each animal was given a turn at being walked for exercise, and Lottie told Hennie there was a schedule for bathing the animals—but that was sometimes dependent on the weather. While one stable hand exercised a horse, another would clean out the stall and put down fresh, clean straw so the horse could return to clean quarters, where it would then be brushed so that each and every horse would be ready when needed—either for a member of the family to ride, or to be hitched to any one of the carriages or wagons in the carriage house to be used whenever necessary. Hennie learned that certain horses were owned by certain members of the grand and wealthy family who occupied Ivy Manor, and other horses were specifically trained to pull wagons or carriages. Every animal was treated like royalty, and Hennie already loved her job even before lunch. Caring for these noble creatures was far easier and more satisfying than serving drinks and food to drunk or impatient customers, always under the watchful eye of the cynical Grenville. Mr. Parsons was in and out of the stable, occasionally checking Hennie's work, but offering kind encouragement and even complimenting her, which only made her want to work hard and do a good job.

Within a week Hennie felt so comfortable with her new life that she couldn't imagine why she'd hesitated even a moment when Lottie had shown up at the inn with such a bizarre proposal. Pretending to be a man had become natural and easy, and even though there was some teasing and bantering with the other stable hands about Lot and Hen being the scrawny ones, their hard work was respected, and Hennie felt safe among these men. The trickiness of maintaining privacy wasn't as difficult as Hennie had thought it might be, and true to Lottie's word, Miss Atkins was efficient and kind in helping them deal with feminine matters. She'd come up with a clever plan that would never arouse any suspicion or create any challenges that anyone else might notice.

On Sunday Hennie and Lottie went to the stables and did their part in helping to feed and water the horses, but other work on their behalf was not performed on the Sabbath. They went back to their rooms and cleaned up, so they could attend church with many other members of the staff. Lottie loaned Hennie a jacket and waistcoat that she added to her usual attire to appear more appropriately dressed for church, and Lottie told her that as soon as she received some wages, they would go into town and she could get her own clothes that would be suitable for church. Noting that Lottie wore a finer shirt, breeches, and boots to church made Hennie want to be able to do the same. Not since her childhood had she been able to experience Sundays the way her mother had taught her to do. While the day had technically been observed at the orphanage and the workhouse, the occupants had never actually left the premises to attend any kind of service. Instead, they had been sternly lectured, as if those in charge were using the Sabbath as little more than an excuse to put the fear of God into those who were in their care and barely surviving, using the specter of God's wrath as a wicked weapon to keep everyone in line. Hennie had always been grateful for her mother's teachings; she had firmly believed in a loving God who heard the prayers of all His children, even though He Himself was required to honor the natural laws of the universe, the agency of mankind, and the laws governing good and evil. Hennie had grown up knowing in her heart that the bad things in her life were not God's fault, and that if she strived to honor Him by the way she lived, all would be made right eventually—in the next life if not this one. Hennie had taught Lottie her beliefs, since Lottie had never been taught anything except for the distorted messages delivered by the people responsible for keeping children trapped in deplorable circumstances. Together Hennie and Lottie had whispered in their bed of their belief in a loving God, and their hope for a better life. They had prayed together every day, and now it felt to Hennie as if many prayers were finally being answered. She felt so incredibly blessed to walk into the lovely church building in the center of the village and be surrounded by fellow believers. While she enjoyed listening to the sermon and singing the hymns, she was bathed with memories of attending church in this very building with her mother.

With the extra time off on Sunday before they needed to help with the evening feeding of the animals, Hennie and Lottie locked themselves away in Hennie's room, where Hennie was able to share all that she was feeling and the strangeness of it that was also so incredibly wondrous.

As days passed and Hennie settled more comfortably into her new life and the work she loved doing, she began to allow herself to indulge in other memories of growing up here—memories she had forced herself to completely lock away a long time ago. But now that she was here in this place, how could she not think of her childhood playmates and other people she had closely associated with? She'd known so much then about the family she worked for now, and she wondered about each one of them—how they were doing, *what* they were doing—one of them in particular. Working in the stables was like existing in a separate world. She didn't go anywhere in the house that wasn't specifically designated for the servants, and there were other stable hands who saddled the horses for family members when they wanted to ride. Hennie and Lottie were on the lowly end of the staff in the stable, doing the menial tasks and always purposely kept out of sight of the nobility for whom they worked. And Hennie was more than all right with such an arrangement. She didn't necessarily *want* to see any of them; she only felt curious. Her mother had been a maid who had done a variety of tasks, essentially stepping in wherever she was needed when there was extra work for a social event, or perhaps when another maid was ill or had taken time off. Sometimes she'd worked in the kitchen, sometimes the laundry, and sometimes she'd even assisted the ladies in the house with the prestigious tasks associated with being a lady's maid. Even though it only happened occasionally, Hennie knew that working directly with one of the ladies in the noble family was a high honor among servants, and her mother had enjoyed it very much. She had talked of teaching Hennie the skills of a lady's maid so that Hennie could eventually attain the best possible employment available to a woman who lived a life of service. Hennie had wondered a thousand times what she might be doing now if her mother had lived. Imagining herself as a lady's maid when she was disguised as a man and working in the stables could actually make her laugh inwardly. It was ironic if not humorous. Perhaps one day it might still be possible, she often thought. For now, she found joy in the work she was doing and simply worked hard and did her best to avoid any undue attention, which served both her and Lottie well in trying to remain inconspicuous.

Hennie quickly realized there was a distinct lack of any gossip among the servants that might satisfy her questions about the family for which she worked. After a couple of weeks contending with her growing curiosity, she finally just asked Lottie—when they were alone in her room—what she might know, given that she'd been here for more than a year. Hennie felt a relief so deep that it brought her to tears when she learned that the tyrannical master of the house who had shipped her off to an orphanage had died some years ago, and his son had taken over the management of the estate. Lottie encouraged Hennie to talk about the possible reasons she felt so emotional over such news.

"I suppose I just always felt like he was more responsible than anyone for the misery I endured. You know that I would never trade away any of it if only to have your friendship, but I think I've spent my entire life—since I left here—blaming him more than anyone else. The cruel and deplorable people who made our lives miserable every day certainly created a great deal of anger inside of me; we've talked about that. But I will never forget the day Mrs. Reeves and Mrs. Helton sat down together to speak with me, each of them telling me how they'd pleaded with the master to allow me to stay, but he just wouldn't have it, and I was being sent away. They both cried, which made me cry. And I sensed they were afraid for me, even though they were trying to put on brave faces and assure me that everything would be all right." Hennie sighed deeply and wiped at her tears. "I love being here . . . working here . . . but for some reason it feels all the better knowing that this man I've despised—even though I'd barely seen him a handful of times—is now dead. I'm far more comfortable knowing his son is in charge."

"Do you think you've forgiven him?" Lottie asked. It was a fair question, especially since they'd discussed countless times the need to forgive all people in their lives who had treated them so cruelly. And Hennie had just admitted that she blamed this man more than any other for her misery.

"I've tried," Hennie said. "I think so. But to be completely truthful, I still think of him sometimes and feel . . . upset, perhaps even angry. So even though I've prayed a great deal to be able to forgive him, I wonder if I truly have—and if I haven't, I'm not sure exactly how to do that."

"Give it time," Lottie advised gently. "I know myself how difficult forgiveness can be when people have inflicted such suffering on others—particularly us in this case. But we both know it's a burden *we* carry—not the people we need to forgive—and we'll be all the better off and happier if we can let go. Still, it isn't easy." Lottie squeezed Hennie's hand. "We'll keep working on it together."

Hennie nodded gratefully. "And what of the rest of the family? I know the lady of the house passed on when I was a child. As I recall, she never had a strong constitution, and each childbirth wore her down a little more, although I believe it was a cold that turned into pneumonia that took her. But there were five Hannaford children," Hennie said, surprised at the way her heart quickened to recall how well she had known those children—some more than others. And this was the first time since her return that she'd actually spoken the family name aloud, as if just doing so made them more real in her memories—and in the present—a reality that left her decidedly uncomfortable for reasons she couldn't quite define. Hennie's age had fallen right in the middle of the five Hannaford children, and she was among a very small group of the children of servants who sometimes played with them. The five children of noble birth had been taught by their father that it was unseemly to associate with the children of servants, but there had always been a great diversity in the personalities of the Hannaford children, and they had no other children to play with except for the other children being raised beneath the same roof—even if the separate quarters and living conditions left a huge chasm between their worlds. Despite their father's stark disapproval, he generally remained aloof, oblivious to his children; therefore, it required only a few simple precautions to make certain he never found out that three of his five children had made friends among the servant children, and the other two were indifferent to their father's edicts—since none of the children had any fondness at all toward him—and they were therefore supportive of keeping the secrets of their siblings. It seemed they all had secrets they kept from their father to avoid his wrath.

Because the Hannaford children were mostly being raised by the governess and nanny, along with the influence of many members of the serving staff, they were all taught the importance of respecting their father and living up to the expectations of their birth; but they were also taught the values their father completely overlooked—or completely disregarded—of having integrity, being kind and respectful to others regardless of their social status, and seeking out the real seeds of happiness in life rather than getting caught up in the counterfeit sources of money and power—which seemed to be the very things that had made their father such an unkind and difficult man.

Hennie's memories of being a friend among the Hannaford children were mostly pleasant. It had been an ongoing game to avoid being found out by their father, and they learned to play it well. The servants were all in on it, apparently united in solidarity over the desire to allow the children to play like normal children, and to be raised to respect the serving class—in contrast to most children of nobility who mostly grew up to be arrogant and self-absorbed, which only caused grief for those who worked for them—a principle that certainly fueled the servants' efforts to protect the children from their father's tyrannical attitudes.

Hennie listened to Lottie talk about what she knew of these people who were all now adults, trying to mingle the present with the past—which was made more difficult by attempting to put herself into both. The little girl who had played with and known them well was now pretending to be a man working in their stables and hoping to never be found out. Still, she was curious to know what had become of their lives and was glad that Lottie had some information in that regard. Leah, Sarah, and Rebecca had all grown into very lovely ladies—as Lottie described them, even though she'd had only a few glimpses of Rebecca, who was still unmarried and lived here in the manor, and was known for her love of riding, which brought her to the stables frequently. Lottie had only heard of Leah and Sarah since they'd both married and moved far away, but the servants who had known them well spoke of them with love and respect, and as being beautiful and refined. It was as if each of the servants who had been here long enough to have taken a part in raising the children and seeing them grow felt a degree of pride in how well they'd turned out. The three sisters were all considered kind and fair, and that was talked about with more pride than anything else. This idea warmed Hennie, and she was also pleased to hear that Leah and Sarah had five children between them, although Lottie had no idea which one of them had three and the other two.

"And the sons?" Hennie asked, her heart quickening even more, but she fought to conceal her emotional investment in the question—which wasn't easy, considering how well Lottie knew her.

"One of them has taken over the running of the estate, obviously," Lottie said. "He's a good man, fair and kind—although I've only encountered him twice. He rides frequently, but as you know I'm not among those hired to help him with his horse. I hear he often saddles it himself, anyway."

"That sounds like Jack," Hennie said more to herself, hardly realizing she'd said the name aloud, while to herself she recalled how he'd preferred Jack over the more formal name of Jonathan.

"Jack?" Lottie echoed, clearly confused.

Hennie forced herself away from her nostalgia and looked directly at her friend. "The oldest son. He went by Jack; he preferred it over the lengthy name with which he'd been christened. One of his names is Jonathan, and he chose the nickname Jack when he was about seven. He liked it; said it sounded strong— like a knight or a great explorer."

"Goodness!" Lottie exclaimed. "You knew the Hannaford children well enough to know something like *that*?"

Hennie felt briefly embarrassed for some reason, perhaps because she and Lottie were so close, but Hennie had never talked about this part of her past. She wasn't certain why; maybe she'd simply felt that holding on to the most tender memories would keep them safer. Or maybe it was more painful than tender, given the reality that she'd been torn away from that life.

"I did," she said, and while she knew Lottie now deserved a more thorough explanation, for the moment she settled on simply adding a truth that was difficult to comprehend. "Jack was my best friend."

"Unbelievable!" Lottie declared.

"Are you angry with me?" Hennie asked.

"Angry? Why would I be angry?" Lottie asked, incredulous.

"That I didn't tell you before? That I didn't share this part of my past with you?"

"Of course I'm not angry," Lottie said firmly. "Just . . . surprised. You told me all about being raised in a big manor house, and your mother working there, and how kindly you were treated. But being friends with the children of such a noble family? I never imagined!"

"Well, it's true," Hennie said in a faraway voice that expressed the way her mind had been drawn to a long-ago happier time. "Despite Lord Hannaford's odious attitudes, the servants conspired in solidarity to allow his children to play with the few children of servants who lived in the house, so that they could grow up with a more balanced perspective of life. Even though I was very young, I remember hearing those words spoken many times. Although, as children, I don't think any of us really comprehended what that meant; we just wanted to play. I was comfortable with all five of the Hannaford children, and I don't recall feeling any differently about them than I did the three other children of servants who were among our playmates. But for some reason, Jack and I gravitated to each other. We would sometimes hide from the others just so we could talk, but I'm certain our conversations must have been ridiculous, given how young we were."

"I'm certain they must have felt very important to you at the time," Lottie said in a way that left Hennie deeply appreciative of her insight and under-standing over something that Hennie had always chosen to keep to herself—and had now become immensely significant given their current situations.

"Anyway," Hennie said, forcing herself more fully to the present, "we were friends; that's all. I remember that we both cried when we said good-bye; we were both angry with his father for sending me away, but we were also both sad, knowing we would probably never see each other again—and as children there was nothing we could do about it. I think part of the reason his father was so firm on sending me away was that he'd found out how much time his children had been spending with the servants and he wasn't pleased; it was as if I was being used as an example."

"Or a scapegoat!" Lottie said vehemently. "Don't get me wrong. I would have died a long time ago if you'd not been there to help me through, but the very thought of you being torn away from all this . . ." She motioned wildly with her arms to indicate the grand home in which they were living and all it repre-sented. "Well . . . it infuriates me." She blew out a lengthy, ragged breath as if to let go of anger that served no purpose. "But the important thing is that you're back, and it *cannot* be coincidence; there must be some greater meaning to your being here now."

"Or maybe it *is* just coincidence and we shouldn't let our imaginations run away with any thoughts of this being anything more than it is. We've been blessed with good employment, and a safe place to live, surrounded by good people—and let's not forget that the food is heavenly."

"We can't forget that!" Lottie chuckled.

"So, let's be grateful for what we have and not make something out of nothing. And we can be grateful that Jack is in charge, and not his father. You've told me what the sisters are doing, but you've said practically nothing about the brothers. Do you know anything of Jack? And his brother, George? Are they married? Do they have children? Are they—"

"One question at a time," Lottie said, "and bear in mind that I actually know very little. But I do know *one* thing over which you are making huge assump-tions that are absolutely false."

"What?" Hennie demanded, unable to imagine what that might be.

"Jack is *not* in charge here; it is George overseeing the estate."

"What?" Hennie repeated more loudly and emphatically.

"Hush!" Lottie insisted. "We won't be overheard speaking at a normal volume, but don't go getting all upset and inviting any undue attention."

"Very well," Hennie said, feeling upset and confused but speaking more quietly. "Jack is the oldest brother, the rightful heir. Given how close we once were, I can't help but feel concerned over what possible reasons there could be for him not to be in charge." All kinds of worries assaulted her simultaneously. Was he ill? Had he died? Had there been some kind of terrible family rift prior to his father's death that had created problems? There had to be a very good reason for Jack to not be in charge. He was responsible and committed to his home and family. It just didn't make sense.

"All I can tell you is that Jack disappeared."

"Disappeared?" Hennie echoed, astonished; but at least she kept her voice down.

"That's the story around here. Their father died, and Jack just up and left and no one knows where he's gone; no one has heard anything from him in years."

"Good heavens!" Hennie murmured and put a hand over her heart, suddenly overcome with such worry for her childhood friend that she could hardly breathe. "What on earth could have motivated such a decision?"

"Well, if you knew the answer to that, you might be promoted to royalty around here. It seems to be the biggest question among everyone who lives here. George is a fair man and well-liked from what I hear; much better than his father according to what you've told me—and well, I've heard that from gossip around here, as well. I've seen him a couple of times in the stables but not up close, and we've never spoken. I must say that he *is* handsome."

"That's not a surprise," Hennie said, still distracted by what she'd just learned about Jack's disappearance. "They were all beautiful children; not only did I think so when I knew them, but I recall people referring to them that way. I thought Jack's sisters looked like princesses. Of course, they had servants who curled their hair and styled it so lovely, and they wore such pretty dresses. But they all had beautiful faces; they looked to me like dolls that had come alive. I remember wishing to be half as pretty. I told my mother so more than once; she assured me that if I were all prettied up the way they were, I would be even more lovely. But she was my mother, and mothers say things like that to their children."

"I'm not certain I disagree with her," Lottie said to Hennie's surprise. "You have lovely features, my dear friend."

Hennie said with part sarcasm and part humor, "A lot of good that does me in my present circumstances." She made a scoffing sound. "Now my features likely make me a pathetic-looking man."

"We're the scrawny ones," Lottie said with the same humor. A minute or more later, Hennie hadn't realized her mind was wandering until Lottie asked, "Where are you? You're not even listening to me."

"I'm sorry," Hennie said, looking at her friend to prove she was paying attention. "I just can't believe that Jack left in such a way; I feel . . . worried about him. I know I haven't seen him for more than a decade, but . . . why would he do such a thing?"

"You've already asked that question, and we've already established that no one knows."

"I understand, but . . . it troubles me," Hennie said.

"Of course," Lottie said with compassion. "I can understand why." She sighed and added, "From what I understand, George is a good man and very duty bound regarding the estate, but not at all pleased about his brother's disappearance. I think he'd do anything to be able to find him and bring him back. I even hear he's done everything possible. He's hired investigators and exhausted every known possibility. But as I see it, if a person doesn't want to be found, they will find a way to remain hidden—especially given the fact that he probably left here with a great deal of money. That's one thing this family is not short on—which I'm grateful for because it means they can provide us with good jobs and a comfortable situation. Anyway," Lottie sighed, "that's all I know, my friend. I wish I could be more helpful."

"Clearly there's nothing to be done about it," Hennie said. "I'm just . . . surprised, and . . . unsettled. I hate to think of him in some faraway place, hiding for reasons I can't begin to understand, when I know how much he loved his home and family. You say that Rebecca is the sister who remains unmarried . . . who still lives here?"

"That's right," Lottie said. "As I told you, I've only had a few glimpses of her, and she is indeed very beautiful—at least from a distance. But the riding habits she wears could make even an old crone attractive, in my opinion."

This comment made Hennie laugh, and their conversation shifted elsewhere, but as Hennie lay in bed that night, still troubled and puzzled by what she'd heard about Jack, she had to finally settle on simply praying that he was all right, knowing there was absolutely nothing more she could do for him. She wondered what he would think if he knew that she was now back here at the home where they'd been such close playmates—working as a man, no less. He might be disgusted by her role-playing, which was certainly deceptive no matter how one might look at it. But Hennie believed he would more likely find the situation amusing—unless he had changed a great deal.

Hennie finally slept in the midst of praying for Jack and awoke to the usual knock on her door to begin another day working as a stable hand—but she didn't mind at all. It only took her a moment to recall how it had felt to begin a day's work at Grenville's—or worse, the workhouse—for her to be filled with enthusiasm for the prospect of relatively simple—even enjoyable—work, which she could do while being treated with respect. And every meal was a delight in the kitchen of Ivy Manor.

Spring warmed into summer while Hennie settled more comfortably into her new life, where the routine became downright easy to the point that she almost forgot she was pretending to be a man—but never to the point that she would ever let on to the truth. She and Lottie simply became very good at playing their parts and doing their jobs.

From a distance, Hennie saw Rebecca in the stables a couple of times and could only admire how beautiful she was with her dark curls hanging beneath a stylish little hat that coordinated with a magnificent red riding habit. She almost looked like a queen while she waited for her horse to be saddled, chatting with an equally elegant friend who had come to share an outing on horseback. Hennie had to force herself to stop staring at the two beautiful women and get back to work, shoveling old straw out of a stall so that the floor could be cleaned and new straw laid down in its place. It wasn't the first time she'd thought that the horses here lived better than she'd lived in the workhouse—or the orphanage. Then her thoughts wandered to Rebecca. Hennie had never been close to Jack's sisters—at least in the respect that they never shared secrets, and she'd never played one-on-one with any of them. But the children had all played many games together as a group, and Rebecca had usually been involved. A part of her wanted to run over to this woman and hug her and declare that she'd come back, but she knew the idea would be preposterous even if Hennie were not working here in disguise. Rebecca probably wouldn't even remember Hennie, and likely wouldn't care that she'd come back; it wasn't that the woman would be unkind, but she hadn't known Hennie well enough for them to share any kind of reunion.

But seeing Rebecca took Hennie's thoughts again to Jack, no matter how hard she tried not to allow her mind to wander to any thoughts of him. Doing so only left her frustrated and concerned; therefore, she attempted to avoid thinking of him at all.

A few days later, Mr. Parsons entered the stables and hollered loudly enough for everyone currently busy with various tasks to be able to hear him. "Joe's not feeling so good today." Hennie knew he was one of the oldest stable hands; she felt concerned but not surprised that he might not be able to keep up with the hard work she'd seen him doing. "I need someone to take Sally May into town to the smithy to have her shoes changed. Any volunteers?" Hennie was startled to hear the absolute silence that followed Mr. Parsons's question when she believed that volunteering for a task was something that would keep an employee in better standing.

Another moment of silence provoked her to holler, "I'll do it . . . as long as you tell me where to go."

"That'll be no problem," Parsons said, sounding relieved and pleased.

Since Hennie didn't know how to saddle a horse, and she'd told Parsons so from the beginning, he saddled Sally May for her, and told her exactly where to go in town to find the blacksmith whom Parsons preferred working with.

"He'll be expecting you," Parsons said, as Hennie put her foot in the stirrup and hoisted herself into the saddle that was too big for her. "Feel free to walk about town or get yourself a bite to eat while he's working; no need for you to stay there while the blacksmith does his work."

"Very well," Hennie said and nodded.

She was surprised when Parsons asked, "Do you have any money?"

Hennie hadn't even thought about that. "Not on me at the moment, but I've got wages in my room and—"

"Here," Parsons said and pulled some money out of his breeches pocket, handing some to Hennie. "The pub just around the corner from the smithy has a fine venison pie. You can pay me back tomorrow."

"Thank you," Hennie said, tucking the money into a pocket.

"Thank *you*," Parsons said, again surprising Hennie. "Most of these blokes don't like the job of taking a horse to the smithy, but it has to be done on a regular basis, and at least one horse a week has to go into town."

"I'm glad to help wherever you need me," Hennie said, and Mr. Parsons smiled at her before he motioned for her to get going.

Hennie walked the horse out of the stables and then eased her into an easy gallop once they were on the road. She enjoyed the fresh air and peacefulness of the ride so much that she wondered if Mr. Parsons might allow her to make this a part of her regular duties. Or perhaps Joe enjoyed this aspect of *his* duties, and once he was feeling better, he would be expecting to resume this facet of his responsibilities. For Hennie, the idea of simply riding a horse into town once or more a week, and then to be able to wander about while the blacksmith did his work, was more than appealing. She reminded herself that the weather wouldn't always be so favorable, but she now owned a good hat and coat that were suitable for rain, and before winter came she would be well-equipped for cold weather as well.

Hennie enjoyed riding Sally May so much that she arrived at the village more quickly than she'd expected. She dismounted outside the smithy, which was mostly exposed to the open air with flaps of canvas that could be rolled down and tied in less favorable weather. The blacksmith—a well-built man perhaps near her own age with dark hair and a heavy beard—was hard at work hammering a piece of red-hot metal against an anvil. Then he stuck it into water with the large tongs, which held it safely and firmly in place, while steam hissed out of the water. He glanced toward her and said, "Parsons send you?"

"Yes," she said, and the blacksmith stuck whatever he was working on back into the hot coals to heat it up again.

"I thought I recognized Sally May." He then spoke to the horse in a funny voice. "How are you Sally, old girl? I'll be with you shortly." He said in a normal voice to Hennie, "You must be new. It's usually Joe who comes."

"Yes," Hennie said. "I go by Hen. Joe's not feeling well."

"Nothing serious, I hope," the man said.

"Not from what I was told," Hennie said and laughed softly, "but I'm not told much."

"I'm Ollie," the man said and nodded to his left. "You're welcome to tether Sally May there, and I'll get to work on her in a few minutes. There's no need for you to stay. She'll be ready in about an hour."

Hennie wouldn't have minded staying; she'd never watched a blacksmith work before and thought it might be interesting. But she sensed that perhaps he didn't *want* her to stay; perhaps he preferred working without an audience, so she tethered the mare and said, "I'll be back in about an hour, then."

"See you then," Ollie said, and Hennie meandered away from the smithy, wandering idly through the village with no particular destination in mind. She'd come into town previously with some of the other stable hands when they'd been given time off to procure anything they might need, and Lottie had taken Hennie to purchase some necessary clothes. But they hadn't had time to wander, and the men's clothing shop had certainly not been a familiar place to Hennie. But now Hennie became awash with memories of her mother doing simple errands with a basket over one arm while she used the other to hold tightly to Hennie's hand. Hennie passed a candy shop that looked almost exactly the same and stared through the window while she recalled vividly how her mother would allow her to pick out one special treat to savor on the way home. She repeated the ritual in front of a bakery that also appeared unchanged, thinking of how her mother would alternate between the candy shop and the bakery on their visits into town, where she would buy something for each of them to enjoy as a conclusion to their excursion. The memory became so clear that Hennie was almost salivating at the recollection of the iced buns and savory biscuits that had been her favorites. She then realized that she was standing right there with money in her pocket and decided that purchasing a few baked goods to eat for her lunch appealed to her more in that moment than going to some noisy pub for the recommended venison pie. Perhaps she'd try that another time.

With her purchases in a small bag that felt familiar in her hand, Hennie found a little bench that she had often shared with her mother on the high street. She sat there and ate her delectable baked goods, marveling that they all tasted exactly as she'd remembered. The tastes and aromas of her little indulgence, combined with her surroundings, took her back in time so completely that she had a moment where she almost believed she could turn and see her mother sitting beside her.

When the clock in the tower of the town square chimed, Hennie realized that her hour was almost over, and she hurried to finish eating what she'd purchased. After carefully using a handkerchief to wipe away any possible traces of her lunch from her hands and face, Hennie walked back to the smithy and found Sally May tethered in the same place, except that now she was sporting new shoes and contentedly nibbling on something out of a bucket, as if she'd been given her own lunch as a reward for enduring the change of shoes.

"How did she do?" Hennie asked Ollie, who was as busy now as he'd been when she'd arrived earlier.

"She was a very good girl," Ollie said, barely taking time to toss a smile in her direction before he put his full attention to his work. "There's water for her there." He nodded toward a large bucket of it while his hands remained busy. "Give her a good drink before you set out."

"Thank you, Ollie," she said, and he quickly tossed her another smile.

"Of course," he said. "Glad to help."

"Is there anything else I need to do?"

"Not a thing," he said. "Mr. Parsons takes care of my bill on a monthly basis."

"Very well," Hennie said and untethered Sally May to guide her to the bucket of water, which the horse took advantage of. Hennie had no further exchange with the blacksmith, since he was working hard and very focused on his task. With the extreme heat necessary to be able to form the metal, Hennie believed he needed to be especially careful and could understand why distraction might be dangerous. So she just mounted Sally May and rode out of the village toward Ivy Manor, passing through familiar meadows and beautiful wooded areas, where nothing seemed to have changed since her childhood, except that the trees had grown taller—and so had she.

Throughout the summer Hennie settled so comfortably into pretending to be a man that she began to wonder how difficult it might be to someday merge back into life as a woman—although her present circumstances were so good in every respect that a part of her didn't ever want to leave the sanctuary of her employment at Ivy Manor. The meals were excellent and satisfying, the accommodations were safe and comfortable, and the work was fulfilling without being overly taxing. Hennie and Lottie had time together every evening in one of their rooms, where they could completely be themselves and talk about anything and everything that might come to mind. Sometimes they read aloud to each other, and sometimes they talked about books they were reading individually during little snatches of time here and there. On Sundays they went to church, where Hennie thoroughly enjoyed being part of a congregation, and she found the vicar's sermons to be uplifting and rarely boring.

Gradually, Hennie was able to use her wages to buy more things for herself—the most important being suitable clothing. After purchasing a suit that was appropriate to wear to church and feel as if she were not being disrespectful by attending improperly dressed, the next priority was to get some warm winter clothing in anticipation of the colder weather. Only after she'd made these purchases did Hennie feel she could indulge in buying luxuries—such as books. And she always put a portion of her wages away in a safe place, saving for the possibility—or perhaps inevitability—of being found out and having to leave this place and find work elsewhere, someplace far enough away that no one would know how she and Lottie had posed as men to deceive an entire community.

While Hennie recognized that her life was good in many respects, one of her favorite aspects was the opportunity to ride a horse into town to the smithy and leave it there while she wandered about town all alone, and sometimes ate at the nearby pub—where the venison pie was indeed extremely delicious. Following her first assignment to have a horse fitted for new shoes, Mr. Parsons had taken her aside to inform her that Joe's health was not going to improve, given that he'd been diagnosed with an ailment that would only worsen. Hennie was not told what that ailment actually was, but she did find out that Joe was even much older than he'd appeared. She felt badly for the man, even though she barely knew who he was; but she knew that it was standard procedure here at the manor for employees to be cared for in times of illness, even if that meant a lengthy terminal illness. Parsons then asked Hennie if she would like to officially take over Joe's responsibility of seeing that each of the horses had their regular visit to the smithy in a predesignated rotation, which meant her taking a horse into town once, sometimes twice a week. Hennie gladly agreed, fighting to subdue her enthusiasm since she didn't want to behave in a way that was unseemly, or perhaps come across as a little too girlish in her excitement.

Hennie didn't mind any of the work required of her, even though she considered mucking out stalls to be the least pleasant chore. She loved to clean and brush the horses, and she had quickly grown accustomed to their different personalities. Those that were owned and ridden by members of the family were more high-spirited and grew restless easily. Even though George and Rebecca were the only Hannaford family members living at Ivy Manor, horses belonging to the other girls—and even two that were specifically owned by Jack—were still being cared for in these stables, and Hennie had come to know them all by name, and she often whispered quiet, one-sided conversations to the horses as she cared for them. The horses that had been trained to pull carriages and wagons had calmer temperaments and were also a bulkier breed—even though Hennie knew nothing about the differences in breeds or how that affected their appearance and capabilities. Hennie loved them all, which made her love her job. But the opportunity to ride into town on the back of one of these magnificent creatures was absolutely the best part of her life. Even when it rained, Hennie just wore her hat and coat and found that even being chilled and wet didn't feel at all disagreeable, being out in the open as she was, and feeling the freedom that riding offered. Riding such fine-quality horses was a rare privilege that only the wealthy classes enjoyed—except in the rare case of having a job such as Hennie's, where she was being entrusted with the care of these horses on behalf of their owners. And knowing that Mr. Parsons was pleased with her work made it even more gratifying.

Chapter Five

THE BLACKSMITH

THE PASSING OF MONTHS ESCORTED the hint of cooler temperatures into the air, and the leaves on the trees began to change color. Hennie had lost track of how long she'd been at Ivy Manor except for recalling that it had been spring when she'd arrived. And she'd lost track of how many times she'd taken a horse into town for Ollie to change its shoes and make certain during the process that the horse's hooves were healthy and in good condition. Of course, Ollie had been trained in the art of being a good farrier as well as a blacksmith. Hennie had learned from sharing tidbits of conversation with him that any farrier would be required to have enough of the skills of a blacksmith to shape a horse's shoes properly, but there were many blacksmiths who specialized in other work and didn't have the training to care for a horse's unique feet. Hennie hadn't known that before, and when she commented on that fact to Ollie, he seemed surprised—which made him ask her about her background. She remained truthful but vague and simply told him that she'd lived in an orphanage following her mother's death, since her father had died many years earlier. She told him she'd been in a workhouse for some years before finding work elsewhere, until a friend had found her and brought her to Ivy Manor.

"You've had a difficult life," he stated while he continued his work.

"I try not to think about it like that," Hennie said. "I just do my best to be grateful for all that's good; it could always be worse."

He seemed surprised by the comment, even though he barely glanced at her between his hammerings. Hennie felt mildly uncomfortable and made a graceful exit as she always did after she'd tethered the horse in the usual place and they'd chatted for a few minutes. Unable to stop thinking about Ollie and their brief conversations here and there, Hennie impulsively purchased two mutton hand pies from a vendor, along with some iced buns from the bakery, before she returned to Ollie's place of business and conveniently found him sitting down and guzzling water from a large pewter tankard.

"I've rarely seen you actually sitting," she said, meaning it as a compliment in regard to how hard he worked.

He looked pleased to see her and replied, "And I've never seen you return this quickly. I've not even started on Zeus yet."

"Well, that's good . . . because I brought you some lunch; I hope you haven't eaten yet."

"I haven't, no," he said, sounding surprised. "Why would you bring me lunch?" he asked, sounding even more surprised.

"Because I've enjoyed our conversations and thought I might be able to enjoy more if I fed you."

"I won't argue with that," he said and motioned for her to sit in a chair that was obviously meant for customers to use while they waited. "Just give me a minute to wash my hands."

Hennie nodded and allowed herself to look around more thoroughly than she ever had before. The place was every bit practicality and perfectly organized. The coals, which had to be kept very hot to temper the metal, were as always putting off a great deal of heat, but an autumn breeze counteracted its effect agreeably, and Hennie actually moved her chair a little closer to the wide opening of the smithy to get more access to the fresh air. A minute later, Ollie appeared, holding *two* pewter tankards of water.

"Here you go," he said, handing one of them to her before he moved a different chair close to hers where he sat down, and she gave him one of the hand pies, which was wrapped in brown paper. "Oh, it smells good," he said. "You're very kind."

"I got some iced buns as well," she said. "I confess I'm terribly fond of them. I've always thought It's nice to share the things we enjoy with a friend."

He looked momentarily taken aback, and she wondered why. He offered somewhat of an explanation when he said, "It's nice to have a new friend."

"Yes, it is," Hennie agreed, wondering what he'd think if he knew she was actually a woman. Bringing him a simple lunch might have been construed much differently, but then she never would have been here in the first place if she were actually living as her authentic self. She'd made friends—at least in a minimal way—among the men she worked with. Surely there was no harm in sharing some friendly conversation with Ollie during her regular visits to his place of business.

"Oh, this is very good," Ollie said after taking a bite of his pie and chewing enough to be able to speak without sounding offensive. "You must have gotten this from Mel."

"I'm afraid I don't know his name," Hennie said after chewing her food sufficiently, "but I dare say he makes the only mutton around here that isn't too tough to chew."

Ollie laughed. "That's exactly what I was going to say." He took another bite and made a noise to indicate he was enjoying his lunch, although Hennie now thought that she should have purchased *two* pies for him, since he was certainly bigger than Hennie and his work was very physical.

"So," Hennie said after she swallowed another bite, "what made you want to do this kind of work? Did your father—"

"Oh, no!" Ollie said after taking a long drink of water. "My father assumed I would become something prestigious and respectable, but I've found I rather enjoy physical labor. It can be very satisfying. I was an apprentice for a black-smith in the next county. Even though I found him somewhat disagreeable, he was good at what he did and taught me well. I picked up on it rather quickly, I might say, if that doesn't sound like bragging." He chuckled.

"Not at all," Hennie assured him.

"One day a traveler in need of help with a slipped shoe on his horse mentioned that the blacksmith here had died, and his daughter was looking to sell the place and move elsewhere. I had some money put away from an inheritance; I'd saved it with that very thing in mind. So I came here, and I'm here still . . ." He took another bite and added with a chuckle and his mouth full, "Very much enjoying this pie."

"I'm glad of it," Hennie said, enjoying her own.

After finishing their pies, Hennie got out the iced buns, and Ollie was clearly pleased, making it evident that he shared Hennie's love for them. They chatted about some happenings in the village and the weather, nothing of any consequence to either of them. But Hennie enjoyed her lunch with Ollie; she enjoyed even more how appreciative he was of her thoughtfulness. She was pleasantly surprised when he said, "We'll have to do it again; next time I'll buy."

"I wouldn't argue with that," she said and tried to laugh like a man, knowing the result was likely pathetic—but then everyone who knew her and believed her to be male likely found her odd. But she was well-liked regardless of that, so she didn't really care. She felt more socially accepted in this village and the nearby manor than she ever had before. Despite outwardly appearing to be a man, she did her best to be her genuine self—to express her own opinions, and to maintain her integrity. She believed it was these traits that determined whether she found friends among her colleagues and acquaintances.

Ollie set to work on Zeus, a horse well-known for his strength in pulling the supply wagon back and forth to the village on a regular basis. Not wanting to outstay her welcome, Hennie excused herself, insisting she had a few errands to take care of—even though she didn't. She returned to find Zeus ready to go, and Ollie thanked her once again for lunch as she was leaving.

Sharing lunch with Ollie became a habit, and as autumn lurched into winter, they enjoyed sitting closer to the always-hot coals of the blacksmith's fire while the heavy flaps of the front of the smithy were pegged to the ground and tied closed to keep out the wind and snow. Hennie truly enjoyed her friendship with Ollie, even though they both avoided talking about their pasts—as if he sensed that she didn't want to discuss such a horrible upbringing, or perhaps in some way he understood it; she wondered more than once if he'd had a difficult childhood himself, especially by the way he avoided talking about it. But they still found plenty to talk about, and they often made each other laugh. Hennie took to remaining in the smithy while Ollie did his work, which was a blessing since she didn't want to be wandering around the village in cold weather, and she would far rather be visiting with her new friend than sitting alone in one of the local pubs just to stay warm.

Since Hennie and Lottie told each other everything, Lottie knew about Hennie's growing friendship with the blacksmith, but it took Hennie by surprise one evening when Lottie asked, "Is he handsome?"

"What do you mean by that?" Hennie countered abruptly, taken aback by the defensiveness in her own voice.

Lottie chuckled. "I think it's a fairly straightforward question. Is he handsome? I'm guessing he is by the way you just got all riled up by the question."

"I did not get all riled up!" Hennie said, even more defensively, which made Lottie laugh more deeply.

"There you go again," Lottie said.

"I . . . I . . . haven't even paid attention to such things since we came here," Hennie insisted. "You and I are in no position to be looking at men with any kind of romantic interest when we are so fiercely hiding the fact that we are women."

"That doesn't mean we can't assess whether or not a man is handsome," Lottie said with a little giggle. "So, is he?"

"I suppose he is," Hennie said. "His beard is too thick and bushy for my taste, but . . . yes, I suppose he's handsome. He's certainly very strong," Hennie went on, trying to be practical in answering Lottie's questions, if only to dispel her initial defensiveness and what Lottie might read into that. "I can't deny that I enjoy watching him work; he's very good at what he does."

"And what he does requires a great deal of physical strength," Lottie said with a little smirk, making it evident that she *knew* Hennie had certainly taken notice of Ollie far more than she was trying to let on.

"Yes, it does," Hennie said and went on to just address the issue directly. "And whether or not I think he's handsome is irrelevant. He can never know the truth about me, Lottie—never! How can I gain a person's trust and form a friendship over the course of months and then declare that I'm not even a man?" Hennie chuckled satirically. "As long as you and I are living this way, we need to keep any such ideas completely out of our heads. It's plainly evident that until we are able to move very far away from here and resume our true selves as women, there will be no discussion or even thinking as to whether or not we might find a man attractive."

Lottie sighed, long and loud, making it clear without any words that she couldn't argue with Hennie, but she knew her declaration to be true. "I only asked if he was handsome," Lottie said, and they changed the subject.

But that night as Hennie lay in her bed, attempting to sleep while a vicious wind howled outside, her thoughts were ignoring her own edict. She simply couldn't stop thinking about Ollie. He *was* handsome. Despite his beard, which Hennie didn't necessarily like—she'd always preferred a clean-shaven appearance on men—she couldn't deny that he was very attractive indeed. Her preoccupation with that fact left her feeling unsettled and practically squirming in her own skin. She was a woman! She had been created to feel attracted to a man—especially a man she knew to have deep integrity and kindness. She'd come to enjoy his company very much. But it was Hen the stable hand whom Ollie had become friends with. And she meant what she'd said to Lottie. He could never know the truth! Never! A day would come when she and Lottie would leave this area and start their lives over elsewhere. Then and only then could she ever hope to find romance in her life. Whether or not she was ever able to marry—destined to a life of servitude as she seemed to be—remained to be seen, and it would be a good, long time before the possibility might even be considered.

Hennie absolutely knew in her mind the way things needed to be, but something was sparking to life in her heart that was in complete disagreement, which left her heart and head battling each other so fiercely that she had to simply banish any thought of Ollie, making it possible to get the sleep she needed.

Through weeks of bitter cold weather, Hennie kept doing her job and was proud of herself for the way she was able to discipline her thinking and focus only on her need to keep up the proper appearances and simply do all that was required of her. Riding into town in the cold wasn't enjoyable, but she'd learned to bundle up properly, and she always had the warmth of Ollie's smithy to look forward to. The extremely hot coals, which often made the smithy far too warm in the summer, created a pleasant reprieve from the weather on such bitter cold days.

As Hennie continued her friendship with Ollie, she was also proud of herself for the way she was able to completely banish from her mind any minuscule thought of him that wasn't purely friendship—man to man. Winter finally released its bitter grip, and the temperatures began to warm up, bringing with them evidence of spring, with color starting to burst up out of the ground and onto the limbs of the trees. As Hennie continued her regular trips into town to keep the horses' feet properly shod and cared for, she often found herself recounting the fact that she'd been employed at Ivy Manor for approximately a year now, and while it wasn't at all difficult to recall how much she'd hated working for Grenville at the inn, she could feel nothing but gratitude for being able to now live in conditions that were so much better. She often told Lottie how grateful she was that her friend had come to rescue her. And even though the circumstances of their necessary deception were less than ideal, they'd settled into having the ability to do it well, and not a single person had ever seemed even the slightest bit suspicious. Miss Atkins continued to be their friend and confidante, assisting them with any personal matters that might create challenging circumstances. All in all, Hennie considered her life to be good—even though she knew it had to be temporary. Both she and Lottie vehemently agreed that there were times they desperately missed just being able to live as women and show their authentic selves to the world. As much as they enjoyed their life at Ivy Manor, and appreciated the security and comfort it offered, they knew a day would come when they'd have to move on. And they both hoped and prayed they would have the foresight to know when that time might be, so they could leave with dignity and not be forced to leave because their deception had been discovered.

Hennie was glad to arrive at Ollie's smithy to find the heavy canvas flaps rolled up and tied securely, allowing the spring breeze to flow into the smithy. Ollie was sweating anyway as he vigorously pounded a hot horseshoe with his hammer. But it was rare to see Ollie *not* sweating, given the kind of work he did, and how closely he had to remain to those furiously hot coals.

"Hello," he said, tossing a smile in her direction as she was dismounting today's recipient of new shoes.

"Hello," she replied and tethered the horse in the usual place. "How are you today?"

"I'm well," he said, "and you?"

"The same," she answered. "Should I go and get us some lunch?"

"That would be grand," Ollie said, sticking the horseshoe into water with the tongs he held, creating a cloud of steam that filled the smithy with a familiar aroma completely unique to this atmosphere of fire and metal and water. But Hennie had come to like this place so much—mostly because of Ollie's company—that the aroma had become comforting.

"You want anything in particular?" Hennie asked, even though they had only shared food from two different places, and they both preferred the same old items from the bakery. Perhaps if Hennie came more frequently, they would add variety to their menu.

"The usual, if that's all right with you," Ollie said. "It's my turn to buy," he added. "You know where the money is."

"Of course," Hennie said. She *did* know where he kept a small amount of money, and they'd established a firm rule that they took turns buying the food they shared. Hennie opened a cupboard and went on her tiptoes to reach the tin can from which she took some coins and left the smithy, returning a short while later with mutton hand pies and iced buns. Ollie had already washed up and had placed two chairs in a comfortable spot where they could look out upon the narrow street and enjoy the spring weather while they ate. He also had the standard two tankards of water sitting on the ground beside the chairs. Their routine had become familiar, and Hennie was quick to make herself comfortable and stretch out her booted legs as they began to eat, chatting about any news either of them might have heard about people in town or the goings-on at Ivy Manor. Hennie had come to know the people of the village better in the year she'd lived here, and she was always interested in who might be getting married, who'd had a baby, who was ill, or who might have died. And Ollie seemed to enjoy hearing about news from the manor, even though he was only vaguely acquainted with a very few of the people who worked there.

Since Hennie and Ollie rarely, if ever, talked about their pasts—given the fact that neither of them seemed to have much to say that wasn't dismal—Hennie was surprised to hear Ollie start reminiscing about a pleasant experience from his childhood. He got on to the subject after they'd witnessed some children skipping down the cobbled street, laughing as if they were enjoying the best day of their lives.

"I remember," Ollie said, "this particular afternoon when I was . . . oh, I think seven or eight perhaps. The weather was much like today; perhaps that's why I thought of it. I had a good friend, a girl who was about a year younger than myself, I think, and we snuck away to enjoy the sunshine, both of us ignoring our chores . . ." he chuckled, ". . . which I'm certain meant that we were both in a great deal of trouble later in the day." He chuckled again and sank more deeply into his chair, as if reminiscing was far more important in that moment than getting back to work, even though he'd finished eating. "My friend and I began collecting some lovely smooth stones from the edge of a wide stream that ran through a meadow, and we started stacking them carefully so they created a wall . . . and then one wall became four, so we made this enchanting little fortress; it wasn't very big—only about the size of a large book—but we were completely invested in making it perfect." He laughed again while Hennie just listened, wondering why his story was tickling something in her own memories; she just couldn't quite place it.

"For some reason," Ollie went on, "we decided that the fortress needed to be hidden from an evil king who was bent on destroying it. I must confess I had quite an imagination as a child, perhaps because imagining things was far better than the reality of life." A moment of sadness quickly passed into finishing his story. "To keep the fortress hidden from the evil king, we gathered up handfuls of ivy leaves, because ivy grew everywhere, and we completely covered the little fortress with ivy."

Hennie's heart began to pound before her mind even knew why Ollie's story was so significant to her. She turned slightly to see him better, at the same time using every bit of willpower she could muster to conceal the effect his story was having on her. Because she knew what he was going to say next, and she knew why. *A heart-shaped rock was placed in the center of the little fortress—the fortress of stone and ivy.* Hennie could hardly breathe, but she had to make certain Ollie didn't notice. She just remained quiet and waited for him to finish.

"We'd found this rock a couple of days earlier that was shaped like a heart; well, it was an oddly proportioned heart, but it still looked like a heart. And we put the heart into the center of the fortress, pretending that it held magical powers and It was the heart that the evil king was really after, but the heart would be protected by the mighty fortress." He chuckled once again. "We called it the fortress of stone and ivy!" he concluded somewhat dramatically and laughed once more. "Silly story; I don't know why I thought of it. Just a pleasant memory, I suppose."

Hennie swallowed carefully and cleared her throat in an attempt to keep her voice even as she said, "It's a grand story." She cleared her throat again, hoping Ollie wouldn't notice how tightly her hands were gripping the sides of her chair. "Whatever happened to your friend?"

"Oh." He looked down abruptly, but not before she saw a distinct shadow cloud his countenance. "She . . . moved away a few years later after her mother died. I never saw her again."

"How tragic," Hennie said, while inside she was screaming, *It's me, Jack! It's me!* And this was Jack! Oliver Jonathan Spenser Hannaford. She knew his full name because she'd been his best friend. But he'd hated the formality of his name, and his friends and his siblings called him Jack, even though his father had always insisted on referring to him as Jonathan. Jack had gone missing; his disappearance was a mystery to everyone who knew him. And here he was, hiding behind that beard in the village closest to his home. *But why?* Hennie wanted to ask him a thousand questions, but she couldn't even let on to the fact that she'd figured out his true identity, not without revealing the ridiculous truth that she was pretending to be a man so she could work at the manor, which legally belonged to him. Here they were, childhood friends, both hiding their true identities from the world, unable to even talk about it.

Hennie felt so overcome that she had to put all her focus into breathing normally and not letting on how his story had affected her. She felt nothing but relief when he abruptly stood, saying, "Yes, it was tragic, but it was a very long time ago." He chuckled, but it was more tense than humorous. "Enough reminiscing for one day. I need to get to work. Do you have errands to see to while I—"

"Yes," Hennie declared abruptly, moving her chair back to its proper place. Grateful for an opportunity to not be in his presence so she could take in what she'd just realized, she hurriedly added, "I'll be back in about an hour . . . as usual. Thank you for lunch."

"A pleasure as always," he said, tossing her a smile. It *was* Jack! She'd never seen the resemblance because she hadn't been looking for it. She hadn't seen him since they were children, and she never would have expected to see him working as a blacksmith. The fact that they'd changed a great deal since childhood had worked in her own favor since she certainly didn't want him to recognize her as the Hennie he'd once known. But his assumption that she was a man would make it ludicrous for him to look at her and see his childhood friend.

Hennie hurried out of the smithy, around the corner, past the pub, and into a narrow alley, where she was relieved to find herself completely alone. She pressed her hands to the cold wall and hung her head between her arms, now gasping for breath in delayed reaction to what she'd just learned. When she'd finally managed to get control of her breathing, Hennie turned and leaned her back against the wall, looking upward as if heaven might somehow give her the answers to the most obvious questions. She thought of how often she and Lottie had talked about their mutual belief that there was no such thing as coincidence, that even the most difficult circumstances life dished out had purpose and meaning if a person was willing to look for them. How well Hennie recalled the day Lottie had brought her to Ivy Manor, with no idea that this was where Hennie had grown up. She'd declared then that Hennie returning to this place surely could *not* be coincidence, that there had to be a reason for it. A year had passed, and Hennie hadn't given any thought to that idea in a very long time. But now she had found Jack, the missing heir of Ivy Manor—her precious childhood friend.

Hennie slid her back down the wall and sat on the ground, just trying to let her mind catch up to this unexpected revelation. What were the odds that she would end up back at Ivy Manor, of all the fine houses and estates where Lottie might have found work? And what were the odds that Hennie would have been the one—of all the stable hands—to take over Joe's job of riding the horses into town to meet their appointments with the blacksmith? And what were the odds that she and Ollie would become friends, comfortable enough for him to share a tender childhood memory with her? How well Hennie remembered the little fortress of stone and ivy, protecting the enchanted heart from the evil king! No one else knew that story, because they'd sworn each other to secrecy over it, which had added to the magical effect of their imagination and the precious time they had been able to spend away from the manor to play as children should.

Hearing the chimes of the clock tower in the town square, Hennie was forced to compose herself and settle the proper façade into place. She needed to return to the smithy and interact with Ollie—a man she now knew to be Jack—as if nothing at all had changed between them. She put her mind to the task of assuming the appropriate facial expressions and engaging in the minimal conversation necessary to get the newly shod horse and be on her way, reminding Ollie that she had work back at the stables waiting for her. She *had* been gone longer than usual, given their lengthy lunchtime chat; therefore, her need to be quickly on her way was completely legitimate.

Hennie ignored how startled she felt to return to the smithy and just see Jack there; now that she knew it was him, she couldn't see Ollie anymore, which meant it would take a great deal of discipline to interact with him in the future and not let on to the truth of what she'd figured out. She was proud of herself for the way she spoke casually with him as they concluded the day's business as usual—forcing herself to not even think about how they were both living in disguise.

Hennie rode quickly out of the village and toward home, glad the horse knew how to stay on the road and find his way with little guidance. Her mind was still finding it difficult to grasp this new revelation. And the most prominent question that pounded through her head was a huge, resounding *Why?* What reason could there possibly be for Jack to take such drastic measures in leaving home following his father's death, learning the trade of a blacksmith, and hiding under a different identity right here in this village so close to his home?

Assaulted with so many overwhelming thoughts and feelings, Hennie had to stop in a wooded area, where she quickly tied the horse's reins to a tree before she sat on the ground and started to cry for reasons she couldn't begin to comprehend. As she considered the unexpected death of her mother, soon followed by being torn away from her home to end up in that horrible orphanage, she found herself crying with the grief she should have been allowed to experience then. But she'd not dared to even start crying, fearing she wouldn't be able to stop; and the adults around her in the orphanage had made it clear they didn't look fondly upon crying children. Hennie cried as she never had for the loss of her best childhood friend, and all the good memories she shared with Jack. They'd taken for granted that they would grow up together and remain friends for the rest of their lives, never anticipating such a dramatic change over which children had no control. Hennie cried over her horrible years in the orphanage and the workhouse, and even how much she'd hated working for Grenville. Her friendship with Lottie was the only good thing that had come out of those years, and for all that she treasured having Lottie in her life and would never want to be without her, Hennie couldn't deny the enormous dark cavity of grief inside of her related to all she'd had to endure since she'd left Ivy Manor. And now she'd come upon Jack under circumstances so strange that she could hardly believe it was real. He'd been raised with privilege and wealth, and she knew how difficult a man his father had been and how the absence of a mother in his life had been a source of much sorrow for him. And now she knew there were difficulties in Jack's situation that had propelled him to make outlandish and dramatic decisions which had brought him to the present—living in disguise and performing manual labor when he should have been overseeing the estate that was his rightful inheritance. Hennie simply couldn't begin to imagine the reasons, and it wasn't as if she could just have a conversation with George or Rebecca and find out what they knew. Hennie was known to them as a lowly stable hand—a scrawny, odd-looking man—who would have no business inquiring over personal matters in the Hannaford family.

Struck with the passing of time, Hennie gathered some composure and hoped by the time she arrived at the stables, her face wouldn't reveal how much she'd been crying. She forced all of her questions and concerns to the back of her mind and rode quickly home, knowing she would be long past her expected time of return. She dismounted just outside the stables and led the horse by the reins to its stall, well aware of Parsons looking in her direction, his brow furrowed, but he said nothing. Not wanting any tension in the air between them, Hennie simply said, "Sorry for the delay. Ollie was behind today; it couldn't be helped."

Parsons nodded, seeming to appreciate a reasonable explanation—and perhaps Hennie's willingness to at least acknowledge her tardiness. "It happens," was all Parsons said. "Get on with your work, young man."

"Of course," Hennie said and did just that, trying very hard not to think about the fact that she knew the answer to the enormous mystery that hung continually over Ivy Manor and all who lived and worked here; she knew where Jack Hannaford was, even if she didn't know why.

Hennie managed to get through the remainder of the day by focusing on her work and then on the hearty, delicious supper she enjoyed in the kitchen, with Lottie sitting at her side as usual. She wanted to just stand up and let the words burst out of her mouth that Jack Hannaford was alive and well, but she couldn't possibly betray Jack's trust in any way. In fact, by the time supper was finished, she knew she couldn't even tell Lottie—at least not yet. Lottie was such a dear and close friend, and they'd never kept secrets from each other—ever— the friendship she'd shared with Jack in their childhood had been at least as dear to her, and they too had shared a special trust that Hennie realized she had to honor, simply on the assumption that the passing of time and the change of circumstances had not altered it. Until she understood more about what was going on and why, she needed to keep this completely to herself. She could only pray that her acting skills might be strengthened enough to avoid having Lottie even suspect that Hennie's day had been extraordinarily strange and shocking.

Hennie prided herself on the way she was able to behave completely normally during the usual time she and Lottie spent chatting that evening before going to bed in their separate rooms. But long after Lottie had left and Hennie had gone to bed, her thoughts kept whirling with memories and questions. She finally fell asleep but woke up earlier than normal with the realization firmly set in her mind that she could not spend time with Ollie during their visits and not let on that she knew his true identity. And she couldn't tell Jack she'd figured out his secret unless she told him the truth about *her* secret. The very idea felt utterly terrifying! But at least she didn't have to face him until the following week, which gave her time to think everything through very carefully—and even pray over the matter—so she could approach the situation with confidence. After a few days of stewing and praying, her confidence grew in knowing she had to reveal herself to Jack—even if she felt somewhat terrified of what his response might be. But even if he was angry with her regarding her own deception, or upset with her for reasons she might be unable to predict, she had the certainty of knowing that he would never reveal *her* secret since she had the leverage of knowing *his* secret. She predicted that he might be shocked, and his shock might initially manifest itself as anger. But unless he'd changed far more than she could ever imagine, she believed she knew Jack Hannaford well enough to believe he might be glad to see her again—as strange as the situation might be—and he might even be glad to not have to bear the burden of his secret alone. Having to constantly pretend she was someone other than her true self was a burden she often disliked, even if she chose not to think about it most of the time. But she had Lottie with whom she could share that challenge. Did Jack have anyone else who knew the truth, or was he truly alone in his life as Ollie the blacksmith? As far as she knew from her friendship with Ollie, he was well-liked about town, but he'd told her he mostly preferred to keep to himself, and there wasn't anyone with whom he shared any kind of close relationship. She wondered if at least part of his motivation to keep to himself was his hope of not being recognized or found out. There were so many questions she wanted to ask him that she feared once she was finally able to cross the bridge of getting their secrets out into the open, she would gush with curiosity to the point of embarrassing herself. In carefully trying to figure out the best way to handle the situation, she kept reminding herself to remain disciplined and not do or say *anything* that might cause either of them any embarrassment.

When the morning came that Hennie was scheduled for one of her regular trips into town to visit the blacksmith, she decided she was as ready as she could possibly be to speak with Jack, and she had rehearsed over and over in her mind the best way to approach him about the situation, to achieve what she hoped would be the least amount of risk for him to be upset. She could only pray that it would go well, and given the reality that she had no control over the outcome, she prepared herself for what she considered might be his worst possible response. And she'd decided she would take on his reaction to the best of her ability by remaining as dignified and self-controlled as possible. Still, all of her prayer and mental preparation did nothing to alleviate the nervous churning in her stomach, and the way she kept having to switch the reins from one hand to the other in order to wipe her sweaty palms on her breeches.

Hennie had debated whether she should try and talk to Jack—or Ollie, as she'd come to know him; in her mind it was becoming difficult to keep track— before she went to get them lunch, or after they had eaten. She was leaning toward getting it over with, not certain she could eat at all in this condition, but she still wasn't certain which would be best until she arrived and found Ollie sitting down with his usual tankard of water, taking a rare break from his work. She decided she would get no better opportunity than this. They exchanged the usual greetings while she dismounted the horse and tethered it in the usual place. Hennie took a deep breath and forced a calmness into her countenance that was entirely contrary to her inner turmoil.

"I'm glad to catch you taking a break," she said, approaching him. "I wonder if you and I could talk . . . privately." At that last word, his brow furrowed with concern. "Is there someplace private we could speak? Where we wouldn't be overheard?"

Ollie stood up and set his tankard aside. He motioned to the open doorway of a room that Hennie knew was used for storage as well as for maintaining his tools. She'd never been in there, but she'd seen him go in and out a great deal. In a quiet voice he asked, "Are you in some kind of trouble?"

"No, nothing like that," Hennie said, "but . . . well, we . . . just need to talk."

Ollie just motioned again with his arm, and Hennie led the way into the room. "Have a seat," Ollie said as he closed the door, but Hennie felt hesitant since there was only one stool in the room. Ollie leaned against his workbench and folded his arms as if he were perfectly comfortable there for whatever this conversation might entail. At least they were facing each other directly, but Hennie noticed again the furrow of concern in his brow, and it took her a long moment to once again gather her courage. And now that they were face-to-face this way, she didn't see Ollie at all—only Jack. He'd grown up to be so tall and strong and thoroughly masculine, but there was no mistaking that these were the same eyes of the child she'd known so well.

When she had mentally taken herself back to her memorized opening for this conversation, Hennie just forced herself to begin and get it over with. "What I have to say might be somewhat shocking; therefore, I ask you to be patient with me and hear me out. Just . . . listen to what I have to say . . . and then I'll answer any questions you want to ask me."

Jack's entire countenance took on a silent expression of concern as he asked, "Are you certain you're not in trouble?"

"No," Hennie insisted. "Just . . . hear me out."

Jack put up his hands. "All right, I'm listening." He folded his arms again and waited.

Chapter Six

REUNION

HENNIE TOOK A DEEP BREATH and forged ahead. "When . . . you told me the story about the little fortress you built as a child—the fortress of stone and ivy—I realized something that I simply can't remain quiet about. You see . . . I know for a fact that there was a little hole beneath the heart-shaped rock, and in that hole were twelve carefully chosen pebbles—one for each month of the year—and each of them had been assigned a different magical power, powers that the evil king wanted for himself."

Jack looked every bit as astonished as Hennie had imagined he would. She waited until his astonishment understandably turned to confusion. "How could you know that? No one knew that except . . ."

"Except?" she asked. "You can say it, Jack. No one except Hennie." He gasped, but she could tell he was fighting to maintain a composed demeanor, perhaps ready to deny being Jack when he was so obviously determined not to be discovered. "And you know Hennie would never tell anyone because you swore each other to secrecy—especially about the stones hidden beneath the heart-shaped rock." She could almost feel him trying to come up with a way to claim he had no idea what she was talking about, if only to maintain his disguise; but she also sensed his confusion. She hurried to reassure him by saying, "It's all right, Jack; it must be some kind of destiny that made you tell me that story, because . . . it's me, Hennie." He gasped and looked even more confused. "I know the story because I was there. I've been living dressed as a man so that I could get respectable work." He turned his head sideways while he kept his eyes fixed on her, looking skeptical and disbelieving. Hennie impulsively removed the little string of leather she used to tie her hair back in a plait. She shook her hair out and leaned a little closer to Jack. "It's me, Hennie. Ask me anything you need to ask so I can prove it to you." He made a noise that indicated he was barely managing to breathe, and Hennie added, "I think I understand how you're feeling; I felt much the same way after you told me that story last week.

How could it be possible after all this time for you and me to end up together again—friends once more while we're both pretending to be someone else? It has to be a miracle, Jack; there's no other possible explanation."

"Hennie," he finally muttered, but it sounded more like a statement than a question.

"Yes, it's me," she said while he continued to stare and said nothing more. "Ask me anything."

Jack cleared his throat loudly, as if he had to do so to clear away his disbelief. "What nickname did we give my father that no one else knew about?"

"The court jester," Hennie answered immediately. "Because he drank too much and regularly made a fool of himself—especially at parties; and we always used to hide in that alcove on the east side of the balcony above the ballroom whenever there were parties, so we had a perfect view of just how foolishly he behaved."

Jack took in a loud, harsh breath—as if he no longer had the ability to try and hide what he was feeling. He took a good, long look into Hennie's eyes, and the next thing she knew he had practically lifted her off the stool, wrapping her in his arms, hugging her impossibly tight while he muttered her name over and over near her ear, and she realized his voice was quivering with emotion. "Oh, Hennie! I thought I'd never see you again."

"And I thought the same," she murmured back, returning his embrace. "But I never would have dreamed that . . ."

As if to finish her thought, he drew back and took hold of her shoulders. "You're pretending to be a man?"

"Well . . . obviously," Hennie said with some sarcasm, already feeling as if the years had fled and she was again with her best friend when she'd been eleven and he was twelve.

"And why? What did you say?"

"So that I could find respectable work," she said. "It's a long story. Well, actually I've told you the story. The only thing I omitted was the fact that my friend had already been working as a man at the manor because there had been no available positions for women, and when she came to find me, she convinced me to do the same. You already know the rest—except that I didn't know the place where she'd found work, the place where she was taking me, just happened to be where I'd grown up until my mother's death, before I met Lottie at the orphanage."

"An orphanage?" Jack said, looking as if he might cry. His expression became more pained as he obviously recalled other parts of the story she'd already told him. "The workhouse? Oh, Hennie! If my father were still alive, I'd—"

"Hush!" she insisted. "It's all in the past. The important thing is that we found each other again—or more accurately, it seems to me that God just shoved us back together; it doesn't seem you or I had anything to do with actually finding each other."

"It's incredible," Jack said before his demeanor turned to deep concern. "But Hennie, you mustn't tell anyone where I am! No one! No one can know it's me!"

"Of course I won't tell anyone," she reassured him. "I would never betray your trust. Besides that, we both have great incentive to keep each other's secrets. If anyone were to find out I'm actually a woman, I would be sent packing—and none too kindly, I daresay."

"Good heavens!" Jack said breathlessly. "I can't believe it . . . after all this time."

"I have trouble believing it myself," she declared, "and I've had several days to think about it." She sat back down but was still close enough to take hold of his hand, relieved when he immediately squeezed it, showing that he was comfortable with such a gesture. "Jack," she said gently, "I don't understand. I can't even begin to imagine why you would disappear and leave everyone wondering where you are . . . and all the while you're right here, so close to your home. Why would you take such drastic measures, Jack? I pray you still trust me enough to tell me."

He seemed taken aback by the question—and she couldn't blame him. She didn't understand the reasons for what he'd done to put himself in this situation, but he wouldn't have taken such desperate measures if the circumstances were not severe. She gave him time to consider her plea and wasn't surprised by his answer—despite being somewhat disappointed. "I can't think of a single reason not to trust you," he said, "but we've both lived a lifetime since we saw each other last . . . and this is so much to take in. I can't deny feeling a little unsettled to realize that someone figured out who I am, although if anyone could do so, it would be you. I need some time, Hennie, time to think . . . to consider all of this. We'll talk soon . . . I promise, but . . . I can't promise I'll tell you everything; for your own sake as well as mine, it might be better if you don't know the entire situation." He coughed and looked down for a long moment before he looked at her again. "As for now, I have work to do, and you can't be away for too long."

"Of course," she said. "And it's vital that we continue on as normal . . . that we not allow anyone to see even a hint of anything being different . . . of anything that might arouse suspicion."

"Exactly," he said, seeming relieved that she understood without him having to make that point. He squeezed her hand, then surprised her by kissing it quickly. "I'm so . . . overwhelmed right now, Hennie, but . . . I'm so glad to see you . . . to have you back in my life." His voice took on a barely detectable quiver.

"You're the best friend I've ever had. I never imagined a miracle such as this; I truly believed I'd never see you again . . . but I've never stopped wondering where you'd gone." He then kissed her brow, and Hennie wanted to just take hold of him and never let go. He represented some of the best memories of her life, a time when she'd felt safe and cared for. But he was right: a lifetime had passed since they'd last seen each other; Hennie had literally more than doubled in age, which meant he had as well. It would be foolish to allow herself to become too emotionally attached, based on childhood experiences. Everything was different now, and they were in the strangest of circumstances. She had to be careful to not get carried away with making this situation into something more fanciful than it was in reality. There was no denying the miracle that had brought them back together, but simply knowing each other's true identity didn't necessarily mean anything was going to change. When she had no idea of his reasons for living this way, she couldn't possibly imagine how this revelation could alter circumstances for either of them. For now, she just enjoyed the remarkable actuality of their reunion and impulsively hugged him again, soaking in the strength of his embrace and how it seemed to fill her with the same peace she'd felt during the time they'd spent together as children.

"I must get to work," he said, looking directly at her while he held her shoulders. His gaze was long and penetrating, as if he were still trying to reassure himself that this was real. She knew the feeling. Hennie nodded, and he left the room. Hennie had to just sit there on the stool for a few minutes and try to breathe normally as the intensity of their reunion overtook her with a delayed reaction. She finally managed to take even breaths and felt the beat of her heart slow down to its usual rhythm. Hearing the familiar pounding of the blacksmith's hammer reminded Hennie that she needed to make certain everything went on normally so as not to arouse any suspicion. She hurriedly pulled her hair back and tied it into the usual plait before she took a deep breath and returned to the main area of the smithy, saying over her shoulder, "Lunch is on me today. I'll be back soon."

She barely heard him acknowledge her comment as she hurried away, unable to imagine how they would go forward from here—now that they both knew the truth about the other's secret identity. As she walked the short distance to the bakery, it occurred to her that there might not be any change at all in the way they were living, and they would simply go on, week after week—perhaps year after year—living this way, with no way out of the false lives they'd created for themselves. They had their savings, but what if something happened? After purchasing some iced buns and heading out to purchase the usual hand pies, she thought that at least they could now be friends at a more honest level, and even with the rare amount of time each week when they sat and talked, they could be real with each other when they were unable to do so with anyone else. Hennie had Lottie, but her friend couldn't know about Jack, and she suspected Jack had no one with whom he could talk about his real self and his real feelings. While she loved the idea of their friendship becoming closer and more comfortable, the very idea of their needing to carry on this way felt ludicrous and all wrong. But without knowing Jack's reasons for hiding right here under the noses of those who knew him best, she couldn't find a way to consider any other possibility.

Hennie tried not to feel discouraged as she returned to the smithy with lunch. Her conversation with Jack had gone as well as she could have ever hoped; she'd been reunited with her childhood friend, and it truly was a miracle. She needed to focus on the positive aspects of this situation and not worry so much about what might happen in the future.

They sat down together as usual, their chairs situated with a view of the street. Hennie didn't know what to say, and apparently, Jack didn't either, so they began eating in silence.

"Is this really happening?" he finally said as if he'd commented on the weather. "It's really you?"

"I think that's already been established," Hennie said with a chuckle that lacked any humor.

"I know, but . . . I can't believe it's real."

"As I said, I've known since last week, and I'm still having trouble believing it."

More silence followed, as if he needed to allow his mind to catch up to what he'd learned since her arrival today. She decided to just let him think, certain he would speak when he needed to. She was nearly finished eating her mutton pie when he asked, "How on earth do you manage pretending to be a man?" He glanced in her direction for a long moment, then looked back toward the street and chuckled in disbelief. "I admit that when we met I thought you were a little odd-looking."

"I daresay everyone I've encountered thinks that. At the stables they call me and Lottie the scrawny ones, but everyone has been fairly respectful—mostly because the stable master won't tolerate anything less."

"That's good, then," Jack said. "But . . . how do you manage?"

"Is that question rhetorical?" Hennie asked, trying to maintain a nonchalant expression as people passed by. "Or are you asking for details?"

"I'm certain that the details are likely none of my business," he said, "but I'm a grown man, Hennie; I'm not naive to the differences between men and women. This can't be easy for you."

"No, it certainly is not easy, but it's been worth it."

"How is that?" he asked, sounding more concerned than curious.

Hennie cleared her throat and gave him a simple, straightforward response. "Let's just say that when you've lived in a workhouse and worked in a pub, being female seems to automatically equate to being vulnerable and often treated badly by men."

He turned toward her abruptly, looking momentarily horrified. "Has anyone ever . . . hurt you?"

"No," she reassured him firmly. "But I always had to be on guard, and I can't say the same for other women I've known. Being a man has eliminated certain problems from my life, even though it definitely has created others."

"Like what?" he asked, appearing relaxed again now that she'd reassured him nothing terrible had ever happened to her—at least not within the category they'd been discussing.

"Well, as you said . . . you're a grown man, and I'm a grown woman . . . so to be quite frank, I have to tightly wrap my chest every morning, and it's not comfortable."

"I wouldn't think so," he said, not sounding at all embarrassed—more compassionate, truthfully.

"We have to wear clothes that are baggy to disguise that we're shaped differently than a man, and that just makes us look scrawnier, I suppose. There are other, more personal matters which I will *not* discuss with you," she chuckled lightly, "even if you are one of my best friends. But we've figured everything out and we manage. One of the maids is a friend and she helps us."

"I'm glad you have someone to help you," he said as if he'd truly been worried about her. Given the brief amount of time he'd had to take all of this in, she found it touching that his most prominent thoughts seemed to be concern on her behalf. But given how concerned she felt for *him* and the situation he was in, she saw that as evidence that their friendship had not waned despite the years since they'd seen each other. "And I'm glad you have a friend—Lottie—someone you can trust completely, someone who shares your challenges."

"I'm more grateful for her than I can say," Hennie said. "She knows everything about me; she always has. And she is always full of love and support, and completely without judgment."

"Does she know about me?" he asked, his expression showing more curiosity than concern—but he couldn't disguise his concern.

Hennie reminded him firmly, "I already told you I hadn't told anyone, and I won't! Do you not trust me enough to—"

"It's not that," he said. "At least I think it's not that. I just . . . well, I think I'm still in shock." He chuckled tensely. "And in all honesty . . . perhaps a little unnerved to realize I've been discovered, when it's so important that no one know that truth—at least for now."

"No one but me could have figured out it was you, Jack," she reassured him.

"Except that you haven't seen me for half your life. Of course, we never would have recognized each other under the circumstances. But there are people around here who have known me as an adult, and aside from the beard and hiding behind the sweat and dirt and the hard work that most people would simply assume a gentleman would never do, I can't help fearing that I'll be recognized."

"Then, why are you *here?* Why so close to home?"

"It's a long story," he said.

"And you need time," she stated, honoring his previous request.

"Yes," he said. "I need time. But . . ."

"What?" she asked when he didn't finish.

"Will it not be difficult for you to keep such a big secret from your friend? If the two of you are so close, will she not be able to tell you're keeping something from her?" He sighed slowly. "When we were children, I think I would have been able to tell if you were keeping something from me, and if I'd asked, I wouldn't have wanted you to lie about it."

"I've kept her from being suspicious since I figured it out last week," Hennie pointed out. "And . . . if she suspects something . . . if she asks . . . I'll just tell her there *is* something that's happened, but I can't tell her, so I won't be lying. I'm certain she'd feel frustrated, but she would respect my request to not talk about it."

She heard him sigh again before he stood up and said, "I have work to do, and more than enough to think about for one day."

"Of course," she said, unable to tell if he was upset. But surely, she just needed to give him time to adjust to everything he'd learned in the last hour. Perhaps he had good reason to be upset; given her ignorance regarding his reasons for living this way, she couldn't possibly assess how he might be feeling. She put the chairs back in their usual resting place and left the iced buns for him that he hadn't eaten. Casually she said, "I'll be back as usual."

He nodded toward her in a way that was completely Ollie. He'd taken on the demeanor of the blacksmith, behaving toward her as he always had before she'd assaulted him with such huge revelations. She just hoped she would have more opportunities to actually speak with Jack in the future.

When Hennie went back to get the newly shoed horse, Ollie was hard at work on another project, and she just waved and hollered a quick, "Thank you!" before mounting the horse.

Her foot was barely in the stirrup when she heard him say, "Wait!"

Hennie put her foot back on the ground and turned toward him as he approached. His expression remained solid and unreadable, but his voice held a hint of tenderness as he said, "I'm so glad to have you back in my life, Hennie; I truly am. It's just . . . complicated."

"I know," she said, so grateful to hear Jack speaking to her again, expressing appreciation for their friendship—in spite of its complications. "I understand."

"Be patient with me," he said.

"Of course."

"We'll talk some more . . . next time you come." He chuckled uncomfortably and glanced at the ground. "Perhaps by then I'll have become accustomed to . . . this." He nodded toward her attire and lifted an eyebrow while smirking in a way that dissipated the tension.

"Don't get too used to it," she said. "Regardless of what you see, I'm still a woman beneath these ridiculous clothes."

She'd said it lightly, hoping to add to the lighter mood between them, but he replied with severity, "And I'm still Jack—the same Jack you knew so well; I swear to you that I am."

Hennie returned his intense gaze. "I have no doubt about that," she said firmly, and he seemed relieved, as if he needed her to see the real him. She suspected he felt very alone in this situation, and likely disoriented by all the pretending. She certainly had empathy for that.

"I'll see you next week, then," he said and nodded again.

"Yes," she replied, and he returned to his work. She watched him for a moment before mounting the horse, which she rode quickly away, not wanting anyone to accidentally observe anything that might seem strange or out of the ordinary.

During the ride home, Hennie's mind went wild once again as she attempted to make sense of all that had happened and the torrent of associated emotions that made her want to both laugh and cry. But she didn't want to be late again, so she pushed her thoughts *and* emotions aside and rode as quickly as the horse would carry her, loving the wind in her face that helped force back any threat of tears. She felt such a deep joy to have found Jack and to be reunited with him; but at the same time, their circumstances were tainted with a great deal of sorrow. For all that she had no idea why he was hiding behind the guise of a blacksmith, his sorrow was readily evident, and her heart ached for him.

That evening after supper was over and Hennie and Lottie had both gotten cleaned up and ready for bed, they sat in Lottie's room to talk and catch up on another day of living a life of deception. They'd joked about it a great deal, and

Hennie had become accustomed to it. Neither of them could deny that the benefits far outweighed the risk—especially when time had proven they were managing their playacting without raising even an inkling of suspicion. Or perhaps if anyone *was* suspicious, they didn't care since Hen and Lot were both good workers and keenly reliable.

Hennie always looked forward to this time of day when she and Lottie could be themselves and talk and giggle—sometimes like the little girls they'd not been allowed to be in the orphanage. But Hennie felt distracted tonight, which made it difficult to enjoy herself. Of course, it was difficult to keep her thoughts away from Jack. His joy when he'd realized it was really her and the way he'd hugged her so tightly kept jumping into her mind. It had perhaps been one of the greatest moments of her life! Bits and pieces of their conversation also kept recurring like stones being thrown into the ever-flowing river of her thoughts. But ironically, she was most distracted by the things he'd said about keeping this secret from Lottie—and here she was with Lottie when she should have been putting her greatest efforts into not arousing any curiosity in her friend over the fact that something in her life had changed dramatically—and Hennie knew she was failing miserably, even before Lottie said, "Where is your mind, miss? I don't think you've heard a thing I've said for the last ten minutes."

"I'm sorry," Hennie said, and quickly added a lie. "Truth be told, I'm not feeling very well. I have rather a headache." Hennie gave herself an added dose of self-recrimination over the way she'd insisted she was telling the truth right in the midst of the lie.

Lottie quickly touched Hennie's face to check for fever. "Oh, it's nothing like that, I'm sure," Hennie insisted.

"Is it your monthlies?" Lottie asked.

"No," Hennie said, but to be more convincing she added, "but that could be coming on; I've honestly lost track."

"Either way, you should get yourself to bed," Lottie said, entirely convinced by Hennie's lie. And Hennie was relieved. Surely by morning she would have settled her thoughts and could do better at assuming a more convincing façade that nothing had happened, and nothing had changed.

Being the good friend she was, Lottie made certain that Hennie had everything she needed, and she quite literally tucked Hennie into bed. Lottie had often said it was a woman's intuition to mother another woman who needed some tender care—especially women who had grown up without a mother.

"Sleep well, my friend," Lottie said, extinguishing the lamp. "I hope you feel better tomorrow."

"Thank you," Hennie said and breathed out a long sigh of relief once the door was closed. She held her pillow in her arms and looked toward the moonlight radiating through the window while her mind revisited every bit of her interaction with Jack today—over and over until she practically had it all memorized. But she didn't want to forget, not ever. He'd been her dearest childhood friend, and someone she had missed desperately all these years while she'd wondered every day how and what he might be doing. Never in any realm of imagination could she have conceived of the life he was living now. She wondered what each and every person in this household might think if they knew what she knew. She couldn't fathom Jack being able to continue living this way for long, and she wondered if he had any kind of plan for returning to his home and becoming his old self again. But how could she even begin to consider such a possibility when she had no idea over the reasons for this madness to begin with? She hoped and prayed that when she saw him again, he would be willing to tell her his story, that given some time to consider the situation, he would realize that despite the passing of years, he could still trust her completely.

When Hennie realized how many hours she'd just been lying in bed with her mind wandering, she felt certain that tomorrow she would *really* have a headache due to lack of sleep. To try and avoid thinking about Jack at all, she silently sang a song in her head that her mother had taught her, trying to remember the sweet sound of her mother's voice singing the lyrics. She'd reverted to doing this literally thousands of times in the years since her mother's death, when the memory of her mother singing was the only thing that would shut out the horror of her surroundings and give her any peace at all. The method worked, and she was soon asleep, waking up to see the room far more filled with light than it ever was when she got awakened by the usual knock on the door. She sat up abruptly, shocked with panic until she saw that a note had been slid under her door. She jumped out of bed to get it, then had to sit down on the floor when some mild dizziness made it clear she'd jumped up a little too quickly.

Opening the folded paper, she read: *I told Parsons you're under the weather, and he said to let you sleep. We'll all pitch in to cover your chores. I'll come check on you at lunch. There's a breakfast tray outside your door. Didn't want to wake you. Lot*

Hennie couldn't deny being immensely relieved. A glance at the clock let her know she'd been able to make up for much of the sleep she'd lost last night, and this would give her a little more time to let her thoughts settle so she could do better at keeping them to herself. She found the tray on the floor of the hallway just outside her bedroom door, with a cloth draped over it. She took it to her bed and sat there to enjoy scones, butter, jam, and sausages—which were still delicious even though they were no longer warm. There was also tea, even though it too had cooled, but it still tasted good to Hennie and made her feel rejuvenated.

Noting she still had more than an hour left before lunchtime, Hennie went back to bed for a short while but was up and dressed in time to take the breakfast tray down to the kitchen and express her appreciation to Mrs. Helton before lunch was served. Not wanting Lottie to waste time by going upstairs to check on her, Hennie made certain she got to the stables before any of the stable hands left to eat.

"There he is!" Parsons said, noticing Hennie first from where he sat polishing a saddle. "Feeling better?"

"Yes, thank you," Hennie said. "Just haven't been getting enough sleep, maybe."

"Happens to all of us," Parsons said. "And you've not once asked for an hour off since you've come here; if anything, you work longer than expected most days. You certainly earned an extra morning in bed. If you need more time, then—"

"No," Hennie insisted, "but thank you; I'm right as rain now."

"I *did* hear you," Lottie said, approaching from the direction of the stalls with some of the other hands. They all knew that Mrs. Helton expected them to arrive promptly for meals, and therefore they kept close track of the many clocks dispersed throughout the stables.

Hennie walked beside Lottie into the house and thanked her for her thoughtfulness, assuring her that she felt much better after a good night's sleep. And Hennie *did* feel better; she'd grown more accustomed to the reality that she knew Jack Hannaford's secret—and she needed to guard it at all costs. This didn't keep her from thinking about him far too much, but she was proud of herself for behaving as if nothing was out of the ordinary.

Throughout the days that followed, Hennie became increasingly skilled at not letting on to Lottie that something extraordinary had happened, which she wanted desperately to be able to talk about—especially when Hennie couldn't force Jack out of her mind at all. She fell asleep thinking of him, woke up thinking of him, and unless she was distracted by some manner of conversation that kept her engaged, she thought of him almost every waking minute. When she went to bed one night with the realization that she would be seeing him the following day, she actually felt fluttery inside at the very thought. Staring toward the ceiling of her room through the darkness, she put both hands over the fluttering as if she might be able to command it to cease, but instead it only increased—so much so that she gasped aloud and was glad to be alone. She convinced herself that it was nothing more than a reaction to the clandestine nature of what they knew about each other's lives, or perhaps simply the notion that her childhood friend had miraculously become a friend now in her adulthood. Perhaps it was both, she concluded, and fell asleep.

The following morning during her ride into town she was assaulted with the same sensation again—and again. And that was on top of the three times it had occurred between her coming awake and actually leaving the stables. But Hennie ignored anything beyond her desire to simply be able to have a conversation with Jack, hoping he would be willing to tell her his reasons for running away from home and hiding behind that ridiculous beard.

Hennie felt nearly furious with herself when the fluttering increased dramatically as she dismounted in front of the smithy and tied off the horse's reins. She stood there for a good minute watching Jack work, since the sound of his hammering had prevented him from hearing her arrive. She wondered if it was hard labor or simply the way he was built that had made him so broad-shouldered and strong—probably both. But he'd been so skinny as a child, and since she'd been a little bit chubby, they'd likely made a comical-looking pair of friends.

"Hello," she finally said. He stopped hammering and turned toward her in one quick movement. After staring at her for a long moment, he laughed and shook his head. "Is something funny?" she asked, moving closer so that no one passing by might overhear whatever they might wish to say to each other.

"It's just . . . I've been trying to just think about you as this . . . stable hand who . . . How did you put it? Scrawny? Odd-looking?" He chuckled again. "It never would have occurred to me that you're a woman hiding in men's clothing, but now that I know the truth, all I can see is Hennie, and . . . I suppose it's funny."

"So glad I could offer you some amusement," she said, trying to sound offended, even though she wasn't. Her efforts failed completely when she laughed herself and added, "Well, as long as we're expressing our opinions on these disguises we're wearing, I find your beard most despicable. Do you not trim it? Ever? It looks like a bush growing on your face." Again, her attempt at severity failed when she laughed, and he laughed with her.

"Despicable perhaps," he said, "but it does well at hiding at least half my face."

"It doesn't hide your eyes," she said more seriously.

He darted his eyes away for a moment before he asked lightly, "And what of *your* beard? How do you explain away the complete absence of any hint of hair growing on your face?"

"No one has ever commented," she said, "and I snip bits of my hair so I can leave a basin with soap and hair in my room every day. Actually, most days there isn't much hair because can't cut too much at a time, but I still have to leave the mess made by the shaving soap to keep up appearances."

"How very clever," he said.

"Lottie's idea," she admitted, and then they were staring at each other. "How are you?" she asked.

"Better, I think," he said. "I admit to experiencing some . . . shock."

"Yes, I understand."

"But I do believe I've had some time to get used to it, and as you said, it can't possibly be coincidence. In truth, sometimes I've wondered if God has ever really heard my prayers—ever. But when I consider the way you came back into my life, I don't think I can doubt that He's been listening—not without being struck by lightning, or something."

Hennie was so thoroughly touched by his sentiment that she had to fight back a temptation to cry. She could recall his words later tonight when she was alone in her bed, and she could cry all she wanted. For now, she had to be strong and act like a man. She focused instead on how she loved seeing him behave more like the Jack she knew—or rather the grown-up version of the Jack she'd known. She'd seen a glimpse of that man the previous week, and she'd felt entirely and surprisingly comfortable with him, as if the core of his character had never changed. She found it ironic now to be able to see that Ollie the blacksmith had always been Jack, perhaps a quieter and more subdued version of him. But then, Ollie was a man living in disguise, without close friends or confidants. Facing Jack in that moment, Hennie saw a man who was pleased to have been reunited with an old friend—a friend with whom he could be himself. She was grateful beyond words for the undeniable evidence that he felt that way, because she felt that way too.

"I think," he said, "that you and I have a great deal to talk about; much to catch up on."

"I would agree," she said, hoping that meant he intended to tell her the whole story.

"We don't want anything to appear too out of the ordinary to anyone who might see us talking," he added, as if he'd given it a great deal of thought. "Perhaps it's unfortunate that the smithy is so open to the street and people who pass by regularly can see exactly what's going on here." He chuckled. "If it were winter, we might have more opportunity to talk privately since the front of the smithy would be staked down and tied shut. However . . ." he drawled, "I don't think there's anything suspicious about us being just a little slower eating our lunch or taking a few extra minutes to talk when you leave and arrive. I think that's a fair place to begin this new version of our friendship. What do you think?"

"I think it's all perfectly reasonable, and I look forward to every minute we can spend catching up on everything we've missed."

"Good," he said and seemed pleased. "Now, lunch is on me today; you know where to find the money. I'll finish up what I'm doing while you go get it, then we'll talk while we eat."

"I'm looking forward to it," she said and resisted the urge to loiter before heading out, confident they would be able to enjoy some good—and hopefully enlightening—conversation when she returned.

Today Hennie decided to go into the pub around the corner and get two of their famous venison pies instead of getting the usual mutton pies. It wasn't the first time they'd splurged on this option, and they'd taken turns paying for the extra indulgence. The venison pies were made at the pub every day and could either be served on a plate with some gravy or taken out wrapped in brown paper to be eaten elsewhere. With the pies in hand, Hennie went to the usual bakery, but instead of purchasing their favorite iced buns, she instead got two large slices of Madeira cake, which were wrapped carefully in a more lightweight brown paper. She thanked the young girl who often worked selling the baked goods her parents were always busy creating in the kitchen.

Approaching the smithy with her purchases in hand, Hennie was once again assaulted with that fluttering in her stomach. She fought to suppress it as she stepped inside, where Jack was hard at work, but a quick glance toward him only worsened the problem. She tried not to look in his direction at all as she set the food down and put the chairs in their usual lunchtime places, and she also filled the customary two tankards with water. She considered how comfortable she had become here, and how their routine of sharing an occasional meal had practically become a ritual. But they'd become comfortable as the blacksmith and the stable hand, two men chatting about the weather and village gossip. Now they were childhood friends reunited, and while the lunchtime ritual itself hadn't changed, everything else had, and Hennie could feel nothing but pleasant anticipation for every possible minute of conversation they could press into their usual routine.

Chapter Seven

CARDS AND DRINKS

JACK SMILED AT HENNIE AS he set down his tools. He went to wash his hands while Hennie made herself comfortable and waited for him to return, considering the fact that she'd not actually felt this happy since her mother's death. She'd been blessed with much happiness and joy through Lottie's friendship, a gift she could never take for granted. But she'd truly missed Jack, and being here with him like this—with the opportunity to just enjoy a simple meal and some good conversation—truly seemed like a miracle, and she could never take *that* for granted either.

"I decided on extravagance today," she said as he sat down beside her, and she handed him his venison pie.

"Ooh," he said, unwrapping the brown paper while he inhaled the aroma, "you read my mind. Thank you."

"Don't thank me," she chuckled. "You paid for it."

"You went to get it," he countered, chuckling himself.

They ate in silence for a few minutes before he asked, "How is everything at the majestic house of stone and ivy?" Hennie didn't miss the mild sarcasm in his question. They had called the manor house by those exact words in their childhood, when their play had centered around using their imaginations to make everything grand and splendid beyond reality, often attaching titles and magical powers to people or simple inanimate objects. Hennie doubted that he had uttered those exact words in reference to his home in years, because no one besides herself would understand the reference. But like her, he had probably recalled their secret name for the manor house a thousand times. She felt deeply sad for a moment over the way their childhood games and fantastical ideas had all faded into the harshness of life, bringing them both to live in a way they never could have imagined.

Hennie pushed her sadness away and just answered the question. "Everything is fine as far as I know. No gossip among the servants beyond the usual trivial matters."

While Hennie wanted desperately to hear the story of how Jack had landed himself into working as a blacksmith, she could understand his need to ask, "And what of George? And Rebecca? Are they well?"

Hennie heard a sadness in his voice that perhaps exceeded what she was feeling. He'd always been close to his siblings; being separated from them in such a ridiculous manner likely caused him deep heartache.

Hennie tried to keep her voice light as she said, "It's not as if I have any personal interaction with them—me being a lowly stable hand and all." More seriously she said, "I've seen brief glimpses of Rebecca when she goes riding; I've not once personally seen George. But from everything I hear, they are both well. That's all I can tell you." She cleared her throat and ventured to add, "I've heard a number of servants frequently comment that they worry about you . . . that they wonder where you are and what's happened to you."

"Well, they're going to have to keep wondering," Jack said with a subtle bite to his voice.

"Why?" she asked, actually turning to look at him. "Can you tell me even a little bit of why this situation is necessary? I can't begin to imagine the reasons, Jack. Of course, it's up to you whether or not you tell me, and I won't keep bringing it up if you ask me not to. But I hope you believe me when I tell you that you can trust me implicitly."

"I *do* trust you, Hennie. It only took about a day for me to know in my gut that you would never lie to me, and you meant it when you said you wouldn't tell anyone."

Hennie breathed a deep sigh of relief. If he trusted her, they would be able to move forward with their strange friendship in a far more positive way.

"It's just . . . complicated," he went on, "and perhaps I've become so accustomed to *not* talking about it—not talking about that part of my life *at all*—it's difficult to even know how—or where—to begin."

"I can understand that," she said, "but . . ."

"But?" he echoed when she hesitated, trying to find the best words to express herself.

"But . . . I know from my own experiences how hard it is to feel completely alone. Maybe the situation can't be remedied—at least not for the time being; I don't know because I don't have any idea what the problem entails. But if you truly must live this way, would it not be better to have someone to talk to without having to hold back? I just . . . well . . . sometimes I feel like it's exhausting trying to keep such a big secret, but at least I have Lottie to talk to, and . . . I admit that I'm worried about you. You're obviously fine physically; you're working hard, your needs are met, you're safe. But are you happy? Are you even close to happy?"

"I am right now," he said, glancing toward her with a distinct warmth in his eyes that provoked a little burst of laughter from Hennie.

"Well, I am too," she said, "but . . . you can't base your happiness on sharing lunch and conversation once a week or so."

"Nor can you," he said, sounding irritated.

"I have Lottie."

"Well, perhaps you should introduce the two of us, and I could also enjoy the benefits of conversation with *her.*"

"Perhaps I should," Hennie said and realized they were arguing. She recalled a few arguments with him in their childhood, but it had been about things like which one of them would pretend to play the horse in a particular make-believe scenario, or whether spring was preferable over autumn. "Except . . . oh, wait . . . I can't introduce you to her when I've promised you that I wouldn't even *tell* her about you."

"Fair point," he said more calmly.

After giving herself a few seconds to calm down, Hennie stated what seemed obvious, "Apparently the issue at hand is not a comfortable topic for you."

"Nor for you," he replied.

"I'm concerned about you; it would seem I have good cause to be." More gently she added, "I just don't want you to be alone in all of this, Jack. Did you ever consider the possibility that perhaps God brought me back here so you *wouldn't* be alone?"

She heard him sigh loudly and noted they were both holding their hand pies while hardly eating them. He then set his down on the paper on his lap as if he didn't want to be distracted by it. "If you must know, I *have* considered that. I think I already admitted as much."

"So you did," Hennie said, now recalling what he'd said earlier about his believing that her appearance in his life was evidence God had been hearing his prayers. "Forgive me. I'm just . . . concerned."

"And I appreciate that," he said. "Forgive *me*; I can't deny the issue is . . . sensitive to say the least. I feel angry, Hennie—but my anger is not toward you, and I shouldn't behave as if it is."

"Why don't we just . . . put all this aside for now, and . . . you let me know when you want to talk about it . . . *if* you want to talk about it."

"I'm ready to talk about it," he said so quickly that it surprised her. "But it's far too long of a conversation to have now . . . like this."

"And what other option might there be?" she asked.

"You have your evenings off, do you not?" He picked up his pie again and took a big bite.

"I do," she drawled, feeling skeptical. "But how exactly do you suppose I would go about getting away from the estate with a reasonable explanation, and how would we—"

"Funny you should ask because I've given that some thought." He tossed her a self-satisfied smile. "You've told me you spend your evenings after supper with Lottie, so she's the only one who would notice a change in your routine if you left."

"Except that I would need to use a horse from the stables, and I can't do that without an explanation to Mr. Parsons."

"Ah," he said. "Well, that's all right . . . because you can just tell them both the truth."

"What truth?" she demanded, knowing full well he didn't want her telling them the *real* truth.

"That your friend Ollie has invited you over to play some cards and have a few drinks. It's a normal enough social experience among men. Parsons won't question it. Will Lottie accept such an explanation?"

Hennie couldn't keep from laughing at the thought, and Jack turned toward her, silently questioning such a reaction. But she decided to keep to herself how Lottie might read into the situation that Hennie was perhaps attracted to the blacksmith—even if she could only be so in secret. She could deal with Lottie, even if it might be more difficult to keep Jack's identity a secret when her need to lie about the situation was growing bigger.

"I'm sure I can get away for . . . cards and drinks." If it meant having the time for Jack to tell her his story, she would do just about anything. "When?"

"Will this evening work?"

"I don't see why not," Hennie said.

"And you could leave right after you've had your supper?"

"Yes."

"Good," he declared. "I'll see you then." He popped the last of his pie into his mouth and stood up to get back to work.

Nothing more was said between them that wouldn't have been said long before she'd known his true identity. As she left with the newly shod horse, she pointed to where she'd left the wrapped Madeira cake for him and said, "Something special for dessert. Enjoy."

"Thank you," he said.

"You paid for it." She smiled at him and rode away.

By the time Hennie arrived at the stables, she was so excited by the prospect of her evening plans with Jack that it took extra self-control to keep a smile off her face as she got to work doing the usual chores. When Mr. Parsons passed by, she stopped him and asked if she could have permission to borrow one of the horses to go into town after supper. She knew the other hands did it all the time, so it was certainly not an unusual request—except that Parsons had never gotten any such request from her. "You got some special plans, young man?" Parsons asked with a little smile.

"Nothing too exciting," she said, trying to appear indifferent. "The blacksmith invited me over for a few drinks . . . and some cards."

"Ollie's a good lad," Parsons said, seeming disappointed that Hennie's plans sounded indeed relatively boring. "Enjoy yourself, then," he added. "Don't drink too much or stay out too late."

"I won't," Hennie said, and Parsons walked away. Hennie then turned around to find Lottie standing nearby; she tried not to look guilty or surprised—even though she was both.

"What's that?" Lottie asked. "Drinks and card games with the blacksmith?"

Hennie shrugged. "I've told you we've become friends. I don't know that he *has* any other friends. He asked, so I said yes."

"Did you now?" Lottie asked with a little wink, which made Hennie glance quickly around to make certain no one was nearby. She wanted to remind Lottie that they had strictly agreed to never even hint at their deception unless they were alone in one of their rooms. For Lottie to imply that Hennie might have a romantic interest in the blacksmith was utterly ludicrous when—as far as Lottie believed—Hennie was portraying herself to Ollie as a man. But for her to even hint at it here in the stables—when they had no idea who might be around and what they might hear or see—actually made Hennie mildly angry.

"We'll talk later," Hennie said.

"After you get back from town?" Lottie called after her as if she found the matter amusing.

"Maybe," Hennie said. "Don't wait up."

Hennie ate supper quickly and excused herself before anyone else was done—mostly because she didn't want any more teasing from Lottie. It was an entirely different experience riding into town in the dark, but thankfully the horse didn't seem to care. Each and every one of them seemed to know the road well and had no tendency to stray off of it. The village also looked and felt different in the dark. Except for the pubs, all the businesses were closed, and it was eerily quiet. Approaching the smithy, it was difficult for Hennie to imagine it as the same place. There was no noise, and no burning coals that let off a red glow and a great deal of heat.

Hennie dismounted and tethered the horse in the usual place. She stood there for a moment wondering what to do until she heard Jack say, "So you came."

"I said I would," Hennie replied, seeing him step out of the darkness. "And I am a man of my word." Jack chuckled at her declaring herself a man and motioned for her to follow him. As she did, she realized for the first time that there was a door at the back of the smithy. She'd never noticed it, but even if she had, she might have assumed it went outside. But as Jack opened it and she stepped through, she could see that this was his home. Until now she hadn't even wondered where he lived. With the way he monopolized her thoughts, this realization seemed rather silly. Now she found herself standing in what could be called a common room, given that it was a kitchen, dining area, and parlor combined—even though it was remarkably small.

"Make yourself comfortable," Jack said, motioning to the little round table circled by four chairs. "Under any other circumstances I'd help you with your chair, but I think you can manage."

Hennie chuckled. "No, please don't help me with my chair—or attempt any other gentlemanly gesture."

"I wouldn't dream of it," he said and sat across from her. There was a deck of playing cards on the table, a bottle of some kind of liquor, and two glasses, but he leaned back and folded his arms over his chest, making it clear that his reasons for inviting her here had nothing to do with cards *or* drinking.

Somewhat facetiously he motioned toward the cards and asked, "What game do you prefer, young stable hand?"

"I've not once played cards in the whole of my life," Hennie reported. "If your intent is to truly play cards, you'll have to teach me . . . young blacksmith."

He smiled slightly. "I've set out the port to drink, but if you prefer something stronger . . ." He motioned toward the kitchen area as if to imply he had other liquor there somewhere.

"The port is fine," she said, knowing it was a mild wine that she could sip enough to quench her thirst without having it impair her judgment. She didn't care at all for anything stronger. "Although water would suit me fine, if you must know."

"Then water you shall have," he said and stood up to retrieve a pitcher of water from the counter. He set the pitcher on the table and sat back down, resuming his comfortable position by sliding down in his chair, crossing his booted ankles, and folding his arms over his chest. Hennie wondered how to initiate the conversation she so desperately wanted to have, and was relieved when he said straightaway, "I know you've come because we need to talk about what's happened since we last saw each other, and I know you can't be out too late. We both have to start work early, so it would be prudent for me to get over my hesitance to talk about such things and just get on with it."

Jack sighed, shifted slightly in his chair, and went on. "I've thought about this a great deal since you let me know who you really are . . . and that you'd figured out who I really am; I've thought of little else. I want you to know that I *do* trust you, Hennie, but I still need to hear you say it one more time—that you'll not repeat any of this to anyone—not anyone!"

"I swear to you, Jack; nothing you tell me will ever pass through my lips. My knowledge of your being here is equally confidential. I promise you."

Jack sighed, a mixture of relief and trepidation. "Thank you," he said and sighed again. "I suppose to start where we left off, you should know that when I was told you'd been sent away, I nearly lost my mind. I would never presume to compare what I experienced to your trauma of losing your mother and being carted off to an orphanage, but I can tell you that I felt as if one of my limbs had been amputated. For a twelve-year-old boy, losing my dearest friend so abruptly and without warning sent me into a strange . . . melancholy that now seems like a foggy dream in my memory. It was Mrs. Helton who got me through it, although she didn't explain where you had gone. In fact, she really didn't seem to know. She talked me into eating when I had no appetite whatsoever. Bless her heart, she gave me the mothering I needed so very much. She taught me that bad things happen, that life is not fair, that we more often than not have no control over our circumstances; we can only control how we respond to them. Gradually, with her love and guidance, I managed to find some kind of normalcy in my life, even though I felt like you had died—except it was worse in some ways, because if you had died, I wouldn't have had to wonder where you were and what you might be going through."

As Hennie listened to Jack's heartfelt experiences regarding their separation, memories of how all of that had been for her came flooding back. She fought hard to hold back the tears that stung her eyes, until they refused to be vanquished and forced their way down her cheeks. She knew that wiping them away might only bring more attention to them, and she just hoped that in the dim light he wouldn't even see her tears.

"Why are you crying?" he asked, reaching for her hand across the table, dashing her hope that he might not notice.

"Just . . . the memories," she managed to say without bursting into a fit of unseemly sobbing. "It was all so horrible, Jack, truly horrible. But even with all

I experienced, which I do *not* want to talk about . . . I worried about you too. And it took me a long time—years perhaps—to let go of my anger over the fact that it never needed to happen that way. My mother's death couldn't have been prevented, but I was old enough to work; many children my age were paid servants and workers. Did you know that Mrs. Helton *and* Mrs. Reeves both pleaded with your father to let me stay? They both offered to take responsibility for me and had promised him I would earn my keep, but he refused their pleas and sent me away."

"I *did* know that," he said, sounding angry. "They both spoke to me about it, trying to help me understand, to come to terms with letting you go. Even as kind as they were, I felt as if they were trying to tell me I was only a child, and I would surely find another friend to play with. How could I have ever explained—at my age—that our friendship wasn't just about having someone to spend time with?" He blew out a ragged breath and added with even more anger in his voice, "The entire matter became far more confusing and upsetting the following year when another servant died who also had a child. Do you remember Albert? He was a little younger than you."

"Albert? The freckle-faced ginger who loved following the gardeners around?"

"That's him," Jack said. "His father worked at the manor for years as an under-butler. I barely knew him personally, but he contracted pneumonia and passed away, leaving Albert an orphan. But Albert was *not* sent away."

"What?" Hennie demanded, her heart pounding as she understood why Jack was sounding progressively angrier. "What . . . happened?"

"He was given a reasonable amount of work assisting the gardeners and was put into their care." Jack shook his head and made a sound that reminded Hennie of the way a hot horseshoe would steam when dipped into water. "I was glad for Albert—even though I didn't know him terribly well—but I was so *furious* given the fact that *you* had been sent away, and the situation was exactly the same. My father just yelled at me and told me I didn't understand such things. Any attempt I made to talk to the servants about it only made them uncomfortable, and they had no answers that made any sense—because not one of them could understand why my father would send *you* away and allow Albert to stay."

"I can't believe it," Hennie said, finding it difficult to not dredge up the horror and fear she'd experienced when being dragged from the only home she'd known, with so little explanation.

"Nor can I," Jack muttered. "To this day, I cannot believe it!"

"What happened to Albert?"

"He learned such excellent gardening skills that he acquired a position as head gardener for a large estate in Cornwall."

"I see," Hennie murmured, unable to say anything more while she allowed herself to consider once again how different her life might have been if she'd been able to remain at Ivy Manor.

Jack let out a weighted sigh. "You must tell me how you managed to let go of your anger, because I'm *still* angry!" He shifted again in his chair, and Hennie could see the muscles in his face tighten. She knew he had more to say and didn't want to hinder his momentum, but she also felt afraid to speak without letting on how her anger had just been rekindled.

"Although," he continued, "I suppose my anger toward my father has had many reasons to grow over the years. You know very well how much I detested him even when you lived at the manor and we were very young. I was embarrassed to know he was my father. In fact, my earliest memories are of him belittling and demeaning me, as if his children were somehow scapegoats for his own deplorable behavior. And I clearly remember observing him in his drunken conversations with his friends—I suppose you could call them friends; I think most of the people who surrounded him only wanted the food and drink and favors he doled out with the delusional idea that doing so would earn friendship. But he seemed content with his delusions. Whatever he convinced himself to be truth was truth; there was no argument to sway him into even considering that his ideas about the life he lived were ridiculous and deplorable."

Hennie could feel a hard knot growing in her stomach as she listened to what he was saying, and the way his breathing became shallower as he spoke. He leaned forward and placed his forearms on his thighs so that he could drop his head into his hands, as if it had literally become too heavy.

Following some grueling moments of silence, he went on. "I admit that I spent my youth far too preoccupied with hating my father; and mixed into that there was always—almost constantly—this ongoing worry about you, wondering where you were, what had happened to you, all the while trying to accept that I would likely never know. No one at the manor who actually cared about me had any idea where you'd been sent; if they had, I would have gone personally to find you once I was old enough. I even spoke to the constable, wondering if records were kept of where children were sent under such circumstances. He told me they weren't, and he'd not had any involvement in the situation. He was very kind, but couldn't help me. By doing some digging, I found out that my father had simply asked one of his solicitors to arrange having someone come to collect you, but that particular solicitor was dead by then, and there were no records. Nothing. Nothing." Jack tugged at his hair with his hands while he kept his head down, and Hennie continued to cry silently, glad that at least he wasn't looking at her.

Jack blew out a loud, ragged breath as if he were trying to maintain his composure against incredible odds; then he did it again. And Hennie just waited, knowing he needed to keep talking, and also certain that she couldn't even comment without letting on to her own emotional state.

In a softer voice, Jack admitted, "I felt like a wicked person, Hennie; from the day you were taken away and all the way into my adulthood, I felt wicked. Ironically it wasn't because I *did* anything wrong. According to the sermons taught at church, I did everything right. I considered myself wicked because of the way I felt toward my father, because of my thoughts concerning him. I wished him dead a thousand times and more, certain that when he died I would be set free from all of this anger and hatred I felt toward him."

When he paused to once again catch his breath, Hennie managed to say, "Obviously that didn't happen; his death didn't change the way you felt."

"No, it did not!" he declared as if he resented the fact. He sat up again, and Hennie hurried to wipe her cheeks dry with her hands before he noticed. Folding his arms again, he said with fervor, "All those awful, wicked thoughts and feelings were still there. I wanted to spit on his grave; he was the bane of my life, and even after his death, I was plagued by the way he'd taunted me my entire life, by the pain and suffering he'd caused me. And I wondered what was wrong with me . . . because my siblings endured varying degrees of the same treatment from him, but they were able to let bygones be bygones. They all admitted some relief over his death and not having to answer to him anymore—which is sad, truly sad. I remember standing over his open grave and wondering if the ghost of him had any awareness of how there was not a single person who felt sorrow over his death, only relief—or perhaps indifference. What kind of life does a man live to have it end with no one feeling any sorrow or grief?"

Hennie pointed out what she felt was important, despite it being obvious, "It's as Mrs. Helton said: we often have no control over our circumstances; we can only control how we respond to them."

"Do you think I don't know that?" he asked, shooting her an angry glare, but she knew his anger wasn't toward her. "Do you think I haven't told myself that thousands of times? I don't know *why* I feel so angry, Hennie. I don't know why I can't even force myself to let it go. I've tried; I've tried so hard. I admit that having you come back feels like . . . well, it feels like God finally gave me evidence that He has compassion for my grief, my loneliness . . . and that He is even merciful in regard to the wickedness inside of me."

"Forgive me, Jack, but what you keep referring to as wickedness is just . . . well, I don't agree. Your father was a cruel, selfish man—and he hurt us both terribly. I too struggled with hateful thoughts and feelings toward him for a very long time. But I never thought of it as being wicked. Surely God understands our human emotions . . . our need to come to terms with them. The ability to forgive someone doesn't happen just because we want it to; it takes time and a great deal of effort. But for you it's extremely complicated—which in no way makes what you feel and think wicked. Perhaps you simply have a more tender heart than your siblings; perhaps his being responsible for sending away your best friend compounded your feelings. Or perhaps . . ."

"What?" he demanded when she didn't finish.

"It's just a thought, but . . . perhaps the fact that you were his heir attracted more negative behavior from him. Maybe your experiences with him were far worse than your siblings experienced, and therefore they could never fully understand. None of that makes you wicked, Jack. You're a good man."

"How can you say that and mean it?" he asked, sounding emphatically skeptical. "We've not been a part of each other's lives for over a decade. How can you know what kind of man I've grown up to be?"

"How can you ask me that?" she retorted, hoping he could hear in her voice how insulted she felt. "I consider myself a very good judge of character. A great deal of my survival experience depended on my being a good judge of character. We became friends again long before we realized the truth. And you just admitted that you never *did* anything that would qualify as wickedness. So, is there something you're not telling me? Are you a thief besides being a blacksmith? Have you become a philandering blackguard? Do you drink excessively and wake up with no recollection of what deplorable things you might have done in your drunkenness?"

"No," he said in a voice that expressed humility and enlightenment. He let out another of those weighted sighs and once again leaned his forearms on his thighs. "I believe you might be right. Perhaps I've spent far too much time with all of this rolling around in my head . . . and no one to talk to who could give me perspective." He sighed again. "I know I need to forgive him, but I'm not certain how to do that, when . . . I can't even think about him without . . . feeling furious." He clenched his fists, then forced them open and looked at his hands. More calmly he added, "I feel like two different people, Hennie."

"You *are* two different people," she pointed out. "Just as I am."

"Yes, I know," he said, sounding mildly disgusted. "But that's not what I mean. There's a part of me that sincerely tried to be a good man and always do the right thing. I believe in God, and I believe His hand is in my life and He's watching over me somehow. I would never want to disappoint Him. I imagine Him to be everything my father was not—loving, compassionate, merciful. I truly think that's who I am in my core, Hennie; it's who I try to be."

"I couldn't agree more," she said. "I know that's the kind of child you were, and I can't believe that the core of your personality and character are not as they've always been. I think you believe the same about me, or you wouldn't trust me enough to be talking about such things."

"I can't argue with that," he said.

Following an awkward silence, Hennie said, "Now that you've told me your story up to the point of your father's death, you must tell me what happened after that; something dramatic must have happened to warrant your running away and changing your identity. And don't think I'm leaving here until you tell me."

Jack shot her a brief glance that let her know he intended to tell her, but he needed a minute to gather his thoughts. Hennie poured herself a glass of water and asked, "You thirsty? Water or port?"

"Water is fine, thank you," he said, and she poured some into his glass as well.

Jack shifted in his chair and took a few sips of water before he set the glass down and said, "Of course it was always taken for granted that I would inherit the estate. That's the way it works. I'm the oldest son. You know all of that; we all knew that. You know me well enough to know that I had no interest in the money or the title, but I have a deep love for the manor, the estate, the people. One thing that gave me some peace . . . some hope . . . was thinking of how I could be so much better at managing those responsibilities than my father had ever been. I wanted to be respected and admired simply for being known as a good and generous man, someone the people within my stewardship would know they could depend on to have integrity and to treat them fairly. I believed that when my father *did* die, I might be able to somehow redeem myself by filling the role I would inherit in a way that would bring me fulfillment and the confidence of knowing that I was using my privilege in a way that would allow me to stand before God with a clear conscience." Jack sighed and squeezed his eyes closed and shook his head. "And then his last will and testament was read to us—me and my siblings—by his solicitor, and I felt as if my every hope for redemption in that regard came crashing down around me. Even in death he cheated me, persecuted me, punished me. It was as if he loathed himself so deeply that he believed his heir should be equally loathed. And the way he loathed me made it difficult not to loathe myself—especially in light of his last act against me."

"Are you saying he left everything to George?" Hennie asked, astonished. "That he—"

"No, it's much worse than that. George didn't want to inherit the position. He begged me not to go. He's a good man, my brother; he understands why I had to leave, and he promised me he would do his very best to honor the position well, even though he didn't want it. I know from local gossip that he's kept his word, and I'm grateful to him for that."

"I know from local gossip that he misses you . . . worries about you."

Jack sighed. "That goes both ways."

More silence allowed Hennie to consider everything he'd said and ask the obvious unanswered question. "What exactly *did* your father's will stipulate? I'm assuming that's the reason you left."

"Yes, that's the reason," he said and leaned his elbows on the table, looking directly at Hennie when he had mostly avoided doing so throughout this difficult conversation.

Following still more silence, she asked impatiently, "Well, are you going to tell me?"

"Eventually," he said. "I think it's hard to say without spitting and hissing—or perhaps using foul language—and I would never want to do any such thing in the presence of a lady."

"You're more than welcome to do so in the presence of a lowly stable hand. The other stable hands certainly do."

"But I could never . . . because I know the truth, that you *are* a lady."

Hennie chuckled uncomfortably. "I am female, yes, a woman through and through. But we both know that I was not born to be a *lady* and I never will be. No lady ever came out of a workhouse."

"Perhaps sometime we should discuss what I consider to be the attributes of a lady," he said as if he'd just told her the world was round when she might have always believed it to be flat.

"Perhaps," was all she said, not wanting to stray from the important points of this conversation.

"I just admitted to sometimes using foul language," he said almost lightly. "Does that make me wicked?"

"You also admitted to never doing so in the presence of a lady," she said with a smile. "That's between you and God, but I'm certain He understands. In my own opinion, certainly not. Now stop trying to stall and just tell me why you left."

"Very well." He sighed even more loudly and leaned back in his chair, once again folding his arms over his chest, as if doing so offered him some kind of protection. "First let me point out that we live in the nineteenth century, in a part of the world that is far from primitive."

"Yes," Hennie drawled, having no idea how such a statement could be a necessary preamble for what he needed to tell her.

"Therefore, imagine my astonishment—and that of my siblings—when we were told my inheritance of the estate was based on the stipulation of an arranged marriage."

"What?" Hennie blurted and gasped at the same time, resulting in a very unfeminine cough.

"That's right," Jack said. "My father and *her* father had decided on it when we were young children. I inherit nothing unless I marry a woman I would not trust to do my laundry—as if she would ever even step foot into a room where something so dreadful as laundering clothes was taking place. She's the kind of woman who has some delusional idea that dirty clothes and linens just somehow magically become clean again and are returned to her quarters, the same way she believes her meals are likely prepared by fairies or elves in the kitchen who are—or should be—nothing but delighted to make her life comfortable in every possible way, and they deserve no gratitude from her because living for the benefit of her comfort should be thanks enough." He made a growling noise that seemed intended to add vehemence to the point he was making. "Can you imagine, Hennie, for even a moment, that I could spend my life with such a woman? That I could have a family with such a woman? With my determination to live my life in a way completely opposite to the way my father lived, he was forcing me to marry a woman who was exactly like him." He threw his hands in the air before folding his arms again. "So I left. Thankfully, George agreed that it was my only choice, and I was able to leave with plenty of money. But I needed to find a profession and learn it quickly; I needed to make some kind of life for myself. Our hope was that this . . . young crone . . . I had inherited would quickly give up on me in my absence and marry someone else. If that were to happen, the stipulation in the will would become null and void; the solicitor told us so. But to this day she remains unwed, portraying herself to the community as a brokenhearted victim of my selfish abandonment, waiting patiently for my return—which she seems to believe is inevitable."

"And you know all this because . . ."

"Everyone knows all this, Hennie. She shares her woes with anyone who will listen: the dressmaker, the cobbler, every shopkeeper and churchgoer."

"Why have *I* never heard any of this . . . when I live at the manor?"

"Because Mrs. Reeves mandated after my disappearance that it wasn't to be spoken of, that she would not allow any gossip to take place at all. And you know well enough that Mrs. Reeves is not a woman to be reckoned with."

"And you know this because . . ."

"Because George and I exchanged a few letters after I first left, but then I was found *because* of those letters, and it became evident that the woman who calls herself my fiancée had hired an investigator to find me. So, I sent my last letter to George while I was on the run, trying to find a different place to live . . . trying to start over once again . . . and I told him it was necessary for us to have no further communication."

"This is unbelievable in so many ways that I . . . I can't even think what to say." Hennie shook her head and made a noise of frustration, but she still couldn't come up with any appropriate words.

"Amen to that," Jack said. "So . . . here I hide!" He briefly raised his arms for emphasis, his voice dripping with bitterness. "So close to my home and family, but completely unable to have any contact with the people I care about . . . and completely unable to fulfill my rightful duties on behalf of the estate."

"It's ludicrous!" Hennie spouted, as if he didn't know. "Does this woman have no self-respect? No decency?"

"No on both counts," he declared cynically.

"Has she not picked up on the obvious message that you don't want to marry her? What kind of woman pursues a marriage this way when it's so evident a man is not interested?"

"A woman who wants to marry wealth and title," he replied. "She has no interest in love or trust or respect in marriage. She was raised to believe marriage is for gaining status and riches. The relationship aspect of such a union is irrelevant to her. But as long as she remains unmarried, I have no choice but to remain in hiding. And every hour of every day, I feel more and more angry with my father for doing this to me—as if I hadn't had plenty of reasons to be angry with him *before* he died and willed me to this woman like some kind of trophy."

"Well . . ." Hennie felt the need to admit, "I told you I'd let go of my anger toward your father, and I suppose in regard to his power of deciding my fate as a child I have—or I *had*—but . . . well, it's more accurate to say that I've tried very hard to do so, and I've made progress. Coming back to Ivy Manor stirred up some of those old feelings, and I'm still working on it, but now . . . Oh, Jack! I feel *furious!*" She actually had to stand up and start pacing, afraid she would start shouting otherwise. "I cannot *believe* this! Why would he do such a thing? Why?"

"I can't begin to understand his reasons . . . other than what I've already said. I can't think of him as anything more than a selfish, cruel monster. I don't want to feel that way about my father, Hennie, but I do. He's condemned me to a life of imprisonment, of hiding and running. It's as if he *knew* I would do his job better than he ever could, and he had to find a way of making certain I would be miserable, just to spite me."

"Well, we have to figure out a way to solve this!" Hennie insisted, still pacing. "There has to be a way around his ridiculous edicts! There has to be!"

"If you have any ideas I haven't already thought of, I'm listening." He said it with a sarcasm that made it evident he'd truly exhausted every possibility. Hennie could also hear despair in his voice, and she forced herself to sit down and focus on the heartache of her friend rather than her own growing fury toward his father.

"I'm so sorry, Jack," she said gently.

"It's not your fault."

"I'm not apologizing; I'm just . . . telling you how badly I feel . . . about all of this. It's horrible. I mean . . . you make a fine blacksmith and all, but . . . this situation is . . . unconscionable."

"I couldn't have said it better myself." He sighed and apparently felt the need to talk about something else when he asked, "And how exactly did a woman from the workhouse learn such refined speech?"

"It took a great deal of effort, if you must know," she said. "But I *learned* to speak at Ivy Manor, if you'll recall. However, I quickly noticed that at the orphanage I was beginning to pick up on the way most of the other children talked. And Lottie had no education. So we would listen to people speak on our breaks and then practice more proper English when it was late at night and the lights were out; we would whisper back and forth until we fell asleep. Doing this helped me remember how my mother had taught me to speak. She always told me that the way a person spoke always left an impression that was difficult to undo, and refined speech was more likely to get me better employment." She sniggered. "Fat lot of good it did me. I went from the workhouse to an inn to being a stable hand."

"Through no fault of your own," he reminded her.

"I know, but . . . that doesn't change the way things are."

"And so we're both hiding . . . both living in our own kind of prison."

"It's rather pathetic, isn't it," Hennie stated.

"Yes, it is!" Jack said emphatically, then he softened his voice and reached for her hand across the table to squeeze it. "But at least we've been blessed with the miracle of coming back together. Our circumstances are certainly pathetic, but we're in them together. I consider that to be nothing short of a miracle."

"Amen," Hennie said and squeezed his hand in return.

Chapter Eight

THE QUEEN OF TOOKLE-BERRY

"So," Hennie asked, trying to keep her tone light, "who is this evil witch who has turned you into a blacksmith?" Reverting to the way—as children—they'd always put everything and everyone into the context of imaginary tales seemed appropriate at the moment; if nothing else it could perhaps help ease the strain of this insufferable situation. "Do I know her?" Hennie added the last facetiously, well aware that she knew practically no one from his privileged world—especially since they'd not even been a part of each other's lives for more than a decade.

"You do, actually," he said and completely surprised her.

"Who?" Hennie asked, sitting up a little straighter, frantically trying to recall any girls who might have been around when they were children, who could have grown up into the despicable woman he'd described.

"Rebecca's dearest friend since they were six," Jack stated.

It took Hennie a long moment to attempt piecing more memories together. And then when it *did* come together, she gasped as if she'd been tossed into a cold pond. "No!"

"Oh, yes!"

"Letitia Tewksbury?" She practically choked on the name. "You're talking about Letitia Tewksbury?"

"The very same," Jack said, sounding as if he would be dragged to the gallows at any moment.

Hennie laughed, but it was a macabre, humorless laugh. "Of all the women in the county," she said with a bitter edge, "your father's dying wish was to shackle you to the Queen of Tookle-Berry?"

"Well," Jack said without any humor whatsoever, "he obviously didn't know that you and I had dubbed her that—a queen who possessed two completely different personalities, which she could use to manipulate and torture her victims. Isn't that how it went?"

"That's how I recall it," Hennie said. "And with good reason." She made a scoffing sound. "How many times did we see her shove another child to the ground, or even hit them, and then cry and tell the adults she'd been attacked? How often did she say cruel and vicious things to the children she disliked, and immediately transform herself into a perfectly kind and loving princess so that certain people would always believe that's who she was?"

"Yes, that's her."

"And she manipulated no one more than . . . Rebecca."

"Still does," Jack stated. "Right up until my father's death, I was regularly disgusted by how blind Rebecca is to Letitia's manipulation. But I had no idea this . . . *disaster* . . . was already a part of my father's will. I'm certain now that if I'd begun to show any interest in a woman while he was alive, he would have marched me to his study and made me aware of the provision, to make certain I married the woman of *his* choosing. We both know the Tewksbury family is extremely influential, and I suspect this deal was manufactured for my father to remain in the good graces of Old Man Tewksbury—and the other way around."

Hennie gasped again as a new realization came to mind.

"What?" Jack asked.

"I've seen her," she said. "Only a few times . . . in the stables . . . and only from a distance. But I've seen a woman with Rebecca. She wasn't close enough for me to recognize her, not that I necessarily would have, considering how long it's been, but . . . it's always the same woman who goes riding with Rebecca; it must be her."

"I'm certain it is," Jack said with chagrin. "Through the years Letitia has made certain that Rebecca doesn't have *any* other friends, as if socializing with anyone else would be a personal insult. Even when we were younger, I pointed this out to Rebecca numerous times, and how it's an indication of Letitia's attempts to control Rebecca's life. But Rebecca is convinced that I just don't like Letitia, and so I made all this up just to be cruel. Of course, she *would* see it that way. That's the way people behave when they're under the spell of the Queen of Tookle-Berry."

"And naturally, Rebecca was present when your father's will was read."

"Of course," Jack said. "She was thrilled; she thinks it would be nothing but wonderful to have her best friend become a member of the family and live under the same roof. Rebecca doesn't believe she'll ever get married; she thinks she's too old. I think Letitia has discouraged and disrupted any possible romantic involvements for Rebecca because that would mean losing her friend whom she can manipulate to her heart's content."

"That's terrible!"

"It's evil, Hennie. When a person uses and abuses someone for their own gain or to buffer their own ego, it's evil. She's ruining Rebecca's life, but because they've been friends for most of their lives, Rebecca simply can't see it. To give Letitia the benefit of the doubt, I think she's a product of the way her parents raised her, and she likely doesn't even realize how badly she behaves; she simply follows some strange instinct inside herself to do whatever she has to in order to get what she wants. But whether or not it's intentional or rational is no excuse for it to be tolerated."

"I agree," Hennie said, overcome with a combination of compassion and fury.

"And what of your other siblings? What is their opinion on the matter?"

"George agrees with me completely," Jack went on. "He too has tried to convince Rebecca to be rid of Letitia and to seek out more worthy social attachments, but she's convinced that her brothers are a couple of senseless oafs who are just being cruel for the sake of being cruel—like our father; yes, she compares us to our father and believes we are just like him, and yet she is still all in favor of Letitia marrying me. Try to explain how *that* makes sense, because I certainly can't."

"And what of Leah and Sarah? What do they think of all this?"

Jack sighed and pushed his hands through his hair, tugging at it briefly as if it might release the pressure on his brain. "Neither of them expressed any opinion at all. It's as if being able to get married and move away from here was such a huge relief that they've separated themselves emotionally from anything at all related to the home and family they left behind. I think they know Rebecca is being hoodwinked, but they won't stand up to her. That's how my father raised his daughters—the same way he treated our mother before she died— to be submissive and keep their opinions to themselves because they are of no consequence."

"So, explain to me how you and George turned out to be such good men— so completely opposite of your father—when he was your example of manhood growing up?"

"Oh, I can answer that easily enough, because I've actually thought about it a great deal. For all that my mother was not allowed to speak her mind in my father's presence, she had no qualms about teaching her children personally and privately that she'd not married our father by choice, and she didn't want us to grow up believing that his behavior was all right. Even though she died when we were still young, she always taught George and me the power and importance of treating all people as equals, of being respectful to women, of having integrity. And since my father's lack of character was so obvious and such an embarrassment to the family, I believe it was easy for us to take in her quiet lessons. I know she taught my sisters to be very careful in choosing a husband, and made them aware of the signs to watch for so they would avoid marrying a man who might turn out to be anything like their father. The servants who were heavily involved in our lives were well aware of our mother's teachings and perpetuated them as they cared for us following her death. I'm glad to say that Leah and Sarah are both married to good men. I believe they're happy and doing well, and I don't blame them for wanting to separate themselves from the difficulties at home—especially when their sister is so obviously being foolish but there's nothing anyone can do about it. I can certainly understand why they wouldn't want to say anything to Rebecca that might come between them."

Jack sighed loudly. "I don't know what else there is to say, Hennie. That's the situation. Letitia is certain that with time I will come to my senses and return home, and I think Rebecca is convinced of the same, since she thinks my running away was some kind of childish tantrum meant simply to rebel against my father."

"There has to be some way to rectify this, Jack," Hennie said. "There has to be!"

"Well, I'm open to ideas, because I can't think of anything. It's not that I mind working as a blacksmith; I really don't. But I want to live *my* life, not someone else's. This is not who I am; not who I was meant to be."

"No, it's certainly not."

"And how strange it is that you would not only end up here now, but that you actually have some real empathy for how it feels to live in disguise, always pretending, constantly wondering if someone will notice."

"Yes, I have empathy for that," Hennie said, giving him a wan smile.

They talked a good while longer, each of them comfortably able to express their emotional response to all that had happened during the years they'd been separated, and how it had impacted the present. Both Hennie and Jack agreed about having difficult feelings toward his father, but they also agreed that they needed to work on coming to terms with those feelings and finding peace; neither of them wanted to give the old man any power over their lives—especially from beyond the grave.

A pause in the conversation brought Hennie to a sudden awareness of how much time had passed, and she insisted that she needed to return home. Jack agreed, not wanting her to get into any trouble with the stable master, and also not wanting her to get too tired before she had to ride home in the dark. Before she left, he hugged her tightly, and Hennie allowed his embrace to fill her with strength. His coming back into her life was one of the greatest blessings God could have ever given her. They understood each other in so many different ways that she could never count them.

"Thank you," she said as they each stepped back from their embrace.

"For what?" he asked, looking genuinely confused.

"For trusting me enough to tell me all that; you didn't have to, but I'm glad to know what's going on in your life. I wish I could do something about it, but . . . at least I can perhaps be more supportive by knowing the whole story."

"That's the way it should be with friends," he said with a little smile, then he jokingly punched her lightly in the shoulder, the way one man might do to another. It didn't hurt at all, but it forced her to take a step to the side to catch her balance, which made them both laugh.

"I'll see you next week," she said.

"Unless we're blessed enough to have a horse throw a shoe, or some other fortunate event that might require an extra visit."

"We could hope," she said, and he walked her back to where her horse was tethered, waiting patiently as if he'd been napping on his feet—which he likely had.

All the way home, Hennie recounted everything Jack had told her and felt freshly astonished over such a ludicrous state of affairs. Back at the stables, she found a single lamp left burning, which she knew was standard procedure when any of the horses were still out. In fact, she knew there would be a lamp for each absent horse, and a lamp should be extinguished after that horse had been cared for and settled in for the night. Only one lamp meant that Hennie was the last to return. She took care of the horse properly, extinguished the lamp, and found her way quietly into the house, where she found another lamp that she lit and used to guide her up the back stairs and to her room. She knew Lottie would be asleep by now—along with everyone else in the house. But Hennie was glad to avoid Lottie tonight. It was becoming more and more difficult to keep secrets from her dear friend—especially when the secrets were growing bigger and more emotionally significant.

It took Hennie a long time to fall asleep while she recounted once again all that Jack had told her, and she feared that she might have a difficult time getting through her work the next day without appearing tired—which might bring more attention to the fact that she'd stayed out too late.

Hennie came awake abruptly in response to the usual knock at the door and was glad to note that she'd slept well once she'd fallen asleep, and it only took her a minute to carefully place all the secrets she shared with Jack into a private space in the back of her mind, where thoughts of him would hopefully not interfere with her normal routine.

"Good morning," Lottie said brightly when they met in the hall to walk downstairs together and out to the stables to do the early-morning chores that had to be completed before breakfast.

"Good morning," Hennie replied.

"And how was your evening out?" Lottie asked, as if Hennie might have attended some kind of fancy, high society ball.

"It was fine," Hennie said. "We just talked. I have no gossip to offer." She thought of how she certainly knew things that would be considered the most delectable gossip among the household, but she'd been honest in stating that she had none to offer; she'd promised Jack absolute confidence, and she would not compromise the trust he'd put in her.

"But you like him?" Lottie asked in a quiet voice, even though there was absolutely no one nearby.

"He's a good friend," Hennie insisted. "Don't forget that I am pretending to be a man." Again, she clarified to herself that she'd told the truth. Even though Jack knew she was a woman, it was certainly a fact that she was pretending to be a man. "You're not jealous, are you?" Hennie asked with a little laugh. "I mean . . . I do have your permission to have more than one friend?"

Lottie laughed. "You may have as many friends as you need to make you happy—as long as I know that I'm your best friend."

"Lottie," Hennie said and stopped abruptly, feeling the need to stand still and face her as she said firmly, "no one but you could ever understand what it was like to grow up the way we did. No matter how our lives might change in the future or what might happen, you will always be dearly precious to me; I will always need you—and don't you ever forget it!"

Lottie's eyes actually glistened with moisture before she turned to look both directions on the stairway to be certain they were completely alone. She then hugged Hennie tightly but briefly so as not to be caught hugging like a couple of girls when they needed to appear as manly stable hands.

"And the same to you," Lottie said as she began walking again, going a little faster to make up for the minute they'd just lost.

As they arrived at the stables and got to work, Hennie felt deeply grateful for Lottie's friendship and support, and her healthy attitude about Hennie having other friends. Throughout the day she thought often of Rebecca, and the way Letitia had manipulated her into a strange kind of isolation, where it seemed that Rebecca could not have any other friends, or even be close to her family members. Hennie felt deeply sorry for Rebecca, and increasingly angry with Letitia. She tried to do as Jack had suggested and give Letitia the benefit of the doubt, considering the way she was raised. Still, Letitia was a grown woman, and surely she had some awareness of the difficulty she was bringing into other people's lives. Surely she had to see how her determination to find Jack—convinced that he should and would marry her—was simply ridiculous. What kind of woman would want to marry a man, fully aware that he did *not* want to marry her, so much so that he'd made great efforts to leave home and go into hiding?

When Sunday came, it occurred to Hennie that she'd never seen Jack at church. She knew that spiritual worship was important to him, and she wondered why he didn't attend. But it took her only a few moments' thought to realize that he would avoid people as much as possible so that he wouldn't be recognized, and church was a very social occasion, given the way people interacted before and after the service.

As the day approached when Hennie would be riding into town to visit the blacksmith, that fluttering sensation began to happen inside her again—only worse. She tried to just ignore it and decided to not even try to analyze why she would feel such a thing—especially when she'd never experienced such a feeling in her entire life. She simply looked forward to seeing Jack and sharing lunch and some conversation, just as they'd been doing for many months— except that now there were no secrets between them, and they could talk about their lives realistically within a context of complete honesty.

Hennie enjoyed the ride more than usual, since the weather was perfect, as was the temperature. Spring had settled in fully, and the scenery was dotted with color from wildflowers coming up out of the ground and trees bursting to life in response to the warmth. Some were filled with blossoms of white or pink, and others were becoming vibrant green as new leaves sprouted and spread out to take in the sun's light.

When Hennie arrived, she was surprised to see Jack just sitting with his long legs stretched out, his booted ankles crossed, and his arms folded over his chest. As she dismounted, he said, "Slow day."

Hennie tethered the horse in the usual place and sat in the empty chair next to Jack. He'd obviously placed it there in anticipation of her arrival. "Is that good or bad?" she asked.

"If I needed the money, it would likely not be good, but I don't, so I can say that it's nice to have a break—especially since I now have your company."

"It's strange how we've come to sit here where we can see a little of what's going on in the village and watch people go by, and no one takes any notice except for an occasional wave. And I wonder sometimes . . ." she laughed softly, ". . . if they only knew the truth."

"I think about that every day," he said and laughed as well. "We could both cause quite a stir if the truth were known." He sighed. "Which is exactly why we will both be very careful about keeping each other's secrets."

"Yes indeed," Hennie said and then commented on what she could see as an obvious change. "You trimmed that ghastly beard; it's somewhat less ghastly now."

"It's necessary now and then," he said very seriously and then chuckled, which let her know he was mostly joking. "I must maintain a proper balance between remaining in disguise and not appearing too ghastly."

"Yes indeed," Hennie said again with a chuckle.

"How have you been?" he asked.

"Fine," she replied. "I've had a lot to think about, certainly. And it's still difficult to believe. But everything at the manor just goes on as usual. How have *you* been?"

"The same," he said. "I saw you at church."

Hennie turned to look at him in surprise. "I was going to ask you about that. I know you enjoy going to church, but I assumed I never see you there because you don't want to interact with people who might recognize you."

"That is all true," he said. "So, I arrive just after the service has begun, sit at the very back of the chapel, and hurry out the moment the vicar gives his final amen. But I saw you, and I assume it was Lottie sitting next to you."

"Yes."

"Now I know what she looks like," he said.

"I'll have to introduce the two of you one of these days—given that you're both very dear friends. I'm certain she'd like to meet Ollie the blacksmith. Maybe she'd even like to join us for cards and drinks."

He chuckled. "Except that we'd actually have to *play* cards, and maybe even drink something."

"Maybe," she said, and they fell into a lull of silence.

"Hennie." The way he spoke her name to break the quiet caught her attention, and for some strange reason it caused an enormous eruption of that fluttering inside of her. "May I speak to you . . . privately?"

Hennie glanced briefly toward him, wondering why this request seemed unusual. "No one can hear us," she reminded him.

"That's not what I mean," he said, and she honestly had no idea what he *could* mean.

"Will you just . . . come with me . . . into my work room? Just for a few minutes?"

"Very well," she said, and they both stood up. She followed him into the room with the workbench and supplies where Hennie had told him she'd figured out his true identity, and that she was in truth his childhood friend. The memory of their reunion warmed her as he closed the door behind them.

"Is something wrong?" she asked, turning to face him.

"No, Hennie," he said, "nothing is wrong; at least I don't think so. You might disagree with me."

"I don't understand," she said, confused by the intensity of his gaze, especially when it heightened the fluttering in her stomach and quickened her heart.

"Neither do I," he said and surprised her by reaching up to pull off the leather string that held her plait in place. Before she could ask his reason for doing such a thing, she looked up at him and realized how close he was standing. His height in contrast to her own had never been so obvious as it was in that moment. Even though he was taller than the average man, it was no wonder the other men she worked with considered her scrawny and small.

"That's better," he said and wrapped the string around one of his fingers. "Although, I've never seen even the tiniest resemblance to a man since you told me the truth. I only find it a little strange to see a woman wearing breeches—even though I think I've gotten used to it, and in a way, it suits you."

"They're much more practical," she said, her heart quickening to an even faster pace as he moved closer still, and she began to wonder if his purpose might actually be what she both hoped and feared it might.

"I can understand that," he said, "but I didn't bring you in here to talk about the way you dress." She gasped when he took her face into his hands, as if he refused to let her look anywhere except at him while he said whatever it was he felt he needed to say. "I'm going to come straight to the point. I can't stop thinking about you, Hennie. I don't think a minute passes without you there in my mind, and . . . what I feel is unlike anything I've ever felt. The situation we are in is ludicrous, but I've realized I can't let that keep me from admitting to my true feelings. We've been completely honest with each other over everything; how can I be with you at all and try to pretend I don't feel this way?"

"Jack," she murmured as he leaned a little closer and she instinctively took hold of his upper arms, fearing she might topple over otherwise. Feeling the tightness of his muscles beneath the fabric of his shirt, she was both impressed with the effect of all his physical labor, and even more aware of why she and Lottie were viewed as so scrawny.

"What?" he asked in a breathy voice when she said nothing more. While she attempted to contend with her own breathlessness and heart palpitations, her mind swirled with what he was trying to say and what it meant. And she was entirely surprised—though she figured perhaps she shouldn't have been—to realize he had just explained and validated everything *she* had been feeling but had apparently been too imperceptive—or perhaps too afraid—to acknowledge. She realized now she had been trying so hard to only think of their relationship as being friends—just as they'd been when they were children—that she'd not even allowed herself to consider any other possibility. But now he was here, so close she could feel his breath on her face, declaring feelings for her that were the same as her own. She could hardly believe it, and she certainly didn't know what to do about it. But knowing their opportunity to enjoy this private respite would be brief, she decided to stop trying to analyze what was happening and just enjoy what had to be the greatest moment of her life.

"Say something," he said when she still hadn't uttered another sound. "Tell me I'm a fool. Tell me you could never feel for me as I feel for you, and I'll leave you in peace, but—"

"I could never tell you that," she muttered.

"Why not?" he asked, as if he needed to be certain he hadn't misconstrued her meaning.

"Because it just wouldn't be true," she said and allowed herself to look into his eyes—really look into his eyes—as she'd never done before. And what she saw there prompted the tingle of tears in her own eyes. She closed them in an attempt to hide her tears, and a moment later she felt his lips on hers. His kiss caught her by surprise, but she had no trouble responding by leaning forward to press her lips a little more tightly against his.

Following their brief first kiss, she opened her eyes to look at him and had no control over the tears that slid down her cheeks. She saw his brow furrow as he asked, "Why are you crying?"

"I'm not sure," she whispered, "but I think it's something to do with . . . feeling too much joy to hold it all inside."

He smiled, apparently liking that answer, then he kissed her again, letting go of her face to wrap her in his arms. She returned his embrace, pressing her hands tightly against his back, realizing she'd never imagined that anything in this world could be so perfectly blissful.

Their kiss ended slowly, as if he felt as reluctant as she for it to conclude. She opened her eyes reluctantly, wanting to hold on to the dreamlike sensation surrounding her. She found him looking at her with the same kind of dreaminess she felt.

"I think we have a problem," he said, and one corner of his lips twitched upward. "I'm a blacksmith, and you're a stable hand. I don't think there is any established protocol about courting in that regard."

Hennie laughed softly and touched his hair, realizing she'd wanted to for a long time, glad to be able to do so now. "And when did either of us ever care about established protocol?"

"Neither of us . . . ever," he said. "However," he added, drawing out the word, "in the interest of keeping our secrets, we can't be seen together in public *at all* beyond our established habit of eating lunch together at the front of the smithy."

"Well," she said lightly, "we could go to the pub for a tankard of ale, and I could do my best to guzzle it down like a man and belch loudly afterward."

Jack laughed, but he still didn't put any distance between them. "We could talk about hunting game and other such important matters that men are meant to discuss."

"We could," she said, "but . . . I think I prefer being with you *here*." She initiated another kiss which ended with him chuckling and rubbing her nose with his.

"And what do you suppose passersby might think of our strange disappearance?"

"I doubt that anyone is paying attention enough to notice," she said, "and quite frankly I don't care."

"Nevertheless," he said with a self-composing sigh, "there is work to be done, and everything must appear to be business as usual." He smiled at her and added, "I'm just ever so glad you didn't reject what I had to say; I confess I was terribly nervous, but I knew I couldn't keep the truth to myself any longer."

"I'm so relieved you made it possible for me to understand and acknowledge what I've been feeling."

He smiled again and took her hand to kiss it before he said, "I'm not sure how we're going to manage—or where any of this could possibly take us—but for now we'll just enjoy the moment." Then he handed back her leather hair string.

Hennie returned his smile and nodded in agreement before she watched him open the door and leave the room. She stood there for at least a minute, basking in all she'd just experienced. Joy and elation flooded her, and she resolved to hold them close, to keep the memories prominent in her mind to help her get through the mundane goings-on of daily life while they remained in hiding.

Hennie tied her hair again and left to get lunch. She had to wait longer than usual to get the meat pies and also the buns at the bakery. It seemed that everyone in town had decided to make similar purchases at the very same time. While she stood around, waiting for her turn to be helped, Hennie kept thinking of Jack's tender confessions and the thrill of his kisses. She had to will herself not to blush as she pondered what this might mean regarding their future. She only had to think about it for a few minutes to realize that—under their current circumstances—this relationship could go absolutely nowhere. Something had to change, but in truth she didn't really know what his intentions were beyond the confessions he'd made. Perhaps he didn't know either; he'd likely felt the need to share his feelings and hadn't taken the time to think anything through beyond that point. A number of problems came to Hennie's mind—some being more critical and urgent than others—and she was stewing with concerns by the time she finally returned to the smithy with lunch.

"Did you get lost?" Jack asked, sitting down again.

"Just lots of people; had to wait." After offering the most minimal explanation, she sat down beside him, and they began their ritual of sharing lunch. "And the horse?" Hennie added, nodding toward the animal she'd brought with her.

"Hind feet are done; still need to do the front."

Hennie took another bite of her mutton pie and realized how ridiculous it was that they were sitting there talking like a couple of mere acquaintances. She'd become accustomed to the way that men generally spoke to each other with very few words and short sentences. But no one was anywhere near enough to hear them, and not so long ago they had been in the back room kissing.

"Jack," she finally said, "what are we going to do?"

"I don't know," he replied in a tone that indicated he *had* thought about it, and he knew well the messy situation they were both in.

"There's one concern I have and . . ." she chuckled ironically, "well, obviously there are many concerns, but I suppose when I consider taking on what seems most urgent at the moment, I need to talk to you about one concern in particular. I suppose we'll have to work things out one step at a time."

"I'm listening."

"It's just . . . Lottie and I are so close; she's very perceptive. I don't know how I can keep this from her without damaging our friendship."

Jack shot her an alarmed glance and said with his mouth full, "You can't tell her who I am; no one can know."

"No, of course not. I know that, but . . . can I not tell her a portion of the truth? She knows I've become good friends with the blacksmith. She's joked about it becoming something romantic, which I've reminded her is ludicrous when you believe I'm a man—even though you've known for some time now that I am not. Anyway, I think I should tell her that you have known for a while now that I'm a woman, and that something romantic *has* developed between us; by us I mean . . . between me and the blacksmith. There's no reason she has to know any more than that. But at least this way I can talk to her about my true feelings, and she'll be more supportive in helping me get away so that I can see you more often, and . . . well, what do you think?"

"I think that sounds perfectly reasonable," Jack said, much to Hennie's relief, "especially since I know she has her own incentive to keep secret the fact that the both of you are pretending to be men. I know from what you've told me that she can be trusted, and she would never want that secret getting out."

"Exactly," Hennie said and laughed softly. "And after all that Lottie and I have been through together, how could I not tell her about you and me? I can't tell her that we were childhood friends, but I can tell her how things are now."

"Of course," Jack said, and they shared a lengthy glance that made it clear they were both wishing they could share a kiss. Instead they finished their lunch, and Hennie took care of a quick errand while Jack finished putting new shoes on today's equine customer.

As she was preparing to leave as usual, they exchanged all the normal comments, both of them trying to ignore that *everything* had changed between them. Hennie could almost believe she'd imagined what had taken place between them privately, except that she never could have imagined such a wondrous experience. She was relieved when he stepped close to her after she'd mounted the horse to leave, asking softly, "When can I see you again? Can you get away tonight?"

Hennie wanted to very badly, but instinctively she knew that asking Parsons for the use of a horse and leaving for the evening too frequently would draw undue attention to the situation. None of the men went into town for any reason more than two or three times a week. She also knew it was important to have some time to talk to Lottie, and since she'd mostly been avoiding her friend—not wanting Lottie to be able to sense that Hennie was keeping secrets—she knew it was important to make an effort to spend some time with her, and to use their precious time between supper and going to sleep to catch up on this remarkable turn of events in Hennie's life. So Hennie resisted the temptation to tell Jack she'd meet him later and said, "Not tonight, but I think I can get away tomorrow."

"There's no need for you to come all the way into town," he said, indicating he had thought this through as well. "Remember the tree, the enormous tree we used to walk to?"

Hennie gasped; she'd honestly forgotten about it until now. "The tree out in the middle of the meadow, all by itself. I *do* remember. At least I do now."

"Can you meet me there tomorrow? Just after dark so we won't be seen."

"I'll be there," she said and wished she could bend over to kiss him good-bye. She nodded and smiled instead, adding a little wink, which she hoped he interpreted as a *wish* for a kiss. He winked back, and she believed they were thinking the same thing.

Hennie rode away, feeling as if her entire life had changed since she'd come into the village today. Even though she couldn't begin to imagine where all of this might lead her, she knew that nothing would ever be the same.

Chapter Nine

KEEPING SECRETS

HENNIE DIDN'T SEE LOTTIE UNTIL supper, since Parsons had sent her on some errands. When they sat down next to each other in their usual places, Hennie whispered, "I need to talk to you as soon as we're done here."

"I'm glad to hear it," Lottie whispered back, "because I need to talk to *you*." Lottie lifted her eyebrows briefly and gave a quick smile. "I know you've been keeping something from me, and I've been wondering for days if I should insist that you tell me. Today I decided that I should, so I hope you will."

"We must be thinking the same thoughts," Hennie said quietly, "because today I decided that I need to tell you what I didn't feel I could tell you before."

"Well, I'm glad that's settled," Lottie said, seeming relieved. Perhaps Hennie's secrets about Jack had been more evident to Lottie than Hennie had believed. She certainly didn't want any tension between them, or any strain on their friendship; she was glad to know she could at least share enough to not feel alone in this situation. "And it wouldn't be the first time we were thinking the same thoughts," Lottie added. "I've lost count of how many times *that* has happened."

"Indeed," Hennie said, and they both focused on enjoying their meal and the light banter and pleasant conversation taking place at the table.

After Hennie and Lottie were both in their nightshirts and ready to settle in for the night, they sat on Lottie's bed, where Lottie immediately said, "I'm waiting, and I'll not wait another minute."

Hennie took a deep breath. "First of all, I admit that I probably should have told you sooner, and I apologize for keeping it from you. I think that . . . maybe I didn't think anything would come of it, and then when it did, it all happened so fast and . . ."

"Just get to the point," Lottie insisted.

"Very well," Hennie said and took another deep breath. "Ollie knows that I'm a woman, and—"

"He knows?" Lottie interrupted, astonished. "For how long?"

"A while now; I'm not sure. We just . . . got so comfortable in our conversations, and I knew I could trust him, and . . . it became too difficult not to tell him." Hennie was careful to avoid even a hint of how this had come about because she'd figured out that Ollie was in fact the heir of Ivy Manor. "I know you and I had promised we wouldn't tell *anyone,* so perhaps I was a little afraid to admit I'd broken that promise, or—"

"No need for that," Lottie insisted, easing Hennie's discomfort. "I trust your judgment. I do wish you'd told me sooner, but I understand; truly I do."

"Thank you!" Hennie said earnestly. "I knew you would understand. It's just that . . . now, you see . . . just recently . . . he admitted he has feelings for me, and . . . I can't deny that I've had feelings for him for quite some time, but I've been trying to disregard them, and . . . well, that's all, really."

"That's *all?*" Lottie said and laughed. "That's amazing!" Hennie marveled that with all the horrors Lottie had lived through, she still believed in the notion of finding happiness and true love, of seeking out a better life and believing it could be found. She reacted as if Hennie had stepped into some kind of fairy tale, and she knew her relationship with the blacksmith would surely come to a glorious happy ending.

"Don't be getting ahead of yourself," Hennie pointed out. "For all that I believe this is a good thing, the situation has complications, and we certainly need time to be prudent in getting to know each other better. And might I add that *courting* could be difficult if not impossible while I'm living as a man."

"Then perhaps it's time to make your true identity known," Lottie said as if it were nothing.

"And then what? Be promptly banished from the property without a job? And do you think I can make myself known without compromising *your* secret when everyone knows we're close friends and you're even shorter and scrawnier than I am?"

"You make a fair point," Lottie said. "Although . . . I must confess this is becoming more and more difficult, especially when . . ."

"When what?" Hennie insisted when she hesitated, sensing that Lottie had a secret of her own.

"I must admit," Lottie said, blushing slightly, "I've taken a liking to a fine young man, someone we work with. I suppose it's not unlike how you've told me your friendship developed with Ollie. The difference is that we actually *work* together, and I don't know if I can tell him the truth. I don't know him well enough yet to know if I can trust him with that, or how he might feel about it."

"Good heavens, Lottie! Why didn't you tell me?"

Lottie said lightly, "I don't think you can be asking me such a question, given what you have just admitted."

"Fair enough," Hennie said. "Well . . . who is he? Which man is it? One of the stable hands?"

"Yes."

"Tell me! I'll never let on that I know; you can trust me."

"I know I can. It's just . . ." She actually giggled. "Saying it out loud is . . ." She giggled again, and her skin turned an even brighter pink. "It's Zeke."

"Zeke," Hennie said, recalling the tall, thin man they'd both spent much time working with. He was kind and funny, and his hair was a mass of blond curls, as if no comb could ever keep them in place and he instead just rumpled them with his hands and allowed them to fall where they may. "Zeke!" Hennie repeated his name with more enthusiasm now that she'd let the idea settle in. "Oh, Lottie, that's wonderful! He's a dear man!"

"Wonderful?" Lottie echoed and made a scoffing sound. "He thinks I'm a man! He calls me *mate*."

"Well, eventually we'll just have to find a way out of this," Hennie declared. "And if we're meant to spend our lives with these men, we'll have to find a way to change our circumstances dramatically. For now . . . I'm just going to enjoy getting to know Ollie better . . . even if we have to do so in secret. And you can do the same with Zeke. At the same time, you and I will continue to do our jobs well and keep our heads down and not draw any attention to ourselves."

"Of course," Lottie said, sounding only a little deflated. "But . . . tell me more about Ollie; tell me what he said when he admitted to his feelings."

Hennie felt giddy over the memories and loved telling Lottie how he'd taken her into the storage room and closed the door so that he could kiss her. Lottie became completely entranced by Hennie's romantic tale, and they speculated about how they might one day both be happily married with children and look back on this time of their lives and laugh over the absurdity of this deception and the strange circumstances growing around it.

Lottie was thrilled to learn that Hennie would be meeting Ollie the following evening at a place that was within walking distance from the manor—especially after Hennie assured her that she knew Jack was a perfect gentleman and she wasn't at all concerned about spending time alone with him. Lottie was more than happy to help Hennie get in and out of the house unseen, and to cover for her absence should the need arise. Even though they couldn't foresee any reason why Hennie would actually need help, it was nice to know that Lottie was available should a problem arise.

The two friends talked far too late and finally forced themselves to get some sleep. The following day was as normal as any day could be. Hennie was glad that Lottie's chores kept them distanced from each other; she didn't want to try to hide their tendency to want to whisper and giggle over the romance evolving in Hennie's life. And given how she couldn't keep Jack out of her mind, nor could she control the fluttering inside herself that frequently occurred when she *did* think of Jack, she didn't trust herself to not whisper and giggle at the slightest provocation—which she knew Lottie's intrigue over the situation would surely inspire.

The day dragged for Hennie, but when it came time to actually sneak down the back stairs and out of the house, she was filled with equal amounts of nervousness and excitement. After concluding that she had no good reason to feel nervous, she focused on the excitement she felt at spending time with Jack. Her eyes quickly adjusted to the dark, aided by the glow of a partial moon, and she walked briskly across the meadow and over a hill that sloped down so that the enormous tree where they'd often played as children was not visible from the manor or the road. As its shadow came into view in the distance, Hennie couldn't believe she'd forgotten about it. They'd had so much fun climbing among its sturdy branches, playing all kinds of silly games and fantastical make-believe beneath its boughs through every season of the year. As her memories regarding the tree flowed back into her conscious mind, she felt a strange sensation, as if they'd emerged from some dark cavern where they'd been hidden away, and she wondered *why* she would have stored such precious memories in such a deep crevice in her mind. But she was also struck with a sensation that made her shudder, a vague, barely discernible idea that other memories existed in that dark cavern, and some of them were not nearly as pleasant as the childhood games she'd shared with Jack.

As Hennie approached the tree—which had grown even bigger since she'd last been there—she saw Jack's form as he moved away from the enormous tree trunk, and there was no mistaking that it was him, even in the darkness. He had a very distinct way of standing and moving, and her heartbeat quickened as they stepped toward each other.

"I began to worry you couldn't get away," she heard him say.

"Am I late?"

"No," he said, "I just . . . wanted to see you so badly that I started to—"

"I'm here," she said, standing close enough to touch the side of his face, above his beard.

"Oh, I'm so glad!" he said and kissed her. Hennie went on her tiptoes and wrapped her arms around his neck.

"I'm so glad too," she said, and they kissed again.

After one more kiss, Jack chuckled and said, "I must try to behave like a gentleman and not get carried away. If we're going to meet unchaperoned, we must be especially careful."

"Yes," was all she said as she attempted to consider the implication of his words. She'd never even stopped to think about anything happening between them more than the kisses they'd already shared—perhaps because she absolutely knew nothing like that *would* happen in either of their lives unless it was within the bounds of marriage. She certainly wasn't naive about such things, but she realized in that moment that she didn't really believe that this relationship would ever evolve into marriage. How could it? He was the heir of Ivy Manor, and she was working as a stable hand; she'd grown from a child to a woman in the workhouse. But he took her hand and walked with her, a sensation so pleasant that she pushed away any concerns for the future and decided to simply enjoy this evening as it was.

Hennie wondered where they were going until he sat down in a grassy spot and patted the ground beside himself. "We can see the stars from here," he said, lying back on the ground and putting his hands behind his head.

Hennie lay back as well, maintaining an appropriate distance between them. "Oh, it's beautiful!" she said, wondering how long it had been since she'd just taken the time to enjoy the beauty of the stars. When survival was a constant concern, even looking up at the night sky seemed a luxury she'd not been able to indulge in for many years. Both in the orphanage and in the workhouse, she had barely been allowed outside at all, and never at night. But she didn't want to talk about that right now. Instead she enjoyed listening to Jack explain the different constellations they could see as he pointed them out with his finger. Of course he'd been highly educated throughout his youth in many subjects, while Hennie had stopped receiving any education once she'd left the manor. She knew how to read and write, and she'd always been conscious of maintaining refined speech. She knew very basic math, and she loved to read—which had taught her many things. But she could feel inferior when comparing her education to Jack's. Again, she chose not to think about that right now, but rather to simply enjoy all he was showing her in the night sky that she'd never even imagined existed.

When he'd concluded his discourse on what he called his minimal knowledge of the stars, he took hold of Hennie's hand and squeezed it. "This is nice," he said.

"It *is* nice," Hennie replied, turning her head to look at him.

"I confess that these years of working as a blacksmith have been terribly lonely. It's so good to have you back, Hennie."

"It's good to have you back too," she admitted. "I was blessed to have Lottie's friendship, but that time when I was working at the inn and didn't even know if she was dead or alive, I sometimes felt as if the loneliness would smother me."

"How did you do it?" he asked as if she'd just told him she'd trekked across the deserts of Africa.

"Do what?" she asked, confused.

"How did you even survive an orphanage? A workhouse? I've heard such horrible stories of these places . . . where people are barely alive but hardly living. It haunts me, Hennie, and I can't help wondering how you even came out of there alive—not only alive, but so positive about life."

Hennie cleared her throat as if that might soften the difficult memories. "It wasn't easy, and I can't deny that the stories you've heard are probably true—or worse. I've heard that the orphanage we were in was considered better than most. I look back and wonder what that means about those that were worse. I missed my mother so much; I missed you—and everyone at the manor who had always been so kind to me. I couldn't even imagine that it was possible for life to change so dramatically—to have once been surrounded by so much love and abundance, and then to be living so starkly; everything was dark and dirty and barely livable. And that's what seemed to be the goal: to keep the children barely living."

"Oh, Hennie, it makes me feel sick, literally sick."

"We are in agreement on that," she admitted. "Which is why I've had to put it behind me; I have to force myself not to dwell on such memories."

"I can understand that," he said, "but . . . as I've said . . . it haunts me. Will you tell me just a little more? And then we'll put it away."

"I don't know what there is to tell; the details aren't important."

"Was the workhouse any better?"

"No, It was worse—far worse," Hennie said and heard Jack sigh with compassion. "The work was tedious and never-ending. The place was filthy, and I went to bed every night listening to rats scurrying around the room."

"Oh, Hennie!" Jack blurted. "No child should have to live like that!"

"No, it's true. But that's the reality. I kept holding on with the hope of getting out of there and somehow finding a better life. Lottie made a huge difference in that regard. She has a way of looking to the future with a bright hope that's almost unearthly. It's as if she came to this world with a gift of being able to see the best possible outcome, even when the circumstances feel completely impossible to survive. Even now, she's certain that aside from the fact that we are living this life of deception, we will somehow emerge from it in some kind of magical way that will give us better lives. I want to believe her, but . . ."

"And why shouldn't you?" Jack asked, turning to his side to lean on his elbow and settle his head into his hand. "Why can't we reach toward a better future for both of us? And for Lottie as well?"

"I hate to point out the obvious, Jack, but you are hiding from your life, pretending to be someone other than yourself to avoid marriage to the Queen of Tookle-Berry. We are all in ridiculous circumstances, which are not going to be changed easily."

"You make a fair point," he said with chagrin, "but that doesn't mean we shouldn't *hope* for change . . . for escape. Shouldn't we?"

Hennie looked at the sky and stated a truth she had learned long ago; as dismal as it sounded, she felt it had to be said. "Hope is a fragile thing, Jack. Investing hope in certain things, or certain people, can often leave you shattered. It's as if hope is some kind of beautiful vase; it sparkles in the sunlight and lures you to want to get closer and even try to touch it. But it topples over so easily and breaks into hundreds of unfixable pieces, and it takes everything you have to come up with the ability to find hope again." She sighed and closed her eyes. "I want to hope for something better, Jack, but the reality of our circumstances is . . . difficult to look beyond."

"But we must!" he insisted vehemently and sat up, turning to look at her.

Hennie sat up and leaned on her hand. "And how do you foresee all of this turning out?" she asked, sounding a little too much like a mother speaking to a child—and she knew it. But she considered her concerns valid.

"I . . . don't know, Hennie. But we'll figure it out. Now that I've found you again, I don't ever want to lose you. I *can't* lose you!"

"What are you saying, Jack?" she asked, a little out of breath at his implication.

"We have to be together, Hennie," he declared.

"And again I ask: what are you saying?"

"I'm not proposing marriage, not yet at least, but—"

"How can you think of the possibility of proposing marriage at all . . . unless we both go very far away from here and start our lives over under new identities?"

"If that's what we need to do, then we will," he said with firm resolve.

"Just like that?" She snapped her fingers.

"Just like that . . . if we must."

"But I know you came back to this area for a reason," Hennie said more softly. "I know you're concerned about your home and family; I know you feel responsible because it's who you were raised to be." He hung his head slightly and said nothing; his silence implied his inability to deny the truth in what she'd said. "Jack," she added, taking his hand, "we've been apart for so long, and so much has changed. I know you're as grateful as I am for the miracle that has brought us back together . . . and to feel the way we do, but . . . surely, we need time. We must be prudent and cautious and not make any rash decision simply because our circumstances are so frustrating and often discouraging. We must be patient; we must take some time to get to know each other again. Despite the strangeness of all this, I think . . . Do you want to know what I think?"

"Of course I do!"

"I think we need to have our own version of courting. We need to spend time together and talk about all the important matters of life. We need to carefully evaluate the kind of people we've become and what's important in our lives. And if we both sincerely believe we're meant to be together, we need to find a way to solve these problems the *right* way. Perhaps leaving *is* the best option, but we need to do so thoughtfully and with purpose, not impulsively, not in any way that might one day bring us to regret our decisions."

Hennie watched him turn his head to the side, as if looking toward the manor—even though he couldn't see it from here—might help him think more clearly about the quandaries in his life that existed because of it. Following minutes of silence, he lifted her hand to his lips before he said, "You're right; I know you're right. We need time. We'll just . . . see each other when we can and keep our secrets for now." He kissed her hand again and added in a positive tone, "I'm certain everything will work out the way it's meant to."

"I'm certain it will," she said and kissed his cheek.

Hennie distracted him by repeating her conversation with Lottie about how she'd become romantically involved with the blacksmith, and how excited Lottie was. They speculated a little over how it might be when Hennie and Lottie would find a way to no longer have to pretend to be men, then Hennie felt the need to return home. She was getting sleepy and knew she needed to be refreshed for work tomorrow. She rode more than half the distance to the manor with Jack on the horse he'd brought, but he didn't want to get any closer, and Hennie didn't ask him to explain.

After kissing Jack good night, Hennie hurried home and was in bed a little after eleven. She feared not being able to fall asleep when thoughts of the way Jack had changed her life swirled in her mind with a dreamlike effect. But she was very tired, and her thoughts went with her into her dreams. She woke to the usual knock on the door, feeling rested and even more in love with Jack. Love? The thought that she was in love with him had come so naturally to her mind, but the word *love* had never been spoken between them. Of course, she believed she'd always loved him as a friend—and he her. But this was different, so different. And yet, two people didn't speculate about sharing their lives together unless they loved each other. Did they? Well the Queen of Tookle-Berry might, but not Jack, and not herself. In her heart she knew that she *did* love him, but that didn't change the fact that they needed time. Still, spending time with him and getting to know him again was ever so appealing, and it prompted her to get out of bed and face the day with enthusiasm, knowing every hour that passed was an hour closer to the time she could see him again.

Summer eased smoothly along while Hennie managed more easily than she'd expected to be able to live a dual existence. Whenever she and Jack could maneuver private time together without drawing attention to themselves in any way, she found perfect joy in his company and an increasing desire to never be without him. She had declared the need for time to prove whether or not their relationship was strong enough—and rooted deeply enough in the right things—to withstand the test of a lifetime. And every day she believed they had everything they needed to make each other happy—except for the fact that eventually they had to face up to their true identities, and she couldn't help but see the enormous chasm in their real lives.

The first time Hennie took Lottie into town with her so that she could meet Jack—and *play cards*—everything went even better than Hennie had anticipated. Lottie and Jack—or Ollie as far as she knew him—took to each other almost immediately, and they got along well. Since they were in the common room of Jack's house and could not be overheard, Jack and Lottie loved making jokes about the way the women were living in disguise, and they provoked a great deal of laughter by speculating over how all the people at Ivy Manor might respond if they knew they'd been working with women all this time. Hennie enjoyed the humor, but the very idea of anyone finding out left her terrified, and she didn't want to think about it too deeply.

Since Jack and Lottie had become fast friends, they all spent more time together. Hennie enjoyed her time alone with Jack, and she knew that their being able to talk privately about certain matters was important to the evolution of their relationship. She also knew it wasn't wise to spend *too* much time alone with Jack—especially when the attraction between them was growing stronger, and they were becoming more and more comfortable with each other. To be able to spend time with him and have Lottie there allowed them all to talk and enjoy each other's company, and Lottie made an excellent chaperone. Of course, Lottie knew nothing of Jack's true identity, and at this point in time she simply couldn't. But Hennie knew that eventually she would *have* to know. If Hennie's relationship with Jack turned into a serious commitment, her best friend would have to know the truth. Jack agreed, but he was as hesitant as Hennie to think too hard about what that could entail, so it was a subject they most often avoided.

Despite avoiding certain difficult topics, Hennie felt deep joy and gratitude in her evolving relationship with Jack. Each opportunity they had to spend time together and talk about their beliefs and feelings on every matter in the world they could think of, they always came away with a deeper conviction regarding their ability to share their lives, to have children together, and to raise them well. The problem was that neither of them was in a position to take such steps without making drastic changes in their lives, and no matter how they speculated over how those problems might be solved, every option felt wrong.

"Perhaps the timing is wrong," Hennie suggested one afternoon late in the summer while they shared lunch in their usual chairs at the front of the smithy. The temperature was especially warm, which made it mildly uncomfortable, but occasionally a breath of breeze came their way, offering a moment of relief. The leaves in the trees were just beginning to show hints of changing color, and Hennie knew that the warmth of summer was coming to an end. She dreaded winter in regard to having to brave the cold for her rides back and forth into town, and she also knew that meeting Jack at the big tree was not at all practical when the temperatures were freezing and there might even be snow on the ground. But for now, she enjoyed the warmth of the day and pondered the statement she'd just made, which Jack had only met with silence. Realizing he expected her to explain what she meant, she added, "Perhaps one of the options of solving this problem is the right answer—no matter how difficult it might be. But maybe it feels wrong because it's simply not the right time. If we trust that God will guide our lives and help us find our way out of this—and I know we do because we've talked about it—then we must believe that we will know the right course to take, *and* the right time. Either that, or circumstances might force the truth to the surface whether we like it or not."

"What do you mean?" he asked, sounding panicked, even though his facial expression didn't reflect it. They'd become very good at visibly hiding their emotions when there was any possibility that another person might happen to take notice and consider their behavior odd. They didn't want to bring any attention to themselves at all.

"I don't know." Hennie shrugged. "I suppose I just mean that sometimes a situation becomes so unbearable that you just *have* to change it, or sometimes an unexpected change in circumstances might bring something to light in a way we might not have even considered. That's why we must trust in God; we can't do this alone. I believe if He brought us back together, He has a plan to make it possible for us to *stay* together. And maybe it's just not the right time."

"Maybe," was all Jack said and kept eating, as if to declare that he didn't want to talk about it. At least not right now.

The next time Hennie and Lottie went into town together in the evening to visit Jack, they all exchanged the usual greetings, but instead of sitting down at the table where they usually talked and pretended to play cards, Jack said, "Come along, ladies. There's something I want to show you."

"Very well," Hennie said, and they followed him out a side door from the common room, which she realized went outside. In the remaining light of a summer evening, Hennie could see that just to the right of the door was a narrow set of stairs that went up the side of the house. Jack led the way up, and the women followed. He opened a door and led them inside. There was just enough light coming through the windows to reveal that they were in a tiny room with furnishings covered in dusty fabric. There was a fireplace at one end, and it was easy to see that beneath the fabric were chairs and a table and some kind of small couch.

"What is this?" Hennie asked.

"When I purchased the smithy and its adjoining house, the previous owner told me that part of his large family had used these rooms. He told me that before their family had grown so big, they had rented these rooms as a separate apartment. It's been empty since I came here. I haven't wanted to deal with renters, and I do well enough with my work that I haven't needed the money." What Hennie knew that Lottie didn't was that he'd left home with a great deal of money and he didn't even need what he made working as a blacksmith. He walked through a nearby door that had been left open, and they followed. The furniture in here was also covered with dusty fabric, but it was easy to see two narrow beds, a washstand, a bureau, and a night table between the beds. The room was small and the furniture barely fit, but it was better than most places Hennie had lived. Jack then led the way to another bedroom, which had covered furniture that appeared much the same as the other bedroom, except that it had only one bed that was larger; obviously meant for two people to share.

"It's quite nice, actually," Hennie said.

"Could do with some cleaning," Lottie said facetiously, since her statement was readily obvious.

"But why are you showing us this?" Hennie asked.

Jack hesitated, then said, "Come back downstairs with me and I'll tell you."

Hennie felt a little nervous at the implication that this was meant to be a lengthy conversation and they would need to sit down. She also sensed a mild nervousness in Jack. When they were all seated around the table in his common room he said, "It's an idea I've been mulling around for some weeks now, and . . . it's entirely up to you, but . . . I wanted to offer it as an option."

"An option to what?" Lottie demanded, looking thoroughly confused, while Hennie could see exactly where this was going, but she remained silent, preferring that Jack explain.

"An alternative to living as men," Jack said, "when you should be able to live as who you really are and stop pretending. I must admit that I worry about the two of you; women should be able to live as women. I believe in women being treated equally and with respect; you both know that. But the fact is that men and women are different; we have different needs and different abilities." He looked more at Lottie as he said, "Hennie hasn't told me details, but I know it can't be easy for the two of you to deal with feminine matters in this situation, and . . ." He absently motioned toward them and made only a quick glance toward their chests before he cleared his throat and said, "Forgive me if I embarrass you, but I worry about the way you have to bind your chests every day. It just seems so wrong, and I worry that maybe it's not even healthy; it's not the way you're meant to live."

Both women remained silent. Hennie felt somewhat aghast to realize there was actually a feasible option for to being able to stop living as a man. She *had* become very weary of it, and she knew Lottie had too. The binding around her chest *was* uncomfortable, and she too had worried that it might not be healthy. She'd wondered if it might negatively impact her desire to one day have children and be able to properly feed them as any mother should—and she knew Lottie shared the same discomfort and concerns, because they'd talked about it.

When a minute passed and neither Hennie nor Lottie had uttered a syllable, Jack turned more toward Hennie and leaned forward as he took her hand. "Listen to me, Hennie. I'm tired of living this way; we can't go on like this."

"I agree with you," Hennie said, realizing she'd almost said the name *Jack*, which wouldn't have been good with Lottie present. Sometimes she found it truly difficult to keep track of this man with two names. But they had to take on revealing their secrets one step at a time. "But I don't understand exactly how this would work. What exactly are you proposing? You're talking about us being able to live as women, but . . . no matter how we might dress or style our hair, our faces are well-known here in the village. People from the manor come into town all the time. How are you suggesting such a change is possible simply because you have a place for us to live respectably? And I can think of other challenges as well, but let's start with *this* one, because it's no small thing."

Jack leaned back in his chair and folded his arms. "If you don't agree with me, I completely understand, but . . . it's my thought that you should just . . . come clean. Tell Parsons the truth."

"He'd fire us on the spot!" Lottie declared.

"Exactly," Jack said. "And it would be great fodder for gossip over half the county that two women had actually been living and working as men all this time. And once everybody knows, there's nothing to hide and nothing to be ashamed of. You both know why you did what you did; you don't have to apologize to anyone. And you have a place to live. I'll make certain you both have everything you need."

"Lord have mercy!" Lottie exclaimed in a trembling voice before she stood up and turned her back as if she were overcome with emotion and didn't want the others to see.

"What is it, Lottie?" Hennie asked, standing beside her.

"It's just that . . ." Lottie's voice trembled more, and there was no hiding that she was crying. Hennie tossed a concerned look toward Jack, whose expression was filled with concern and compassion. Hennie focused again on Lottie as she explained with tears running down her cheeks, "I've become so very tired of all this. I've been praying for a way out of this mess I got us into, but I didn't see any possible solution."

"You didn't get us into a mess, Lottie," Hennie reminded her. "You saved us. It was a brilliant idea, and it's served us well. But clearly it is no longer serving us as well as it once did. Perhaps it's time for a change." Even though Hennie felt deeply concerned and hesitant, Lottie's reaction made her more open to considering the possibility. "Come sit down and we'll talk about it. I don't know if this is the answer, but let's talk about it some more, and we'll see what we can work out."

Lottie nodded and wiped her hands over her cheeks. Hennie chuckled in an attempt to relieve the tension and said, "It's all right if you cry in front of Ollie. He won't mind."

"Not at all," the man with two names said as he deftly appeared on the other side of Lottie, gallantly holding out a clean handkerchief toward her.

"Thank you," Lottie said, and they all went back to their chairs, Lottie still dabbing at her eyes.

Since Lottie seemed too emotional to perhaps think all of this through, Hennie turned to Jack and said, "I admit that it feels somewhat . . . frightening . . .

to think of telling Parsons the truth and having that truth out in the open . . . but to think of getting beyond the initial shock of all that, I believe we would both feel so much relief that I'm guessing it would quickly outweigh any challenges. However, there are some obvious challenges I can think of that we need to discuss. We can't do this unless we've planned it all out very carefully."

"I agree," Jack said.

"For one thing, we can't just live here, appearing to be renting an apartment from you without people being able to see that we are paying our own way. If there's any cause for the public to think that you are supporting us, then rumors which we do *not* want to contend with could stem from such ideas. We must be able to support ourselves—or at least *mostly* support ourselves, which means I'm admitting that I'm willing to lower my pride enough to allow you to help us some, but not completely. You can't support us entirely, Ollie." She was proud of herself for inserting the correct name to be used in Lottie's presence. "We need to be able to work, to maintain our self-respect. And who is going to hire us if we're the source of this great scandal of having duped the entire staff of Ivy Manor all this time?"

"I've actually thought about all that," Jack said with a confidence that Hennie hoped was not unfounded. "I might be wrong, but I believe this *scandal* could work in your favor. Even though there are generally no ill feelings between the villagers and the Hannaford family, there is still a lot of joking about them among the villagers. It's mostly in good fun, but the men in the pubs enjoy making light of their wealth and privilege." Hennie understood how such a truth might be viewed through Jack's eyes, in contrast to him saying it as a blacksmith—a man pretending to be one of the villagers. "I sincerely believe the shopkeepers and pub owners would *love* to hire the women who duped the entire Hannaford household. I know for a fact that the Hawk's Nest just lost one of their best servers since she's quit to have a baby that's due to come soon. I hear she worked a lot of hours and she was very reliable and will be missed. Even if the two of you could *split* the time she worked, you'd at least both be working. And I think I could convince the owner to consider taking you on."

Hennie knew the Hawk's Nest was only a five-minute walk from the smithy. She'd gone there with Ollie in the guise of a man to sometimes have a drink and try to make herself fit in. She could hear a great deal of logic in what Jack was saying, but she also felt the need to point out, "It all sounds like a reasonable plan, but it's also full of risks. You're assuming that people will see this as something positive, that they'll be willing to give us work. But what if the opposite happens? There is risk involved."

"Is there not always risk involved with change, Hennie?" he asked with a fierceness in his eyes. "The worst that can happen is the two of you will not be able to get work here in the village. You will still have a place to live that's safe and warm and dry, and you'll have your needs met. If people speculate over that and find reason to gossip, what of it?" He leaned forward and became even more intense. "I want to court you properly, Hennie. And I can't do that under the present circumstances. That's far from the only reason I believe the two of you should stop living this charade, but it's still a big part of my incentive. If you make this decision and unforeseen problems arise, we will all leave here and start over somewhere else. With any luck I can convince you to marry me, and Lottie will find equivalent happiness—either here or wherever we all choose to go. The future is not something we can see or predict, Hennie, but right now we can make a choice to improve the situation. Please. Think about it, but know how very much I'm hoping and praying that you will cease all this nonsense and take what I'm offering. I'm blessed enough to have the means to provide for both of you, so allow me to do so. You've both suffered far too much in your young lives; you deserve to have someone actually do some good on your behalf. Don't you?"

Hennie felt implications sink into her heart that he hadn't been able to say in Lottie's presence. It was his father who had sent Hennie away into a life of terrible hardship. He was declaring that he wanted to make up for that—for her and for the precious friend who had helped her survive through those terrible years.

"I'll think about it," Hennie said, and Jack let out a slow sigh of relief.

Chapter Ten

FACING THE WORLD AGAIN

"I DON'T HAVE TO THINK about it," Lottie said, looking at Hennie with pleading eyes. "What is there to think about? I don't want to live this way anymore; I *can't* live this way anymore! Are you forgetting how it's become more difficult to deal with my monthlies since I've been tending to feel ill the first day or two and . . ." She stopped as if she realized what she'd just said and had forgotten a man was present. She turned toward Jack, looking embarrassed and said, "I'm sorry. That was inappropriate and—"

"It's all right, Lottie. Men are aware of such things, I assure you. I'm not at all embarrassed. It's just a fact of life, and one of the many things that has concerned *me* as I think about the way the two of you are living. It's a perfect example of how men and women *are* different, and in this regard both of you should certainly be in a position to deal with the issue appropriately each month and not have to hide it."

Lottie smiled wanly at Jack, then looked again at Hennie. "He's right, Hen. He's right about everything. It feels like a miracle to me. I don't have to think about it."

Hennie felt put on the spot and frightened, even though she couldn't figure out why, exactly.

"Talk to us, Hennie," Jack said. "Tell us what concerns you. We can't work out the problems if we don't know what they are. If there's something I've overlooked, then speak up."

Hennie thought about it for a long minute. Then another. She finally had to say, "I feel some fear, but . . . nothing truly legitimate. I think it's simply a general fear of the unknown."

"Given your past experiences, I believe that's understandable," Jack said, "but I promise I will take care of you—both of you. We'll take on any problems as they arise."

"I'm thinking if there's a job available right now at the Hawk's Nest," Lottie said, sounding enthused, "then we should just do this and get it over with."

"Oh, good heavens!" Hennie exclaimed and erupted to her feet, only to feel a little lightheaded, which made her lean one hand against the wall while she put the other over her quickened heart, lowering her head and trying to catch her breath.

"What is it?" she heard Jack ask softly, at the same time feeling his hands come over her shoulders.

"I . . . I know it's the right thing to do; I can feel it—as if my spirit just leapt inside of me, telling me I have to move forward." Hennie struggled to even out her breathing, grateful to feel the strength of Jack's hands; his strength helped her feel like he wouldn't let her fall—literally or figuratively. For the first time since her mother's death, she felt as if someone was there to help take care of her, that she wasn't on her own in the world. She and Lottie had often talked about the fact that despite their close friendship, the circumstances of their growing-up years had incited an internal desperation for survival that often made them feel alone; even knowing they had each other's love and support didn't mean they could have done anything to prevent increased hardship in each other's lives. And now Jack had stepped in, offering them a solution to escape their current deceptive situation. She appreciated the way he was willing to help but he wasn't overbearing or insistent; he was simply allowing them an option and giving them the opportunity to make new choices based on new alternatives. And Hennie knew in her heart she would be a fool not to follow Lottie's lead and just move forward with the faith that everything would work out somehow.

"I can't disagree with anything either of you have said," Hennie finally managed to say, turning to look at them. She impulsively leaned her head against Jack's shoulder, and he wrapped his arms around her. "And if we're going to do it, I think we just need to get it over with. I don't think I can hide my nerves from anyone I work with."

"Everything will be all right," Jack said, and Hennie believed him.

Jack lit a lamp since the room was becoming dark, and the three of them sat for a while longer discussing details of the best way to go about doing what needed to be done, now that they were all in agreement that they had to just go forward. When they all agreed that their conversation with Parsons—and their actual leaving—would be better done when it was dark, the matter suddenly became urgent, and Hennie and Lottie left with the purpose of returning to the manor as quickly as possible, packing up their minimal belongings, and telling Mr. Parsons the truth. Jack would meet them at the big tree with extra horses and escort them to their new home under cover of darkness so that no one would see the two men who moved into the apartment over the smithy, and the two women who would be living there the following day.

"You have *extra* horses?" Hennie asked Jack, never having heard of such a thing.

"Yes, my dear," he said with a smirk. "You never would have noticed unless you'd gone down the alley on the opposite side of the shop from the apartment stairs, but this is also a livery. I sometimes board and care for people's horses, but I have four of my own."

"Hmm," Lottie murmured, sounding impressed. "A wealthy man, indeed."

If she only knew, Hennie thought, wondering how long it would be until her friend learned the full truth about Jack. She didn't believe that *any* secret could be kept forever, and if they were going to be living in such close proximity with Jack, she doubted he could manage to keep up his acting skills continually. Or maybe he could. At least he was living his life as a man.

"Wait a minute!" Hennie said as she realized they had a problem. "We don't have any women's clothes. We got rid of everything; we didn't want anything to be found in our rooms that would arouse suspicion."

"And everything we had before we came here was pathetic anyway," Lottie interjected.

"Well," Jack said, "you should be proud to know I thought of *that* too. A few days ago, I purchased some women's clothes at the secondhand shop; and I even got some hair pins." Both women looked at each other in astonishment, and then at him. "Yes, a man can purchase women's clothes without creating any scandal. The shopkeeper hardly noticed. She didn't ask *why* I was making such a purchase, but I was prepared to lie and say that I was sending them to my sisters in some far corner of England."

"Good thing she didn't ask," Lottie said. "That was entirely unconvincing."

Jack smirked at Lottie and added, "Nevertheless, I believe I have sufficient clothing for you to manage for a day or two—and I think I was able to guess your sizes enough that they will work—and you can go buy more for yourselves as soon as you've settled in."

"We do have a fair amount of money put away from our wages," Lottie added, and Hennie appreciated her friend's ability to speak when she felt mostly numb and a little afraid. "In fact, our saved wages could justify how we're able to afford rent for a time even if we don't find work right away."

"You see," Jack said more to Hennie, "everything will be fine."

Hennie could only give him a wan smile, appreciating his positive attitude—as well as his help. He leaned forward and kissed her quickly, ignoring Lottie's presence. Following his kiss, Jack kept his face close to hers and just looked into her eyes with an intensity that had become familiar to her. She could see his love for her glowing as brightly as it ever had. And because he loved her, he was making it possible for her and Lottie to dramatically improve their situation. She touched his face with silent appreciation, now able to offer him a more sincere smile, not caring that Lottie was there as she kissed him again.

"Everything will be all right," Jack said with a confidence that gave Hennie strength.

Focusing on the need to step into a new season of life with too many unknown factors to even imagine, Hennie rode quickly with Lottie back to the manor. They were riding too fast to be able to share conversation, but that suited Hennie fine. She needed time to think all of this through and try to adjust. Earlier this evening they had been riding in the opposite direction to spend a pleasant evening with Jack. Now they were on the brink of changing everything, and once Mr. Parsons knew the truth, there was no going back.

They arrived at the stables to find them quiet and devoid of any human beings. While they were unsaddling their horses and caring for them, knowing it would be the last time they did any such thing within the walls of these stables, Hennie felt an urge to cry. She'd enjoyed the majority of her experiences in this place, and leaving felt difficult and uncertain. But she forced herself to think of the future, of being able to be seen as a woman again, of being able to spend more time with Jack—properly and without any strange deception on her part.

Still saying very little, Hennie and Lottie went up to their rooms, and they each had their belongings packed in a matter of minutes. Hennie's concerns felt less prominent as she thought about actually being able to wear a dress again, with a chemise and petticoat underneath. Holding to that idea, she felt braver as she and Lottie left the manor house for the last time and walked together toward the back of the stables, where Mr. Parsons had a small apartment and his office. Light emitted from the office windows, and they knew he was likely there finishing up the day's paperwork, which he kept meticulously.

"Let's get this over with," Lottie whispered, took a deep breath, and knocked on the door. She set her bag on the ground against the wall and out of sight, and Hennie put hers with it.

The door came open quickly, and Mr. Parsons looked surprised to see them. "Good evening, lads," he said. "What can I do for you?"

"We apologize for bothering you so late," Lottie said, "but we need to speak with you."

"Come in, come in," Parsons said, not sounding at all put out. "Have a seat and—"

"We prefer to stand," Hennie interjected, not wanting Lottie to think she had to completely take charge of the conversation. And if they remained standing, she hoped their conversation would tend to be briefer. "We won't take up too much of your time, but . . . we have a confession to make, and we're certain you'll be disappointed in us."

When she paused, Lottie took the next step. "We apologize for that . . . for disappointing you, because you've been more than fair with us in every way."

Parsons chuckled uncomfortably. "I can't even begin to imagine what you might be trying to tell me, boys. Have you been stealing from me or—"

"No, nothing like that!" Hennie declared. "It's just that . . ." She took a deep breath and just said it. "The reason we are scrawnier than most men is that . . . we are not actually men."

Parsons furrowed his brow and narrowed his eyes, looking even more confused. Lottie added quickly, "We are in fact women. When I first came here in search of work, there were no positions available for women, but there were jobs available in the stables. Since most of the staff had been away that day, I realized I could come back as a man and try that. After growing up in an orphanage and a workhouse, I was desperate for work and didn't figure living as a man could possibly be any worse." Lottie hurried on as if she wanted to get this explanation over with as quickly as possible, and Hennie was in complete agreement.

"After I'd been here about a year," Lottie said, "and you mentioned that you needed to hire more help . . . and you told me you wished you could find someone who worked as hard as I did . . . that's when I went to find my dear friend, who was working at an inn where the conditions were dreadful. And so I pulled her into my deception. We've been treated so well here, and life has been good for us . . . except that . . . we've simply reached a point where trying to pretend to be what we are not has become too difficult." Lottie took a deep breath as if a huge weight had slid off of her. "We offer our sincerest apologies, and of course we know that we can't stay."

After a grueling stretch of silence, Parsons said, "I can't believe what I'm hearing, and I can't imagine how the two of you managed to be so convincing." He sighed and looked at the floor a long moment before he looked at them again, his expression more regretful than angry. "It's true that I can't let you stay now that I know the truth. You know His Lordship requires absolute honesty from all his employees; he would simply never stand for something like this."

"Of course," Lottie said at the same time Hennie said, "Yes."

"But I do wish I didn't have to let you go. You truly are two of the best workers I've ever had. I've never had to worry about either of you doing what was asked of you, and doing it well."

Hennie wanted to thank him for the compliment, but she couldn't get her tongue around the words. Lottie remained equally silent.

"What will you do? Where will you go?" Parsons asked, sounding genuinely concerned.

Hennie knew honesty was the only option; they had all agreed on that before leaving the smithy. "The blacksmith and I have become friends over time as I've taken horses in regularly," Hennie said. "He has an apartment over the shop that is available to rent, which he's gladly offered."

"He's a good man, Ollie," Parsons said. "Funny how I've never actually met him, but I've never heard anything but praise—both for his work and his fine character. He's a good man to have as a friend, I would think."

"He is indeed," Lottie said. "We have saved a fair amount of money, and we'll look for work in the village—as women."

Parsons shook his head, looking at them as if he'd never seen them before. "Now that you've told me, I can see it, but . . ." he chuckled ironically, "I never would have imagined." He shook his head again before he said, "Before you leave let me give you the last of your wages." He walked around a desk, opened a drawer with a key, and took out a small stack of paper notes, counting out what was owed to them since they'd last been paid. Hennie and Lottie both thanked him as they took the money.

Hennie felt compelled to add, "Thank you for everything, sir. You've been so kind . . . so very fair. It's been a pleasure working for you."

"Amen to that," Lottie said.

"The pleasure has been mine," Parsons said, then added thoughtfully, "Do you prefer I not tell anyone about this or . . . I mean . . . people will wonder why you left so quickly, and—"

"We're ready for the secret to be out," Lottie said. "We'll be living in the village, and it's not as if our faces won't be recognized, even if we'll be wearing dresses. Tell people whatever you must."

Parsons nodded thoughtfully and asked, "How will you be getting into town? Do you need to borrow some horses or—"

"Ollie is meeting us nearby," Hennie said, "but thank you; again, you are so very kind when you have every right to be angry."

Parsons said with compassion, "I don't believe anyone can judge too harshly the actions of those who come from those deplorable workhouses. I was blessed to never have to endure such a place, but I've known others who have, and it's a pitiful thing, truly pitiful. You've both shown a great deal of integrity and you've more than earned your pay. I'll judge you on those merits and let the rest be forgotten." He reached out a hand to shake each of theirs, as if he felt it was important to part respectfully.

After Hennie and Lottie had stepped outside and the door was closed behind them, Hennie whispered, "I never would have imagined that to go so well."

"He's a good man," Lottie added as they both retrieved their bags and began walking briskly away from the stables and across the meadow to the big tree where Jack would be waiting.

As they came over the crest of the hill, Hennie could see the tree in the distance, and the outline of three horses. She couldn't see Jack but suspected he was relaxing on the ground until they arrived. When they got close enough for him to hear their approach, he jumped to his feet and declared with dramatic humor, "You've successfully made your escape from the majestic house of stone and ivy!"

"Indeed we have," Hennie said, wishing she could tell Lottie that this was her beloved childhood friend Jack, and he was referring to what they had called the manor when they'd been playing games of make-believe many years ago.

It took only a minute for them to secure their bags to the saddles and be on their way, riding quickly toward the village since it was late, and they were all tired. Upon arriving at their new home, they each took care of their own horses and settled them in for the night in the livery that Hennie hadn't known existed until this evening. Jack then insisted on carrying their bags as he led the way around the back of the building to the other side and up the stairs, joking about how he was now going to behave like a gentleman and be more helpful now that they could stop pretending they should be treated like men.

"Obviously we'll need to clean this up better tomorrow," Jack said as they all came through the door where he'd left a lamp burning so they could see. He set down their bags and turned up the wick on the lamp so it burned more brightly. "For now, let's just make it livable enough for you to be able to get a good night's sleep."

"*We* will clean tomorrow," Hennie said, "and we will manage just fine in making it livable for tonight. You've already done so much."

"Fine," Jack said, pretending to sound insulted. "I'll . . . get you some fresh water."

"That would be lovely, thank you," Hennie said, smiling toward him.

Jack smiled back. "Now that you're going to be a woman again, are you going to use more words like *lovely*? Because I think I would enjoy that very much."

"Go get the water!" she said as if it were an order. He laughed and walked out the open door.

"You should marry him," Lottie said the moment he was gone.

Hennie was a little taken off guard but couldn't deny that Lottie was probably right. For now, however, they just needed to adjust to a new way of living and hope the results of these changes would go as smoothly as possible.

Lottie and Hennie worked together to remove the fabric covers from the furniture they needed to use. Lottie wisely pointed out that they should carefully fold the fabric so that the dust remained inside and didn't have any opportunity to get into the air and then settle where it would have to be cleaned up. They set the folded fabric outside the door on the large landing at the top of the stairs. It was pleasing to find that beneath the dusty coverings, the beds were all made with linens and blankets. When Jack returned with water and a bag containing the clothing he'd purchased, he told them the bedding had all been clean before the beds had been covered. He left the water and clothing and told them both good night, declaring that they should sleep as late as they wished the following morning, and he would leave some breakfast for them in his kitchen downstairs. Hennie appreciated his thoughtfulness, especially when they didn't have a morsel of food yet in their own tiny kitchen.

"Sleep well, ladies," Jack said with a smile before he closed the door behind him.

With clean water in the washstands and clean beds to sleep in, Hennie and Lottie each shook out a dress to be worn the next day and got ready for bed. Lottie insisted that Hennie take the room with the larger bed, while Hennie argued that the size of the bed didn't matter at all, as long as they both had a place to sleep. Hennie finally gave in, and as she relaxed into the spacious bed in a safe and comfortable room, it occurred to her that tomorrow morning she didn't have to hurriedly bind her chest, and she didn't have to ever pretend to be anything different than who she truly was. A warm contentment enveloped her as she drifted to sleep, loving the idea that Jack was sleeping in the house downstairs. Just knowing he was nearby made her feel safe and more content. And with any luck the next few days would go well—as she and Lottie took the necessary steps to start their lives over again as women.

⌘

Hennie awoke early, realizing her body was accustomed to doing so and going back to sleep wouldn't be possible. She listened to the sounds outside, which were so different from those surrounding the servants' quarters of Ivy Manor.

The distant bustling of the villagers coming awake and going about their business had a pleasant warmth to it.

Suddenly excited to actually appear as a woman again, Hennie jumped out of bed, freshened up, and put on the clothes Jack had acquired for her, impressed with how well he had guessed her size. She brushed through her hair and managed with the tiny mirror on the wall to pull it back in a way that was much different than the masculine plait she'd been wearing for so long. She was grateful she'd never had her hair cut too short when she was able to manage pinning it into a bun at the back of her head. She was putting the last pin in place when Lottie appeared in the open doorway of her room with her hair fixed much the same way. Lottie had let her own hair grow long enough to be worn in a plait, for which she now admitted she was very grateful.

"Shall we?" Lottie asked.

"Face the world again, you mean?"

"Exactly!" Lottie said. "And I'm starving!" she added with a chuckle. "I hope Ollie is a good cook."

"Not bad," Hennie said, having eaten food he'd prepared a few times. "But I'm afraid he won't measure up to Mrs. Helton's standards."

"I doubt that *anyone* could do that," Lottie said, and they left their new apartment, walked down the stairs together, and knocked at the door to Jack's little house.

"Come in!" they heard him call at the same moment Hennie was wondering if he would have already left to begin his work.

Hennie stepped through the door with Lottie right behind her. Jack had his back turned as he worked at the stove, cooking something that smelled delicious and made Hennie's stomach growl.

"Good morning," Hennie said as Lottie closed the door.

"Good morning," Jack replied and glanced briefly over his shoulder before he immediately set down the spatula he'd been holding and turned abruptly to face them. His eyes roamed quickly over both of them before they came to rest on Hennie's face. "Well, hello there, Henrietta," he said as if he'd not seen her for years. "You look so . . ."

"Different?" Hennie offered, startled to hear him speak her real name. She wondered if she'd ever heard it spoken since she'd left the manor as a child.

"Beautiful," Jack corrected, then laughed, not with humor but delight. "It's so good to just see . . . the real you."

Hennie smiled and tried in vain not to blush, but she could feel the adoration in his eyes, and it felt so good—not only to *be* herself, but to be admired as a woman.

Lottie cleared her throat and said lightly, "Should I leave the two of you alone for a minute so you can share this romantic moment and—"

"Don't be silly!" Hennie said and moved toward Jack. "Whatever you're cooking smells delicious. Can we help?"

"Not today," he said. "It's almost done. Just . . . sit down; make yourselves comfortable. You've both spent enough time here to feel at home, I would hope."

"We do indeed," Lottie said and knew where to find the dishes, which she began setting out on the table. Hennie was only vaguely aware of Lottie doing so as she found herself facing Jack while they shared a long, meaningful gaze—and again she could only relish being admired as herself, rather than having him only see her in disguise. She was glad when he kissed her, then she heard Lottie clearing her throat loudly, and all three of them laughed as Hennie stepped away from Jack and Lottie said, "Don't be burning our breakfast, Ollie."

"All is well, Lottie," he said, winking at her. "No need to worry."

The three of them sat together to share a simple but hearty breakfast of boiled eggs, buttered bread, and sausages that were perfectly crisp on the outside and steaming savory goodness on the inside.

"You *are* a fairly decent cook," Lottie said to Jack, and Hennie nodded in agreement with her mouth full.

"Perhaps," he said. "I have learned to cook well enough to sufficiently take care of myself, but the variety of my knowledge is extremely limited. As long as we're on the topic of food, I was thinking that it would be more practical if we just share our meals. We all know it's no more work to cook for three than it is for one, and if we all pitch in . . . take turns . . . I don't know; whatever the two of you think is the best way for us to share the work. No one from the street is going to be able to see when the two of you come and go from here—or how much; not that I would care if they did. So, what do you think?"

"I think it's an excellent idea," Lottie said, and once again Hennie nodded, wishing that her need to comment wasn't always coming up just after she'd popped food into her mouth. "We're going to do some errands this morning, mostly to get ourselves some much-needed new clothes. We'll visit the grocer and the butcher while we're out, and Hennie and I will cook supper tonight."

"If you think we can remember how," Hennie said with a little laugh. "Truthfully, neither of us has ever done much cooking. This could be an adventure."

"I'm certain we'll manage," Jack said lightly.

"And we'll figure out some kind of schedule," Lottie added.

Once they had eaten, they all pitched in to clean the dirty dishes and put the kitchen in order before Jack disappeared through the door into the smithy, and the women went out through the other door and up the stairs to their new apartment. They freshened up sufficiently to go out, resolving to spend some time later doing necessary cleaning to rid their quarters of its years of accumulated dust.

Together they set out down the street, and Hennie was glad that no one seemed to pay any attention to them. She saw a few familiar faces but no one she'd ever interacted with directly, and she doubted that anyone would notice the change in her appearance. They went to the shop of a dressmaker that Hennie knew to be a woman who made clothing for the villagers and common people, rather than another dressmaker in town who catered mostly to the wealthy clientele. Since Hennie had been living as a man, and all of the clothes she'd purchased while living here had been in a different shop, the two women who worked here didn't recognize Hennie or Lottie at all. And she was more than fine with that. She figured that with time, the rumors would spread regarding the women who had disguised themselves as men, but she preferred to gain some confidence in becoming a woman again before taking that on.

Both Hennie and Lottie were able to find two dresses each that were ready-made and fit rather well. They also purchased some new underclothing, nightgowns, and stockings. They purchased new shoes at a different shop, so they wouldn't have to wear masculine boots beneath their skirts. They were still left with a fair amount of cash they could live on for quite some time, but neither of them knew yet if they would be able to find work. And even though Hennie knew Jack was secretly a very wealthy man, and he would make certain they never went without, she didn't want to take advantage of him in that way. She hoped eventually they would come to the decision to marry, but they were presently in the midst of too many changes—and too many complications—to be making any such decisions. And until she was officially his wife, she would not have him bearing the burden of responsibility for her. Beyond graciously being willing to accept his generous offer of allowing them to live in the apartment that had otherwise been sitting empty for a very long time, Hennie was determined that she and Lottie would provide for themselves. She discussed her feelings with Lottie as they completed their errands, and they were both in agreement.

After putting their purchases away, Hennie and Lottie sat at the front of the smithy with Jack to enjoy mutton hand pies and some cake from the bakery for lunch. Hennie found the situation so ironic that she kept laughing for no apparent reason. When Jack questioned her, she simply said, "I wonder if anyone has noticed that the man who used to sit here with you and share lunch occasionally is actually a woman."

"It's delightfully scandalous," Lottie said, and they all laughed.

"It feels good to be seen as a woman again," Hennie admitted, "even if no one notices."

"Amen to that," Lottie said.

"I certainly like it," Jack said, winking at Hennie.

After they'd eaten lunch, Hennie and Lottie carefully removed the fabric covers from the rest of the furniture in the apartment, and all the fabric was carefully folded and stacked on the landing outside the door to be laundered and put away properly at another time when other matters were not so pressing. After a couple of hours with the two of them sweeping, dusting, and scrubbing, their new apartment was in pristine condition and had everything they needed— although the little kitchen actually had no dishes or pans, which made their plan for sharing meals with Jack all the more practical. Hennie recalled that he'd told her the previous owner of this place had used this apartment for some of his children; hence, they wouldn't have been cooking up here.

"That's about as good as it gets," Lottie said with satisfaction as they walked through the rooms to admire their work. "I like it very much."

"As do I," Hennie declared. "I especially like that our men's clothing will no longer be needed." She nodded toward the pile of it in the corner of Hennie's bedroom, which would be laundered and taken to the secondhand shop in the village, along with the boots and braces they had worn.

"Amen to that," Lottie said, and they freshened up again before walking together down the street and around the corner to the Hawk's Nest, purposely arriving at a time in the afternoon when pubs were generally less crowded. Jack had told them the owner's name was Lester, and they should speak with him. It was Jack's opinion that they tell Lester straight out about the situation, and simply hope for the best. Lester had a reputation for being fair and honest, and they had all agreed that being honest with him up front was the only option they could live with. They all knew that men from the manor came to the pubs in the village when they had time off, and they needed to be prepared for facing up to being recognized and perhaps even scoffed at or made fun of, and if someone was willing to give them work, they had a right to be prepared for such a possibility.

"Here we go," Hennie said, briefly squeezing Lottie's hand as they hesitated outside the door to the Hawk's Nest.

"If it doesn't work out, something else will," Lottie said with a ring of optimism that Hennie tried to take hold of. She would prefer to have this work out, and then they could move forward confidently, knowing they had employment.

Stepping inside, Hennie was relieved to see that there were only a few customers, and a couple of serving girls were relaxing at the bar. A middle-aged balding man was seated not far from the door, reading a newspaper that was opened on the table in front of him. He looked up to see who had come through the door, and immediately asked, "What might I do for you ladies?"

His interest in assisting anyone who came through the door indicated that he was likely the owner, but Hennie still said, "We're looking for Lester."

"That's me!" he said proudly and came to his feet.

"We heard you might have work available," Lottie said.

He offered a smile and at the same time briefly inspected them more thoroughly, as if he were assessing whether they were the kind of women he might hire. "Let's talk," he said and motioned toward two chairs on the opposite side of the table where he'd been sitting. They all sat down, and Lester folded his newspaper and set it aside, along with the eyeglasses he'd been wearing.

"Your names?" he asked.

"I'm Hennie," she said, "and this is Lottie." Hennie had hardly used or even acknowledged her surname for as long as she'd known Lottie—who didn't even *have* a surname. In their world it hadn't much mattered.

"A pleasure," Lester said in greeting, as if he only needed to know what to call them. "Who sent you?" he asked as if it were very important. "You knew to ask for me, so who was it that—"

"Ollie . . . the blacksmith," Hennie said. "He's a friend. We're renting the apartment above the smithy."

"Oh, I see," he said as if that information pleased him. "Ollie's a good man."

"He is," Hennie added.

"Do you have experience serving in a place such as this?" Lester asked.

Hennie sensed Lottie's nervousness and answered for both of them. "I do. I worked for about two years serving meals and drinks. Lottie doesn't have actual experience, but she's a hard worker and can learn anything quickly. I can teach her."

Lester made a thoughtful noise and again looked intently at both of them, as if a good, firm gaze might give him necessary information. After some tense moments of silence, he said, "I recently had one of my girls leave, so I only have one position to fill, but she worked long hours—wanting to earn extra money. Having her gone has put an extra burden on the other girls. If the two of you would be willing to split the hours she was working, I'll try you out."

"Oh, that would be perfect!" Hennie said. "Perhaps at first the two of us could work together so that I can help Lottie learn, and then we'll work whatever shifts you need us to."

"Let's try it for two weeks and see how you do," Lester said. "I never hire anyone permanently until I can see how they work."

"Of course," Hennie said.

Lottie put a hand briefly on Hennie's arm before she said, "We appreciate your willingness to give us a chance, but there's something we need to tell you first. We are in a rather strange . . . situation . . . and we need to be honest with you; we don't want to cause you any trouble."

"Oh my goodness," Hennie said more to Lottie. "I'm afraid I got so excited I completely forgot." She was relieved to see that Lottie intended to tell Lester, and she waited with her heart pounding to see how he might respond. The job offer he'd just given them could well be revoked in the next minute or two.

"You see . . ." Lottie began and cleared her throat nervously, " . . . I'll just get straight to the point and then fill in the details if that's necessary." Hennie knew what she meant was that if getting to the point made Lester not want anything to do with them, any details of their story would be irrelevant. Lottie took a deep breath. "We have been working in the stables at Ivy Manor . . . pretending to be men . . . because there were no respectable jobs available for women at a time when we needed work." Lester's eyes widened but he didn't comment, and Lottie went on. "Ollie has known the truth for quite some time, and we've become rather weary of all the pretending, so he offered us the use of the apartment, which has been empty for years, and we came clean with the stable master. Of course he had to let us go, although I believe he would vouch for how hard we work and that we are reliable employees. Beyond this one deception, which we realize is no small thing, we are honest and respectable. But it would be ridiculous to believe that people won't hear the rumors of what we did, and it's highly likely that you have customers who will have known us as men, and we don't want to cause any problems, so . . . that's the truth of it. You can take back your job offer, or you can ask us any question you like, or you can—"

"Exactly how long did you get away with this?" Lester asked, but he asked it with a smirk, as if he found their story amusing.

Lottie and Hennie took turns answering his questions, and Hennie felt increasingly less nervous as it became evident that Lester was curious but not necessarily put off. He finally said, "Well, the two of you might be somewhat of a novelty around here; you might even bring in more business with rumors flying about." He looked briefly alarmed and added, "I don't mean to say that I'd use you like that. I don't let anyone treat my girls badly, and the customers know it."

"That's very good to know," Hennie said. "I confess it wasn't that way where I worked before."

Lester concluded firmly, "If the two of you are brave enough to admit to what you've done and show your true selves to the entire county, then I'm more than happy to stand by what I already told you. Let's try it for a couple of weeks and see how it goes."

"Thank you so much!" Lottie said with a little laugh of relief.

"Yes, thank you," Hennie added. "We won't let you down."

Lester walked them to the door and told them to be there the following morning at ten, so he could show them around and explain their responsibilities before the lunch crowd started filling up the place. They thanked him again and left the Hawk's Nest, barely managing to get around the corner before they both exploded with laughter. Hennie felt so much relief and joy to simply be herself again and to be employed in a situation that was completely honest, by a man who by all accounts was fair and decent. Added to that, she would be seeing Jack every day, and they no longer had to hide their feelings for each other when anyone else was around. She just felt completely happy, and Lottie admitted that she felt the same. They both agreed that they hoped it would last.

Chapter Eleven

GOSSIP

JACK WAS UNDERSTANDABLY THRILLED TO hear from the women that Lester had agreed to hire them, and none of them were worried that he might change his mind in the next two weeks, because they all knew that Hennie and Lottie could work hard enough to prove they were a good investment as employees.

That evening Hennie thoroughly enjoyed cooking a meal with Lottie and sitting down to share a relaxing supper with the two people who meant the most to her in this world. It was nice to be wearing a woman's clothes and to not feel restricted. It was nice to think that she didn't have to ride back to the manor this evening. And she loved the deep relief that was really settling in of how she and Lottie were no longer living a lie. As long as those who had known them as men didn't cause any problems for them now, everything would surely be all right.

After supper they all worked together to put the kitchen in order, then Jack asked Hennie if she would take a walk with him.

"I know when I'm not wanted," Lottie said in good humor. Then she took on the demeanor of an overprotective parent, "Just mind your manners and don't stay out too late."

"I'll be a perfect gentleman," Jack said to Lottie and surprised her with a quick kiss on the cheek. "I promise . . . *Mother*."

Lottie made a scoffing sound and then laughed before she headed out the door and up the stairs to the apartment. Jack took Hennie's hand and led her outside and away from the house through quiet back streets of the village and into a meadow, guided by a nearly full moon. They walked in silence while Hennie wondered if he had anything in particular he wanted to say, or if he'd just wanted to share some quiet solace with her after all the busyness that had been going on.

At the very moment she became certain it was the latter, he stopped walking and turned to face her, taking both her hands into his. "There's something I have to tell you," he said in a way that made her mildly nervous. Were there more secrets in his life? Some other dilemma they might need to contend with? "Now that you're no longer living a secret life, and you and Lottie are living where I can help watch out for you . . . and also that . . ." He cleared his throat nervously and looked at the ground, seeming to gather courage before he looked at her face again. "Now that some time has passed and we've been able to truly get to know each other again—as adults—I can't hold the words inside any longer." His voice lowered and became slightly husky as he admitted, "I love you, Hennie. I do. I've loved you my entire life—as my dearest friend. I've held that love in my heart through all those years we were apart, wondering where you were. I never forgot about you; I never went a day without thinking of you. It's a miracle that you came back into my life, a miracle I will never take for granted. Hennie, you are the best thing that's ever happened to me. And you just . . . need to know that I love you. I love you and I love having you in my home, sharing simple tasks and meals and conversation. I want it to always be this way. I know it's probably too soon since you've just barely come out of hiding, but I want you to at least consider . . . to think about . . . the possibility of becoming my wife."

Hennie gasped, caught off guard by that last statement. She felt a deep relief to know that he shared her feelings—feelings she had pondered a great deal during the months they'd been spending time together—but she also had concerns she couldn't ignore. Sensing his vulnerability after such a confession, she hurried to reassure him, saying earnestly, "I love you too, Jack; I do. I always hoped I could find a love that was real and true—but I didn't know if it would be possible. What we've come to share is a miracle for me too, and yes, Jack, I want to be your wife." She heard him laugh softly with relief and felt him relax, even by the way he held her hands. "But we *do* need more time. Under the circumstances we can't rush into marriage too quickly. As you said, I've barely come out of hiding, and we still have no idea how that is going to impact our lives. Perhaps it will be intolerable, and Lottie and I will need to leave here and—"

"Then I will go with you," he said firmly.

Hennie sighed, realizing more and more that of the two of them, she was the practical one. He could be impulsive and react to a situation based solely on his emotions. She was more likely to think things through and consider all possible options and outcomes. She inhaled a breath of patience and said gently, "Jack, leaving might be the best option, but we can't know that right now."

"Of course," he said. "I just want you to know that I'm willing to do whatever we need to do to be together and for you to feel safe, and Lottie as well. She's family to you, and that makes her family to me. I mean that from my heart, Hennie."

"I know you do, and I'm so grateful for that." She pondered for a moment if this was the right time to bring up her greatest concern, and decided that it needed to be said, rather than waiting in dread for the right time. This was as good a time as any. "Jack, I need you to know that I'm not nearly as concerned about whether Lottie and I stay here or leave, as I am *your* reasons for making that same choice."

"What do you mean?" he asked, sounding defensive—but she had expected that.

"I know very well this is your least favorite topic to discuss, which is why we haven't talked about it nearly as much as we should, but we *need* to talk about it, Jack. I have come out of hiding, but you have not. Sometimes I think you would prefer to just leave here and start over somewhere else . . . except you did that once, and you ended up coming back here. But I don't think you ever really came to terms with your reasons for doing so. I think you are drawn to being close to home; you miss your family, the manor, the life you had there. And I think that leaving again would only be running from problems that should be faced and dealt with."

Jack abruptly let go of Hennie's hands and stepped back. "Dealt with?" he echoed, sounding less angry than she knew he felt. "How exactly am I to *deal with* such a ridiculous situation?"

"I don't know, Jack. But we're never going to figure it out if we don't talk about it. I know how it feels to live a false identity, to wake up every morning and look in the mirror and feel out of sorts with the face looking back at me, because it's not who I really am. I fear that in time it would eat away at you, and your unhappiness would only grow."

"My unhappiness?" he countered, now sounding angrier and *more* defensive.

"Yes, Jack," she retorted in the same tone. "Do you think I can't see it? Feel it? You appreciate all that's good in your life, and I know what you and I have come to share brings you happiness, just as it does me, but there is a deep lack of peace in you, Jack, and it will come between us if you don't come to terms with it—especially if you get angry every time I bring it up. You will never convince me that you're happy being a blacksmith. Never!"

"If it's the Lord of the manor you want to marry, Hennie, it's never going to—"

"Don't you dare turn this around and make it about what *I* want! I want *you*, Jack! You should know me well enough to know that I would prefer to avoid that kind of life. I'm not sure a woman like me could *ever* fit into the world you came from."

"You came from that world too," he said, but he still sounded angry.

"From the servants' quarters!" She wanted to shout but kept her voice low enough to not be overheard, given that they weren't terribly far from the homes at the edge of the village. "It's not the same—not even *close* to the same, and you know it. I don't care if I marry a blacksmith or a farmer or a prince, as long as I marry the man I love. But I need to know that the man I love is at peace with himself, because I refuse to live my life haunted by the ghosts of unanswered questions and unresolved issues that would surely erode any amount of love and happiness under which they are buried. If you choose to leave this place for good, then do it for the right reasons and in the right way. And don't use the possibility of me and Lottie needing a fresh start elsewhere as an excuse for you to run away from here again—to leave your brother worrying and wondering. And however selfish and arrogant the Queen of Tookle-Berry might be, she deserves to know beyond any doubt that you will *never* marry her, so she can stop living in her ludicrous delusions and get on with her life."

Silence followed Hennie's outburst. When it grew too long, her nervousness increased, and she began to actually wonder if Jack would refuse to face up to the difficulties in his life and allow it to come between them. The very idea felt impossibly heartbreaking. Thoughts of having to let Jack go filled her with despair to the point that she was startled when he finally spoke.

"Well," he said, not sounding angry *or* defensive, "I don't think I've been put in my place like that since my mother died. My father was always full of criticism and ridicule, but that's not the same thing, is it." He stated it in a way to indicate he clearly recognized the difference. "I know you're right, Hennie; I do. And I love you more for having the courage to set me straight. I *have* been hiding, avoiding it—mostly because I just don't know what to do."

"I've been praying very much for the right course to present itself."

"I'm ashamed to admit that I've been praying for a way to escape; praying that George and my sisters would just forget I'd ever existed and find peace with accepting my absence."

Hennie couldn't help her mildly scolding tone as she said, "Well, no wonder you're not getting any answers. If you want God's help, Jack, you need to pray for the right thing. He has a purpose for your life, and I believe we know in our hearts when we're living in alignment with God's purpose—or when we're running from it. Don't be like Jonah in the Bible, Jack; don't try to run and hide. It didn't go well for him; I think there's an obvious lesson in the story."

He sighed loudly, and then sighed again. "I'm not sure I like the comparison—mostly because it's uncomfortably accurate. I certainly don't want to metaphorically end up rotting in the belly of a whale until I learn my lesson." He stepped forward again and wrapped Hennie in his arms, as if holding her close might soothe his spirit. Hennie wrapped her arms around him as he said, "Oh, my love. I don't know what to do. No matter how I look at the problem, I can't find a way around it—which I suppose is why I keep avoiding it. But I know you're right; I know I need to make peace with it and not leave the people I care about helplessly wondering—*or* the Queen of Tookle-Berry." He drew back to look at her. "I promise you, Hennie, that I'll find a way. As long as I know I have you by my side, I'll find a way to resolve the problem. If I need to leave, I'll make certain I handle it the right way."

"*We* will find a way," Hennie corrected. "I *am* by your side, and you're not in this alone. You've helped me and Lottie make the changes in our lives we needed to make to be who we really are, and we will help you find your own freedom to be who *you* really are."

"And you'd be all right with being a blacksmith's wife?"

"More than all right with it," she said, "as long as I know you're choosing to be a blacksmith because it can offer you fulfillment and happiness—not because it's a means for you to hide." She touched his beard and laughed softly. "Besides, I look forward to the day when you can shave this off and I can see you for who you really are."

Jack laughed as well, and Hennie was glad to hear no evidence of the anger he'd been feeling only minutes ago; she was also relieved that they'd been able to talk about the problem. With a tangible hope that he was committed to actually doing something about it, she felt more inclined to indulge in the hope that they could be married and not have the tension between them of having to keep secrets in the way they lived.

"Oh, how I love you!" he said, taking her face into his hands.

"I love you too, Jack," she replied, and he kissed her in a way that had become familiar but never less magical.

"When I think of the miracle of God bringing you back into my life," Jack said, "it gives me hope that perhaps he has another miracle in store for us; perhaps there is a way out of this, and I *have* been praying for the wrong thing. I'll work on that, I promise."

Hennie smiled and kissed him again before they walked back to the house, holding hands. Jack kissed her at the foot of the stairs and watched her as she ascended. Before opening the door, she turned and blew him a kiss, and he returned it. Once inside, she locked the door behind her and leaned against it for a long moment, allowing hope for a better and brighter future to wash over her.

Tomorrow she and Lottie would start their new job, and she felt surprisingly calm about all it might entail—even the possibility of facing the men she and Lottie had worked with in the stables. Being able to face the world as a woman again gave her a surprising amount of courage and strength. Perhaps looking back over all she had survived had increased her confidence. Whatever the reasons, she felt more than ready to begin a new life. And sharing that life with Jack—even though they had some problems yet to face—just made her utterly and completely happy. She forced herself to go to bed, knowing she needed her rest, and she drifted to sleep, content with thoughts of one day becoming Jack's wife. Whatever kind of life that might lead her to, she prayed she could take it on with the same confidence and courage she felt about facing her forthcoming adjustment from stable hand to barmaid. At the very least, her life certainly wasn't dull.

⚬⚬⚬

Jack stood at the opening of his place of business, leaning his shoulder against one of the sturdy posts there, watching Hennie and Lottie walk away to begin their first day on the job at the Hawk's Nest. The worry he felt for both of them caused him once again to marvel over his recent awareness of how quickly and deeply he'd come to feel responsible for their well-being. He'd been feeling that way about Hennie ever since she'd come back into his life, and once he'd had the opportunity to get to know Lottie, he'd come to feel responsible for her as well. It was as he'd told Hennie: Lottie was like family to Hennie; therefore, she was like family to him. He'd felt a deep relief at helping them come out of hiding and live right here where he could watch out for them. The only negative aspect of the situation was their employment in a place where men gathered to drink. Even though men and women alike also went there for meals, most of the customers were men seeking respite from their lives by drinking. He knew Lester was a good man and would not allow his employees to be treated badly, or he never would have recommended that these precious women seek work at such an establishment. He hated their having to work at all, especially when he had plenty of money to meet their every need and desire. But he understood why they needed to do it; he respected them for their insistence on being self-reliant and earning their own way. He just hoped it didn't always have to be this way. Considering the loving lecture Hennie had given him the previous evening, he hoped and prayed he could find a way out of this situation. And in the meantime, he hoped and prayed that Hennie and Lottie would be safe and well in their new work environment. He reminded himself they were strong and capable; they'd both survived a great deal of hardship long before he ever showed up in their lives.

But he just couldn't suppress his instinctive male desire to be their protector and defender. However, once they were out of his view, he had to force himself to get back to work, looking forward to them returning before supper. In fact, he looked forward to it so much that he wondered how he had ever managed to live in such solitude for so long. And now it was as if all that time being alone had accumulated into an almost desperate need to *not* be alone. Reminding himself to keep his life and his emotions in proper balance, he kept very busy and forced himself not to keep glancing at the clock, which was in plain view for the purpose of keeping him punctual with his work. But today it moved only too slowly as he wondered if everything was going all right at the pub.

His growling stomach forced him to eat a quick lunch, after which he put a leg of lamb in the oven to roast slowly through the afternoon in preparation for a fine supper—even if that meant only adding some scrubbed potatoes and carrots later, which was the best of his culinary skills. Then he got back to work, wondering exactly when the women *would* return. Lester hadn't told them how many hours he'd actually expected them to work today, so he had no idea.

Jack was focused on the rhythm of his hammer as he pounded out hot metal to reshape a horseshoe when he heard a man say, "Excuse me, sir."

Jack stopped and turned to see a man near his own age, with blond hair that was very curly. He was a little taller than Jack, and thinner. But what Jack noticed most was how nervous he seemed.

"Can I help you?" Jack asked, sticking the horseshoe into water, which made steam hiss into the air.

"I hope so," the man said. "I understand you know something about the two women . . . who were working as men . . . at the manor."

Jack set down his tools and put his hands on his hips, asking a little too vehemently, "Depends on why you're asking."

"I'll be completely honest with you, sir," the man said.

"I would hope so," Jack countered, noting that the man seemed even more nervous due to Jack's efforts to intimidate him. But until Jack knew this man's intentions, he wasn't willing to offer any information.

"The news came as quite a shock to the whole lot of us . . . by us, I mean, those of us who have been working with them all this time. Mr. Parsons—the stable master that is—"

"I know who he is," Jack said, wanting him to get to the point.

"He told us the situation and made it clear that if any of us ever caused either one of these women any grief he'd see that we were out of a job the same as they were."

"Did he?" Jack asked, wanting to personally thank Mr. Parsons for *that*. But he knew such a thing would be impossible.

"Not that I would ever do anything of the kind," the man went on. "You see . . . I'd become rather good friends with one of them, and . . . even though it's quite shocking to learn the truth . . . I've quickly realized that I very much miss that friendship, and I would just like the opportunity to tell him . . . I mean her . . . that I understand why she did what she did, and I don't hold that against her, and . . . well, I'd just like to talk to her."

"Which one?" Jack asked, not necessarily keen on the idea of Hennie having a close friendship with another man. But then, he felt certain if she'd had any real friends besides Lottie, she would have told him.

"Lot," the man said. "I don't suppose that's her real name."

"It's close," Jack said, feeling more relaxed. This man's explanation made perfect sense, and his genuine humility was evident. "Her name is Lottie, and both women are renting an apartment from me."

"Oh!" the man said with overt relief, his countenance lighting up.

"But they aren't here right now," Jack said. "They're at work."

"They've found jobs so soon?" he asked, seeming pleased.

"I'm not sure when they'll be back," Jack said. Rather than telling this man where to find them, he preferred to have Lottie encounter her *friend* here where he could be close by. He had no idea whether Lottie would want to see this man; that would have to be up to her, but if she wanted to let him know their friendship was something she wished to put in the past, Jack wanted to be around in case she needed any help convincing him. For the moment, he gave this man the benefit of the doubt and simply added, "You're welcome to wait." He motioned toward an empty chair. "But as I said, I don't know how long they'll be."

The man thought about it a moment and said, "Perhaps I'll go and see to a couple of quick errands and come back."

"As you wish," Jack said, and the man stepped forward, holding out his hand.

"Zeke," he said, introducing himself.

"Ollie," Jack said, surprised at how close he'd come to introducing himself as Jack. Having Hennie call him that whenever they were alone had made it more difficult at times to keep track of his separate identities.

"A pleasure to meet you, Ollie," Zeke said. "And might I offer my gratitude."

"For what?" Jack asked.

"For giving them a place to go. This can't have been easy for them."

"I'm glad I could help," Jack said.

Zeke nodded. "I'll be back, then." He walked away, and again Jack wondered whether Lottie would be pleased by Zeke's visit. He also wondered for about the hundredth time since they'd left how their first day of work was going.

Zeke hadn't been gone long when Jack caught movement from the corner of his eye and looked up from his work to see Hennie and Lottie approaching the smithy, talking and laughing. They didn't look at all as if they'd been traumatized by their hours at the Hawk's Nest. He set aside his work to just watch them, deeply grateful to think of sharing supper and conversation with them this evening.

"Hello," they both said in almost perfect unison when they saw him.

"Hello," he replied. "How did it go? Don't leave me in suspense."

"Very well, actually," Hennie said as both women plopped into chairs meant for customers. Jack scooted another chair over to where he could sit down and face them. "Lester is patient and kind. Lottie has already learned to serve meals and drinks with great finesse." She laughed, and Lottie bowed dramatically as much as she could while sitting down. "And we actually encountered a few of our old workmates who told us that Parsons had threatened every one of them with their jobs if he caught wind of them being unkind to us."

"Yes, I heard about that," Jack said.

"You did?" Hennie asked, but before she could press him further, he asked another question.

"And what did your old workmates think of the way they'd all been duped?"

"They thought it was hilarious," Lottie answered. "At least the ones we saw today. But if that's the general attitude, I don't think we have anything to worry about."

"How did you hear about what Parsons said to them?" Hennie persisted.

Jack smirked toward Lottie and said, "A friend of yours came looking for you. He'll be back . . . soon, I think. He wants to talk to you."

"Who?" Lottie demanded, looking both hopeful and terrified, which made Jack wonder just how good a friend this Zeke might be.

"Zeke," was all Jack had to say to have his every question answered. Lottie blushed and put her hands to the sides of her face, squeezing her eyes closed.

"You *like* him!" Jack declared with a little laugh.

"Oh, she does!" Hennie said and laughed as well.

"It's not funny!" Lottie insisted. "All these months we've been *friends* and I couldn't tell him the truth! It's been horrible!"

"But now he *knows* the truth," Jack said, "and it's kind of funny, you have to admit."

"I suppose that depends on how he feels now that he knows the truth," Lottie said and looked firmly at Jack. "How was he? Did he seem upset? Is he angry with me? Did he—"

"Calm down," Jack said, unable to keep from laughing again. "He was perfectly kind and respectful about the situation. He told me he misses his friend." Jack chuckled and slid down more comfortably into his chair. "Maybe now that he's had a couple of days to get used to the idea, he might have realized he actually likes the idea that his *friend* is a woman."

"If he hasn't realized it by now," Hennie said, "I suspect he'll start to feel that way once he sees her for who she really is."

"I would have to agree," Jack said.

"I think I've had enough of you two making fun of me," Lottie declared, pretending to be more insulted than she really was. She stood up and walked out, declaring, "I think I need to freshen up. If he comes back while I'm gone, tell him to wait."

"Your wish is my command," Jack hollered and laughed, loving the way he and Lottie had become good enough friends to tease back and forth the way they did.

Now that he was alone with Hennie, he admitted, "I missed you. I'm afraid I've quickly grown far too accustomed to your company."

"I missed you too," she said, leaning forward to take his hand. "The wonderful thing is that we'll always be able to see each other every day, instead of having days in between."

"That *is* wonderful," Jack said, wanting to elaborate on how much that really meant to him, but instead he just stared at her.

"What?" she asked with a little laugh, staring back but clearly confused.

"I just want to look at you all the time," he said and squeezed her hand. "I'm still getting used to the new you, but I can't deny that I like the changes very much."

"I'm glad to hear it," she said. "I would certainly feel insulted if you told me I look better dressed as a man."

"Never!" he said and chuckled.

Hennie returned his gaze in a way that made him want to kiss her, but they were sitting in public view, and he knew such a gesture wouldn't be appropriate, given that they weren't yet married.

"What?" he asked just as she'd done a moment ago in response to the way she kept staring.

"I'm looking forward to seeing the new *you* when you get rid of that ghastly beard."

"Your flattery is touching," he said with sarcasm.

"You should know me well enough to know I won't be anything less than honest," she said with a little laugh, but her eyes made it clear she felt as attracted to him as he did to her—despite his ghastly beard.

"I could just . . ." he began but looked up to see Zeke approaching.

"Oh, this is suddenly awkward," Hennie said to Jack so that only he could hear.

"Just think how awkward it will be for Lottie," Jack whispered back as they both stood.

"Oh, my," Zeke said, peering at Hennie to take in the changes. "It really is true. Now that I know the truth, I don't know why I didn't see it before."

"That's what *I* said when *I* found out the truth," Jack said, feeling more relaxed with Zeke now that he knew Lottie cared for him. If Lottie knew him well and liked him, he surely had to be a good man.

"Hello, Zeke," Hennie said. "I hope you're not too terribly shocked by all of this."

"It's taken some getting used to," he said. "I just hope Lottie will be glad to see me." He chuckled. "Strange to say her name like that."

"I don't think you have anything to worry about," Hennie said to him just before Lottie appeared. She just stood there, wringing her hands, looking at Zeke somewhat sheepishly, her nerves showing as clearly as if they were red spots all over her face.

"My goodness!" Zeke said, taking in her changed appearance. "It's really true!" He chuckled, clearly nervous himself. "It might take some getting used to, but I must say the change suits you well."

"I should hope so," Lottie said, "since this is my true self." She cleared her throat and added, "I apologize, Zeke, for deceiving you, but it was necessary . . . for a time, at least. I hope you can understand."

"I do, actually."

"I wanted to tell you, but . . . I just couldn't. I hope you can forgive me, and—"

"No need for that," Zeke said. "I'm just hoping we can get to know each other again . . . without any secrets."

Lottie visibly relaxed, and Hennie shared a warm smile with Jack as they observed this tender interaction that exhibited many signs of a potential romance.

"I'd like that very much," Lottie said. "I assume this is your day off."

"It is," Zeke said.

"Would you like to take a walk?" she asked. "It's not far to a lovely meadow."

"I'd like that," Zeke said with a smile, also appearing more relaxed now that the awkward facets of their reunion were over.

"And why don't you stay for supper?" Jack said. "Hennie and I will cook tonight," he added, winking discreetly at Lottie, glad to see by her smile that she'd caught it.

"If it's no trouble," Zeke said. "I don't want to cause any extra—"

"It's no trouble at all," Hennie said. "You two run along and we'll see you at supper."

Lottie nodded and smiled at Hennie, then turned and walked away, with Zeke following her.

"Well, that was interesting," Jack said, "if not entertaining."

"Indeed," Hennie said. "I suspect Lottie's relief could make her faint if she's not careful." She laughed softly at the very idea. "She's liked Zeke for quite some time, but of course she couldn't say anything."

"And I daresay Zeke seems to prefer knowing his friend is a woman."

"It would seem that way," Hennie said and turned to Jack. "And what about you? Do you prefer knowing the friend you made from the stables is actually a woman?"

"Oh, I prefer that very much!" Jack said with a smirk and a wink.

"Did you put the leg of lamb into roast as you were supposed to?" she asked in a motherly tone.

"I did!" he said proudly.

"That's good. Our plans for an extra nice supper tonight worked out well, considering we'll have company."

"How very serendipitous!" he said in a histrionic tone that made her laugh.

"So, why don't you get back to work, and I'll go prepare the potatoes and carrots and lay the table with our finest china."

Jack made a scoffing sound, knowing he had one set of dishes and they were nothing but common and practical. Hennie surprised him with a quick kiss on the cheek, which made him smile. With her face close to his, she said, "I love you, Jack Hannaford."

He managed to hide how uncomfortable it felt to hear his surname used at all. He'd completely lost touch with being a Hannaford, but Hennie had given an argument that was more than fair in regard to him making peace with all of that; he just had to figure out exactly how to go about doing something that currently felt impossible.

"I love you too," he said and kept his other thoughts to himself. "How lovely for you to be here with me, off to the kitchen to finish cooking supper. I think I would like to make this a permanent arrangement."

"We'll see about that," she said with a smile that let him know she wanted the same, but she would also be adamant about him following through on the things they'd talked about; she would not marry a man who was hiding and running, and if he had any hope of earning her favor enough to become his wife, he had to find a way to face up to the challenges of his life and come to terms with them. While he respected Hennie for her insight and courage in demanding such a condition, the very idea also left him terrified. But he pushed those thoughts away and got back to work as soon as Hennie left through the door that led into his home behind the smithy.

Hennie felt delightfully content as she worked on preparing supper in Jack's kitchen. She'd actually enjoyed working at the pub today. Lester was a kind and good man, and the people they'd encountered—even those they had worked with in the stables—had been kind and respectful, and the revelation of Hennie and Lottie's secret seemed to have become a grand joke the entire village was enjoying. But they weren't laughing over it in a way that was unkind toward Hennie and Lottie; rather there seemed to be a kind of respect toward these two women who had pulled off this impressive scheme and had had the courage to come forward and be honest about it when other options opened up for them. Now, as Hennie scrubbed and cut potatoes and carrots to go with the lamb, she thought of Lottie and Zeke walking together in the meadow, and how their conversation might be going. She felt joy on Lottie's behalf that her friend could now be herself and be able to admit to her true feelings for Zeke, and it had been blatantly evident that Zeke was nothing but pleased to know the truth. It seemed that—at least for the moment—life could be no better. She only hoped and prayed that Jack could find a way to rectify the fact that he was still in hiding, and they could find a way to go forward in their lives with no secrets hanging over them. But that would take time, and for now all was well.

Zeke and Lottie returned just after Jack had closed up the smithy and washed up for supper. Hennie was slicing the lamb while Jack was drying his hands when Lottie and Zeke entered the room—holding hands—and Hennie exchanged a discreet smile with Jack. Jack leaned closer to Hennie and whispered, "Romance is in the air."

"Us or them?" she asked lightly.

"Both," he said and kissed her cheek.

Supper was delicious and especially enjoyable. Hennie marveled at how quickly Zeke had adjusted to the change in Lottie's identity, but she wasn't at all surprised by how well they got along. Their friendship had been going on for a long time. She *was* surprised, however, by how well Zeke and Jack got along, and how comfortable they were talking and laughing. But perhaps she shouldn't have been surprised at all. With as close as she and Lottie were, it stood to reason they would fall in love with men who would have a great deal in common and get along well. But Hennie wondered what Lottie and Zeke would think if they knew they were actually conversing with the mysteriously missing Lord of the manor, and that Jack's true identity put him in a world the rest of them couldn't begin to relate to. Still, Hennie knew that Jack's character and personality would never change, no matter his surroundings or circumstances or position. Her knowledge of that was the one thing that allowed her to believe they would be happy together no matter what path his life ended up taking. The uncertainty could be unnerving, but she loved Jack, and she knew he loved her. And she knew him, heart and soul. Surely they would get through this, and God willing, they would be blessed with a miracle.

George Hannaford was on his way to the stables when he saw his sister approaching from the opposite direction. He was always pleased to see Rebecca, but the added presence of her friend Letitia made him sigh with frustration, and he couldn't suppress the weighted disgust that rose inside of him. But he knew Rebecca would not be convinced of Letitia being anything but loyal and perfectly wonderful, and he was committed to resisting any further attempts to convince her otherwise, which only ended in their arguing without accomplishing anything positive. He forced a smile and greeted his sister with a kiss on the cheek, and he nodded graciously toward Letitia.

"Have you ladies been out riding already? So early?" he asked.

"It's a beautiful morning," Rebecca declared. "The leaves are changing color more in the hills and it's lovely. We must enjoy such nice weather while it lasts."

"I can't argue with that," George said.

"Oh, and have you heard . . ." Letitia interjected, and George wanted to crawl out of his skin; he couldn't count the times she'd begun a conversation with those exact words, since gossip was her favorite topic—whatever the subject might be. "Surely you *must* have heard!" she added. "After all, you're in charge of everyone here." She said it as if she resented the fact, and he knew exactly *why* she resented it. She wanted to be married to his brother; *she* wanted to be in charge, believing that if Jack had done right by her and married her, she could manipulate him into doing things *her* way, and all they owned and cared for would become hers.

George pushed that thought away—along with all its accompanying uneasy emotions—and pretended to be interested in what Letitia was saying, although he felt the need to clarify her erroneous perceptions. "There are far too many people working here for me to keep track of them and what they're doing." He resisted the temptation to add that he really didn't care what his employees and tenants did with their personal lives, as long as they did the work they were paid to do and remained loyal.

"Still," Letitia went on, like a cat playing with a mouse. Rebecca looked indifferent, and George wondered for the thousandth time why his sister couldn't see how shallow and selfish this woman could be. "Something as scandalous as two of your stable hands actually being *women* and pretending to be men, working here for who knows how long—until Parsons found them out and sent them packing."

"What?" George laughed, suddenly finding this particular bit of gossip interesting, but his laughter seemed to displease Letitia; apparently, she had expected him to be angry. "That's the most incredible thing I think I've ever heard. *However* did they manage to get away with it?"

"Who knows?" Letitia said as if she were disgusted by the entire situation. "Can you imagine?" she said more to Rebecca. "Living like a *man?*" She said that last word as if men were a species to be loathed. He didn't doubt she probably felt that way. He firmly believed she saw men as creatures to be manipulated and used to do her bidding. It was one of many reasons he could barely tolerate the woman.

"Perhaps they had their reasons," he felt inclined to say, certain Letitia couldn't comprehend the plight of the majority of humankind. Realizing he had no desire to continue this conversation—and suddenly anxious to talk to Parsons about what he'd just heard—George wished the ladies a lovely day and hurried on toward the stables.

Chapter Twelve

THE Lord of the manor

GEORGE WENT AROUND THE BACK of the stables to Mr. Parsons's office, hoping to find him there so they could speak privately. He wanted to hear the stable master's version of the story, not Letitia's gossip. He knocked lightly and heard Parsons call for him to enter.

"Oh, hello, good sir," Parsons said and stood when George entered.

"Please, sit down," George said and closed the door before he sat down himself.

"What might I do for you? Going to any parties? Need a carriage readied for some courting?" Parsons said it lightly, since it had become somewhat of a joke between them that George had become mostly reclusive since his brother's disappearance, and for reasons that were difficult to explain, he had no desire to socialize at all.

"I'm afraid not," George said. "I'm just curious regarding an incident I heard about just now."

"I'm guessing that would be the two women we've had working here, pretending to be men," Parsons said. "I meant to tell you about it when we had a chance to meet, but I've not seen you since you returned from London."

"That's fine," George said, not wanting Parsons to think he needed to tell George every little thing. "You know I trust you to handle everything according to your best judgment; I'm not worried about that. I'm just . . . curious. I heard you found them out and sent them packing."

"Is *that* what you heard?" Parsons asked with a chuckle.

"Those exact words, yes," George said.

"I did *not* find them out, nor did I send them packing. They came to me and told me the truth. They were respectful and apologetic and told me they knew they needed to leave because they were well aware that honesty was expected here, and they had finally found the means to live as their true selves. Of course,

I told them I *did* have to let them go, but I wished them well. They were hard workers, and I never had an ounce of trouble from either one of them."

"Remarkable," George said and chuckled himself. "However did they manage to pull it off all this time?"

"Well, they were certainly the scrawniest men who have ever worked here." Parsons laughed again and shook his head.

"Oh, I've seen them!" George said. "From a distance, anyway. I did think they were rather small and thin, but . . . I never imagined."

"No one did," Parsons said. "And as I told you, they were reliable and worked hard." He shrugged. "Why would I question *that* when it's not always easy to find such qualities in the men I hire?"

George still felt immensely curious and asked, "Did they tell you *why* they did it?"

Parsons sighed as if the answer to George's question saddened him. "The two of them went together from an orphanage into the workhouse, and since then I think they've had trouble finding work a woman could do and be treated fairly. I can understand that. Poor lads—I mean girls. I admit that I miss them. Still haven't found anyone to replace them and—"

"Do you know where they are?" George asked, jumping to his feet.

"Why?"

"So we can hire them back, of course," George said as if it were obvious. "I don't care whether or not men or women work in my stables. And if they don't want to work in the stables, I'll find something else they can do."

Parsons was obviously pleased by George's idea. "They told me the blacksmith would be renting them the apartment above the smithy."

"I've never met him," George said, which he figured should have been obvious, since he had servants aplenty who took care of such things for him.

"Nor have I," Parsons said. "Ollie is his name. I've only communicated with him through some written messages back and forth, and the stable hands I've sent there with our horses. But he does fine work, and his prices are fair."

"And where exactly would I find this Ollie?" George asked, very much wanting to speak to these two women who had created such a stir.

Parsons told him where to find the smithy. George thanked him and went to the stables, where he saddled his own horse—as he usually did—riding quickly toward town, rehearsing what he might say to these women who had been working in his stables in disguise for who knew how long. He found the very idea surprisingly delightful, perhaps because his life was so terribly boring and devoid of variety or surprise. Or perhaps he found the idea of women doing something so unusual in order to simply find respectable work to be incredibly brave. Knowing only what he did about these women, he couldn't keep himself from comparing them to a woman like Letitia. His sisters had led sheltered lives of privilege, but they were still kind and respectful to others, no matter who they were and what kind of life they'd led. But Letitia was arrogant and spoiled, and she continually made it evident how she looked down upon anyone who didn't share her social status. Even without meeting these women who had worked as stable hands, he already respected them so much more than he could ever respect a woman like Letitia.

⬥

Jack quickly got back to work after seeing the women off to work. This was their third day working at the pub, and so far, it had been going well, apart from a few minor challenges. Yesterday they had both gone in to work a few hours at lunchtime when the crowds were heavy, and they'd gone back in the evening to work a few hours more for the supper rush. They were enjoying the work, especially being able to work together, but Jack didn't enjoy having them absent during mealtimes, when he'd quickly grown accustomed to sharing their company. They'd decided this morning to alter their mealtimes so they could all eat together before and between their work shifts, which suited Jack fine, even if that meant grabbing a snack to tide him over while he retrained his stomach to expect to be fed at a different time of day.

While Jack worked he could feel evidence in the breeze that autumn was closing in. But he liked the coolness of it when he had to work near the constant heat of the coals. When he stopped pounding for a minute, he could hear that it had started to rain, and he turned for a long moment to just watch the rain fall. It was a light sprinkling, but it smelled good and felt comforting for reasons he couldn't define. He forced himself back to work but remained aware of the pleasant weather, so much so that he was startled to hear a man say, "Forgive me for intruding, but I'm looking for Ollie; I assume that's you."

Jack stopped the pounding of his hammer, but his heart took over, thumping hard in his chest. He knew that voice; he knew it so well. But why on earth would his brother be *here*?

"That's me," Jack said, trying to sound indifferent as he gripped the tongs more tightly and stuck the hot horseshoe into water where it hissed, and a plume of steam rose into the air. He pretended to need to watch the steaming horseshoe closely, so he wouldn't have to turn and look at this unexpected visitor. "What might I do for you?"

"I'm actually looking for two women who were working in my stables, and now I understand they are renting an apartment from you."

Jack wanted to shout, *Why on earth would you come looking for them personally?* But he kept his calm demeanor and simply said, "They aren't here right now. Would you like me to give them a message?" Jack pulled the horseshoe back out of the water and hammered on it lightly enough that he could still engage in conversation. His hammering accomplished nothing except for allowing him to appear busy so he wouldn't have to turn and face his brother. Then it occurred to him that perhaps he *needed* to face his brother. Could this possibly be some kind of miracle that had guided George here? Could it be the answer to Jack's prayers, an opportunity to force him out of hiding—at least in regard to his brother? He pondered those questions while his heart beat even harder and his stomach tightened.

"I'm George Hannaford," Jack's brother declared, "and I—"

Before he could finish, Jack let out a strained chuckle and couldn't resist saying, "Ah, the Lord of the manor. Why would you come personally in search of two women who were only in your employment because of their deception?" He wondered then if George would recognize *his* voice. He wasn't doing anything to try and disguise it, but then George simply wouldn't be expecting the local blacksmith to be his own brother; at the very most he might have been thinking that Ollie's voice reminded him of his brother.

"Let's just say," George answered, "that when I returned from London to learn of what had happened, I found the courage and ingenuity of these two women . . . inspiring. I wanted to personally let them know I'm more than happy to provide work for them, regardless of the unique situation."

Jack stopped tapping with his hammer. He just stood there for a long moment, reminded of his brother's kindness and generosity. He shouldn't have been surprised, but he'd honestly forgotten. It had been so long. He suddenly felt the urge to just reveal his true identity and embrace George—as two brothers long lost to each other would do after being reunited. Needing another moment to decide what to do—or not do—Jack commented casually, "They are indeed courageous women, and their ingenuity is rather impressive. I think they'd be pleased to know that you recognize and appreciate such qualities. Life hasn't been easy for them."

"So I was told," George said, "although I know very little. Still, I would very much like to speak with them and let them know they are more than welcome to return and—"

"They've already found work elsewhere," Jack said, still looking at the work in front of him even though he wasn't actually doing anything; he only wanted to avoid looking at George. He felt glad to be able to tell George this; the thought of Hennie and Lottie going back to the manor was not at all pleasing. He liked having them close by and being able to spend time with them.

"Already?" George said and chuckled. "They are certainly resourceful, then."

"Yes, they are," Jack said.

"Still, I would very much like to speak to them," George said. "Do you know where I might find them? Or when might be a good time?"

"They're working at a pub," Jack said, purposely not telling him which one. "But I'm not sure having the Lord of the manor show up to speak with them in a public place would necessarily be anything but awkward . . . no offense intended."

"None taken," George said, "but I appreciate your insight. Will they be returning here any time soon or—"

"Not sure," Jack said, while a voice that seemed separate from his own shouted at him out of the darkest recesses of his mind that he needed to face his brother, and he needed to do it now. The opportunity was far too brimming with serendipity for him to ignore; he knew he would regret it later if he didn't speak up. He didn't know how George would respond, or what might happen after this, but he had to take *this* step, and he had to do it now! "However," Jack said, "as long as you're here, there's something you should know."

George was quiet for a long moment, implying some confusion, which was evident in his voice when he finally said, "Very well. What might that be?"

Jack set down his tools, took a deep breath, and turned to face his brother, putting his hands on his hips. "It's me, George. I never expected you to find me here, but you *are* here, and I have to believe there's a reason."

George narrowed his eyes, and his brow creased with deep furrows. He looked Jack up and down, then gazed into his eyes as if doing so might verify that what he was seeing and hearing might actually be real. Jack's nervousness increased, wondering if George would be glad to see him—or angry with him for running away and hiding the way he had. Probably both.

"It *is* you!" George said and took a step forward, as if he intended to embrace Jack.

"Stop!" Jack said, quietly but firmly. "People can see us; you can't do anything to draw undue attention."

George's expression was mostly one of confusion; his eyes betrayed a combination of relief, tenderness, and frustration. "What are you doing *here,* of all places?" George growled in a voice too quiet for any passersby to hear. "And how long have you been here . . . right here . . . . doing what? Shoeing my horses? Making friends with my stable hands? But you couldn't let *me* know that you were here? That you were all right?" Despite the frustration in his voice—bordering on anger—tenderness and relief still showed in his eyes.

"I owe you a thousand apologies, brother," Jack said, "and I can only say for now that my reasons are complicated at the very least. But I've been praying for a way to work all of this out, even though I have no idea how that's possible. Still, I have to believe the fact that you're standing here right now must surely be the answer to my prayers." Jack heard a quiver in his own voice as he admitted, "I've missed you so dreadfully."

George offered a wan smile, and his anger dissipated as he said, "And I've missed you. I'm so glad to know you're all right. I just . . . I don't want us to have to go on like this, Jack."

"Nor do I," Jack said, "but . . . now that it's gone on this long . . . I don't know how to turn it around. And the situation is the same as it was when I first left. Is there *anything* at all we can do to change any of that?"

"I don't know," George said, shaking his head, almost looking as if he might cry; but Jack understood because he felt the same way. He and George had always been close, and here they stood, unable to even acknowledge each other as brothers or to enjoy the kind of reunion that should have been appropriate. It was all so full of madness!

When the silence grew uncomfortably long and charged with tension, Jack knew that neither of them wanted to say good-bye, but they couldn't stand here in view of the townspeople and talk the way they really needed to. Jack glanced at the work he'd been doing and felt entirely unmotivated to keep at it, which made him grateful to realize that he had no customers actually waiting for work to be done; no one was scheduled to come in for the remainder of the day. With no pressing matters to attend to, he impulsively said to his brother, "If you'd like . . . you can discreetly walk down the alley just north of here." Jack nodded in that direction. "Go around to the back of my place to the door, and I'll meet you there in a few minutes."

George nodded and smiled, his eyes brimming with enthusiasm over such a suggestion, which Jack took to mean that his brother didn't want to leave, and he too longed for some privacy. "Thank you," he said and hurried away, walking past the alley and down the street, which Jack figured was an attempt to deflect any undue attention from his going there.

Jack rolled down the canvas flaps at the front of the smithy and tied them closed. It wasn't often he closed down his business during the day, but it happened now and then when he didn't have any specific appointments scheduled. There were two other blacksmiths in the village, which meant a person could get help from one of them if they needed it. Going into his little home and through it to the back door, Jack's heart began to pound again. He'd been reunited with his brother, and now they could share a proper greeting. It all felt a little too remarkable to be real, which made him think that his prayers were being heard; he desperately needed to find a way out of this imprisonment of hiding beneath the guise of a blacksmith—or to make peace with maintaining the status quo—and it made sense that he could never take either course without making peace with his brother. But he wondered if he ever could have found the courage to just go find George and face him. Now George had inadvertently found *him*, and Jack would never need to summon that kind of courage.

Jack took a deep breath and opened the door to see George pacing nearby. Jack's appearance seemed to briefly startle him, then as if they were of the same mind, they both glanced in one direction, then in another to be certain no one was nearby—and no one was. Jack knew it was rare for people to be back here, but he still didn't want to start any strange gossip. The Lord of the manor visiting the blacksmith might not have normally aroused any suspicion, but given that everyone around here knew that George Hannaford's brother was mysteriously missing, any odd behavior on George's part could prompt people to start making unusual speculations.

"Come in," Jack said, motioning with his arm.

George stepped inside, and the moment Jack closed the door, his brother threw his arms around Jack and held to him as if George had believed Jack to be dead, and perhaps he had. Jack returned his brother's embrace with fervor, not surprised to feel the burning of tears in his eyes, but more inclined to not try and hold them back when he heard George sniffling.

"I feel very prodigal right now," Jack said as they finally stepped apart and both men wiped their sleeves over their faces to dry their tears. "Although in the Bible it's the father who embraces his son, offering love and acceptance, and the brother isn't necessarily happy about it."

"In *this* story," George said, "it is the other way around."

"Even though I've handled all of this terribly? Even though I've been hiding practically under your nose and didn't have the courage or respect to let you know?" Jack heard a mild defensiveness in his voice and knew that he feared his brother was angry somewhere underneath his obvious joy over their reunion.

"I've been very worried, Jack," George said, "which means I am now very relieved to know you're all right." He shook his head. "I can't say that if the situation were reversed I wouldn't have done the same thing; therefore, I would be a fool to judge the way you've handled this."

"Thank you," Jack said. "I admit some of my fear in facing you was the belief that you'd be angry; and since I wouldn't at all blame you for being angry, it seemed likely."

"I'm not angry," George said.

Jack nodded, not knowing what else to say.

"Sit down," Jack said, attempting to break the strained silence; and he motioned toward one of the chairs facing the small table near where they were standing.

"Thank you," George said, and they sat down across from each other. George leaned his forearms on the table and smiled at Jack—a genuinely happy smile that made Jack smile in return, deeply grateful for this miraculous reunion, especially now that they'd gotten past Jack's fear of his brother being angry.

"Tell me everything," George said. "I want to know all that's happened since Queen Tookle-Berry had you found, and you stopped writing to me." He said it with a harsh cynicism that let Jack know his brother shared his disdain toward Letitia over the way she was making a difficult situation so much worse.

Jack sighed and took his mind back to when he'd realized that Letitia had been paying someone to find him, and they'd somehow gained possession of one of the letters George had written to Jack. Jack had written one final letter to George to explain the situation before he'd quickly left—under cover of darkness—the town where he'd almost begun to feel at home, as much as he possibly could while being far away from his loved ones. He'd become good friends with the blacksmith who had taken him in and had efficiently trained him in all the best skills necessary to work the trade, and Jack had found fulfillment in being able to pick up on those skills rather naturally. But Letitia had found him, and so he'd had to say good-bye to his new friends and leave. He'd traveled carefully for days, making certain he wasn't being followed, until he found a village where a blacksmith had agreed to take him on as an assistant, given that he had some experience. Jack had lived there a long while, improving his skills but not as eager to try and make friends, fearing he'd be found again and have to move on. Then, quite by chance, a man traveling through the area had mentioned hearing about a blacksmith in Lancashire who had passed away unexpectedly, and the man's family was moving to live with relatives elsewhere. Jack had known that blacksmith, and he knew exactly the village to which this man referred. Feeling strongly pulled toward home, Jack had once again moved on quickly and had been able to purchase the smithy with its attached house and apartment, where he managed to settle in and establish a good reputation, without a single person taking any notice of his possible resemblance to the absent Jack Hannaford.

Jack told George the entire story in detail, answering questions George inter-jected occasionally. Then Jack insisted that George tell him everything of sig-nificance that had taken place during his absence. George reported there wasn't much to tell. Nothing had changed in his life or in the lives of their sisters. Leah and Sarah were doing well, as far as he could ascertain from their regular exchange of letters, and he continually worried about Rebecca—mostly due to the way she was like a puppet on Letitia's manipulative strings.

"Very good analogy," Jack pointed out. "Which brings us back to the same problem we've had for years. As long as Letitia remains unmarried, I can't make my presence known."

"Yes," George drawled, his eyes growing sad and distant. "I can't even let myself think about it or I become furious—with our father especially, but also Letitia—and *her* father; the man's a demon. He's encouraging her and guiding her in all of this; I'm certain of it. Is what we have really so valuable that they would not be willing to let this go? Do they not have more than enough of their own wealth? I don't understand, Jack; I really don't."

"Nor do I," Jack said. "And I too have to keep myself from thinking about it too much, for fear of being completely overtaken by rage and fury. But I—"

Jack was interrupted by the back door coming open, and the men both stood as Hennie and Lottie came into the room, laughing over something they'd been talking about until they both realized in the same moment that Jack was not there alone, and the room became suddenly very still.

"Oh, my," Hennie said when she recognized George.

"Oh, my!" Lottie repeated, more obviously aghast. She too recognized that this was George Hannaford; she had worked for him—if only from a distance. But Lottie had no idea of their connection. Jack had a feeling that was about to change. It was a good thing he knew he could trust Lottie, or this situation could quickly become a whole new challenge.

"Um . . ." Jack drawled, if only to give him a moment to decide how to handle this. The obvious thing was to make introductions. "Ladies," he said, "you clearly know this is George Hannaford. George," he motioned toward the women, "may I introduce your former stable hands, Lottie and Hennie."

"Sir," both women said at the same time, curtsying slightly, which left Jack uneasy—if only in the way it reminded him of the huge social barrier between his present life and the one he'd been born to live. But he knew they were responding appropriately to meeting the Lord of the manor, and he couldn't help but admire them for being respectful toward his brother.

"Hennie?" George echoed, glancing at Jack and then back at Hennie, squint-ing slightly to look at her in a way that might allow him to see her many years younger. "It can't be so common a name," he added, and Jack knew there was no hiding the fact that this woman had been their childhood playmate. Even though Jack and Hennie had been closer to each other than anyone else in their little group of friends, George and Hennie had known each other well. It would be ridiculous to think—even with the changes of growing from child to adult— that George wouldn't connect her name with her face.

"Hennie?" George repeated. "Is that really you?"

"It is," Hennie said, stealing a quick glance at Jack as if to apologize; they both knew her honesty could complicate the situation, but she certainly couldn't lie.

Before anyone had even a moment to anticipate George's next move, he closed the distance between himself and Hennie and wrapped her in a tight, brotherly embrace, and what could she do but return it? Jack felt that sting of tears in his eyes again as he observed their reunion. For a brief moment, that old anger toward his father rose up inside him. Hennie never should have been sent away; they should have all remained friends through these many years. But at the moment, Lottie's wide eyes and stunned expression made it clear there were more immediate reasons for concern.

George stepped back and took Hennie by the shoulders, laughing softly. "This is a miracle!"

"It is indeed," Hennie said, smiling up at him.

"How on earth did you come back to us?" He laughed again as pieces of the puzzle were obviously coming together for him. "And how on earth did you end up working in the stables?"

"A very long story," Hennie said, "which has a great deal to do with my dear friend, Lottie."

Hennie motioned toward Lottie, who was looking aghast and confused. "Lottie!" George said as if he were meeting the queen. He took her hand and kissed it, keeping hold of it as he looked right at her and said, "It is an unspeakable pleasure to meet you."

"And you," Lottie said, her voice a little squeaky. She glanced at Hennie, then back to George, "And how is it the two of you know each other so well?"

"I told you I grew up at the manor . . . until my mother died," Hennie said.

"Yes, but . . . you didn't mention being so friendly with the *Lord* of the manor."

"I certainly wasn't Lord of the manor back then," George said with a chuckle, "nor did I ever expect to be. My father detested having us play with the servant children, but he hardly paid any attention to us, so it wasn't terribly difficult to get away with doing so. But it was Jack and Hennie who were inseparable—like twins from different mothers, we used to call them."

As George turned to look at Jack—at the same moment talking about him—Jack knew the truth couldn't be kept from Lottie any longer. He realized he was all right with that; in fact, it would be much easier to stop having to pretend with Lottie when she and Hennie were almost always together, and he spent most of his free time with both of them.

Lottie's eyes widened, and her mouth dropped open slightly, but no sound came out. She darted her eyes back and forth between Jack and Hennie as if doing so might answer what was likely a great many questions. She finally managed to utter a single syllable. "Jack?" she asked, looking directly at him. She then found momentum to keep going. "You're *Jack*? The ever-famous, mysteriously missing Jack Hannaford?"

Jack took a deep breath, noting that Hennie looked concerned, George looked confused, and Lottie's expression bordered on angry. "Guilty," Jack said, certainly feeling the word perfectly described his position in that moment.

Lottie took in a sharp breath and again looked at Hennie, then again at Jack, then back at Hennie, her countenance now showing betrayal and disappointment.

"Lottie," Jack said, certain it was up to him to explain this, rather than putting it on Hennie's shoulders, "you of all people should be able to understand how important it can be to keep certain things secret. Keeping my identity hidden has been crucial. Hennie couldn't tell you because—"

"You don't trust me?" she asked, looking back and forth at both of them, making it clear the question was inclusive. "You think I couldn't keep a secret for the sake of your welfare?"

"Lottie, it's not like that," Hennie said. "You must understand that—"

"I need a few minutes," Lottie said, and Jack suspected she didn't want to express her true feelings in front of George when she didn't know him—and could likely feel intimidated by knowing he'd been her employer. She nodded toward George, her expression barely polite, and hurriedly said, "A pleasure meeting you, sir. Forgive my hasty retreat."

"The pleasure is mine," George barely managed to say before Lottie had left and closed the door behind her—none too softly.

After they'd all winced from the slamming of the door, George said, "Apparently there's a great deal more going on here than I realized."

"I'm afraid there is," Jack said, "but it clearly has nothing to do with you, and I'm sorry you ended up—"

"I believe it all has a great deal to do with me," George said to his brother.

While Jack was wondering how to respond, Hennie said, "It's so good to see you again, George. I believe I should go and explain the situation more clearly to Lottie." She looked at Jack and added, "I'll let you fill in the details for your brother." Jack just nodded at her, and she went to the door.

"It's very good to see *you* again, Hennie," George said to her. She offered him a nod and a smile and left, closing the door more softly than Lottie had.

"So," George said with a lilt of drama in his voice, *"those* are the women who have been working for me in disguise."

"That would be them," Jack said. "The situation is . . . complicated at best."

"Then I think you'd do well to give me a fair explanation," George said and once again sat down.

Jack seated himself across the table from his brother and sighed before he told his brother how Hennie had been asked by Mr. Parsons to take over the job of bringing the horses to him—one at a time—to have their hooves trimmed and shoes replaced. George was amazed to hear how Jack and Hennie had become friends while they'd shared simple lunches and conversations, and then how Hennie had figured out who he was when he'd shared a story from his childhood that only Hennie could have known about. George was also amazed to realize that Hennie had not chosen to come back here, that Lottie had been working here a long while before she went with Parsons's blessing to get her friend and bring her back since he needed another reliable employee—and Hennie had had no idea Lottie was taking her to Ivy Manor.

"It can't be a coincidence," George said. "It seems nothing short of a miracle that she would end up back here like this. I've always regretted the way Father sent her away." George became deeply thoughtful, then his expression showed a combination of enlightenment and horror. "You told me these women came from a workhouse. And from an orphanage before that."

"Yes, that's true," Jack said, unable to keep the sadness out of his voice. "Hennie tells me she's grateful for the experiences only in the respect that she and Lottie are such dear friends and they never would have met otherwise. She doesn't think Lottie would have survived without her. Beyond that . . . well . . . it was hell, brother. Simple as that. They've both lived in hell, under circumstances we cannot begin to comprehend."

George looked visibly ill as his eyes assumed a distant expression, and Jack knew exactly how he felt. Jack continued by saying, "Which is one of many reasons I'm very glad to have them in my care—well, in a way. They are fiercely independent and refuse to let me take care of them *too* much. But at least they are living in the apartment above the smithy so I can keep track of them."

George asked with mild panic, "Were they not safe working at the manor? Is there some reason that—"

"They were fine. Parsons demands respect and good behavior from everyone under his supervision. They just grew weary of having to pretend every minute when they were outside their rooms, and it was time for a change. They were fine then, and they're fine now."

"Relatively speaking," George said after another stretch of thoughtful silence. "Apparently my showing up has created a stir." He looked upward as if he could imagine the two women arguing in their upstairs apartment. "I hope Lottie isn't too upset, and I hope you'll forgive me for inadvertently exposing your identity."

"It's all right," Jack said. "I'm relieved to not have to keep it a secret with Lottie anymore. Hennie and I have talked about letting her in on the secret; we just weren't certain how to go about it. Now we don't have to wonder about that." Jack sighed. "And don't worry; their friendship has survived a great deal of drama. I'm certain Lottie will quickly come to understand our motives and forgive us—as I told her, she understands the need to live under a different identity."

"She would certainly understand it a great deal more than I do," George said, looking hard at Jack as if he was trying to figure out what to do with the fact that his brother had become a blacksmith. "How do you do it, Jack?"

"One day at a time," Jack said. "I don't mind the work. But I've missed you; I miss our home. There isn't a day when I'm not tempted to just ride to the manor and reveal myself."

"And why haven't you?" George asked.

Jack made a scoffing sound. "You know the answer to that. I can't *be* Jack Hannaford without being forced into marrying the most despicable woman in the county. I regret how all of this has left such a burden on your shoulders, but it was Father's doing, not mine. And I don't see any way out of this. Besides," Jack leaned back in his chair and folded his arms over his chest, smiling as he brought up his favorite subject, "I have every intention of marrying a common woman. Queen of Tookle-Berry or not, the Lord of the manor marrying a common woman would not settle well around here."

"Why should anyone care?" George asked. "Queen of Tookle-Berry and her father aside," he clarified, "why should anyone care?"

"It's just not done," Jack said, "and you know that as well as I do."

George sounded mildly defensive. "You should know that our family has come far beyond such things since our father's death freed us all from his narrow-minded attitudes and behaviors, and . . ." George stopped, fixed his eyes more directly on Jack, and chuckled. "Wait a minute! You're not speaking hypothetically . . . or in principle alone. You're in love with someone!" He said it as if he'd caught his brother stealing cake from the kitchen, then he laughed as if he found the mischief terribly amusing. George leaned over the table and grinned. "Who? Tell me."

"I'll tell you as long as you can admit that *this* above any other reason makes it impossible for me to come back and assume my real identity. I must marry for love, George—no other reason. I won't be forced into a marriage because—"

"This is a very old conversation, Jack," George interrupted. "I *never* expected nor wanted you to heed that stipulation in Father's will. That's why I don't begrudge you the need to have me fill your position; I know you had to leave. There's no question that you could ever marry Letitia. The only real problem comes down to the legalities of the whole thing. That will our father left is complicated and messy, and it's as if he intended it to be so."

"And *that* is a very old conversation, as well," Jack said. "But I still need to clarify that I will marry for love, and the only way I can do that is to remain a blacksmith. I don't want to move away from here; I like being so close to home, even if I've never been able to actually see you."

"That could change," George said, "as long as we're careful."

"Perhaps," Jack said, "but I don't want to bring any potential hardship into my marriage because of my true identity. And it might be necessary for us to just . . . move away and start a new life elsewhere. Eventually Letitia *will* give up and find another man to be her victim."

"I wish she'd give up *now* and just marry someone else, which would make all of this simply go away."

"I've given up on that," Jack said, "especially now that I want to get married as soon as I can talk her into marrying me."

George's eyes brightened as the topic of conversation turned from the dismal facets of their situation to the fact that Jack had found someone he loved enough to marry. George asked with a smile, "Does she know the truth? About who you are and—"

"Of course," Jack said. "I would never expect to become seriously involved with a woman and not have her know everything."

"Everything?"

"Everything!" Jack said, a little surprised that his brother hadn't pieced together what Jack considered obvious. Not wanting any further drama due to misunderstanding or assumption, Jack hurried to clarify, "She figured out who I really am before we fell in love, and falling in love was easy when we already knew each other so well." George looked intrigued but still had obviously not made the connection. "Why do you think I wanted her to live under my own roof—in a manner of speaking—so that I could help take care of her?" George gasped softly as the truth came to him, but Jack still added, "Why would I want the woman I love to live her life pretending to be a man, which made it impossible to even *think* about trying to court her properly? I might be a blacksmith, but I'm still a gentleman. I love her and respect her, and I need to go about this appropriately—as much as possible under the circumstances."

"This is remarkable," George said, leaning back—as if doing so might help him take all this in. "You and Hennie. Of course, *you and Hennie.* If she'd stayed, you would have ended up together. By some incomprehensible, divine intervention, she's come back, and *of course* the two of you should be together."

"I couldn't have said it better myself," Jack said, adding somewhat snidely, "and if not for the Queen of Tookle-Berry and her evil father, I could actually give her my name when I marry her instead of simply sharing this bizarre alias I've taken on."

"And what surname exactly would that be?" George asked.

"I don't even have one," Jack said. "I've just gone by Ollie, short for Oliver, which is my first given name as you know. That's how I've introduced myself to anyone I've encountered. No one's ever asked. I'm a blacksmith, not a banker." He sighed and tried not to sound too self-pitying as he added, "I'm a man without a name and banished from my home." He sighed again. "I'm confident that Hennie and I can share a good life under any circumstances, and she sincerely doesn't care about my name or my profession or where I live, but *I* care. Sitting here talking to you has made me realize I care a great deal more than I've allowed myself to admit—perhaps because it was too painful, or simply because I couldn't do anything about it."

"Perhaps both," George suggested.

"That's likely true," Jack said and pushed his fingers through his hair. "Hennie's only hesitation in our moving forward with marriage is that she believes I need to make peace over this situation; that if I'm going to live my life in another identity, I need to do so without regrets—or something to that effect."

"She's a very wise woman," George said firmly.

"She is indeed, and I am very blessed to have her in my life—but I want to give her the best life possible, George."

"You know that despite all this you have all the money you could ever need. I'll make certain of that."

"I know that," Jack said, "and I'm grateful, but . . ."

"But . . ." George guessed, "it's not about the money? Dare I say you feel unsettled by simply not being able to be the man you were born and raised to be?"

"An accurate assessment," Jack said, wondering now how he'd managed to go so long without ever talking to his brother. For all that Hennie was compassionate and understanding of his circumstances, George knew him as only a brother could. "In some ways I believe Hennie would be more comfortable living a simple life; she's admitted as much. But I think she underestimates her ability to do very well blending into our world—or should I say *your* world?"

"It's still your world too," George said. "It's as if the house is . . . haunted by you. I feel your absence in every room, at every meal; I feel it every time I sit at the desk to do business or meet with the overseers—just *everything*. I don't mind the work, brother; it just feels like I'm some kind of . . . imposter. It feels like you're supposed to be there and not me."

Jack felt suddenly emotional and leaned his forearms on his thighs, hanging his head with the hope of hiding how deeply his brother's words had affected him.

Chapter Thirteen

THE SCHEME

JACK CLEARED HIS THROAT IN an attempt to steady his voice before he said to his brother, "I've often fantasized about us working together to run the estate. I think we could make a good team."

"I think that sounds marvelous."

"But it's not possible, George; it's just not possible."

"Well, it *should* be!" George hit a fist on the table, which startled Jack. He stood up and started pacing. "There has to be a way around this . . . out of this. There has to be!"

"And do you think if there were, one of us wouldn't have thought of it by now? As I understand from gossip, Letitia is with Rebecca nearly every day, surely convincing her of how unfair we've been to her. Unless Rebecca has changed her mind for some reason, I'm sure she still believes that her friend is a perfect match for me, and she can't understand why I would run and hide."

"It's all true," George said, still pacing. "It's as if she's always there, lurking, scheming, making herself at home while she's planning on how she'll redecorate the whole place once she's the lady of the manor."

Jack made a disgusted noise that didn't begin to express just how deeply outraged he felt. But he couldn't think of anything to say that hadn't already been said many times. He sat there feeling rather sulky while George continued to pace, and Jack wondered how the conversation was going between Hennie and Lottie. He hoped that Lottie would be quick to understand and forgive; he didn't like the idea of there being tension among any of them because of this.

"Hey," George said and stopped pacing abruptly, which again startled Jack. George then leaned both his hands on the table and looked at Jack with a distinct sparkle in his eyes. "You need to marry Hennie."

"I know that," Jack said.

"No, I mean . . . soon. Will your marriage not make all of this go away? Your inheritance of the title and the estate was contingent upon your marrying Letitia.

But you've already let go of those things by leaving. It's my choice to share my wealth with you. I know the title doesn't matter to you. So, your getting married would leave Letitia no choice but to move on with her life. You would be able to come home . . . with your new bride, and it's my choice to share my home with you, and to engage you in assisting with my responsibilities. Our father's wishes will remain legally intact. You marry for love and relinquish your inheritance to me. I choose to share *my* inheritance with you. There. And the new Mrs. Hannaford must absolutely bring her dear friend to live at the manor, as well. We couldn't possibly think of separating such close friends after all they've been through together. It's not as if we don't have the space. Lottie can have a wing to herself and no one will hardly notice. It's perfect."

Jack listened to everything George was saying while his heart quickened and then began to pound. Jack had never considered such an option because he hadn't had anyone in his life he'd wanted to marry. But he couldn't deny that George's plan made perfect sense. In that moment he could clearly see how he'd needed these years away for time to pass so that he could be in this position. And perhaps the separation he and his brother had endured made the possibility of taking this path feel more appealing and feasible than it might have in the past.

"What do you think?" George demanded when Jack said nothing.

"I think it might work," Jack said. "But I know that I can't make any such decision without discussing it thoroughly with Hennie. This isn't just *my* life we're talking about; she must be a part of this decision. It could bring up difficulties we might not even be able to foresee. We would need to consult with a solicitor we can trust, someone who can help us understand if there's anything in the will that would make such a move problematic for you—or anyone else."

"Of course," George said. "You know I fired Father's solicitor the day after he read the will to us. The very fact that he helped craft such a document . . . and the snide way he presented it to us just . . . irks me still."

"That is long in the past," Jack said.

"I know, but . . . I've been working with a different solicitor ever since. He's a good man; I trust him completely. He's gone over the will many times at my insistence. He'll be able to tell me if there are any loopholes that could cause problems. But it's at least worth considering. And, well . . . if it doesn't work, then perhaps you and Hennie *will* have to move away and live elsewhere. But we must find a way to stay in touch . . . to see each other. We must!"

"I agree," Jack said. He was about to add that they would take some time to think this through when he heard two sets of footsteps coming down the stairs just outside the room in which they stood. "Well, it sounds like they are together; I hope that's a good sign."

The men both stood before the door came open. Hennie and Lottie stepped tentatively into the room, as if not wanting to interrupt whatever might be taking place.

"Is everything all right?" Jack asked.

"Relatively speaking," Hennie reported and closed the door.

"Forgive me, Lottie," Jack said. "I never meant to exclude you from the truth of what's going on in my life, and we had every intention of telling you, and—"

"I know all of that," Lottie said, "and I understand; I really do. It's just . . . a shock, I admit." She chuckled tensely. "But I suppose it's no more of a shock than what I gave certain people by revealing the fact that I'm a woman. My being upset would surely make me a hypocrite. So . . . forgive me for getting upset."

"Still friends?" Jack asked, holding out his hand toward her.

Lottie took it and squeezed his fingers. "Always," she declared with a wry smile.

Hennie noticed and said, "Truthfully, I think she's more rattled by *who* you are than the fact that you've been living under a false identity."

Lottie looked mildly embarrassed as she glanced quickly at Jack, then George, then at the floor, letting go of Jack's hand. "I admit it's . . . strange."

"I assured her you're just ordinary men," Hennie said. "I mean . . . you were fairly ordinary children. Jack hasn't grown up to walk on water or anything like unto it." She looked at George and smiled. "I assume that nothing of the sort has occurred in your life since I last saw you."

"I can assure you that I am indeed *very* ordinary," George said. "If anything, the Hannaford name and all its obligations has been little more than a curse."

"Amen," Jack said and motioned for everyone to sit down.

As soon as they were all seated around the little table, Lottie looked at Jack as if she'd never seen him before, and asked with some hesitation, "So . . . should I call you by your real name now, or—"

"When no one else is around to hear it," Jack said, "I would prefer that, yes. I know you and Hennie have a great deal of experience in knowing when to use which name," he said with a wry smile

"Yes, we certainly do," Lottie said, seeming a tad more relaxed, but far from normal. Jack didn't want her treating him any differently now that she knew the truth, and he hoped she would adjust quickly.

"However did you manage?" George asked, still clearly fascinated by the fact that he'd had two women disguised as men working for him and he'd never had a clue.

The conversation lightened as Hennie and Lottie answered George's questions, and they told some humorous tales of situations that had been especially awkward, or things that the men they'd worked with had talked about in their presence, which the women had laughed about when they were alone, certain the men would be mortified if they'd known the truth.

"And now that they know," George said, laughing in a way that made it clear he found this whole situation especially funny, "I wonder if they think back and they *do* feel mortified. If I'd been regularly making comments on how annoying women are, and later found out I'd been speaking to a woman, I think I would surely be embarrassed."

"And yet *you* were always a perfect gentleman," Hennie said.

"Was I?" George asked. "I honestly don't remember. I don't remember encountering either one of you, and I don't know if I'm kind to the people who work for me. I try to be; but I'm often distracted or in a foul mood, and I can't say whether or not I'm difficult to work for."

"I don't think you encountered either of us directly," Hennie said. "Lottie only saw you from a distance now and then, and I never actually saw you at all. But you should know the general attitude among your employees is that you're a good man and a pleasure to work for."

George let out a brief, ironic chuckle. "Well, that's good to know, I suppose. Although I'd far prefer they were working for my brother."

"That will *never* happen," Jack said with a vehemence he'd intended, and a defensiveness that he'd unwittingly allowed to slip through.

"It *could*," George replied, "in a roundabout kind of way; we just talked about that."

"About *what?*" Hennie demanded, sounding alarmed.

Jack remained silent, preferring to have George explain his idea, and curious to see how Hennie would respond. George leaned across the table and took Hennie's hand. "My dear friend," George said. "At least . . . I hope we're still friends; it would mean so much to me to know that we are . . . despite how our father's deplorable choices impacted your life so adversely."

"His choices have nothing to do with you, George," Hennie said, and Jack noticed that Lottie was observing all this with awe. The reality that her dearest friend shared such close relationships with the Hannaford family—for whom she had worked a fairly long time—was likely still difficult to comprehend. "Of course we're friends. I thought of you every day that I worked in your stables, and I'm glad I never actually saw you because it would have been immensely difficult to not just throw myself at you with a big hug, and that would have caused a stir."

George chuckled. "It certainly would have, although if I'd known you were there, I would have found a way for you and your friend to not have to live in disguise. Now that I *do* know, I wish you would have come to me; I would have arranged something more suitable."

"You're very kind, George," Hennie said, "but we had a good life there. We were treated fairly, had good living conditions, and earned a fair wage. Now, let's not wallow any more in the past."

George smiled at her and let go of her hand to lean back in his chair, sighing loudly in a way that Jack recognized as preparing himself to say something important. Before he could speak, Hennie said, "Now, tell me what you were going to say; I want to know what the two of you have been talking about." She glanced at Jack, then back to George. "I'm guessing some kind of conspiracy from that look on your brother's face."

"What look?" Jack demanded lightly, hoping to ease the tension. "This is just my face!"

"I know your face very well, darling," Hennie said and tipped her head mischievously. "Is it all right if I call you darling in George's presence? I assume you told him that you're trying to get me to marry you."

"I told him *everything*," Jack said.

"I'm especially interested," George said, "in the part about your hesitance to marry a man who hasn't made peace with who he is and what he's going to do with his life. Would you say that's an accurate assessment?"

"Fairly accurate," Hennie said, offering Jack a long gaze of compassion before she turned again to face George, adding in a gentle tone, "I want him to be happy, George. However he chooses to live—and whatever name he chooses to bear—I want him to be at peace with it. I don't want him to always feel like he's running and hiding from the life that would make him happy."

"And what of you, Hennie? Could you be happy living at Ivy Manor, married to the Lord of the manor?"

Lottie gasped as if this aspect of Jack's identity in regard to Hennie hadn't occurred to her. Hennie sighed. "I can't deny it would take some getting used to, and it's difficult to imagine myself filling such a role, but . . . I love Jack. I will be happy as long as we are together and *he* is happy. I don't want to spend my life feeling like we're forever living with the results of being cursed by the Queen of Tookle-Berry."

"The what?" Lottie asked. "Who?"

Jack chuckled as he considered how that must have sounded to someone who had not been privy to silly childhood fantasies that had now become some form of a private joke—even if it wasn't at all funny anymore.

Hennie, Jack, and George all took turns filling in details of the reasons they had dubbed Letitia Tewksbury with such a ridiculous name in her childhood, and why she was the reason Jack had gone into hiding—Letitia and her evil father.

"Of course I couldn't marry her; it would be like sentencing myself to the guillotine, and I would be sentencing every person who lives on the estate to her evil ways."

"That's why you left!" Lottie declared as it became obvious.

"Yes, that's why I left," Jack said. "And that's why I can't go back."

"But you can," George interjected with an enthusiasm Jack didn't share.

"How?" Hennie asked with such sincerity that Jack felt overcome with a fresh surge of love for her. He knew she would far prefer to live a simple life and not have their lives entangled in the workings and obligations of Ivy Manor and the Hannaford family. But she loved him. And she knew him well enough to know that a part of him ached to go home—even if he'd been hesitant to admit it too boldly, perhaps because he feared it just wasn't possible.

George surprised Jack—and the women—when he answered Hennie's question by saying, "Marry my brother, Hennie. Soon. Let's just put all of this behind us and get on with our lives."

"What on earth do you mean?" Hennie insisted.

"If Jack doesn't marry Letitia, he loses his inheritance. He already has. The title means nothing to him. It doesn't really mean anything to me either, but taking it on won't change my life one way or the other. I'm already running the estate. But if Jack marries the woman he loves, Letitia will have no choice but to accept that she needs to move on and let go of her delusions. And Jack can come home with his new bride and help me run the estate. It's my choice to share my inheritance with him if I wish, and I do." He looked at Lottie and smiled. "And of course, Hennie must bring her friend with her to live at the manor. Every lady needs a suitable companion. I told Jack you could have your own wing in the house if you like; there's plenty of room."

Lottie took in a sharp breath, then seemed to have trouble letting it out. She just turned to Hennie as if relying on her to handle this might help her breathe. Hennie looked inquisitively at George a long moment before she asked, "Is it really that simple? Are you certain there aren't . . . I don't know . . . other stipulations in the will or something that might cause problems?"

"I'm going to have my solicitor make certain," George said. "He's already studied the will carefully because I've been trying for years to figure out a way to get around this."

A taut silence followed George's words, making it evident that everyone present had far too much to think about, and the hope of solving these problems was still contingent upon acquiring information regarding legal aspects of the situation that were tangled with uncertainty.

Lottie broke the quiet by standing up and declaring, "I'm going to fix some supper. If I'm getting hungry, I assume the rest of you are too."

"I'll help you," Hennie said and stood up as well.

"I'll help too." Jack also stood up, needing something with which to occupy himself for fear of imploding over all that was circling in his mind: the past events leading to this day, all that had changed this day with George's reappearance in his life, and the possibility of everything changing in the future if George's idea was viable. Overwhelmed and a little afraid of how all of this might turn out, Jack began peeling potatoes, which had been previously washed and left in a bowl. He was proficient at the task and could do it without thinking, and potatoes could always be used to add substance to any meal.

"Well," George drawled and came to his feet, rolling up his sleeves, "I'm certainly not going to just sit here while the rest of you are working. I assume that if I *help* with supper, you'll allow me to stay and eat with you."

Hennie watched as the lord of Ivy Manor seemed determined to help them cook here in the tiny common room of Jack's home behind the smithy, and she almost felt as if she were dreaming. But a quick glance at Jack and the subtle smile that passed between him and his brother left her feeling more hope than she'd felt since they'd come back together. She didn't necessarily want to live in luxury at Ivy Manor, but she did want Jack to make peace with his life, and it seemed some huge steps had been taken in that direction.

"You'd be welcome to stay and eat whether you help or not," Hennie said to George, laying slices of salt pork into a pan that was getting hot from the fire she'd just lit in the stove. Once the pork was sufficiently cooked and she could pour out the excess grease into weeds not far from the back door, she would add some chicken she'd purchased earlier at the butcher's shop. Lottie was cutting some raw beets they had washed before bringing them into the house. If they were cut into small pieces, they would cook quickly in the pot of water that was already set on the stove so it could be heating, along with a second pot of water meant to boil the potatoes Jack was peeling. It was a simple meal, but Hennie knew it would be satisfying. They'd already developed a plan for having food ready to cook quickly for supper, since they were all usually tired in the evening and wanted to be able to prepare their evening meal as easily as possible. Sometimes they just had bread and butter with some leftover lamb or beef, and they would eat vegetables raw—if they didn't feel like cooking. But Hennie was glad they had food ready and on hand to be able to make a tolerable meal—since George Hannaford was eating with them. Hennie had to glance at him to reassure herself that he was really here, and that he and Jack had really been talking about plans on how to change Jack's circumstances. Perhaps later, when she was alone for the night, the enormity of what was happening would sink in to the point that she could fully accept it as reality. For the moment she felt mostly in shock, so she just focused on cooking and tried to imagine how life might be if George's plan actually worked.

The four of them engaged in casual conversation while supper was cooking, and they all continued to talk while they ate, remaining at the table long after the meal was over. Hennie noticed that Lottie and George were conversing so naturally that no one would ever guess they'd come from such dramatically different upbringings—nor was it evident that they'd only met not so many hours earlier. Hennie knew that Jack noticed the same by the way he smiled at her while Lottie was telling George a humorous anecdote from her days of working as a man in his stables. George found the entire situation so humorous that he often laughed heartily and made comments to indicate it was likely the funniest—and most exciting—thing that had ever happened at Ivy Manor.

"Short of the Lord of the manor dramatically disappearing?" Hennie asked in a light tone, not wanting the topic to dampen the mood.

"Oh, that wasn't exciting," George said in an equally light tone. "That was dreadful." He smiled at his brother and added, "But it's all in the past now."

"We can hope," Jack said and stood up to begin clearing the table.

George insisted on helping clean the dishes with water that had been left heating on the stove while they'd eaten. He admitted he'd never once done any such chore, but he rather enjoyed washing the dishes in the warm, soapy water and then handing them to Lottie, who rinsed them off before she handed them to Hennie, who dried them before she handed them to Jack, who put them away.

"We make a fine team," George declared, and Jack chuckled.

"If our father could see us now . . ." Jack said and chuckled again, which made George laugh.

"He'd turn over in his grave," George said, "and dare I say that the very thought gives me some kind of wicked pleasure."

"Why wicked?" Lottie asked. "He was despicable enough to send our dear Hennie off to an orphanage . . . to an inevitable life of hardship. I don't think the idea of him finding displeasure in the fact that his sons have defied such an upbringing to become such fine men is anything close to wicked. It's just . . . human. If being decent and generous defies him, then I think the two of you should go on living in a way that would infuriate him."

"Amen," Hennie said emphatically, and George laughed heartily.

"I like her," George said to Jack while he pointed at Lottie with soap bubbles on his hand.

"Yes, we all do," Jack said, laughing with his brother. "And I think it's a worthy goal—to live in a way that would infuriate him."

"Amen," George said, imitating the way Hennie had just said it. "So, let's keep cooking our own meals and cleaning our own dishes, and let's also find a way to blast his last will and testament into pieces."

"We could tack the papers to a board and shoot holes in it," Lottie suggested, and again George laughed.

"That is an *excellent* idea," George said. "And once we've worked our way around all of his ludicrous tyrannical wishes, I think we will do just that."

"Amen," Jack said, imitating the way both Hennie and George had said it. And they *all* laughed.

After George left rather late in the evening, Lottie told Jack good night and went out the back door to go up to the apartment. It had become their normal routine for Lottie to give Hennie and Jack a few minutes of privacy before Hennie went up to the apartment herself. Hennie had quickly come to love these moments alone with Jack at the end of the day when he would tell her he loved her and kiss her good night. During the brief time she and Lottie had been living in the apartment above the smithy and sharing much of their daily routine with Jack, Hennie had become keenly aware of how deeply she loved him. Not only did she love him, but she had come to admire, trust, and respect him the more that she had come to know him as an adult. They had agreed to give their relationship time, to get to know each other again, and to see if the love they felt was based on something valid and stable. Hennie now knew in her deepest self that what they shared had passed every test that mattered to her; she truly believed that no matter where or how they ended up sharing their lives, they could and would be able to make each other happy, and they were meant to be together. But George's visit had brought the hovering struggles in their lives directly to the forefront where they couldn't be avoided and put off any longer. A part of Hennie was glad Jack finally had to face his dilemma and move forward one way or another. His avoidance to do so up to this point had been the one thing holding her back from making a firm commitment to him. But now that Jack's brother was back in their lives, insisting that Jack take some bold steps forward, Hennie felt decidedly nervous over what the outcome might be.

After Lottie left, Jack sat back down and planted his elbows on the table, pushing his hands into his hair with a long, deep sigh. "Are you all right?" Hennie asked, sitting across the table from him.

"Overwhelmed," he said and lifted his head. "Are *you* all right?"

"The same," she said. "I'm grateful George found you, Jack. You couldn't keep hiding from him, and now we don't have to wonder how to bridge that gap."

"It was good to just spend time with him . . . to talk and laugh the way we used to before all this happened."

Hennie took his hand across the table and squeezed it. "So, what do you think of his plan? Assuming the solicitor doesn't find anything in the will that—"

"I don't care what the will may or may not say, Hennie. I think it's high time you and I just got married." Jack said it with such vehemence that Hennie caught her breath. "I know you will stand by me no matter what course my life takes. What else matters? I prefer to be able to go home and share the running of the estate with my brother, but if that isn't possible, we will make another life elsewhere." He leaned both arms across the table, taking both of Hennie's hands and looking into her eyes with conviction and adoration. "Will you marry me, Hennie? I don't want to wait any longer, and I refuse to allow this situation to control my decisions any further. There are some things I *cannot* control; but I can choose whom to marry and when. I know, Hennie, with all my heart, there is no woman as right for me as you are, no one I would rather spend my life with—whatever that life entails. And I swear to you, Hennie, no matter how we end up living our lives, I will do everything in my power to make you happy, and I will always work hard to see that you are cared for in the best possible way." He sighed and tightened his hold on her hands. "Please say yes; please tell me you'll marry me."

Hennie was startled but not surprised by how the rightness of his question surged through her entire body with a warm tingling, affirming what she already felt in her heart and knew in her head. "Yes, Jack," she said with a quiver in her voice. "Yes, to everything."

Jack let out a one-syllable laugh and immediately stood up to reach across the table and kiss her. "Oh, Hennie," he said and stepped around the table as she stood to face him. He took her face into his hands and kissed her again. "Knowing we'll be together makes everything else seem . . . not so important. I pray all of this works out the way it's meant to, but as long as I have you beside me, we'll make the most of whatever happens."

"Absolutely," she said and urged him to kiss her again.

"There is an obvious problem to getting married, however," he said, his brow furrowing. "We can't get married in England without posting the banns, and we can't do that without using our legal names, and we know the result would be Letitia's father coming forward to make a formal protest. Our only safe option is to get married in Scotland."

"Then we must go to Scotland to be married," she said eagerly. Now that the decision to be married was firm, she felt anxious to get on with it and move forward with their lives. The idea of the journey wasn't appealing, but it would certainly be worth it.

He laughed softly and said, "My thoughts exactly; it's as if you can read my mind."

"Lottie should go with us," Hennie said. "And George. I can't think of anyone else I would want to be there when I get married."

"I was thinking *that* as well," he said. "When should we go?"

"The sooner the better," Hennie said, "but . . ."

"But?" he asked, sounding panicked.

"I was just thinking of how Lottie and I just settled into our job at the pub. Lester has been so kind; I don't want Lottie and I to leave him in a bind."

"I'll speak with Lester," Jack said, "and see what we can work out so that we *don't* leave him in a bind, but of course I must talk to George first."

"Lottie will be ecstatic, I think," Hennie said and laughed with perfect delight as she wrapped her arms around Jack and rested her head on his shoulder. She loved the way he held her so tightly, as if he could protect her and keep her safe, from this moment forward. Having Jack in her life made it easier to believe she could put all the horrors of her past behind and truly be happy.

<hr />

Jack left early, before the women were even awake, to meet his brother at a time and place they had decided upon the previous evening. He'd forgotten to tell Hennie, so he left a note in the kitchen, knowing they would come there once they were awake and dressed. The autumn air was pleasantly cool as he rode quickly to the big tree, loving the nostalgia of it, and the way its location was out of view from the road and the manor. He found George already there, sitting on the ground with his legs stretched out and crossed at the ankles, leaning back against the tree.

"Good morning, brother," Jack said as he dismounted and tethered the horse. He then laughed, simply because it felt so good to be able to say those words—and to be here with George.

George jumped to his feet and laughed as well, apparently sharing Jack's enthusiasm. They shared a brotherly embrace that normally would have been brief, but they'd been separated for so long that it only felt right to stretch it out a few extra seconds, as if doing so might make up for lost time.

"Before you say anything," Jack said, sitting on the ground and leaning back on his hands, "there's something I need to tell you."

George resumed his comfortable position, leaning back against the tree. "I'm listening," George said.

"After you left last night . . . and after everything we'd talked about . . . I found the courage to do something I should have done a long time ago." He took a deep breath that filled him with warmth and peace. "I proposed to Hennie—officially."

"Good man!" George said with enthusiasm. "I hope she took enough pity on you to say yes."

"She did indeed," Jack said with a chuckle. "The thing is . . . I realized that it doesn't matter how any of this works out—or doesn't—she's the best thing that's ever happened to me, and we need to be together. She's willing to stand with me whether we end up living at the manor, or she has to change her name and be a blacksmith's wife. She loves *me,* and I know I can make her happy—especially knowing that I can make peace with all of this and be comfortable with who I am, knowing that *who* I am is not directly linked to any inheritance or title, and it certainly has nothing to do with how our father treated us."

"Amen to that, my brother," George said and briefly squeezed Jack's shoulder in support.

"I believe I've known all this in my heart, but I gave in to confusion and doubt rather than taking hold of what's truly important. For some reason, your showing up the way you did, and the things you said . . . your attitude about all of this . . . just made it easier to see the future more clearly, and I know I need Hennie to be a part of it."

"So, does this mean we're planning a wedding?" George asked enthusiastically.

"In a manner of speaking," Jack said; this part was not so easy. "We can't get married here and do it properly, George. I can't post the banns without stirring up a hornet's nest, and I won't marry Hennie under a false name. I don't want anything about our marriage to be tainted in any way—despite present challenges. Therefore, the only viable option is for us to elope to Scotland. And since I've put this decision off too long already, the sooner the better. I know there could be some legal loopholes in the will we may have to deal with, but I realized it doesn't really matter. Once I marry Hennie, we're married; it's done. We will just have to take on the rest one step at a time." Jack took a deep breath now that he'd said everything he needed to say. "So, what do you think? Am I jumping into this too quickly? Is this a rash decision, or—"

"I think it's absolutely the best thing you could do—for many reasons," George said. "And I support you completely."

"Good," Jack said and chuckled, "because I want you to come with us; I need you to stand up with me, be my best man."

"It would be an honor," George said. "When do we leave?"

"Well," Jack chuckled again, "we have a few arrangements to make, but . . . as soon as possible. How can I let you know without causing any trouble?"

They discussed some possible ideas for communicating in a way that wouldn't disrupt their usual routine and finally settled on a plan that would be surprisingly easy for both of them. But given the miraculous way George had come back into his life—and the way it had become the determining factor for Jack to be able to move forward—he shouldn't have been at all surprised to see everything coming together so well.

Jack only visited with his brother a few more minutes, since he had one more stop he needed to make before returning to the smithy, so he could be open for business and have the coals hot before a scheduled appointment at eleven. With any luck he'd have time to eat breakfast sometime before then.

Chapter Fourteen

THE NEW MRS. HANNAFORD

Jack rode quickly to the pub where Hennie and Lottie were now employed. He was glad to know it was open for business early in the day, but there would likely be very few customers. After tethering his horse out front, Jack went inside, pleasantly surprised to find *no* customers, and Lester seated at a table near the door, reading a newspaper. He looked up to see who had entered, then offered a broad smile. "Ollie, my friend," Lester said and stood up, reaching out a hand. "What a pleasure this is! What can I get for you?"

"I came hoping to speak with you," Jack said and glanced around. "It appears to be a good time."

"It is, indeed!" Lester said with kind enthusiasm and motioned for Jack to sit across the table from him as Lester sat back down and pushed his newspaper side. "Now, what do you need?" he asked with sincerity.

"First of all," Jack said, wanting to get straight to the point. "I can't tell you how grateful I am that you were willing to give Hennie and Lottie jobs here. They actually enjoy their work, and given the unusual situation, your kindness means a great deal."

"Not at all! Not at all!" Lester laughed. "They're delightful young women, and hard workers. It's a pleasure to have them working here; I just wish I had more hours to give them." He looked mildly concerned as he added, "And I might have to cut their hours back some; I'm hoping that doesn't cause distress for them."

"Actually," Jack drawled, wondering if moving forward with his plans would continue to offer him an ongoing series of miracles, "I came to respectfully ask if it would be too much of a problem for Hennie and Lottie to be gone for a few days, perhaps as long as a week. You were so kind to give them work, and I don't want their absence to cause a problem for you, but . . ."

"What are you scheming?" Lester asked with a wink and a grin. "I see a sparkle in your eyes I've not seen before, and you've come here something regular for a long time."

Jack chuckled and glanced down for a moment, slightly embarrassed to think his joy might show so clearly. "Well," he said, "I've asked Hennie to marry me, and she's said yes."

"Well, isn't that just the brandy on the pudding!" Lester exclaimed with a jolly laugh. "I'm happy for the both of you!"

"Thank you," Jack said. "The thing is . . . given a number of complications, we've decided to elope and avoid any attention from the community. I'd like to leave as soon as we can make arrangements, and of course Lottie needs to come with us. Hennie can't get married without her best friend there. My only concern is leaving you without the help you need."

"Well, you needn't be worrying about that," Lester said, "because I've turned down two women looking for work just in the last few days. I hired another who came, since her situation is so dire I couldn't turn her away, but taking her on would mean having Hennie and Lottie work fewer hours. I know where to find the other women I turned away; we can manage just fine. Although, I'm not sure how many hours I can give them when they come back, or—"

"Truthfully, Lester, I would prefer to support both of them—especially since Hennie will be my wife. I have enough income to keep us all fed, probably because I haven't spent money on much of anything for years." He chuckled, and Lester winked at him again, since he was the kind of man who understood that spending money that didn't need to be spent was simply a waste. "They keep my house cleaner than it's ever been, and they certainly cook better than I do. They want to work to maintain their self-respect, and I understand that."

"As do I," Lester said.

"But perhaps when we return we could arrange something where they can work just enough to feel good about the situation; maybe they can fill in when you need them. We'll talk about it."

"A good plan, indeed," Lester said and shook Jack's hand firmly.

They chatted a few more minutes before Jack left the pub, amazed and grateful for the way everything was coming together. He arrived back at the house just as Hennie and Lottie were finishing their breakfast.

"Hello," he said, coming in the door.

The moment he appeared, Lottie jumped to her feet and wrapped her arms around his neck, giving him a loud smooch on the cheek.

"What was that for?" Jack laughed.

"It's about time, you old scoundrel," she said with a little laugh. She sat back down as quickly as she'd stood up. "Hennie told me everything, and I couldn't be happier." She stuck a forkful of fried potatoes into her mouth and smiled at him before she started chewing.

Hennie stood up and wrapped her arms around him as they exchanged a quick kiss. "Good morning, my love," she said.

"Good morning," he replied and gave her another quick kiss before he reluctantly let her go. She sat back down after she took a plate out of the oven for Jack and set it on the table.

While he was washing his hands before eating, Hennie asked, "So, where have you been so early?"

"I met George and told him our plans, then I went to speak with Lester, since I don't want to cause any problems for him when he's been so generous." Jack sat down and added, "Hmm. Smells good. I'm famished."

"How did it go?" Hennie asked while both women looked at him, their expressions showing concern; he knew they too didn't want to leave Lester in a bind, but this marriage couldn't happen without their leaving for several days.

While slowly savoring his breakfast of fried potatoes, eggs, and crisp sausages, Jack repeated the gist of his conversations with both George and Lester. The women were pleased with the outcome, and they began making more specific plans about when to leave and how best to go about making the journey to Scotland.

With a plan in place—including arrangements to hire a coach that would drive them to a larger city where they could get passage on another coach that would take them to Scotland—Jack wrote a discreet note to his brother, with no names or any other information that could identify either one of them, and he went to the Hawk's Nest, where he sat at a particular table and tucked the folded note between the cracks in the wood beneath the table, knowing that George would come to the pub later in the day, sit in the same chair—even if he had to wait for it to be vacant—and discreetly take the note. As long as that information got into George's hands, he would be ready to meet them in the next village, where he could leave his horse at a livery and join them on their journey without anyone who knew them observing the fact that they were traveling together.

Having done everything he could do for the moment, Jack returned to the smithy and was able to meet a scheduled appointment with a farmer who needed new shoes for his horse, and for the hooves to be properly trimmed. While Jack worked, he felt as excited as a child to think of running away with Hennie to get married—and having his brother and Lottie along made it feel even more adventurous and enjoyable. He could hardly believe this was happening. There was no way to predict what might happen once they returned, but he knew beyond any doubt this was the right step to take *now*, and he could only pray that the next step would present itself once he and Hennie were married.

While Hennie helped Lottie clean up the kitchen after breakfast, she felt a bubbling sensation inside of her, as if a tea kettle filled with perfect happiness and peace was coming to a boil, and bubbles of excitement and joy were beginning to rumble inside of her every time she thought of the reality that she and Jack would be married—and they would be leaving for Scotland very soon. And since she could hardly keep herself from thinking about it constantly, she felt as if she might burst with the growing and rising of those happy bubbles. She kept laughing for no apparent reason, and Lottie would just laugh with her—rather than questioning the reason for it; she already knew Hennie well enough to understand perfectly.

With Jack's house and their own apartment in order, they went together to the pub to work during the lunchtime rush. During a moment when all the customers were satisfied, Lester pulled them both aside to congratulate Hennie and to wish them both a safe and pleasant journey. He reiterated the arrangement he and Jack had discussed, wanting to make certain it all met with their approval—which it did. But Hennie still appreciated Lester not assuming that he and Jack could make decisions on behalf of Hennie and Lottie without their knowledge.

After the lunch crowd had filtered away and the dining room was cleaned and put in order, Hennie and Lottie left the pub, knowing they wouldn't return to work until after coming home from Scotland—and Jack and Hennie would be married. They stepped outside into a light drizzle of rain, but it wasn't enough to be unpleasant. They just pulled the hoods of their cloaks up over their heads and walked home while they discussed the changes taking place in their lives. Hennie was pleased with Lottie's support, and how she was nothing but happy for Hennie, even though it meant obvious changes in their friendship. There was no reason they wouldn't always be close, but they both knew marriage meant putting a spouse first and foremost in one's life, which would inevitably be an adjustment for Lottie. But her relationship with Zeke was going well and showing promise, and they both hoped it wouldn't be long before Lottie herself would get married, and their lives could move forward on parallel paths.

"Do you think we'll end up living at the manor?" Lottie asked when they were almost home.

Hennie sighed, slowing her steps. "It seems a likely possibility," she said. "Which means we won't be working at the pub anymore, and our going back there—as women . . ." she chuckled more with irony than humor, "and as family rather than servants . . ." She couldn't finish that sentence when the words required to articulate her thoughts just wouldn't come.

"You'll be family," Lottie said. "I'll still be a servant. I'm not complaining; I don't mind, really. To have the job of taking care of *you* is the best thing I can imagine. We could grow old together and still be friends."

"I agree with the last part, but I really don't want you *taking care of me*. We take care of each other."

"But you will be the wife of Jack Hannaford," Lottie said, "and I need to have a respectable place in the household; I can't just live there simply as a privilege of being your friend. I need to stay busy and have a purpose. You will be helping your husband with his work in running the estate, and I will help take care of you—which means we will be able to spend time together every day."

"That makes sense," Hennie said, even though the idea of Lottie *working* to see to her needs felt uncomfortable. But she believed they would adjust, and they could shape their responsibilities and attitudes any way they chose. That would be one of the great advantages of being married to Jack Hannaford. "It's still going to take some time to get used to; that's for certain."

"I can't argue with that," Lottie said and sighed.

"One advantage is that you'll be working in the same household as Zeke," Hennie said with a delighted laugh. "How convenient is that!"

Lottie laughed too. "You think I hadn't thought of that?"

They were laughing when they walked into the smithy, which had the front flaps rolled up to expose the shop to the pleasant autumn air, which was made even more pleasant by the light sprinkle of rain.

"And what are you ladies finding so humorous?" Jack asked, pausing his work to look at them with a warm smile as they pushed their hoods off their heads.

"Just happy," Hennie declared, which clearly pleased Jack. She could see in his countenance that he was happy as well.

"I'm happy too," Lottie said.

"I'm very glad to hear it," he said, and Hennie stepped toward him to give him a quick kiss before he got back to work.

By the end of the day, all the arrangements had been made for their trip to Scotland. While Jack worked through the afternoon, Hennie and Lottie did some shopping, glad to find a ready-made dress for each of them that would be appropriate for an elopement. And they also picked up a few other things they needed to make the wedding as special and memorable as it could be under the circumstances.

Hennie could hardly sleep that night, overcome as she was with the prospect of marrying Jack and being able to share her life with him. She managed to get a few hours of sleep, but not nearly enough, and hoped she would be able to sleep in the carriage so she wouldn't end up facing her wedding day with circles under her eyes due to not getting enough rest.

Hennie got up early since she was wide awake and managed to get ready without disturbing Lottie, who was still sleeping in her own room. She went down the stairs and slipped quietly through the back door of Jack's house with the intention of getting an early start on fixing breakfast, since they'd agreed they needed a hearty meal before they were due to start out later this morning. She expected to find the kitchen empty and quiet, but she entered to the pleasant aroma of salt pork sizzling on the stove, and Jack standing watch over it, holding a spatula as if it were some kind of weapon.

"Good morning," she said and closed the door behind her, suddenly breathless from just seeing him and knowing she would soon be his wife.

"Good morning," he said, smiling with obvious pleasure at seeing her there.

"You're up early," she added, leaning against the door to catch her breath.

"As are you," he stated. "I couldn't sleep. You?"

"The same," she said, then it fully dawned on her that he looked different. He'd trimmed his beard closer to his face than she'd seen since they'd come back into each other's lives. Knowing he considered the beard a method for keeping his face less easily recognized, she wondered if trimming it was a way of getting closer to the point when he could reveal his true identity. She hoped so, if only for the sake of his own happiness and peace. Whatever his reasons, she couldn't deny how handsome he looked, which made her stomach flutter, and that made it more difficult to catch her breath.

"What?" he asked, looking at her closely as it became evident she was somehow stuck to the door and could do nothing but stare at him.

"You just . . . look so handsome. I can almost see your face now."

Jack chuckled and used the spatula to adjust the pork in the pan. "Well, I'm getting married. I prefer to look somewhat like a gentleman for such an important occasion. And hopefully it won't make it possible for anyone to see the real me—at least for now."

"God willing, pretending to be someone else won't last much longer," Hennie said, now able to breathe more normally—at least enough to cross the room and wrap her arms around him while he continued watching over the contents of the pan on the stove.

"God willing," he said and put his free arm around her, pressing a kiss into her hair. "I love you, Hennie."

She laughed softly and tightened her embrace. "I love you too."

"I just don't want you to forget," he said, and she looked up at him. "Since making the decision to move forward and marry you, I have been happier than . . . well, ever. I've never been this happy."

"Nor have I," she said. "Well . . . perhaps when you and I were children and we had those rare times we were able to sneak away and create our little fantasy worlds and make up stories together."

"Yes," he said with a smile. "That would be close, but this is much better." He bent down to kiss her, then chuckled and said, "Yes, this is much, much better."

⊸⧫⊸

The journey to Scotland went smoothly, albeit long and somewhat tedious. But Hennie slept a great deal, making her realize how all that had been happening in her life had been making it difficult to sleep, and now she felt more relaxed, knowing that she and Jack would always be together.

Both Jack and Hennie found it amusing—if not ironic—how comfortable George and Lottie had become with each other. Lottie even confessed to George about her blossoming romance with Zeke, who worked in his stables, and George heartily declared that he hoped it would work out. He very much liked the idea of the two of them remaining at Ivy Manor for the rest of their lives, especially since he knew Zeke to be a good man as well as a good employee. They were all surprised, however, when the conversation shifted, and George admitted to all of them that he was very much in love with a woman named Clara, whom he hoped to marry. He didn't consider her being a kitchen maid any problem whatsoever, but Clara was stubbornly against the marriage—even though she loved him, and he knew it. It was George's hope to convince Clara that she was perfectly capable of being the lady of the manor, and he seemed somewhat encouraged when Jack pointed out that with him being married to Hennie—the daughter of a maid—perhaps Clara would be more easily convinced that the Hannaford family cared nothing for ridiculous social chasms.

They arrived in Scotland weary from their traveling, but after a good night's sleep, they were all perfectly refreshed for the wedding, and everything fell so smoothly into place that it only heightened Hennie's belief that this was all meant to be—and Jack agreed with her wholeheartedly. Becoming Mrs. Jack Hannaford was by far the greatest thing that had ever happened to her.

⊸⧫⊸

After returning from Scotland, it took only a few days for everyone to settle comfortably within the walls of the smithy and its adjoining house and apartment. Hennie now shared Jack's home as his wife, and Lottie was living comfortably upstairs. The three of them still shared their meals together, and Jack was kind and forthright in letting Lottie know that her presence in their home was a joy to them, and she should never feel unwelcome or out of place. He commented more than once that to him it felt as if Lottie were Hennie's sister, and it felt completely natural to have her as a part of their lives. Hennie deeply appreciated the comfortable, sibling-like relationship that had developed between Jack and Lottie; she wondered how she ever would have managed if her husband and her best friend were at odds with each other in any way. As it was, she felt grateful and remarkably content being Jack's wife and still having Lottie around—very much like a sister, as Jack had observed.

Before they'd returned from Scotland, Jack and George had agreed that Jack would remain living as a blacksmith until they could visit with the solicitor, who was looking more carefully into the will to make certain that Jack's marriage would not create any unexpected problems. Once they had the opportunity to speak with him, Hennie knew it was possible they could all be moving into the manor where all secrets would be made known. More than anything she wanted Jack to be happy and at peace with himself; a part of her knew he would be most content living under the same roof as his brother and sharing the responsibilities of the estate with him, but she knew that another part of him secretly longed for life to just continue as it was. She loved Jack with all her heart, no matter by which name he was called.

Once word had gotten out that the blacksmith had eloped to Scotland and had now returned with his new bride—who was one of the women reputed to have worked as a man at Ivy Manor—many people in the village stopped by to offer congratulations and even to bring gifts. Hennie felt increasingly at home and comfortable being the blacksmith's wife, and she couldn't imagine being any happier than this. Just being able to spend her nights close to Jack, and never having to go their separate ways at bedtime, filled her with a safety and security she'd never known. Being a wife and sharing such a deep and complete relationship with her husband was absolutely the best thing that had ever happened to her. As Lottie continued to spend a great deal of time with Zeke, Hennie wished for them the same kind of happiness.

Hennie and Lottie worked an occasional shift at the pub—just enough to consider themselves employed, and to earn a little bit of money that was their own. Having a great deal of free time, they worked together to keep the apartment and the house perfectly clean and organized, and they spent more time cooking, which made it possible to try a variety of new recipes and to eat much nicer meals. Jack always complimented their efforts—even when some of their experiments didn't turn out very well. But that always gave them something to laugh about. And Jack always helped clean the dishes at the end of the day; he adamantly insisted, even though he'd worked hard hours in the smithy. Hennie came to enjoy the way she and Jack shared the dishwashing routine along with quiet conversation. As if Lottie had noticed the tenderness taking place between the new husband and wife, she had begun to excuse herself and tell them good night as soon as she'd cleaned off the table and put away any leftover food where it would stay cool and could be reheated for tomorrow's lunch. In Lottie's absence, the washing and rinsing of dishes became mingled with a great deal of kissing, and sometimes embracing each other with wet hands, which would cause laughter to erupt between them. During such moments, Hennie often thought that such a simple occurrence as washing dishes together would never happen if they lived at the manor, but at the same time she knew Jack's greatest desire was to return there—and she couldn't blame him. She simply had to believe that everything would work out the way it was meant to, and she did her best to put the matter in God's hands and simply enjoy the life she was living now with all its joy and humble beauty.

Jack had made a daily habit of taking a break from his work to go to the Hawk's Nest during a slow time of day, so he could sit at the same table each time, knowing that George would go to the same pub at a different time of day and always sit in the same place. It had now become their practice that if they had anything to communicate to each other, they would leave a note underneath the table between a place where two slats of wood came together, and no one would ever find it unless they turned the table upside down and were looking for it. Most of the time, the notes Jack received consisted of simple comments such as: *All is well.* Or: *No news yet.* Hennie noted that Jack was surprisingly patient when he had always been somewhat restless over the fact that he was living in disguise. He admitted that being married to her had made his life much more comfortable, and he had come to believe he could be happy anywhere as long as they were together. Hennie deeply appreciated knowing he felt that way, even though she couldn't shake the feeling that when all was said and done, they would end up back at Ivy Manor, and she would be required to make huge adjustments in the way she lived her life.

Nearly two weeks after their return from Scotland, Jack returned from the pub with a note from George that had put him on edge. He came straight to the kitchen with it, where Hennie was scrubbing some carrots, staying close to the warm stove since there was a chill in the autumn rain outside that seemed to announce winter was on its way.

"What's wrong?" she asked, setting her task aside and wiping her hands on her apron.

"Where's Lottie?" he asked.

"She went to the bakery and the butcher," Hennie reported.

"Good," he said. "I need to talk to you alone."

"What is it?" Hennie asked, sitting down, not certain if his distress was due to something having gone wrong, or if he was simply nervous over the uncertainty of their future.

Jack sat across the table and slid the note over to Hennie. She opened it and read: *Solicitor has new information. We need to speak to him together. Bringing him to you after supper.* Hennie read it through twice, knowing the time and place of the meeting were kept cryptic on the chance that if anyone else *did* see the note, they would have no idea when or where some secretive meeting was taking place. George knew how to discreetly come to the back door of the house without being seen, and he knew approximately when they were generally finished with supper.

Hoping some conversation would calm her own pounding heart, Hennie asked her husband, "Do you think this is good news or otherwise?"

"I have no idea," Jack said and stood to pace the narrow width of the room.

"Which explains why you're so nervous," Hennie observed.

"Does this not make *you* nervous?" he asked, tossing her a severe gaze that didn't break the rhythm of his pacing.

"I admit that it does," she said and ventured to expound on her feelings. "I know how important this is, Jack; I really do. And you know I'll stand by you no matter what. But I must confess that . . . I like the way our life is now, and changing it . . . frightens me." She couldn't help the tremor in her voice as she added, "I don't want anything between us to change."

Jack proved his selflessness and sensitivity to his wife when he immediately sat back down and took both her hands across the table, looking into her eyes. *"Nothing* is going to change what you and I share," he insisted. "Nothing! I promise you. And I will not make any decision without consulting you."

"I know," she said and would have wiped the tears that leaked down her face except that he was holding both her hands and she didn't want to let go. She laughed softly, hoping to ease the tension. "Does that mean we can wash dishes together at the manor?"

He laughed and lifted her hands to his lips, kissing them both. *"If* we go back to the manor, I will absolutely order the maids to leave the dishes to us anytime we wish to do the task ourselves."

"In that case," she said and sniffled, "everything will be all right."

"Yes," he said with a smile, as if the issue of washing dishes was the most crucial matter at hand. Seeming more relaxed over the prospect of George and the solicitor coming later this evening, he added, "Everything *will* be all right. I have *you* in my life, Hennie, which is tangible proof to me—every day—that God is mindful of us, He loves us, and He will guide us in the right direction." He kissed her hands again. "Yes, everything will be all right."

Hennie smiled at him, wanting to believe him but not willing to admit that a part of her feared the inevitable changes in their future. Being *all right* was relative. She wasn't worried about her and Lottie ever going hungry again or having to submit themselves to any kind of degrading work just to survive. Jack would always take care of them, and he would always respect the friendship she shared with Lottie. She wasn't worried about her relationship with Jack in any way; blacksmith or Lord of the manor, he was a man without pretentiousness or arrogance. He would always love her, and she felt confident the tenderness they now shared would always be there. Beyond that, she had no idea what to expect, and for reasons she couldn't quite discern, some part of her felt terrified to return to Ivy Manor and to live in that house. But she kept those thoughts to herself, wanting to be supportive of her husband. Surely everything *would* be all right. She simply had to keep reminding herself of that.

Chapter Fifteen

EDICT OF THE EVIL KING

WITH LOTTIE'S HELP, HENNIE HAD supper ready a little earlier than usual. Jack had agreed that since the actual time George and the solicitor might arrive was vague, it would be better to eat early and get the kitchen cleaned up, since it was the only place they could all reasonably sit to visit. While they were eating their meal in unusual silence, Lottie had barely hinted that it might be better for her to be absent for this meeting before Jack was quick to say, "All of this involves you, Lottie, and we have no secrets. I'd prefer that you stay, if only so Hennie doesn't have to try and repeat everything that was said."

"I prefer that as well," Hennie said, giving Jack a wan smile, which she hoped expressed her appreciation for his sensitivity.

The decision to eat early proved a good one when a light knocking on the door occurred just as Hennie wiped dry the last plate and set it into the cupboard. Jack opened the door while Hennie and Lottie stood with their shoulders touching, as if they might be able to help hold each other up considering the nervousness they were both feeling. Or more accurately, Hennie believed Lottie was trying to be supportive. She'd admitted to not really caring if they stayed here or moved into the manor or left this place altogether. As long as she and Hennie could remain friends, and she could have Zeke with her, she would be fine. And Zeke had made it clear to Lottie that he could find work anywhere if they came to the decision to marry. Even though he knew nothing of the complications involved with Hennie's marriage to the blacksmith, Lottie had told Zeke her friends had considered moving away, and Zeke was completely supportive of not wanting Lottie and Hennie to be separated. But there was an unexplainable anxiousness in Hennie over the whole matter, and Lottie was sensitive to it—even if she didn't understand it. But then, Hennie didn't really understand it either. She only knew she desperately preferred to never go back to Ivy Manor. For some reason,

living there as a man and working in the stables had been fine, but the thought
of being a part of the Hannaford family and residing there in such an official
capacity had created a growing anxiety that frequently tightened her chest and
made her stomach smolder.

Hennie suppressed her anxiety and consciously willed herself to simply hear
what George and the solicitor had to say, and to trust that Jack would never
make any decision regarding this situation without discussing it with her. Feeling
somewhat as if she were dreaming, Hennie observed Jack inviting the men into
the house. She responded with a forced smile and a nod when he introduced
her and Lottie to the solicitor. Mr. Cunningham was much shorter than Jack
and George, thin and wiry with brown hair that seemed to have protested any
attention from a comb. But kindness was evident in his eyes, and Hennie didn't
feel uncomfortable in his presence; it was the topic they were meant to discuss
that unnerved her. Once introductions were complete, they all sat around the
little table that felt much smaller with a fifth person present, sitting on an extra
chair that Jack had brought in from the bedroom.

"We'll get straight to the point," George said, and Hennie was shocked out
of her dreamlike state when she noted the gravity of his countenance. Something
was wrong. Her heart quickened, and she instinctively reached for Jack's hand;
the way he squeezed it let her know he sensed it too. "The news is not necessarily
good."

"But it's not all bad," Mr. Cunningham hurried to say. "It simply will require
more . . . patience on your part."

"What do you mean?" Jack asked, not hiding his concern.

George leaned back and folded his arms, letting out a loud sigh of disgust.
"You tell them," he said, nodding at the solicitor. "I don't think I can bring myself
to even utter any more details of how that man continues to torment our lives."

"Which man?" Jack asked his brother. "Our father? Or Tewksbury?"

"Both, actually," George said, his voice sad but his eyes flaring with anger,
both of which provoked an uncomfortable tightening of Hennie's stomach, and
she felt Lottie take her other hand beneath the table, squeezing it hard in silent
support.

Jack looked at Mr. Cunningham and said, "You were going to get straight
to the point."

"Ah, yes," Cunningham replied. "The heart of the matter is that after studying
the will extensively—over and over—I realized that its language is somewhat
ambiguous, which means that it's as if it was purposely written in a way that left
it open to interpretation or personal opinion."

"Which means what, exactly?" Jack asked, sounding as impatient as Hennie felt.

"Which means that if it were taken before a judge, for instance, any decision a judge might make could be solely based on his own interpretation of what the will states; it's filled with implications while very little is stated clearly—with the exception of your inheritance." He nodded at Jack. "It relies completely on the condition of your marrying Miss Tewksbury." Cunningham sighed in a way that indicated he was about to delve into bad news. "Given the ambiguous nature of the will, I took the liberty of showing the will to a judge I'm well acquainted with and asked him to give me his opinion on what problems might arise if the heir were to marry someone else. More specifically, I asked if that would make the will void once the heir had relinquished the inheritance."

"And?" Jack asked. The somber expression on George's face seemed to be making his brother more agitated.

"He said it was impossible to predict exactly what Tewksbury might do, because the wording of the will leaves it open to a number of possible interpretations." Cunningham leaned his forearms on the table and looked directly at Jack, then Hennie, then Jack again. "After gathering all the information I possibly could without actually speaking with the solicitor who represents Tewksbury—a Mr. Hobbs, the man who once represented your father and is also the man who constructed this despicable document—my greatest concern is that if Tewksbury learns you are married, he will legally demand an annulment—possibly because he could argue that the marriage was an act of fraud—and as horrible and ridiculous as that sounds, he might actually convince a judge it's the right course. Given the fact that we're never sure which judge a case might come before, there's no way of knowing which way the pendulum might swing."

"Wait a minute," Jack said, letting go of Hennie's hand to lean his forearms on the table too, as if looking Cunningham more closely in the eye might help him understand. "Are you telling me that a judge could declare our marriage null, and order it *undone* simply because the will states I'm supposed to marry that . . . that . . ."

"Don't say it," George ordered, as if he knew the possible unfavorable terms that might be floating around in Jack's mind, and it would not be seemly to speak any one of them—especially in the presence of ladies.

"Yes, that's what I'm telling you," Cunningham said gravely.

"But . . ." Jack stammered, while Hennie felt decidedly ill, "how can a marriage be *ordered* undone? How can that be right in *any* respect? Legally? Religiously? *Ethically and morally?* We are husband and wife, which I will be blunt enough to say means we share an intimate relationship. How can that be undone? Declared null and invalid as if it had never happened?"

Hennie squeezed Lottie's hand more tightly as the meaning of all this settled in more fully. Initially she hadn't known what an annulment meant exactly, but Jack had made its meaning explicitly clear, and she could hardly believe what she was hearing. She felt every bit as horrified as Jack sounded.

"It's deplorable, in my opinion," Cunningham said. "I cannot say for certain that Tewksbury would even think to pursue such a thing, but I know his solicitor well; Hobbs is a shrewd man, and Tewksbury pays him handsomely. He's like a bloodhound, always sniffing out any legal way to serve his employer's best interests; and might I say that in this business, I have seen many things that might be legal, but that doesn't necessarily make them ethical. So, I am here to advise you to continue to keep your identity hidden until some more time passes. Being married longer makes the possibility of an annulment much less likely. And if you will forgive me . . ." He cleared his throat. "I don't wish to sound presumptuous or intrusive, but I know you want my complete honesty and best opinions on how to protect the both of you and your marriage."

"We do," Jack said, once again taking Hennie's hand. "Speak candidly . . . please," he said, almost as if it were an order. When he talked like that, it was easier for Hennie to imagine him as the Lord of the manor.

"Once there is a child . . . or even the imminent arrival of a child . . . the possibility of the marriage being declared null and void is practically impossible. In that situation I could confidently defend your case before any judge and know that the marriage would be declared valid—no matter *how* angry Tewksbury might be."

After Cunningham finished doling out the necessary but despicable information, Hennie could actually *hear* Jack breathing, as if each breath were laced with fury. He looked at Hennie with a deep apology showing in his eyes, which contradicted his angry countenance. "I'm so sorry about all of this," he said. "If I'd known . . ."

"If you'd known, then what?" Hennie countered as if no one else was in the room. "If your knowing this might have prevented our marriage, then I am entirely glad you did *not* know because I have no regrets. Our life here together is not so bad." As she said it, she felt a deep relief that she didn't want to admit to Jack; she felt anything but pleased with the idea of living at the manor, and this would delay their doing so for a long while—and perhaps they would never be able to return. While she understood Jack's desire to do so, she couldn't deny her own relief at having more time to come to terms with the possibility. "No one knows who you are except for those of us in this room, and we'll keep it that way. We're safe here, and the estate is safe in George's hands. We'll follow Mr. Cunningham's advice and let some time pass."

"And what if time passing does not produce a child?" he asked, still talking as if no one else was present. But Hennie didn't mind. They were all discussing openly some very personal matters that applied to the situation, and feeling embarrassed at doing so would accomplish nothing. She far preferred being open and honest, however delicate the topic might be. "Some people wait months or even years for pregnancy to occur," Jack went on. "Some people are never able to have children. I can't begin to tell you how much I hate all of this possibly resting on whether you and I are able to have a child—and when that might happen. It's despicable to have such personal matters tangled into legal loopholes."

"It *is* despicable," Hennie agreed, "but it is the way of it, and I refuse to let it interfere with our happiness. We have people here who care for us and will help see that we are protected, and our best interests served. We simply need to give the matter some time. So calm down and consider that we should be grateful for Mr. Cunningham's insight and advice—which will help us avoid possible problems—rather than being angry over a situation we cannot control."

Jack took a very loud, very deep breath. Then another. "You're right," he said to Hennie and leaned over to kiss her brow. "You are the wisest and most insightful of the two of us, for certain."

"Amen to that," George said with a lightness that made it evident he was trying to ease the tension of such a difficult conversation.

"Forgive my anger," Jack said, briefly glancing at everyone present before he focused on Mr. Cunningham directly. "Thank you for your efforts, and for being so candid in a way that *will* help keep us protected."

"I wish the news were not so grim," Cunningham said with compassion. "I will do my best to remain aware of anything that Tewksbury might be up to and keep you informed; or rather, I will keep George informed, since I meet with him regularly regarding many matters relating to the estate, and our appointments will not arouse any suspicion. If there is anything noteworthy, he will let you know."

"Of course," Jack said. "Thank you."

The solicitor came to his feet, and the other men did the same, but Hennie felt too weak to stand and was glad that Lottie remained sitting beside her. They exchanged a long stare that had begun back in the orphanage as a silent means of declaring to each other that they had much to talk about, but it would have to wait until they had privacy and wouldn't be overheard. They had been children then, sharing their secret hopes and fears, words that would not be tolerated if spoken aloud in such a strict and terrible place. Now they were grown women, still sharing secret hopes and fears even while they were embarking on new lives that included the men they'd grown to love.

Hennie didn't realize Mr. Cunningham had left until she heard the door close. She looked up to see George and Jack standing close together, facing each other, talking quietly enough that they couldn't be overheard. But it wasn't difficult for Hennie to guess the gist of their conversation. They were both frustrated and discouraged—even disgusted—by the need to continue keeping secrets while they could only hope and pray that the passing of time would allow Jack and Hennie to come out of hiding.

When they'd stopped talking and were both just standing there, looking as if the world might come to a disastrous end at any moment, Hennie said to them, "It will be all right. It's not what we'd hoped for or expected, but we've been managing fine and we will continue to do so." She came to her feet. "However, standing there looking so glum isn't going to change anything." Opening a cupboard door to remove a tin painted with a bright floral design, she added, "I think the cake Lottie brought home from the bakery this afternoon might be helpful." She set the tin on the table. "I wish I could say that one of us had baked it, but the truth is that neither of us ever learned any baking skills, and if we want to truly enjoy any baked delicacies, we need to rely on the experts."

Opening the tin let loose the aroma of the Madeira cake inside. "Oh, that smells heavenly," Jack said, taking a seat, which inspired George to do the same. While Lottie retrieved a bottle of port and some glasses, Lottie got plates and forks and a knife with which to cut the cake. Jack said mostly to George, "When I thought Hennie was a man and she'd go and get lunch for us to share while we chatted, she sometimes brought me a slice of Madeira cake."

"That's a tale to tell your grandchildren," George said with a smile that made it evident the tension left in the wake of Mr. Cunningham's visit had dissipated.

Jack smiled at Hennie as she was seated. "I suppose Madeira cake will always remind me of that time."

"And me," Hennie said.

"Why do you think I chose it?" Lottie asked, serving up portions onto the plates while Hennie poured the wine. "I know those stories too."

"Of course you do," Jack said, and they proceeded to enjoy their wine and dessert with no mention whatsoever of Mr. Cunningham's visit or the continual oppression in their lives that had been left behind by the late Mr. Hannaford. His cruelty and control of his son's life—even from beyond the grave—were pathetic and abhorrent. But Hennie watched her husband and his brother laughing together over something trivial, and she felt a deep hope that they would find their way past all of this, that their father would not dictate the outcome of their lives—no matter how much he may have wanted to.

⁂

After George left and Lottie had gone upstairs to her apartment for the night, Hennie got ready for bed, then sat with the covers over her lap, leaning back against the headboard, waiting for Jack to change into a nightshirt and clean his teeth. She mentally tallied the situation they had discussed with Mr. Cunningham while she wondered why it seemed to be pushing open some kind of heavy, reluctant door in a far corner of her mind. She didn't know what was behind the door—and in fact she hadn't consciously even thought about the fact that there were likely many hidden memories locked away behind such a door—but it frightened her. For reasons she didn't understand, she had no desire to discuss it with Jack, but she doubted it was wise to keep something like this from her husband. Still, it was difficult to know what to say when she hardly knew what it meant.

"Are you all right?" Jack asked, startling her as he climbed into bed beside her and snuggled up close to her, putting his arm around her and urging her head to his shoulder in a way that had become typical as they spent this time before falling asleep recounting the day and sharing their thoughts and feelings. And today had been unexpectedly eventful. Mr. Cunningham's visit had not been lengthy, but it had certainly brought to light an entirely new perspective to their situation.

"Just . . . so much to think about," she replied.

"Indeed," he said and was silently thoughtful a long moment until he added, "Hennie, I want to have a family with you. I know you already know that; before we got married, we talked about having children. I can't imagine anything bringing us more joy than having a baby together."

"I agree with that, of course," she said, looking up at him without relinquishing her comfortable position.

"But . . ." he added with a tinge of frustration; she'd known there would be a *but* in what he was saying. "But . . . having all of that twisted into these demeaning legal matters just feels so very . . . crass and unsavory . . . and I don't like it at all."

"I don't like it either, Jack, but . . ." she drawled that last word with an emphasis that made him look directly at her, "it's up to us how we choose to handle the situation. These legalities are annoying, and I know how much you want to come out of hiding, to be yourself, to return home; I do know it, Jack, and I have compassion for that. But none of that changes the love we share, the fact that we *are* married—and we will *remain* married—even if that means having to leave the country. I will go where you go, Jack; I will always be with you. And we *will* have a family. If my becoming pregnant helps put these legal matters to rest, so be it, but we both know that's not the reason we want to have a baby, nor will it ever be. As long as we keep our relationship—our family—the most important thing, I believe it will all work out the way it's meant to. We must have faith . . . and hope; and we must always put each other first. That's how I see it."

Jack sighed and pressed a lengthy kiss to her brow. "You are so wise . . . so strong. What did I ever do without you?"

"I have no idea," she said lightly, and they both chuckled before he kissed her brow again.

They relaxed together in silence, even though a lamp was still burning, and they'd not yet told each other good night in a way that would conclude their conversation. Hennie's heart quickened as she considered telling Jack about the uncomfortable feelings she'd been contending with. Suddenly not wanting to carry the burden of those feelings alone any longer, she sat up abruptly so that she could turn and face him. He looked startled by her sudden movement and concerned as he picked up on the evidence that she had something important to say.

"I need to share something with you," she began, wondering why she heard a tremor in her own voice. Was it so difficult to express what had been going on in her mind?

"I'm listening," he said when she hesitated far too long.

"It's . . . difficult to put into words," she admitted. "It's . . . a feeling more than anything; but it's vague, almost impossible to define except to say that I feel . . . uncomfortable and perhaps even . . . afraid. It feels as if something is locked away in the back of my mind and it's trying to make itself known, but I can't quite get hold of it . . . and it's making me . . . uneasy, and . . ." she chuckled with no humor, "I don't know if I'm making any sense at all."

Jack sat up as well and took her hands into his, a gesture that already made her feel a little better. He wasn't dismissing what she'd just said, even though it made little sense. That alone meant a great deal to her.

"What are you saying, Hennie?" he asked, his brow furrowed, indicating that he sincerely wanted to understand.

"I don't *know* exactly what I'm trying to say," she told him. "I just feel . . ." She took a deep breath and decided to just tell him exactly what had triggered these thoughts and feelings initially, which was the very thing that kept urging them forward. "Jack, I can only say that the very thought of living at Ivy Manor makes me . . . afraid . . . uncomfortable." He looked both surprised and concerned—and disappointed. She hurried to state the obvious, "I know how much it means to you to go back there; it's your home. And I'm not saying I would refuse to go there with you—if it works out that way. I meant it when I told you that I will go where you go; I will stand by you no matter what. But . . . I need you to know that I'm having a difficult time with the very idea, and I don't understand why. I know that I will *never* understand why if I don't talk about it, and you're my husband, so we *need* to talk about it, even though I'm not even certain *what* to say—any more than what I've already said. I just feel . . ." she actually shuddered, "so uncomfortable."

"And afraid?" he asked gently. "You said the thought of it makes you afraid." She nodded, and he asked, "Why?"

"I don't *know* why," she blurted, wondering why she would feel *angry* over the question. "Forgive me," she said immediately and more softly. "I don't understand why simply discussing it makes me so . . . agitated. I suppose that's why I've put off talking about it."

"How long have you felt this way?" he asked.

"I'm not sure," she admitted. "The thoughts and feelings came on slowly; I suppose they coincided with our decision to marry and the possibility that I could end up living there."

"But you *have* lived there," he said. "As a child, and more recently as—"

"As a stable hand," she interrupted, again sounding abrupt and irritated, but relieved to note by Jack's expression that he understood she wasn't irritated with *him*. "I lived in the servants' quarters; and it was the same when I was a child. If we go back, it will be entirely different. I never went into the rooms in the house where the family resided and socialized; it wasn't allowed."

"Except there were times when we sneaked into the library or the conservatory," he reminded her, and she felt a little stunned by the memory.

"I'd forgotten," she said. "We *did* sneak in there to play occasionally . . . when we knew your father was away."

"Yes, we did," he said while Hennie's mind felt very busy trying to connect this new memory with whatever was trying to push its way past that barrier of her subconscious. Something else occurred to her, and she said, "I remember now that my mother would sometimes let me come with her while she was cleaning. It was a big job for her to thoroughly remove every speck of dust from the library, and she would let me read or draw while she worked, but I had to remain hidden behind one of the sofas so if anyone came in they wouldn't know I was there—because having me there was against the rules." Hennie was startled by a subtle but sudden smoldering in her stomach, and she abruptly put her hands there as if doing so would have a calming effect.

"What is it?" Jack asked.

"I don't know," Hennie admitted. "It's just . . . recalling that . . . thinking about that . . . makes me feel more afraid; more uncomfortable." She looked directly at her husband. "What is it, Jack, about being in that house? Why would it make me feel this way?"

"I don't know, darling," he said, pressing a hand to her face, "but we're going to figure it out. If we keep talking about it, perhaps you'll remember more. Perhaps something happened that upset you. I know I overheard many conversations my father had with visitors . . . and the servants . . . that made it clear the kind of person my father truly was. That was often *very* upsetting. I'm certain I've pushed away many of those memories because they're despicable. But it's just common sense that everything we've experienced is there in our mind somewhere, isn't it?"

"I would think so," Hennie said, suddenly having the sensation that her skin was on fire and she might die if she had to face whatever was hiding behind that door in her mind. With no warning, she jumped off the bed and began to pace, abruptly and sporadically, shaking her hands as if doing so would shake off the literal sensations in her body that seemed directly connected to the memories being dredged up from a place inside herself she hadn't even known existed.

"Hennie," Jack jumped out of bed as well, "what is it? What's wrong?"

"I don't know," she said and tried to explain what she was feeling, but it came out sounding mostly like nonsense, and she just ended up crying uncontrollably. At first, she didn't want him to touch her, but after standing there crying for several minutes, she found that his hands settling gently on her shoulders had a soothing effect. He very carefully moved his hands down her arms and back up again, with a light touch that implied he would respect the boundaries of her present unsettled state of mind—even if he didn't understand it. But she didn't understand it either.

Eventually she was able to calm down and she sank into his arms, allowing him to tuck her into bed. He doused the lamp and eased carefully into bed himself, asking her if it was all right for him to hold her. Comforted by his presence and the safety and security he represented, Hennie eased into his arms, where she became aware that she was trembling. But Jack just held her, whispering soothing words and stroking her hair until she finally relaxed while forcing herself to think only of pleasant memories. She'd done enough delving into secrets and lost memories for one day. She'd confided in Jack, and she felt some relief in knowing that she wasn't in this alone, even if talking to him about it had plummeted her deeper into her discomfort. But instinctively she knew she had to go deeper still; she would never find peace over what was troubling her until she uncovered these strangely suppressed memories and came to terms with them—whatever they might be.

Hennie asked Jack to tell her stories from their childhood, of building tiny castles and fortresses with smooth stones and lush leaves of ivy—imaginary places where battles of good and evil took place. But in those stories, Hennie had always felt safe and happy, and hearing Jack repeat those stories allowed her to relax—both mentally and physically—and she fell asleep to the mellow sound of her husband's voice.

It took only a few days for life to settle back into the normalcy of the days prior to Mr. Cunningham's visit. Jack, Hennie, and Lottie had spoken of the matter only enough to be mutually reassured that they were all fine with going forward as they were presently living and simply enjoy the blessings they found all around them. They were each determined to try and see the positive aspects of their lives, rather than focus on their frustrations, and they resolved that at each meal they would share at least one thing for which they were grateful. Doing so quickly proved effective in keeping their spirits up. Hennie was able to push away her discomfort and fear, even while she was resolved to remain open to facing any memories that might surface. Jack made her promise to talk to him about *anything* that might manifest itself regarding the matter, and she felt less afraid of the issue, knowing she was not alone.

Hennie also discussed the matter with Lottie over supper one evening while Jack was present, and she was nothing but compassionate as she also expressed her support in helping Hennie come to terms with whatever was making her afraid of the very idea of living at the manor. Lottie shared some difficult memories of *her* early childhood, things that she barely recalled, given how young she'd been before ending up in the orphanage, but disturbing enough to have created some deep unrest within herself. She'd shared some of this with Hennie previously, but Hennie hadn't realized until now just how much these memories had troubled Lottie. Now, however, she had empathy for such feelings, and it felt good to be able talk openly—among the three of them—about difficulties from their early years. While the three of them had little in common regarding the actual circumstances in which their childhoods were rooted, the emotional impact of their distressing memories was very much the same. Hennie was both surprised and pleased at how much Jack was willing to talk in Lottie's presence about the difficulties of his own childhood, and Hennie heard stories she'd never heard before of how his father's ill treatment had been far worse than she'd ever imagined. For all Jack's wealth and privilege, his childhood was littered with the abuse his father had regularly doled out, and the three of them found common ground regarding the emotional impact of having survived the harshness of life.

As winter settled in abruptly—severe and bitterly cold—Hennie appreciated the warmth and security of her home and the life she was sharing with Jack. Being happily married, coupled with having her best friend as an integral part of her life, felt so idyllic that she often wondered if it was just too good to be true. Lottie had a perfect sense of maintaining the balance between being a part of the family and allowing Jack and Hennie sufficient time to themselves to properly become accustomed to married life.

Zeke was coming around more and more, and it wasn't at all a surprise when he proposed to Lottie on Christmas Day, and she eagerly accepted. As the new year began, Hennie loved every opportunity to help Lottie plan her wedding. It would consist of a simple ceremony at the nearby chapel where they attended church on Sundays, with a celebration afterward including only a small number of close friends. George had offered on one of his rare, discreet visits to have the celebration at the manor—since Zeke lived and worked there. But it immediately became evident that Jack couldn't possibly attend, given the fact that many people who worked at the manor might likely recognize him if they saw him up close. It was during this same conversation that Zeke was finally told the truth about Jack's identity. They'd all known it was necessary, with Zeke becoming a part of the family, so to speak. And they'd all known for months now that Zeke was completely trustworthy, and he would never betray Lottie or the people she cared for most. He was surprised at the revelation but declared he would just put that knowledge aside and continue to see Jack as Ollie the blacksmith and treat him accordingly. Given the fact that Zeke wanted Ollie to stand up with him as his best man, and that the few people he worked with who would be invited to the ceremony weren't likely to recognize Jack for who he really was, they decided that the wedding celebration would be held at Lester's pub. Since the wedding would be on a Sunday and the pub would be closed to the public anyway, it could be decorated with ribbons and flowers and candles, and they could share wedding cake, a lovely meal, and even some dancing by simply moving the chairs and tables around. Lester was thrilled to be involved, since he'd grown very fond of Hennie and Lottie, even with the minimal hours they worked for him each week.

Jack told Hennie and Lottie he was concerned that there *would* be a couple of stable hands in attendance at the wedding who had known him very well before he'd gone into hiding. But Hennie assured him that with his beard having grown thick again, and by simply behaving with confidence as a common blacksmith, people weren't likely to pay attention to the resemblance because they wouldn't be looking for it.

"And," Hennie said, "if someone *does* recognize you . . . and says something to you . . . or George . . . you'll just have to ask them to be respectful enough to keep your secret. Do you not think these people would know you well enough to want to help you?"

"Actually, yes," Jack said. "I've never wanted to put anyone in a compromising position, but I can't deny that some of the men Zeke considers his friends are men with whom I once shared a great mutual respect." He chuckled. "I miss the days when I could go to the stables and just chat with the men who worked there as I came and went."

"Then perhaps being recognized might not be such a bad thing; at least it's nothing for you to be afraid of. And if you're not afraid of it, you can relax and enjoy the day."

"I think I will," Jack declared, and Hennie could feel evidence of a gradual evolution that seemed to be leading them to his likely return to Ivy Manor, with all secrets done away. As always, the joy she felt on his behalf came with equal amounts of fear and discomfort—for reasons she still did not understand. But she knew that whatever happened, she and Jack would be together, and they would help each other through any adjustment, whatever it might take.

❦

Lottie and Zeke's wedding day turned out beautifully. The spring weather was perfect, and all their plans came together without a hitch. And no one recognized any resemblance between Ollie the blacksmith and the missing heir of Ivy Manor. Hennie was surprised, however, to realize that one of the people Jack was most concerned about recognizing him was Mr. Parsons, a man he'd known most of his life. Jack had carefully and purposely set up the arrangement of his doing work for Parsons with communication exchanged via written notes or through the employees Parsons sent who had never known Jack. Hennie found it terribly ironic that she had worked for Mr. Parsons and had come to know him well herself. They both agreed he was a kind and decent man, but it was best he didn't know the truth about Jack—at least not yet.

The only negative aspect of Lottie's marriage was the fact that she would be living with Zeke in one of the quaint little houses on the estate, not far from the manor, that were specifically used for servants who were married and had families. Lottie loved her new home—and the very fact that she had a home of her own. And she practically glowed with the happiness of being married to Zeke. Hennie missed having her around much of the time, even though she could see that it was likely good for her and Jack to have more time to themselves. Hennie also missed having Lottie working at the pub with her, but she would only have to think of Lottie's happiness, and her little bouts of sadness were easily soothed. Zeke and Lottie came over two or three evenings a week for supper, which kept their friendships strong and allowed them to enjoy each other's company.

All in all, life felt as good as it possibly could be—except that Hennie knew Jack felt restless in his desire to come out of hiding and be able to return home and work with his brother. And Hennie still felt uneasy about that prospect due to distressing memories she still hadn't been able to recover. It just felt as if something had happened in that house, something she had seen or heard—or both— and it had frightened her. Both Jack and Lottie had suggested it might not be something as serious or severe as she feared; rather it might have simply been an experience that was frightening to a child. Perhaps it was as simple as being somewhere she wasn't supposed to be and almost getting caught. Or perhaps she had been caught and scolded and it had frightened her. Hennie couldn't disagree with the possibility; in fact, she hoped that was the case. But she couldn't get rid of a nagging sensation that there was more to it, and she both wanted to remember so she could be free of these feelings, and at the same she hoped to *never* remember.

As spring rushed quickly into the warmth of summer, it came as a pleasant surprise to all of them to learn that Lottie was pregnant. Hennie was immensely happy for her friend, as she knew Jack was. But as they were getting ready for bed not long after Lottie and Zeke had left after sharing their news, Hennie felt a sadness and concern that she knew Jack shared, and she knew they needed to talk about it—even if they didn't want to.

Hennie got ready for bed earlier than usual, feeling especially tired, which she credited to all the heavy thoughts that had been weighing on her. She sat in the middle of the bed, her knees drawn up to her chest and her arms wrapped around her legs, listening to the sound of a moderate rain outside, accompanied by just enough wind to pelt it against the windows. She suspected there was more wind than rain, but the force of the wind made the storm feel ferocious, which had the effect of making Hennie feel safe inside a warm, dry, comfortable home, with a soft bed to sleep in and more than enough blankets to ward off the cold. The fire burning in the grate kept the room warm enough that she didn't even feel the urge to be underneath the covers; she just sat there, lost in thought, vacillating between her joy for Lottie's wonderful news, and her own sadness and concern over the fact that she had been married for months and had not yet conceived. Was there something wrong with her? And if there was, she couldn't help but consider the horrible irony that she was married to Jack Hannaford, and their having a child together would greatly aid their case in avoiding the possibility of any ridiculous notion that their marriage could be legally annulled.

Even though she and Jack rarely spoke of his desire to return home and be himself again—mostly because there was nothing to say that hadn't been said a hundred times already—she knew it meant a great deal to him and it was likely on his mind far more than he let on. And even though Hennie still felt uncomfortable and even afraid—for unknown reasons—about living in that house, she had become more resolved to simply press forward with courage to do as she had promised and always stand by Jack wherever life might lead them.

"Are you all right?" Jack asked very close to Hennie's ear, startling her since she hadn't even heard him come into the room, nor had she noticed that he'd sat on the edge of the bed and was leaning toward her.

"Just . . . thinking," she said, hoping to completely avoid talking about all that was on her mind.

"About what?" she knew he would ask, and she also knew she had to answer his question honestly. They were committed to complete honesty, and if it were the other way around, she would expect him to tell her if something was troubling him. She looked at him and attempted to smile, but tears welled in her eyes instead, and she knew there was no point in trying to hide them. "Let me guess," he said when she didn't speak. "You're very happy for Lottie, but you're also very sad that the same has not happened for us. You're wondering if it will *ever* happen, and since you want children very much, the idea of that not being possible is frightening and sad. But you're also concerned about the legal implications of what might happen regarding our marriage if we don't have a child, and how much time has passed and we're still living here when you know I would prefer to be myself again and return home."

Hennie touched his face and managed a more convincing smile. "That is a remarkably accurate description of what I'm feeling. How did you—"

"Because that's what *I'm* feeling," he said, "and I know that in most cases you and I think very much alike . . . so it was a fair guess."

Hennie's tears overtook her, and she wrapped her arms around him, pressing her face to his chest, grateful for the way he held her while she cried. When she'd calmed down enough to speak, she settled the side of her face against his nightshirt, wet from her tears. "I want nothing more than to have a baby, *our* baby. And I wonder if something is wrong with me."

"Or me," he said. "There's no way of knowing whose fault it might be, but it doesn't matter, Hennie. We're in this together. We need to be patient and focus on all that's going well in our lives."

"How optimistic of you," she said with light sarcasm, since it was most often Hennie who was trying to get Jack to see the positive side of things.

Jack chuckled and tightened his arms around her. "My wife has taught me a great deal about being grateful for all I *do* have instead of allowing myself to be weighed down by what I *don't* have. And what I *do* have is wonderful. I couldn't ask for a better wife, and the life we're living is good, even if it's not the one I'd prefer to live. We have each other, Hennie, and I really believe that with time we'll have a baby. We shouldn't worry about it."

"And what of the possibility of annulment?" she asked, looking up at him.

"I don't know exactly what to do about that," he said, but he didn't sound concerned. "For now, I'm not even going to worry about it. Let's enjoy what we have and give it time."

"I can live with that," Hennie said, feeling relieved and comforted by the evidence of his love, and how he'd been able to find more peace in his circumstances, in contrast to the impatience and bitterness she'd seen in the past. It was true: their life *was* good; and making the most of it was nothing but a pleasant possibility. She was more than all right with that.

Chapter Sixteen

RETURN TO IVY MANOR

A FEW WEEKS AFTER HER conversation with Jack, Hennie was struck with the irony of their mutual concerns about her not yet being pregnant. She woke up feeling more nauseated than she had the previous morning and was glad that Jack had already gotten out of bed when she had to rush to the chamber pot and throw up. Even though her stomach was empty, she heaved for a couple of minutes, which seemed like much longer. She went back to bed and looked up at the ceiling, asking herself all the questions regarding the most obvious symptoms of pregnancy, and she was pleasantly astonished to realize that she was indeed experiencing every obvious sign. As nausea began to creep slowly into her stomach again, Hennie recalled what Lottie had told her she'd quickly learned as a remedy—which was something she'd also heard from many other women. She needed food in her stomach, and she needed it before she had to experience the misery of heaving again.

Feeling mildly dizzy, Hennie stood up slowly and carefully before she hurried to the kitchen where Jack was standing at the stove, tending the sausages he was cooking— an aroma that had always been pleasant to her in the past, but which now smelled terrible to Hennie.

"Are there still scones left from yesterday . . . that I got from the bakery?" she asked, hearing a desperation in her voice that sounded ridiculous.

"Good morning to *you*," he said and chuckled while he pointed at the scones nearby.

"Oh, praise heaven," she said and grabbed a couple of them, sitting at the nearby table to eat them without any butter or jam, just grateful to have something in her stomach. Gobbling one ravenously, she immediately felt the nausea easing—which she considered another sure sign that she was indeed pregnant. The reality thrilled her—especially now that her stomach was settling.

Halfway through her second scone, she realized Jack was staring at her as if she'd been turned into a frog. "Are you all right?" he asked, which was certainly a legitimate question given her strange behavior.

"I'm fine," she said and took another bite. Bursting with the need to share the news with him, she managed to smile and said with her mouth full, "I think I'm pregnant."

Jack dropped the fork he'd been using to turn the sausages in the pan. He took a sharp breath and let out a bewildered chuckle. "Truly?" he asked.

Hennie swallowed and smiled again. "I have all the symptoms," she said and briefly listed them before she shoved the remaining piece of scone into her mouth, surprised by how her love of food had blossomed just since yesterday. It had such a soothing effect, and now that her nausea had eased, the sausages were starting to smell good.

Jack surprised Hennie by lifting her right up out of her chair, twirling her around the kitchen with his arms tightly around her. Hennie's feet dangled in the air and never touched the floor until he carefully set her down, laughing with a pure happiness that increased Hennie's *own* happiness. It took her a long moment of holding to his arms to steady herself, once again feeling unusually dizzy. He noticed and guided her to a chair before he sat beside her, took her hand, and said, "I'm so happy, Hennie."

"I think that's evident," she said with a little laugh.

"I love you so very much, my darling. To have a child is . . . well, there are no words."

"Even if our child is raised with a blacksmith as a father?" Hennie asked.

"Yes," he said firmly. "However our lives turn out, we will be a happy family, and our children will be loved and cared for in every way."

Hennie leaned forward to kiss him before she said, "Please don't burn the sausages. I'm still rather hungry—*very* hungry in fact."

Jack jumped to his feet to get the sausages out of the pan, and he insisted that Hennie remain sitting while he finished cooking breakfast and put a plate in front of her with the ample helpings she had requested. He kept smiling at her across the table while they shared their meal, speculating over whether their first child would be a son or a daughter, and talking of all the wonderful changes parenthood would bring into their lives.

That afternoon Hennie met with the local doctor, who positively confirmed her suspicions, and that evening Zeke and Lottie came for supper and were thrilled with the news. Lottie was especially excited over the fact that she and Hennie would be pregnant and having their first babies around the same time.

After all they'd shared, she considered the timing perfect and surely the result of divine intervention.

Jack and Hennie decided not to tell George the news until Hennie was further along in her pregnancy and it was visibly evident. The doctor estimated the baby's arrival in April, and by the time winter had settled in, Hennie couldn't possibly disguise her pregnancy. Even though she had months to go, it became difficult to be on her feet very much, which brought on aching in her back and legs. It was at this point when she made the decision to stop working at the pub, even though she hadn't been putting in very many hours. Lester completely understood, and both she and Jack were grateful for his friendship and support.

A day came when Jack sat Hennie down to have a serious talk, and she wasn't at all surprised when he asked her if she felt ready to speak with George and Mr. Cunningham about his coming out of hiding so they could return to Ivy Manor. Despite her ongoing discomfort over living in the house—for reasons she still hadn't been able to discern—she felt undeniably peaceful about Jack finally being able to resume his identity and return home. She assured him that she felt as ready as she would ever be, and they discussed in detail every possible challenge they could think of regarding such drastic changes in their lives. Hennie concluded the conversation by pressing her hand to his bearded face. "The most important thing," she said, "is that you can finally show your face again, and I'll be able to see what you really look like beneath this . . . shrubbery."

They both laughed over what had become a common joke between them. He kissed her and murmured, "You are so very good to me. I don't know how I ever survived without you."

"Nor I," she said and kissed him again.

After Jack had left a message for his brother—hidden in the usual place at the pub—he hoped that George would come to the house after supper, since he couldn't be certain George got the message, and he couldn't go back to the pub for a reply without looking suspicious. Jack suggested to his wife that they have supper a little early so they could be finished and prepared for George's visit on the chance that he *did* come. And Hennie eagerly agreed.

Throughout the afternoon as Jack went about his usual work, he wondered if his time working as a blacksmith was truly coming to an end. There were some aspects of this life he would miss, but not enough to make him regret finally being able to leave it behind. He'd missed his home; he'd missed being able to share a life with his brother the way they'd always believed they would. And most of all, a deep, festering part of him had simply hated living in disguise, not being able to show his real face, not being known by his real name. He ached to just *be* Jack Hannaford again. He imagined the gossip that would surely ripple through the village and the estate when he came forward and the truth was finally made public—especially the part of the story that included his marrying the woman who had once worked in the stables pretending to be a man. Their story certainly wasn't boring, but living in hiding was truly getting very old.

Jack felt nervous—but in an excited way—as the hour drew nearer for his brother's visit, and he sincerely hoped George had gotten the message. He wasn't certain he could deal with this tension for another day, and George could only visit after dark until they had both agreed that it was time for Jack to come out of hiding. Hennie reminded Jack at supper that although she was not living under an assumed identity, it would be a huge adjustment for her as well.

"You realize," she said, "that no one even calls us by our surname—because we don't have one. We're known as Ollie and Hennie—the blacksmith and his wife. I keep wondering how it will be to live as the wife of Jack Hannaford."

"I'm still the same man," he declared.

"I know that; I know our private lives won't change. But the way we *live* our lives will change dramatically."

Jack took her hand across the table and ignored his meal long enough to ask, "Are you still feeling uncomfortable or afraid about living at the manor?"

"Those feelings still come up, yes," she admitted, "but I can't make sense of them. They are certainly not a valid reason to procrastinate moving forward."

They discussed their plans in more detail, each confessing that it was more than a little unnerving to realize how fast everything was going to change once they knew that George agreed with their taking this step. And since they knew gossip would spread quickly, they suspected it wouldn't be long before Letitia's father created trouble. Mr. Cunningham was absolutely convinced of that, but he—like George—now knew that Hennie was pregnant, and that they were just waiting for the right time to return to the manor. Now that time had come, and they would be stepping into a whole new world.

George arrived while Hennie and Jack were just finishing the dishes. As always, he embraced both of them, adding a kiss on Hennie's cheek. He was nothing but thrilled about their decision to finally come out of hiding. He had been even more impatient than Jack about not having his brother and sister-in-law living under the same roof. They made plans for the move to take place the very next day, and Jack could see the growing anxiety on Hennie's face as they discussed the details. He paused the conversation to look directly at her and say gently, "It will be all right, darling. Perhaps what you're struggling with will actually get *better* once we're settled in and you realize there is nothing to fear." Jack was glad Hennie had given him permission to discuss her strange fears with his brother; therefore, George was well aware of the situation and equally compassionate.

"Remember, my dear," George said, "it may be the same house our father once governed, but it is not at all the same. As I see it, the servants work *with* the family, not *for* them, and they certainly don't scatter like frightened mice at my appearance as they did with our father. In my opinion, there's an entirely different spirit about the house—if a house can have a spirit."

"I believe it can," Hennie declared, liking that idea very much.

"The only problem," George went on, "is when Rebecca brings Letitia around. She seems to carry a dark cloud into every room she enters. But one day I hope to convince our sister how blind she's become to her friend's true character."

"One day soon, I hope," Jack added, "I will be free of ever having to allow Letitia into our home again."

"Amen, brother," George declared, and they reviewed their plans for the following day.

Jack and Hennie were both restless that night, but they agreed it was nice to be sharing a bed so they could talk about all they were feeling and hold each other until they were finally able to relax and at least get a little sleep.

The following morning, right after a quick breakfast, Jack put a sign outside the front of the closed smithy, stating it was out of business, with an added reference to the other blacksmiths in town—who would surely be grateful for additional business. Then Jack and Hennie walked together to the Hawk's Nest, having decided that Lester should be the first to know the truth. He'd been a kind and loyal friend, and since he owned a popular pub, gossip would quickly be filtering in and out along with the usual flow of customers. Lester was genuinely surprised to hear the truth, but he found the situation amusing more than anything.

"Just think how people will react," he said with a hearty chuckle, "to realize the missing Jack Hannaford was right under their noses all along. You've really duped them, sir," he added respectfully to Jack.

"I suppose I have," Jack said. "I wondered sometimes if I could get away with it, but it seems I have. I just hope people will understand, and that we won't have any trouble with Tewksbury now that so much time has passed." He glanced at Hennie and smiled. "And so much has changed."

Lester promised to do his best to help keep the record straight when he over-heard people talking about what was about to be made known, and he wished them well in being able to make a good life for themselves.

Leaving the pub with Hennie's hand in his, Jack said to her, "There's no turning back now."

"I keep trying to think how it will feel tonight when we're alone together in the privacy of our room at the manor. The worst will surely be over, and even though I'm certain it will take time to adjust, it's today I dread the most and I long to have it over."

"I couldn't agree more," Jack said. "Although . . ." he drawled, "won't it be lovely to see Mrs. Reeves . . . and Mrs. Helton . . . and to tell them who you really are?" He heard Hennie gasp. "I'm sure they've heard the rumors of the women working in the stables, but do you think either of them has any idea one of them was *you*? It broke their hearts when you left as a child, and I think they'll be thrilled to see you again."

"Oh! I hadn't thought of that." Hennie sighed as they walked slowly, hand in hand. "I can't count how many times I encountered them and wanted to just blurt out that it was me . . . to let them know I was all right." She sighed again. "I can't deny that knowing I'll be under the same roof with people who once helped look out for me makes me feel a little better."

"Good," Jack said. "Then we have something to look forward to, which means today might not be so bad."

"And it's not only me they'll be thrilled to see," Hennie declared, smiling at him. "Do you have any idea how much the people who know you have worried and wondered? They'll be overcome!" She laughed softly. "And Parsons is in for a surprise."

"Yes, I suppose he is," Jack said and laughed as well.

Together they did a little shopping, so they could return to the manor prop-erly dressed. They didn't take too much time, but they were able to buy enough to feel like they could return with confidence, agreeing that Hennie would need more clothes very quickly—especially with the progression of her pregnancy. Jack knew he had a great many fine clothes still at the manor, and he really didn't care if some people might consider them out of style. He'd never been one to care much for fashion, anyway. But he told Hennie he wanted to be certain she had everything she needed to feel comfortable.

They returned home and packed up their clothes and personal items—which didn't amount to much and could be easily carried—and left everything else in order, covering the furniture with the large pieces of fabric, which would prevent it from becoming dusty. Jack knew he'd probably sell the place, but a part of him didn't want to even try to do so until he knew that living at the manor was going to work out. Of course, he could never pretend to be someone else anymore—at least not in this village—but perhaps they would eventually realize that living this life was better. Until they knew how Old Man Tewksbury was going to respond to all of this, the future held a great deal of uncertainty.

The last thing Jack did before leaving this place that had been his home for so long was to shave off his beard. Hennie watched closely as he did so, teasing him incessantly about how glad she was to finally be able to see his face. When he was finished, she looked at him, smiled, and declared with adoration in her eyes and a serious voice, "Oh, you are even more handsome than I could have imagined." She kissed him, making a pleasurable sound that implied how nice it felt to not have his lips surrounded by hair. She put a hand to his cheek and looked into his eyes. "It's nice to have you back," she said and kissed him again.

Jack sighed and forced himself away from her gentle touch and adoring eyes, needing to clean up his shaving mess so they could be on their way, but he held on to the way her love made him feel, knowing that with her by his side he could get through whatever might result from the steps they were taking.

❧

Jack and Hennie arrived at the manor on horseback, neither of them having said hardly a word during the ride from the village, except to comment more than once how strange this felt, and how understandably nervous they both were. Entering the stables and leading their horses by the reins, they were met by Mr. Parsons, who quickly approached Jack and said with a grin and a quivery voice, "It really is you, sir! Your brother told me this morning you were coming back, but I've had trouble believing it could be possible."

"I'm really here," Jack said, shaking Mr. Parsons's hand.

"And it's true that you've been working as a blacksmith?" Parsons asked.

"It is," Jack said.

Parsons chuckled, hesitant to let go of Jack's hand. "It's no wonder you always insisted on our communication never needing to be in person. No need for me to waste my time with such things, you said, when you first wrote to me offering to shoe our horses for a fair price."

"I believe that's what I said," Jack replied, and Parsons finally let go of his hand, although he kept staring at Jack as if he just couldn't believe it.

Jack cleared his throat, which broke the silence, and he turned toward Hennie, saying, "I believe you've met my wife . . . but under much different circumstances."

Parsons turned toward Hennie a little startled, as if he'd been so caught up in seeing Jack again he'd not even realized anyone else was there. The moment he looked at Hennie, his eyes widened, and he let out a sound somewhere between a laugh and a cough. "It's you!"

"It is," Hennie said and smiled as Parsons kissed her hand.

"My lady!"

"No need for such formality," she insisted.

"Well, if this isn't the most fanciful tale I've ever heard!" Parsons said as if he'd just been knighted. "But how did the two of you . . ."

Jack hurried to give Parsons a brief version of the story before Parsons wished them well and once again declared how glad he was to have them back. They entered the house where the servants generally came and went, since they'd decided they absolutely needed to speak personally with Mrs. Reeves and Mrs. Helton before doing so much as lifting a teacup. They both knew that George had already announced the truth about Jack's false identity to the entire staff early that morning when he'd given orders for Jack's rooms to be prepared for him and his wife, and that he expected no unsavory gossip regarding a complicated situation, which few if any of them could fully understand. But as far as they knew, no one had been told that Jack Hannaford's wife was someone most of the staff was already acquainted with—even if they might not recognize the way she'd changed.

Holding hands, Jack and Hennie walked quietly into the kitchen, fortunate enough to find Mrs. Helton keeping watch over something on the stove, alone there except for a couple of kitchen maids who were sitting at a table some distance from the stove, doing something artistic with raw vegetables and paring knives. Jack and Hennie stopped not far behind the cook, and Jack said, "Something smells good." Mrs. Helton turned around with a gasp and put both hands to her face. "But then, it's always smelled good in here."

"Bless my soul, it *is* you!" she declared with tears welling in her eyes. "When your brother told me you were coming home, I didn't dare believe it!"

Jack laughed and opened his arms to share a long, tight hug with Mrs. Helton in a way that would never happen in most households between those of different social classes.

"Oh, my boy," she said, pulling back to look at his face as she put her hands on his upper arms. "You look well. Are you?"

"I am!" he said. "Mostly due to the love and patience of my dear wife." He motioned toward Hennie, and like Mr. Parsons, the cook had been so caught up in seeing Jack that she'd not noticed anyone else standing there.

"Oh, goodness!" Mrs. Helton said. "You must be something special to have won the heart of our precious Jack."

"You're very kind," Hennie said, only willing to wait a moment to see if the cook recognized her.

"Wait a minute. I know you!" Mrs. Helton laughed and slapped her hands on the front of her apron. "You're one of them that was working in the stables!" She looked at Jack and back at Hennie. "And the two of you . . ." She laughed again. "Oh my! I can't wait to hear the rest of *this* story."

"And we will gladly tell you everything you want to hear," Hennie said and took a step closer, "but there's something else you must know first, something I wanted so desperately to tell you when I was working here but I just couldn't."

"What is it, child?" Mrs. Helton asked, concerned.

Hennie was struck by an unexpected rush of tears as she recalled how desperately Mrs. Helton had tried to keep Hennie in her care following her mother's death. She hurried to just say, "We knew each other before . . . a long time ago, when I was a child." She swallowed hard and cleared her throat. "It's me, Hennie."

Through long seconds of dumbfounded silence, Hennie felt Jack squeeze her hand. The older woman mouthed more than spoke the name, "Hennie?" Then more audibly she squeaked, "Our little Hennie?"

Hennie nodded, unable to speak, feeling very much like the child who had been terrified to leave the care of this good woman and her accomplice, Mrs. Reeves.

"Oh, Lord be merciful!" Mrs. Helton muttered and made no attempt to hold back her emotion as she wrapped Hennie in her arms and wept. Hennie wept with her, holding tightly to the comfort of her childhood, allowing it to seep back into her through Mrs. Helton's love. "Oh, girl!" she sputtered and took hold of Hennie's arms to give her a thorough once-over. "You're safe! You're all right!"

"I am," Hennie said with a little laugh.

"I've worried and cried many a tear," she said, stepping back to wipe away her new tears. She then glanced at Jack, then back at Hennie, her expression becoming briefly contorted with confusion and then bursting with enlightenment. "And all that time you were working here without me knowing you was . . ." She didn't finish the sentence. "And the two of you are . . ." She didn't finish that sentence either. But she put her hands to her face again and laughed heartily, which provoked more tears. Hennie ignored the curious stares of the kitchen maids and laughed with Mrs. Helton as they shared another hug, and Jack laughed with them.

She insisted they sit down and have some tea with her and answer some questions, so she could get the entire story straight, and they were glad to do so.

The cook sent one of the maids to fetch Mrs. Reeves immediately so she could join them, and Jack and Hennie wouldn't have to tell the entire story twice. The housekeeper arrived quickly, wondering what might be so important. Jack and Hennie were spared from having to offer a word of explanation as Mrs. Helton quickly told her friend that not only had Jack come back to them, but by some miracle of which they were about to hear, their precious Hennie had come back too—and married to Jack. Mrs. Reeves's reaction was only slightly less dramatic than Mrs. Helton's had been, but she certainly didn't hug either of them less tightly. The cook then sent the maids away so they could enjoy their tea privately, declaring they surely already had plenty to gossip about.

Jack and Hennie took turns telling these two women—who had both been mother figures to them in their lives—the finer points of all that had happened since they'd each respectively left Ivy Manor, and how they had come back together.

"And you've finally both come home," Mrs. Reeves declared.

"It's like a fairy tale, I tell you," Mrs. Helton said on the wave of a sigh.

"I can't deny that what I share with Hennie feels that way," Jack said, smiling at his wife, "but as for our coming back here, we have yet to see if that will bring about any trouble."

Jack and Hennie were both pleased to hear that the general attitude among the servants was sincere pleasure at having Jack return home with a wife. They were pleased to not only know that Jack was safe and well, but to have him back. Both Mrs. Reeves and Mrs. Helton agreed that before supper everyone would know Jack had married one of the women many of them had become well acquainted with when she'd been working in the stables, and they would surely be glad to have her back as well.

They all talked for a while longer before Mrs. Reeves insisted Jack and Hennie probably needed some rest. After more hugs all around, they left the kitchen, and Jack was guiding Hennie up the back staircase and through a maze of hallways and stairs that almost made her dizzy until they came to the rooms Jack had used before he'd left home. Entering Jack's bedroom, they were both a little breathless—Hennie from the long walk, and Jack from the effect of being in the room where he'd grown up.

Hennie closely examined every detail of the spacious and elegant bedroom, declaring with a chuckle, "It's bigger than the entire house we just left."

"I do believe it is," Jack said, watching her closely as she explored the adjacent sitting room as well. "These rooms have never felt more like home to me," he said, wrapping her in his arms. "I hope you'll be comfortable here," he added.

"Oh, it's all so lovely!" she declared. "And as long as you're here with me, why wouldn't I be?"

The possible reasons for that—which they'd discussed many times—were ignored, and they focused instead on putting away the few belongings they'd brought with them before Hennie declared the need to lie down, if only for a short while. Jack sat in a chair near the bed and just allowed his surroundings to seep into his spirit; he really was home.

By the time afternoon tea was served in the main parlor, Jack noticed that Hennie seemed more relaxed than she had since their arrival. She kept looking around at the beautifully decorated parlor as if to take it all in, while George sipped his tea and talked of how grand it felt to have them there. And Jack couldn't disagree.

"And how are you both doing so far?" George asked.

"It's . . . strange," Jack said, "but it feels like home, and it's good to be here."

"And you?" George asked Hennie.

"I'm all right so far," Hennie said. "Better than I'd expected, to be truthful. I'm not sure about the source of all those strange feelings, but as of now I'm fine. I'm certain it will take time for me to adjust to all the changes, but that's to be expected."

"That's very good, then," George said. "If you—"

"Is it really true?" a woman's voice exclaimed, startling all of them as they turned to see Rebecca practically flying into the room. Jack stood up to greet her. She stopped in front of him, took him in with her eyes, and started to cry, "Oh, it *is* true! You're really back! You're all right!"

"I am," he said, and she flung herself into his arms, hugging him tightly while he hugged her in return.

"Oh, I can't believe it!" Rebecca declared and wiped away tears with her hand as she stepped back to get a good look at him. "We've all missed you so much!"

"And I've missed you," Jack said, knowing that now was the moment he needed to introduce his wife. He didn't know how much Rebecca might have heard through household gossip, but he suspected that not one of the servants would have been brave enough to tell her Jack was married—given the close friendship she shared with the woman who was eagerly expecting to marry Jack when he came to his senses.

Jack reached a hand toward Hennie, and she stood up to take it. The motion drew Rebecca's eyes to the fact that it was not only her and her brothers in the room. "Rebecca," he said, "this is my wife, although in truth the two of you already know each other. She was one of our childhood friends. This is Hennie. You remember Hennie?"

"Hennie?" she echoed with breathless astonishment, confusion filling her countenance as she was clearly looking for some recognition and didn't seem to find it, but then Rebecca and Hennie had spent very little time together as children, and many years had passed. Then Rebecca's eyes were drawn to the obvious evidence that Hennie was pregnant, and she gasped as her eyes shot toward Jack with a histrionic expression that he felt certain she'd learned from spending too much time with Letitia. *"Wife?"* she demanded in a way that reminded Jack of his father, which prickled his nerves and pressed him toward feeling angry. "But you have to marry—"

"Rebecca," Jack said, taking hold of her shoulders, "I'm not going to marry Letitia. There is no amount of time, no demands by our father, no legal document that would ever make me marry a woman I don't love. That's why I had to leave. I'm married to Hennie, and we're going to have a child. What's done is done. I've relinquished my inheritance, but I was tired of living in hiding. I missed all of you. I wanted to come home. It's over and done."

"I can't believe you would do this to us!" Rebecca declared in a way that made Letitia's influence even more evident.

Jack exchanged a concerned glance with George; they'd both expected a less than favorable reaction from their sister, but he wasn't certain what to do about it. He was relieved when George said, "Rebecca, darling, I know you disagree with me, but I still believe very much that Letitia is not nearly as good a friend as you think she is. I believe she has less than favorable motives in remaining close to you, and I don't want you to be hurt when—"

"You have no idea what you're talking about!" she snapped at George before she turned harsh eyes toward Jack and added, "And *you* are a fool! I can't believe this." She looked at Hennie as if she had brought leprosy into the house. "I just can't believe it." She left the room in an angry flurry.

Hennie sat down abruptly and turned her face away; Jack knew she was attempting to hide her emotion. He sat down beside her and wrapped her in his arms.

"We mustn't worry about her," George said, "other than the fact that eventually she *will* see Letitia for who she really is, and I fear it will hurt her deeply. We can only hope no *real* trouble erupts from all this."

"We can only hope," Jack said and tightened his arm around his wife, hoping to reassure her that all would be well. He only wished he felt confident in believing it himself.

By the following day, it had become blatantly evident that every servant in the household knew the entire story of Jack and Hennie, but they both agreed they preferred having all the gossip spare them from having to explain their situation to each person they encountered. The overall attitude was a combination of amusement and awe over all the secrecy and pretending that had been going on, and everyone was extremely kind and helpful. It sometimes felt as if one of their childhood fairy tales had become a very real story of romance and intrigue that everyone at Ivy Manor enjoyed being a part of, and Jack and Hennie were treated like royalty.

Hennie loitered in the kitchen after breakfast, helping clean the dishes and visiting with the women there—a few she'd known from childhood, and many she was only becoming acquainted with. When she met Clara, a lovely young woman with dark hair and striking green eyes—who seemed unnaturally shy with the newcomer—Hennie knew this was the woman George had grown to love. She longed to be able to get to know Clara better, even though she knew that as of now, Clara's relationship with George had been put aside due to her insistence that she could never fit into George's world. But Hennie deeply hoped that her own entrance into the family might soften Clara toward the possibility. However, it would take time to get to know her, and even more time when she would hardly speak a word in Hennie's presence. It was as if her determination to not become involved with George branched out to the entire family.

Hennie took the first possible opportunity to walk out to the stables to properly greet Mr. Parsons and everyone else there she had once worked with. She had encountered some of them in town at the pub, but now that she'd returned as part of the family, she didn't want any one of them believing she had returned in a way that put her above their station. Parsons laughed with delight when he saw her again, and they talked amiably about the situation. He was genuinely happy for her, and even happier that Jack had been able to return to his family home. Many of the stable hands gathered around as the ironies were discussed with an air of humor, but all of them were sincere in wishing Hennie the very best. Parsons finally ordered everyone back to work, and Hennie promised she would be seeing them all on a regular basis. When only Parsons was left for her to talk to, Hennie asked him about Joe—the older stable hand who had been having some health challenges. Parsons reported that at George's insistence Joe would no longer be required to work, and even though he'd only been at Ivy Manor for a few years, he would be looked after for the remainder of his life. He had a comfortable room in the servants' quarters, and many of the servants pitched in to help care for him and to keep him company. Hennie was glad to hear that Joe was in good hands, and it warmed her heart to be part of a family that treated their servants with such respect.

Following lunch, Hennie was informed that Miss Atkins would like to speak with her. This dear woman had made it possible for Hennie and Lottie to survive here as men, but she was also officially the assistant to the housekeeper, and she had her own tiny office in the hallway just off the kitchen. Hennie went there and was relieved to be received with a familiar hug from her old friend. They sat together and visited a long while, both as friends and as Hennie's new role in being the lady of the house—at least until George brought home a wife. It was difficult for Hennie to not spill George's secret, especially since she didn't *want* to be lady of the house—but then she suspected Clara didn't want that either.

Hennie was glad to hear how much Miss Atkins treasured her ongoing friendship with Lottie, and how they'd spent time together since Lottie and Zeke had been married. For Hennie, having an established friendship with Miss Atkins—as well as the cook and housekeeper who had been here in her childhood—made her living here at the manor even more comfortable and easier. All things considered, her first day back had come together relatively well.

⸻

The *real* trouble George had predicted showed up the following day when Tewksbury arrived at the house with no warning, accompanied by his evil solicitor, Mr. Hobbs. Both George and Jack were informed that Tewksbury *insisted* on speaking with both of them immediately. As the brothers went down the stairs together, George muttered angrily, "He's got a lot of nerve showing up unannounced and *insisting* on anything at all."

"Yes," Jack said, "he *does* have a lot of nerve—about everything. He's quite accustomed to getting his own way without exception. I wonder if he's ever *not* gotten what he wants."

"Well, he's about to get a lesson in *that*," George said, still sounding angry.

Jack reminded his brother to remain calm, even if he felt that the reminder was more for himself. He felt at least as angry as George sounded.

Jack was not necessarily surprised but certainly shocked to hear from Old Man Tewksbury's shouting that he absolutely intended to see Jack's marriage annulled, and his solicitor, Mr. Hobbs, regularly interjected a flow of legal jargon that made little sense to Jack. But the gist was undeniable. Mr. Cunningham had accurately predicted that this would happen; still, both Jack and George were somewhat breathless after their visitors stomped angrily out of the house. Jack couldn't believe it. They had to appear in court the very next morning, and the validity of his marriage to Hennie was literally going to be decided by a complete stranger.

Hennie wasn't as upset as Jack had expected her to be when he told her the bad news, but neither of them slept very well that night. The following morning, they had to leave early since it was a long ride to their appointed destination, and then they had to wait a ridiculously long time. Hearing Mr. Hobbs tell the judge his client's side of the story, and the legal rights Tewksbury surely had in this matter, Jack, Hennie, and George could only offer each other disgusted and fearful glances, and Jack knew they were praying as hard as he that this would turn out well. Jack felt calmer due to Mr. Cunningham's articulate and comprehensive representation of their case. He felt Hennie squeezing his hand tightly as a heart-pounding silence descended over the courtroom while the judge looked at the papers in front of him, contemplating his decision. Then suddenly he declared in a tone of boredom—as if he considered such matters to be tedious and inconvenient—that it was indeed ridiculous to think that a marriage could be undone in such a way, and that Jack Hannaford had not broken any laws, given the fact that he had relinquished his inheritance, which was the obvious stipulation in the will.

The judge banged his gavel on the high desk in front of him, which startled both Jack and Hennie. But the sound made it clear they had gotten exactly what they'd hoped for, and the matter was indeed settled.

"Oh!" Jack said and impulsively hugged Hennie while she laughed.

George laughed too, and the brothers embraced before they each shook Mr. Cunningham's hand and thanked him profusely.

"So glad to help," the solicitor said with a smile and quickly excused himself, saying he had other clients who needed his assistance.

Their happiness was interrupted by an angry Tewksbury, whose face was a strange shade of purple. He darted his angry eyes back and forth between George and Jack and tossed a disgusted glare toward Hennie as he snarled, "This is not over. You will not deny me what is rightfully mine."

Tewksbury huffed away, with Hobbs following behind him like an oversized bloodhound.

"What on earth is *that* supposed to mean?" George asked. "What is rightfully *his*?"

"Nothing we have is rightfully his," Jack declared with confidence, and they all hurried out of the courtroom, realizing that another case was coming before the judge and they needed to leave.

The three of them shared a hearty lunch at a nearby pub before they started home in the carriage. Jack kept Hennie's hand in his until she began to get sleepy, and he put his arm around her as she settled her head on his shoulder and relaxed. Jack and George talked about their plans for how they would go about working together to manage the estate, and Jack felt more at peace than he'd felt since his father's will had been read to them by Mr. Hobbs—and the horrible reality of what he'd been condemned to had come to light. And it was evident George felt the same. He had been enduring his own version of agony over the impact of their father's wishes, and he was clearly glad to have his brother back. Jack pressed a kiss into Hennie's hair while she slept and silently thanked God for the miracles He had brought into his life.

With legal matters now settled, Hennie found herself settling more comfortably into living at Ivy Manor. She'd put so much thought and energy into dreading the possibility of living here as the wife of Jack Hannaford that she was pleasantly surprised at how easy it was to fill that role and do it in a way that was comfortable for her. Having known some of the servants from her childhood, and many others from working here—despite being known as a man—she was able to quickly rekindle those bonds and feel at home. Communicating directly and openly with members of the staff with whom she worked to manage the household proved effective and comfortable. These people were good at their jobs and seemed more than glad to have her involved with the household routine. Hennie found opportunities to work with them whenever possible, which helped her feel more like an equal to them, and she believed it helped them realize that she hadn't married into the family to raise herself above the social class into which she'd been born.

Hennie very much enjoyed once again having Lottie close by. Being able to spend more time with her friend was a distinct advantage of having moved to the manor. While Jack was busy with his brother, engaged in estate business, and Zeke continued his work in the stables, Hennie and Lottie were able to share long talks much as they'd done through many stages of their lives. Sometimes they visited at the manor, and sometimes at Lottie's little home on the estate, which was very close to the manor house. They could easily walk the distance except when the winter weather was especially bad—although both women were now far enough along in their pregnancies that even the brief walk had become difficult. Therefore, Zeke had been harnessing the trap they owned and bringing Lottie to the manor house each time he went there to work, which gave the women an opportunity for frequent visits. They enjoyed tea together most afternoons, and oftentimes helped here and there in the kitchen or the laundry.

And since they both needed naps every day, a guest room had been specifically prepared for Lottie to use for this purpose when she spent days at the manor house.

They all attended church together, which was likely the biggest source of gossip spreading through the village about the return of Jack Hannaford—along with his wife and a baby on the way. Jack, Hennie, and Lottie had previously attended at a different chapel in the center of the village, where the congregation was wholly made up of commoners, and Jack had been known only as Ollie. Now they were attending with George at the cathedral on the edge of town, where the Hannaford family had always gone to church, and where most of the household and residents of the estate also worshiped. Jack Hannaford showing his clean-shaven face among this particular congregation had sent the word of his return rushing like a wildfire that quickly consumed the entire valley.

The first Sunday they'd attended church, occupying the Hannaford family pew, Rebecca had blatantly ignored Hennie and worn a disgusted expression throughout the entire service, which Hennie simply tried to ignore, the way she knew that Jack was also trying to ignore, even though she knew it bothered him very much. At dinner later that day, Rebecca had once again lectured Jack on how much he'd disappointed her, and George had once again warned Rebecca about not being able to clearly see Letitia's motives, and that he feared she would end up being hurt. Rebecca had stormed off to her room, demanding that her meal be taken there. From that day on, Rebecca hardly showed herself whenever they shared meals or tea. The brothers were concerned for her, but neither of them knew what to do or say to convince her that she'd been a pawn in Letitia's control for so many years that she could likely not even imagine being any other way.

As long as Hennie didn't encounter Rebecca and her bold disdain—or even think about it—she found she had become so comfortable in her new life that she began to wonder what on earth had made her so afraid and concerned about the idea of living here as Jack's wife. Sharing this life with him made her indescribably happy, and with all the people living and working in the house who had become her friends, she felt less lonely and more fulfilled than she ever had. The baby growing inside of her was most fulfilling of all. Her favorite time of day was bedtime when she and Jack would snuggle close together in the dark, where he'd often press his hand over her rounded belly and speculate over whether the baby was a boy or a girl, and what the child's personality might be like. He made no effort to conceal his excitement over becoming a father, which only heightened the thrill Hennie felt about becoming a mother. If she didn't think about the inevitable suffering required to bring a child into the world, she felt nothing but joy.

Chapter Seventeen

THE PROPOSAL

HENNIE'S JOY BECAME UNEXPECTEDLY INVADED by an inexplicable darkness on a bright afternoon in late February following a snowstorm when she and Lottie decided to find the library and explore its contents. Jack had suggested more than once that they would enjoy spending time there, since it was a lovely and comfortable room, and it had more books than anyone could ever read in a lifetime. For some reason Hennie could never explain to Lottie, she had felt reluctant to go to the library, but a day came when Lottie insisted she wanted to see the room, and if Hennie couldn't give her good reason *not* to do so, they were just going to be adventurous and find it.

They found it easily enough, and Hennie loved watching Lottie's expression as they stepped inside and she was overcome with the enormity of the room, with seemingly endless shelves of books from floor to ceiling. The decor was in varying shades of blue, and the draperies were tied back to allow sunlight reflecting off the snow to stream in brilliantly, illuminating every detail of the priceless reading collection, as well as the comfortable sofas and decorative little tables, which were obviously there so the daily tea ritual could easily be enjoyed in this room.

"It's incredible," Lottie said, craning her neck and turning in a circle to take in books that numbered too many to count.

"It *is*," Hennie agreed and took her focus away from Lottie's reaction to absorb the beauty of the room herself. The decor was so familiar that she knew it hadn't been changed since her childhood, but it actually felt disorienting to realize that she'd come to this room many times—mostly when her mother had been cleaning and she would hide on the floor behind one of the sofas to play quietly, out of view of anyone who might come into the room. She recalled coming here more than once with Jack and George and sometimes their sisters. They had played games that had required crawling beneath the tables, or they would sometimes gather around the huge atlas book that was so heavy it took two of them to retrieve it from its resting place. With the book opened on the floor, they would examine maps of other places in the world and talk about what they might be like.

A flood of memories overcame Hennie, most of them pleasant and comforting—which made her reaction to them completely unexpected and frightening.

"Oh, my," she said, suddenly lightheaded. She sat down and lowered her head, which caught Lottie's attention, and within seconds she found her friend sitting right beside her.

"What is it?" Lottie asked, concerned.

"I felt . . . dizzy . . . and . . ." Hennie put a hand over her smoldering stomach. "Sick. I still do. I feel sick."

"We must get you something to eat," Lottie said, "and—"

"Not that kind of sick," Hennie declared as the familiarity of what she felt began to sink in. She stood up abruptly, startling Lottie, her dizziness overcome by a more powerful urgency. "I need to get out of here. I can't be in this room."

Lottie followed Hennie out of the library and down a long hall toward the staircase. Hennie was surprised at how quickly she was able to move, given the limitations of her pregnancy, but she had a feeling that the smoldering sickness that had urged her to get away from there as quickly as possible would—at any minute—leave her weak, and she would pay a price for trying to walk so far and so fast. The expected weakness came with more dizziness, and Hennie hurried into an empty parlor and sank into a comfortable chair, grateful this part of the house had so many rooms intended for relaxing and socializing.

"What on earth is the matter?" Lottie demanded, sitting in a chair right next to Hennie and putting a hand on her arm.

"I'm not certain," Hennie said, her voice trembling, "but . . . I think something happened in that room, something I don't remember . . . but it's as if the memory is buried in my mind, still making me afraid even though I *can't* remember."

"Good heavens!" Lottie said. "Do you think that's why you were afraid to come back here?"

"It makes sense, doesn't it?" Hennie asked, finally gaining control of her equilibrium enough to look up at her friend. In a voice that sounded utterly horrified, she added, "But what on earth could it be? What could have possibly happened to make me feel this way? And to make me forget . . . but not *really* forget? Because it's obviously affecting me. Oh, Lottie! I feel . . . awful. I feel . . . sick."

"Well, we've come closer to solving the mystery, I think," Lottie said as if that might help Hennie feel better, but it didn't. "In my opinion, I don't believe you'll get over these terrible feelings until you *do* remember . . . and once you've remembered, you can come to terms with it."

"You make it sound so easy," Hennie said snidely, knowing that Lottie wouldn't take it personally.

"It's not easy at all," Lottie said. "But people like you and me—coming from such terrible situations—usually have a great many awful memories of experiences that never should have happened. But it's a reality of life that dreadful things *do* happen, and we can only heal and move forward when we have faced those demons and put them away. We overcome our fears of past events when we take power over them by not letting them have control over our future. And you can't tell me I don't know what I'm talking about."

Hennie and Lottie shared a deep gaze that reminded Hennie of stories Lottie had told her of her early childhood, of things that had happened prior to their becoming friends; experiences that had sickened Hennie. But Lottie had indeed faced those memories boldly and had conquered their power over her. She had risen above a deplorable life to make a very happy one, and in that moment, Hennie could be nothing but overwhelmed with gratitude for Lottie's perfect empathy and support. Otherwise, whatever had taken place in the library—an experience deeply rooted somewhere in the dark caverns of Hennie's mind— would have likely left her completely incapacitated.

Lottie helped Hennie up to her room, where Hennie kicked off her shoes and crawled into bed, feeling unusually exhausted. Lottie sat nearby in a comfortable chair, encouraging Hennie to try and remember what might have happened in the library, certain if she could just remember and be able to talk about it, she would understand why it had affected her so adversely, and she would be capable of handling the memories appropriately. Hennie repeated everything she knew—and felt—to Lottie more than once, but nothing new came to light, and talking about it only made Hennie feel more exhausted.

"I think I just need to sleep," Hennie finally said, and Lottie told her she would just sit there and read.

Hennie was surprised at how quickly she fell asleep, which she only realized when she came abruptly awake with something resembling a quiet scream erupting out of her mouth.

"What is it, darling?" she heard Jack ask before she came awake enough to realize he was sitting on the bed beside her, holding her hand. A quick glance showed Hennie that Lottie was still sitting in a nearby chair, and another chair had been moved close to hers. It was easy to determine that Jack had come looking for his wife and had likely been visiting quietly with Lottie until Hennie had awakened and he'd moved to her side. "Did you have a bad dream?" Jack asked, deep concern in his countenance.

"Yes," she said and struggled to sit up, which wasn't easy given the size of her pregnant belly. Jack helped her get comfortable, leaning on a stack of pillows propped against the headboard. Hennie realized she was breathing sharply while Jack and Lottie looked at her expectantly, waiting for anything she might reveal to them.

When she couldn't come up with any words to describe her dream, Lottie said, "I took the liberty of telling your husband what happened in the library."

"Good," Hennie said, "that rescues *me* from having to tell him." She squeezed her eyes closed, as if the dark memories hovering at the cusp of her conscious mind were threatening to destroy her, and yet she instinctively believed that if she couldn't see her enemy, she could never conquer it.

"Do you remember anything from your dream?" Jack asked. "Does it have something to do with—"

"Yes," she declared. "The dream was very hazy, but I was a child in the library, and your father was there. I was hiding; he didn't know *I* was there. I don't know what was happening, but I was *very* afraid." Hennie drew in a ragged breath. "That's all I remember."

"I'm not at all surprised it has something to do with *him*," Jack growled. "A day doesn't go by when I don't marvel over how much damage one man could do."

Hennie squeezed her husband's hand. "And I marvel that his sons turned out to be such good men; so kind and generous."

"Rebellion, I suppose," Jack said with a little smile. "Neither of us wanted to be anything like him."

"How blessed!" Lottie said.

"It's possible my dream is just a dream," Hennie said. "Whatever happened in the library might not necessarily have anything to do with him. You know how dreams are. Perhaps my mind is just mixing up completely unrelated matters."

"I guess we'll just have to see," Jack said and leaned over to kiss her brow. "I just hope these memories of yours will make themselves known and stop haunting you."

"I hope for that too," Hennie said. "I think. I mean . . . I want to remember because I hope that doing so will help free me of this feeling. But a part of me is afraid to remember."

"We'll help you through, dearest," Lottie said, "no matter what."

"Of course we will," Jack said, squeezing her hand and smiling.

※

Through the remainder of the day and into the next, Hennie was surprisingly undisturbed by the strange fears she'd felt earlier. She concentrated on enjoying the usual routine with the people she cared about, and whatever might have happened in the library when she'd been a child hardly entered her mind. She had a strange dream that night, but it wasn't much different from what she'd dreamt earlier, and this time it didn't feel as frightening. She awoke feeling more curious than anything, simply wanting to know if the dreams *were* connected to her hidden memories.

That afternoon during tea, Mr. Hobbs once again dropped by without any prior announcement. He seemed to enjoy catching people off guard. George insisted the maid bring him to the parlor where Jack, Hennie, and Lottie were having tea with him. The solicitor entered the room with heavy footsteps and a huffing sound, as if he might be having trouble breathing; either that or he imagined himself to be some kind of wild beast who had to announce his presence as noisily as possible.

"To what do we owe the pleasure?" George asked with sarcasm as he and Jack stood to greet Hobbs.

"Would you care to join us for tea?" Jack asked with less sarcasm.

Jack's invitation was met with a breathy noise of disgust, as if an offer of tea was insulting. "I did not come to socialize," Hobbs declared, "and my visit is certainly no pleasure to *me*."

"Very well," George said as the man of the house, "get on with your business then before *our* tea turns cold."

Hobbs handed George some papers, which George didn't even glance at before he asked, "What is this?"

"You are being sued, sir," Hobbs said. "Everything you need to know is there." He nodded toward the papers. "And don't be thinking you'll get out of it so easily this time."

"Out of *what*?" George asked, sounding appalled and disgusted.

"Your obligation regarding the agreement between your father and my client. Breach of contract is a serious thing, young man."

"Breach of contract?" George echoed, his voice rising in pitch. "What on earth would constitute such a—"

"It's all there," Hobbs said and once again nodded at the papers he'd given to George before he left the room, heavy-footed and huffing.

Hennie shared an alarmed gaze with Lottie as the two men sat back down, close enough that they could both read the papers Hobbs had delivered.

"Unbelievable!" George rumbled, angry and astonished.

"They can't really expect that . . ." Jack began but kept reading, which left the women ignorant as to what was so upsetting.

"Feel free to keep us apprised at any time," Hennie said, reminding them there were women present.

Jack looked directly at her and said, "It seems that Tewksbury is now insisting that *George* marry Letitia to fulfill the contract between him and our father; otherwise he will sue us for the majority of our assets, which he considers himself legally entitled to receive, based on the agreement."

"And it certainly explains his motivation all along," George said, slapping the papers with his hand. "We've always known it, but this proves it. This agreement has nothing to do with love or marriage; it's a business deal, and Tewksbury has a great deal to gain."

"It's as if some kind of madness drives them!" Hennie exclaimed. "I can't even make sense of it! Surely any judge would reasonably see how ridiculous this is!"

"I'm not certain we can take that chance," George said and stood, hurrying toward the door.

"Where are you going?" Jack asked, following him.

"To look at our father's evil will again. There's got to be a way around this; a way that will get Tewksbury out of our lives once and for all."

Jack glanced back at the women with a silent farewell as he left the room, but Hennie could see in his eyes the depth of concern he felt. Mr. Cunningham had been analyzing the will for years and hadn't found a way to work around it. How could George and Jack find anything new *now*? But she agreed with George; they had to find a way to get Letitia and her father out of their lives for good. She only prayed that might be possible.

⤝⤞

Jack and George remained in the study with the door closed until it was time for supper. They ate without saying much and returned to the study as if they had a great deal to talk about. Hennie hoped that meant they were coming up with some feasible possibilities for getting out of this mess.

Hennie was sitting in bed reading when Jack came to their bedroom, looking thoroughly exhausted and distraught. He kissed her and inquired about how she was feeling before he sat on the edge of the bed to remove his boots.

"Well?" she asked when he curled up on the bed beside her without having changed into nightclothes. "Anything?"

"We have an idea, yes, but I'm far too weary to talk about it anymore tonight."

"Very well," she said, "but I'm glad to hear you have an idea."

"Unfortunately, it requires Rebecca's support."

"I see," Hennie said glumly, wishing she knew exactly what the idea entailed, but respecting his declaration of being too weary to talk.

"We'll speak with her right after breakfast, and hopefully we can convince her to help us."

"Hopefully," Hennie said and resisted adding that while she wanted to believe Rebecca would side with her brothers over Letitia when it came down to such important matters, she really doubted that would happen. But she kept the thought to herself, knowing that Rebecca was deeply ensnared in Letitia's manipulative spell and she might not be easily persuaded.

Jack kissed Hennie again and scraped himself off the bed to go and change into a nightshirt before he returned and crawled between the covers after he'd extinguished the lamps in the room. He held Hennie close and whispered "I love you" before he fell almost immediately to sleep. Hennie's mind swirled with many different possible outcomes of this ugly situation, but the exhaustion of pregnancy quickly overpowered her thoughts, and she too fell asleep.

The following morning Hennie was haunted by the strange dreams she'd had—much like those she'd had previously. She was so distracted by the bizarre feelings they evoked in her that she completely forgot about the plan to speak with Rebecca after breakfast until her husband's sister arrived at the breakfast table—late as usual.

They all exchanged typical morning greetings while Rebecca dished up a plate for herself from the food that had been left out on the sideboard. Rebecca sat down and began to eat while Hennie wondered if she noticed the lack of any conversation in the room. A few minutes after her arrival, George said, "We need to speak with you after you've finished eating."

Rebecca looked at her brother in surprise. "Me?" she asked.

"Yes, you," he said. "It's important. Just . . . eat your breakfast, and we'll go to the study."

Rebecca set down her fork. "I'm not sure I have much appetite after such an announcement. I can't imagine what might be so serious."

"Just . . . eat," George ordered, and she did, almost as if the way he'd said it had implied she was going to need her strength.

The others had all finished eating, since Rebecca had arrived late, but they sat there sipping tea while Rebecca ate her meal, looking as if it might be her last.

"I can't eat any more," Rebecca said and took a long sip of tea to wash down that last bite. "I'd like to know whatever is going on before lunch, so I might actually be able to complete a decent meal."

Both men stood up, and Rebecca did the same. Hennie hesitated, realizing in that moment Jack hadn't been clear about whether this meeting would include her. She desperately wanted to know what was going on, but she didn't want to be presumptuous. She was relieved when Jack motioned toward her and said, "Come along, my dear. This involves you, as well." His comment seemed to make Rebecca more nervous.

A few minutes later, they were all seated in the study. A large desk was the main feature of one side of the room, but nearer the windows was a sofa and some comfortable chairs where they all sat down in somewhat of a little circle. Hennie was glad that Jack guided her to the sofa, where he sat close beside her and put his arm around her shoulders. George sat so that he could mostly face Rebecca as it became evident he intended to do most of the talking, but Hennie was glad to be able to see both of their faces clearly. She also knew that in many ways, Jack was glad for the way George had so honorably taken on the role as head of the household, and that he was willing and more than capable of speaking for the family and taking the lead in addressing any challenges that might arise. And this challenge was about as big as they came.

"Rebecca," George began, his voice kind and brotherly, "why do you think Letitia has wanted so desperately to marry Jack?"

Rebecca looked surprised by the question but quickly said, "Because she loves him; she always has." She looked at Jack and said with an accusing tone that bore evidence of Letitia's influence, "You've broken her heart, you know. I can't believe you would have done this to her." She glanced at Hennie and said with some kindness, "It's nothing personal against you, Hennie. It's just . . . such a mess."

"Yes, it certainly is," George said.

Jack interjected, "Rebecca, you must understand that no matter how Letitia feels about me, I simply don't love her; I never have, and I never will. Love must go both ways, and I can't in good conscience marry a woman I don't love simply because our father wished it. I need you to understand that."

Rebecca looked away and said nothing. It was as if she wanted to argue but couldn't think of anything to say that would have any merit. Hennie considered the fact that no matter how much Rebecca might be upset that Jack had broken her friend's heart, he *was* married, and that couldn't be changed.

"So," George continued earnestly, "you don't believe Letitia's motives had anything to do with money . . . title . . . prestige?" Rebecca looked up at her brother, astonished. "You don't believe her father might be coaching her, perhaps, to help him gain access to our assets, which are far greater than his?"

"That is the most ridiculous thing I have ever heard!" Rebecca declared angrily, and the brothers exchanged a knowing glance. "Letitia's father is a kind and caring man. He would *never* be a part of any such thing!"

Hennie heard Jack sigh in disgust, and she noticed George discreetly rolling his eyes before he said to his sister, "Then perhaps—since you know Letitia and her father better than the rest of us—you could explain the meaning of these papers delivered to us yesterday by the solicitor representing the Tewksbury family."

George handed the papers to Rebecca. She began to read, then looked confused. She glanced at the next page, then the next before she handed them back to George huffily. "I have no idea what this means. The legal jargon sounds like nonsense."

"Legal jargon can be difficult to understand," George said, "but this is very real and *very* legal. It states that Old Man Tewksbury is suing our family, claiming that we are guilty of what's called breach of contract since Jack didn't marry Letitia. This means that he considers himself cheated out of what he believes is his legal right to a very large portion of our financial assets, which he should have gained upon the marriage between our two families."

"That cannot be right!" Rebecca declared. "It can't!"

"It's all right here," George said holding up the papers.

Rebecca snatched them from his hand and began to read more carefully, visibly determined to prove him wrong. While she was reading, George added, "He's giving us one possible option to avoid the legal suit—where a judge would determine whether we are required to *pay* him an exorbitant amount of money to compensate for his daughter not becoming a part of our family."

"And what is that?" Rebecca asked, looking up from the papers.

"The only other possible way for Letitia to become a part of the family," George said, his voice turning acrid. He leaned toward Rebecca and said, "Tewksbury is insisting that *I* marry Letitia." Rebecca gasped. George leaned a little closer to his sister and added, "So, you tell me, Rebecca, if Letitia's motive is based entirely in love, why would she agree to this arrangement of marrying *me*? I barely know the woman. Has she suddenly had a change of heart? A shift of affection? You're her closest friend. We are very much hoping you can explain this to us. You have spent a great deal of time in their home with their family. Is this the kind of people they are?" Again George slapped the papers, even though Rebecca was holding them.

"There must be a mistake," Rebecca said. "Some kind of misunderstanding."

"If that's the case, perhaps you would like to go with us to visit Letitia and her father and clear all of this up."

Rebecca hesitated, looking afraid, which made Hennie suspect that somewhere in the back of her mind, she knew that Letitia and her father were not all they had appeared to be. Perhaps she *would* side with her brothers, given the evidence before her. George and Jack looked undoubtedly pleased when Rebecca said, "I think that's an excellent idea. We should go today and be done with it. I'm certain we can clear this up."

"I do hope we can," George said. "But we have a condition on this visit, Rebecca."

"What?" she asked, sounding terrified.

"Jack and I have discussed this extensively, and we are both well aware of all the legal implications of our father's will. If you believe Letitia and her father are sincere, we want a chance to prove it. We simply want your support in that. We've come up with a little plan that we hope will bring out Letitia's true nature—one way or the other. All we ask is that you help us carry it out long enough for us to be able to know the truth. But you should know that I— like our brother—will only marry for love. And if that costs us a good portion of the family fortune, so be it. But if Letitia believes otherwise, even for a short time, perhaps we can work this out in a way that's honest and ethical." George paused and tightened his gaze on Rebecca. "I assume you have enough loyalty to your family to want what's right and best for all of us."

"Of course I do!" Rebecca declared as if she might lay down her life right then and there for the sake of honoring the Hannaford name.

"Well, then," George said, tossing a quick smile at Jack, "let's talk about the best way to go about this before we visit the Tewksbury family unannounced— as they have proven so good at doing to us."

Hennie just listened as the men proposed a detailed plan that she could only believe was inspired. She was not only surprised at what they intended to do, but how willing Rebecca was to go along with the scheme. It seemed she was so convinced of Letitia's noble motives—and her father's—that she felt certain the plan would only prove her brothers wrong. But Hennie wondered how Rebecca could reconcile exactly what *that* would mean about Letitia, and the inevitable results. Did she believe Letitia loved George enough to justify marrying him to honor their fathers' wishes? How could she possibly even consider such a possibility when George and Letitia barely knew each other, and Letitia had been declaring her undying love for Jack these many years? Hennie just listened and kept her thoughts to herself, praying that some unforeseen problem might not arise to send this plan awry and only create more havoc. One thing was certain: she and Jack leaving to live elsewhere so they couldn't be found was no longer a possible solution to this problem. Tewksbury had found a way to work around their marriage, and it was no longer the issue. Hennie and Jack would be living here for the rest of their lives, an idea she had grown comfortable with—despite her difficult feelings about something dreadful that had happened in the library during her childhood. She only hoped now that Old Man Tewksbury—as the men always called him—didn't find some way to maneuver around this plan and leave George doomed to face Jack's fate of being faced with the choice of either marrying Letitia or running away and living in hiding. The very idea of sharing this house with Letitia Tewksbury made Hennie shudder, and she prayed it would never come to that.

⚮

Old Man Tewksbury's enthusiastic delight over hearing that George would agree to marry Letitia was not lessened in the slightest over hearing that George would do so on the condition that Letitia would be expected to conform to the way the rest of the family lived. Letitia appeared mildly concerned over the comment, but at the same time, she was preoccupied with tossing George flirtatious glances—which he entirely ignored. George insisted that Letitia move into Ivy Manor immediately and become accustomed to their lifestyle so that he could be assured their agreement would work out. Letitia's father completely ignored any evidence from his daughter that she might have an opinion on the matter. He simply assured George that his daughter would gladly comply with whatever might be expected of her. The thought was a little sickening, considering that Tewksbury really had no idea what kind of husband George might be, or how his daughter might be treated. He only wanted what he considered legally his.

George insisted that the old man sign a legal document declaring that if his daughter didn't hold up her part of the bargain in any way, the agreement between Tewksbury and his father would be considered null and void.

After tense minutes of Tewksbury studying the document in his hand, he called for a servant to bring him pen and ink and he signed the paper, handing it back to George, who smiled and said, "We will expect Letitia and her personal belongings at the manor tomorrow before tea."

"As you wish," Tewksbury said with the triumph of a military general who had just won a great battle, oblivious to the lives that had been lost.

A few minutes later, they were on their way home in the carriage, and George said, "I don't think that could have possibly gone any better."

After minutes of silence, Rebecca said with concern, "She doesn't love you, George."

They all looked at her with some astonishment. "I know that," George said, "and I don't love her."

"So . . . what if the remainder of this . . . scheme of yours doesn't go the way you expect it to go? What if Letitia responds to all of this differently than you're expecting her to? Or what if she's more afraid of her father than the reality of life with our family?"

"You know her better than any of us," George said, "or so you believe. What do *you* think she will do?"

Rebecca bit her lip for a few seconds before she looked out the window and said, "I don't know. I honestly don't know." She sighed loudly. "Perhaps you were right; perhaps I don't know her as well as I think I do."

"I suppose we shall see," George said, and he also turned to look out the window.

Hennie shared a concerned glance with Jack before they both did the same and silently turned to take in the view as the carriage drew closer to home.

❧

Before the household settled in for the night, Ivy Manor had undergone very little transformation in its management and work assignments—but it was enough to be prepared for Letitia Tewksbury's arrival the following day. Hennie found it interesting how very little had to be adjusted for their plan to be executed, and she was pleasantly surprised with how eager Rebecca was to completely immerse herself in a new lifestyle, willing to work alongside the servants of the household. Hennie wasn't certain if Rebecca believed all of this would prove Letitia's true character was what she'd always believed it to be, and that her friend would end up marrying George. Or perhaps somewhere deep down, Rebecca knew the truth, and she hoped this would prove her brothers right and they could be free of Letitia for good. Maybe Rebecca had become weary of all the pretending and falseness with Letitia and she longed for a good reason to be free of it. Hennie could only guess because Rebecca wasn't interested in having any serious conversation about it whatsoever. But she made no protests about following through with their plan, and she had a quiet solemnity about her that implied she had a great deal on her mind. Late that night as Hennie and Jack held each other close in the darkness and talked, they both agreed that Rebecca's deep thoughts meant she was coming to see the truth about Letitia and her father. They could only hope, and they knew that tomorrow they would begin carrying out a plan that would be anything but easy. With any luck—and God's blessings—their plan would actually succeed.

Chapter Eighteen

BLACKMAIL

THE FOLLOWING AFTERNOON WHEN LETITIA arrived, she was met only by Mrs. Reeves, who had the young lady's belongings taken up to her room. The housekeeper escorted Letitia to the beautiful bedroom, which wasn't far from the location of Rebecca's room. But on the bed, clothing had been laid out for Letitia to change into so that she could get to work.

For the next three days, Letitia worked alongside Hennie, Lottie, and Rebecca in the laundry and the kitchen, wherever extra help was needed. At first, she remained mostly silent, even though it was evident she felt furious, and she asked Rebecca if this was truly how her family lived.

"We haven't spent every minute of our lives together," Rebecca told her, "so you couldn't possibly know how our family has lived." Hennie overheard and winked at Lottie; it was, after all, a true statement. And Hennie was proud of Rebecca when she added, "I believe it's good for us to all work together—at least some of the time—so we can appreciate all that we have in common, and how very blessed we are."

Letitia finally closed her astonished mouth and got back to work. In the afternoon the family shared tea without changing out of their working clothes, but after some more work, they all cleaned up before supper. Letitia was dismayed, however, that a lady's maid had not been provided for her. George simply told her that he'd assumed her father would have sent someone to assist her, but Letitia made no comment. Apparently her father wasn't concerned about his daughter's personal needs in *any* regard.

Letitia's complaining gradually grew more frequent and boisterous, until on the fourth day she burst out with a tantrum so childish and astonishing that every woman in the laundry could only stare at her as if the entire room had become frozen except for Letitia. At her insistence, she and her belongings were delivered back to her father that very afternoon, and she left Ivy Manor with the declaration that she would rather die than marry into such a family.

Soon after Letitia's dramatic departure, the family gathered for tea, and Hennie was surprised to hear Rebecca say with some relief, "I hope that will be the end of it."

"I truly believe it's at least the beginning of the end," Jack added.

Hennie looked directly at her sister-in-law and said gently, "This must be very difficult for you, Rebecca. You've handled the entire situation so beautifully, but I know it can't have been easy."

Rebecca sighed loudly, and it would be impossible to not see the moisture that rose in her eyes. But she pulled back her shoulders and said, "It *has* been difficult, but a part of me feels more at peace than I have for a long time. I think something in me always doubted her sincerity, but I ignored such thoughts and convinced myself she would never do anything to hurt our family. I know she's afraid of her father and would do anything he asked of her, but I also know she personally coveted all that we have. I look back now and see many signs of how she imagined herself somehow becoming queen of this place, and I shudder to think what that might have been like for all of us."

"The Queen of Tookle-Berry," Jack said with irony.

Rebecca chuckled humorlessly. "I'd forgotten we used to call her that."

"I still do," Jack declared more lightly, and Rebecca chuckled again, this time with less sadness.

"I wonder what will happen next," Hennie said. "I wish I could be in the room when Letitia tells her father how horribly she's been treated here." She couldn't hold back a little laugh. "And I'd really love to see the look on his face when he realizes what this means regarding the document George had him sign. For all that Letitia is intimidated by her father, I believe he also spoils her very much, and he will not be able to force her to go back on what she just announced to us—even if he could do so legally."

"Let's hope that's the case," Rebecca said and turned her attention back to her tea. Since Hennie was very hungry—as she usually was with her pregnancy—she did the same. Jack and George followed her example.

The following afternoon at tea, there had still been no word from Letitia's father or his evil solicitor. After speculating a little about how things might be going in the Tewksbury household, Jack said to his brother, "Do you think this means he'll come up with another way to torment us? Once he's had some time to think about it, I can't imagine him *not* trying some other scheme."

"He can try," George said, "but I truly don't believe there is anything else he can do."

"Oh, I hope not!" Rebecca declared with a vehemence that took the others by surprise, despite growing evidence that she'd changed her opinions. She began to cry before she murmured, "I'm so sorry—so very, very sorry. I pray you can all forgive me."

Jack and George quickly stood up and sat on either side of their sister while words tumbled out of her mouth about her years of confusion and uneasiness regarding her friendship with Letitia, all the while sincerely believing that her friend was deeply in love with Jack. When she could no longer talk, due to all her crying, each of Rebecca's brothers embraced her and offered firm reassurance that they understood, and all was forgiven, which only made Rebecca cry harder. When she had finally regained her composure, Rebecca stood and crossed the room to sit down right next to Hennie. Rebecca took Hennie's hand, declaring with a sniffle, "And I must apologize to you, as well. I can see how happy you've made Jack, and I'm so glad you're a part of our family. I hope you can forgive me for being unkind in the past."

"Of course," Hennie said sincerely, which elicited more tears from Rebecca, but Hennie just put her arms around her sister-in-law and let her cry.

That evening was likely the most pleasant supper the family had enjoyed since Jack and Hennie had come back to Ivy Manor as husband and wife. Despite wondering how Old Man Tewksbury might still try to create upheaval in their lives, they all agreed they had come a long way and the most daunting obstacles were behind them. Rebecca said more than once how wonderful it was to have Jack home again, and to have Hennie with him. Hennie hoped this meant they might be able to grow closer as sisters, but that remained to be seen. For now, she was simply grateful for Rebecca's kindness and acceptance.

The following morning, they were barely finished with breakfast when a maid announced that the evil King of Tewksbury and his solicitor were demanding to see both George and Jack. Of course, the maid didn't call him the evil king, but that's what passed through Hennie's mind, and she felt certain Jack had the same thought. She knew the intensity of her husband's anger toward this man—which was deeply tangled into the anger he felt toward his father. They were both grateful that George—in his rightful place as the heir—was obligated to speak for Jack and the whole of the Hannaford estate; Jack had told Hennie he feared he would allow his anger to take over and he would say something he would regret, and Hennie couldn't deny the same thing had crossed her mind.

"Let's get this over with," George said as he stood and tossed his napkin to the table with force. "You ladies are welcome to join us . . . or not."

"Oh, I'm coming!" Rebecca declared as if she wouldn't miss it.

Rebecca and Jack both came to their feet abruptly, but it took Hennie more effort to stand—along with a little help from Jack. "Thank you," she whispered as they exchanged a brief smile and a quick kiss once she was standing. "I'd never manage without your help," she whispered, "but then . . . it's your fault I'm in this condition."

"Indeed it is," he said, his smile widening, as if facing Tewksbury were the furthest thing from his mind.

They all went together to the drawing room, where their unwanted visitors were waiting. They'd barely entered before the evil king launched into a tirade about how badly his daughter had been treated and he intended to seek retribution. Jack and George stood to face Tewksbury and Hobbs while Rebecca helped Hennie sit down and then sat close beside her on a little sofa where they could observe.

More than once Hennie found it difficult to not laugh as Letitia's father described his daughter's experience at Ivy Manor, and the trauma that had been inflicted upon her. But when she realized Rebecca too was finding it hard not to find the situation funny, Hennie felt a growing bond with her sister-in-law—at least in regard to their disdain of Tewksbury and his spoiled daughter. It was easy to imagine how Letitia must have whimpered and sobbed to her father, likely exaggerating the situation immensely.

Once Tewksbury had finished his angry speech, George calmly reminded him of the document he'd signed, agreeing that if Letitia did not do what was required to live in the Hannaford household, all legalities regarding a marriage between the two families would no longer be valid.

At that very moment, Mr. Hobbs snapped a paper in front of George, stating with his typical snide persona, "We will let a judge determine that, sir. Arrangements have been made for us to appear in court tomorrow. The information is all here."

While George was glancing at the document, Hennie marveled over the amount of influence Mr. Hobbs apparently had with the courts that allowed him to schedule appointments before a judge in so little time. But they had already discussed this possibility, and they knew what to do. Hennie just hoped that *this* part of their plan went as predictably as Letitia's response to being cajoled into doing servants' work.

Before George had a chance to read even a portion of what was written on the paper he was holding, Tewksbury growled in a voice that chilled Hennie so deeply she shuddered and felt suddenly nauseous. "You have no idea of what I am capable of doing to you!"

"I think I'm going to be ill," Hennie whispered to Rebecca.

"Me as well," Rebecca whispered back, but Hennie felt certain her sister-in-law had no idea what was going on inside of Hennie in that moment. It took everything she had to remain focused on what was taking place in the room.

George stepped so abruptly toward Tewksbury that the old man looked visibly frightened. George's advantage of height became evident with the way he looked down at the old man as he said with all the power of the Lord of the manor, and all the courage of a great warrior, "Not without breaking the law. Now, get out of here, and don't you *ever* step foot on Hannaford land again. *Ever!*"

Tewksbury looked unnerved, but he still snarled, "We'll see what a judge has to say about this."

"Yes, let's see about that," George retorted, and the old man huffed out of the house with Hobbs hurrying after him, not looking quite as smug as he usually did.

The very moment their uninvited guests were headed out of the room, Hennie stood and hurried toward a different door, fearing she might lose the contents of her stomach as her thoughts churned so quickly they made her dizzy. Once in the hallway, she regretted standing up so fast when a light-headedness overcame her, and she feared passing out more than the impact of her nausea.

"What is it, dearest?" she heard Rebecca say, sounding far away even though Hennie could feel Rebecca's hands on her arms. "Good heavens!" Rebecca added more loudly as Hennie began to fall and Rebecca barely managed to help keep her upright.

"What's wrong?" Jack demanded as two sets of men's footsteps made it evident Jack and George had noticed the hasty retreat of the women. "Hennie, what is it?" Jack asked, scooping her into his arms.

"She almost fainted," Rebecca reported with concern.

Hennie was aware of Jack carrying her, but otherwise she was lost inside her own mind as frightening memories brutally assaulted her. She felt herself being laid down on a sofa, but had no idea how far her husband had taken her, or which room they were in.

Hennie kept her hand over her eyes in an attempt to regain her equilibrium. She fought to sort out her thoughts and steady her breathing while Jack whispered reassuring words close to her ear. When Hennie finally felt the beat of her heart and the rhythm of her breathing return to almost normal, she slowly moved her hand and opened her eyes, glad to note the dizziness had relented. She looked up to see Rebecca seated on the edge of the sofa beside her, holding Hennie's hand, looking as if she were barely managing not to cry. George was standing nearby, looking as distressed as she had ever seen him—and she had certainly seen him endure a great deal of distress. Jack was kneeling on the floor beside her, looking even more concerned than his brother. When her eyes met his, he asked, "What is it, darling? What happened? Should I send for the doctor or—"

"No, it's nothing like that," she assured him, glad to know she could speak freely with her husband's siblings present. Despite how minimally she and Rebecca had interacted, Hennie knew Rebecca was aware of Hennie's difficulties regarding the frightening memories buried in her mind; it had come up more than once at meals they had shared. Hennie looked at George and said, "Sit down. You're making me nervous."

George immediately did so, as if she were a queen and he was only too eager to follow her orders. Hennie looked directly at Jack again and said, "It all came back to me—all of it. When Old Man Tewksbury said what he did . . . about . . ." She lowered her voice to imitate him. *"You have no idea of what I am capable of doing to you!"* Hennie then shuddered and eased a little closer to Jack, again closing her eyes as if that might help block out the impact of the memory those words had triggered. She forced herself to continue her explanation, even though her voice was trembling. "I heard him say those exact words . . . in the library . . . when I was a child."

"It was *him*?" Jack asked. "He's the one who created this problem for you?"

"He was there," Hennie said, still keeping her eyes closed; she found it easier to talk about this without having to look at the expressions of her loved ones. "But he was arguing with your father." She opened her eyes only long enough to dart a quick glance toward each of the three children of the man who had frightened her so badly that she had forced all memory of the incident into a place in her mind so deep and dark that she had likely hoped to never think of it again. But after many weeks of threatening their way forward, the memories had suddenly exploded into her conscious mind, and Hennie was still finding it difficult to keep from feeling dizzy. Once again, she put a hand over her eyes, as if she could shield herself from the full impact of her memories, even as she repeated them to her expectant audience.

"It's all right," Jack said after too much silence had passed. "You're safe here with us. There's nothing to be afraid of."

"I know," Hennie said and felt tears leak from the corners of her eyes, trickling into her hair. Her hope that they hadn't been noticed faltered when she felt Jack wipe them away with his fingers.

"Just tell us what you remembered and be done with it," Jack encouraged gently.

Hennie nodded but remained hidden behind her hand. "The two men came into the library where my mother was cleaning, and they ordered her to leave, which she did, but she couldn't reveal that I was behind the sofa on the floor, reading. But she'd told me what to do if any such thing ever happened. I crept carefully beneath a table and remained completely silent. I didn't understand what they were arguing about, but they were both very angry. I can't recall the words exactly, but I can remember now that the two of them had both gotten very drunk at a pub while they'd been traveling together, and afterward there had been a brawl with another man on the street. The fight had resulted in this man's death." Hennie heard all three of her listeners gasp in unison, but she kept going before she lost the strength required to get all of this out. "Tewksbury made it clear that your father was the one who had been fighting with the man who'd died and was therefore directly responsible. However, because Tewksbury had been there and witnessed it—and not reported it—he could also be in a great deal of trouble; therefore, they needed to keep each other's secret. However, Tewksbury was threatening your father, holding this knowledge over him as leverage."

"Blackmail?" Jack asked, sounding appalled and angry, but Hennie just nodded to affirm that he was right.

"He insisted on the absolute guarantee that his daughter be married to the Hannaford heir; that it was the only thing that would keep Tewksbury from reporting what he knew."

"That our father was guilty of murder?" George muttered, his tone somewhere between horrified and a child wanting to cry. Hennie heard Rebecca sniffle and knew she was crying.

"I remember hearing Tewksbury saying those same words he said today: *'You have no idea of what I am capable of doing to you!'* And then he left the room. The problem was that I thought *both* men had left the room, so I crept out from beneath the table, only to find your father glaring down at me." Hennie became so upset she couldn't speak; in fact, she could hardly breathe. Jack eased closer and gathered her into his arms, whispering soothing words while the sound of Rebecca's sniffling increased, and Hennie could hear George pacing—as he always did when he was upset.

The full torrent of this traumatic childhood experience came bubbling out of Hennie on a wave of sobbing that made it difficult for her to breathe. Between heaving breaths and torrential tears, Hennie managed to tell her husband and his siblings how their father had lifted her off the floor by holding to her arms so hard that he'd left bruises from his fingers, bruises she had kept hidden from her mother. He'd told her that if she ever breathed a word of what she'd heard to anyone—anyone at all—he would hurt her mother. And he'd insisted that she forget that any of this had ever happened. And so she had.

Hennie felt indescribable relief once she'd shared everything she'd remembered, and the very fact that she *had* remembered added to her relief. She held more tightly to Jack and managed to calm down while he kept her in the security of his embrace. She heard him and his siblings talking softly about what a heathen their father had been, and their astonishment that this entire situation with Tewksbury was rooted in something horrible that had happened when they'd all been children. Hennie agreed with everything they were saying but was too spent to speak. She was finally able to ease away from Jack and sit up straight when she heard him say, "That's why he sent you away, Hennie."

"What?" she asked, disoriented and trying not to feel embarrassed by how upset she had been in front of George and Rebecca.

"That's why he refused to allow *you* to stay here, when he allowed another child in the same situation to stay. You knew something that he desperately needed to remain a secret, and it made him uncomfortable. So, when your mother died, he promptly and conveniently sent you to an orphanage."

"Despicable fiend!" George murmured hotly.

Rebecca added through fresh tears, "It's a wonder any of us survived being his children without turning into monsters."

"It's a miracle," Hennie said, putting her head again on Jack's chest. "You're all so wonderful; I couldn't ask for a better family."

"And I couldn't ask for a better sister," Rebecca said, which urged Hennie to turn and look at her. "I'm so sorry for what you went through, dearest, but we have our whole lives to make up for it."

"Amen," George said.

Jack pressed a kiss to Hennie's brow, then insisted she needed to get some rest. Feeling less dizzy and ill now, Hennie was able to walk up the stairs with Jack's assistance, and within minutes he had tucked her into bed, again kissing her brow.

"Are you all right?" he asked.

"Much better now, if you must know," she said, taking in a deep breath and letting it out slowly. "I feel . . . lighter." She laughed softly. "Contrary to this enormous child of yours growing inside of me."

"It *is* my fault," he said with a chuckle before his brow furrowed intensely. "Hennie, my darling, I'm so . . . so sorry for all the grief my father brought into your life."

"You have nothing to apologize for, Jack. You've never treated me with any-thing but perfect kindness and respect. And that comes from *you*," she touched the center of his chest, "not him."

"Still . . . he was a despicable man."

"Yes, he was. But we are going to forgive him and get on with our lives; we are going to put all this behind us and live happily ever after."

"I hope the judge agrees with you," Jack said, managing to maintain a bright countenance. It seemed evident he'd come to believe all would be well.

⸺✦⸺

Hennie slept better than she had in weeks, with a complete absence of bad dreams. But she still felt immensely tired the following morning and was glad that Jack insisted she remain home and rest while the others took care of what they hoped would be the last of any legal drama with Old Man Tewksbury. Given the new information that had come forth from Hennie's previously lost memories, Jack and George both felt confident that Tewksbury could be easily influenced into letting the matter go—for good.

Not long after Jack left with his brother and sister, Hennie was glad to have Lottie come to visit. While Hennie remained in bed, she was able to tell her friend all that had happened since they'd talked a couple of days ago. Lottie was amazed and compassionate and immensely pleased that Hennie was finally free of what had been haunting her. They shared lunch in Hennie's room before Lottie went to the guest room she often used, and they both took a much-needed nap. Later in the afternoon, they shared tea together before Lottie had to leave when Zeke's shift ended in the stables. Hennie had expected Jack and the others to have returned home by now. She hoped and prayed that all had gone well, and that she would never need to hear the name Tewksbury spoken in this house ever again.

⸺✦⸺

During the journey into town, Jack was able to speak candidly with his siblings about all they had learned about their father from Hennie's memories, and was grateful to have their full support in whatever it took to have Tewksbury expelled from their lives forever. He especially appreciated how Rebecca had come to see the truth; it was obvious that her involvement and cooperation in this endeavor was genuine and heartfelt.

They arrived at the courthouse early as they had hoped, but they hadn't waited in the hallway long when they saw Tewksbury and Hobbs a short distance away.

"The opportunity we were hoping for," George said to Jack. He then said to Rebecca, "You're welcome to join us, or—"

"Oh, I wouldn't miss this for the world," Rebecca said and laughed, which helped Jack feel more delighted than angry.

Even though George—by right of inheriting the title—had taken the lead in nearly every encounter related to this situation, Jack had respectfully asked his brother for the opportunity to say what needed to be said to Tewksbury before they went before the judge—and George had been glad to comply.

With his siblings flanking him, Jack approached Tewksbury and asked, "Might we have a private word?"

"You may speak plainly with my solicitor present," Tewksbury said with his typical snobbish disdain.

"I can assure you," Jack said more quietly to the old man, "you do not want Hobbs or anyone else to hear what I have to say."

Tewksbury looked surprised but waved his hand as if he were flicking away a fly, and Hobbs walked away. "Get on with it!" he snapped.

"Some new information has come to light," Jack said, unable to keep from smirking. "You see . . . it seems you and our father had an argument that preceded the concoction of this ludicrous marriage stipulation in his will—something about someone . . . dying." Tewksbury looked astonished and downright frightened, his face taking on an ashen hue that was a stark contrast to the angry purple he usually wore. "The thing is," Jack said, "the two of you thought you were alone, but you weren't. The child of a servant had been hiding in the library and overheard the conversation. That child is now an adult and recently came forward, more than happy to testify. Of course, with the dozens of servants at Ivy Manor—and those who have moved away but are still aware of the situation—it would be impossible for you to know *who* it might be. And I suspect you would prefer that this person remain silent and not come forward." Still Tewksbury didn't speak, and Jack found himself enjoying this very much—perhaps far too much. "So, this is how it's going to work. You're going to tell the judge the matter is settled—permanently—and you will never cause the tiniest problem for our family *ever* again, or we will be speaking with the police and . . . well, who knows what skeletons might be found in your closets?" Jack lowered his voice and had no trouble sounding menacing as he repeated Tewksbury's own words back to him, "You have no idea of what I am capable of doing to you!"

Tewksbury remained mute and ashen long enough for Jack to smile at him as if they'd just discussed an upcoming social event. He turned and walked away with George and Rebecca at his sides, feeling better about life than he had in a very, very long time.

"Excellent!" George said softly with a chuckle.

"I've never been prouder to be a Hannaford," Rebecca added.

Only minutes later they were informed that their case would not be going before the judge because the legal action had been dismissed. Jack's relief almost didn't feel real. He'd lived with the threat of what Tewksbury could do to them for so long that he hardly knew how to exist without it. But he was looking forward to finding out.

Rebecca declared that after they had some lunch they were going shopping to get some much-needed new things for the baby. Jack enjoyed every minute with his brother and sister, but he couldn't wait to get home to tell Hennie the good news.

When they finally arrived back at the manor in the early evening, Jack hurried up to the room he shared with Hennie and found her sitting up in bed, just as he'd left her, but she looked a little paler.

"Are you all right?" he asked after kissing her in greeting.

"I'm fine," she insisted. "Tell me what happened. I can't bear the suspense another moment."

Jack told her the entire story, finishing with the triumphant declaration, "And so we shall never have to deal with the evil king again."

"Oh, I'm so glad to hear it," she said and grimaced slightly—not for the first time since he'd started rambling about the happenings of the day. "Because I'm in labor," she added with a mischievous smile.

"What?" he demanded. "Why didn't you say something? Are you—"

"Calm down," she said. "The pains are still several minutes apart, the doctor has been sent for, and the maids are gathering everything I will need." She squeezed his hand and smiled. "I love you, Jack Hannaford—and I'm going to have your baby."

"I love you too, Henrietta Hannaford," he said and kissed her, "and nothing could make me happier—except perhaps having it over with."

"I can agree with that," Hennie said and urged him to kiss her again, as if it might give her strength for the inevitable difficulty ahead.

HENNIE GAVE BIRTH TO A healthy baby girl, enduring her labor with Lottie holding her hand, and assisted by women who had been a part of her childhood. Jack and Hennie's daughter was welcomed into the household with so much love and adoration that Hennie somehow believed the happiness of this child's life could literally compensate for all the misery of her own. In fact, while Hennie was contemplating this very thing, Jack admitted to her—while watching his daughter in awe—that he'd found it much easier to let go of his ill feelings toward his father since he'd become a father himself. Nothing would ever make the behavior of Jack's father right, but with the difficult circumstances he'd caused now behind them, it just didn't seem to matter anymore. They had each other, and they had this beautiful child. Hennie doubted that life could ever be better.

Rebecca was so taken with the baby that she often declared being an aunt was one of the greatest aspects of her life. Her sisters both had children, but they lived too far away to be a part of Rebecca's life. While she doted on the new baby, she and Hennie became much closer, and Hennie began to feel as if they truly were sisters. Not only was Hennie pleased by Rebecca's complete acceptance, but she also loved seeing Rebecca so much happier than she had likely ever been.

While Hennie was recovering from childbirth and following the doctor's orders to remain in bed as much as possible, she specifically requested that Clara bring her meals from the kitchen. With George's permission to discuss the situation candidly, Hennie asked Clara to sit and talk with her, and she shared her own feelings about being the daughter of a servant woman, now married to Jack Hannaford. Clara was at first taken aback but quickly softened and began to cry. After they'd had the chance to visit four or five times, Hennie schemed to have George waiting in the sitting room when Clara came to Hennie's bedroom with a supper tray. Clara's initial surprise quickly turned to visible relief, and it was evident she'd missed George and the time they'd once spent together. They left to take a walk, holding hands, and Hennie felt quite pleased with her matchmaking skills, and she hoped George and Clara would be able to work out their differences and find happiness together.

Lottie and Zeke had also received their own daughter, and as soon as the new mothers were recovered enough to travel back and forth, they relished caring for their babies together while their husbands were busy with their work. Never in all their wildest dreams could they have imagined becoming mothers at the same time, nor had they ever envisioned living such a grand life. Zeke continued working in the stables—but it was common for Jack and George to spend time there working as well. Zeke and Lottie began sharing more meals with the family on the days he worked, and they became more and more like a part of the family.

As the babies grew and both became adorably plump and full of smiles, Rebecca began making more of an effort to get out and socialize. She attended ladies' teas and fancy balls, where she made more than one new friend and also gained a few possible suitors. Hennie was pleased to see this change in her sister-in-law's life and was especially pleased with the way that Rebecca felt completely indifferent about what Letitia might be doing with *her* life. Although none of them were surprised to hear that Letitia was being courted by a baronet. The family discussed it for about a minute, only long enough to agree that they felt sorry for him.

After the smithy had remained empty and unused for months, Jack finally got a response to the regular advertisements he'd been putting in numerous newspapers. He was able to work out a fair deal with a blacksmith who had come with his wife and five children quite some distance after having lost nearly everything in a fire. Jack and George not only made certain they received a warm welcome, they organized a project in the community to gather donations, so that the new blacksmith and his family had everything they needed to start over in a new location. The situation prompted Jack and Hennie to reminisce over their many good memories at the smithy and its attached living quarters, but they agreed it was obviously the right home for this new family, and they were both glad to now be settled at the manor and not living under false identities.

On the first really warm day of summer, the entire Hannaford family—which now included Zeke, Lottie, and their daughter—walked the short distance from the manor to the beach. Hennie had recently mentioned to Jack how her mother would often take her to the beach for a picnic on her day off, and she'd not once been there since her return. When she'd been working as a stable hand, she'd been afraid going to the beach would only awaken difficult memories. And the weather had been cold when she'd returned here as Jack's wife. Now that they had a perfect day for such an outing, the family was making a rather elaborate event out of the opportunity. They talked and laughed throughout the trek away from the manicured gardens of Ivy Manor and down to the beach, where the waves rushed in and out over the sand with methodical rhythm.

Once they had picked a pleasant spot and had blankets spread out, Rebecca asked, "Where is George? I'm ashamed to say I didn't even notice he was missing until now." She giggled like a child. "But don't tell him."

"He's coming," Jack reported. "He had something to take care of, but I believe he'll be here soon."

They all sprawled out on the blankets beneath large umbrellas that protected them from the sun while they ate the food they'd brought with them in hampers packed by Mrs. Helton and her assistants. The babies—as usual—were the center of attention, with every funny noise or silly expression drawing great interest from the adults. A bout of laughter was interrupted by George calling, "You can start the party now; I'm here."

"The party is over, brother," Jack said the same moment they all realized George hadn't come alone. The men jumped respectfully to their feet as George approached, holding Clara's hand in his.

"Hello," everyone said almost at the same time in a haphazard chorus.

"I believe you all know Clara," George said, "or know of her."

That haphazard chorus was repeated.

"And I believe she knows all of you—or knows of you," George added, looking at Clara, who nodded slightly in apparent agreement. "But what you *don't* know is that she has finally taken pity on me and agreed to be my wife, so . . ."

George couldn't get another word out as everyone jumped to their feet in a flurry of excitement, overwhelming George and Clara with congratulations and hugs. Hennie noticed how overcome Clara seemed initially, but within a few minutes she was seated on a blanket next to George with food being passed to them while lighthearted conversation ensued, and Clara seemed to relax. Hennie knew it would take very little time for Clara to realize how comfortable they could all be together, even as mixed-up of a group as they were. Within minutes it became evident Clara was beginning to realize that very thing, and she seemed completely relaxed.

While Hennie was admiring the obvious adoration George and Clara had for each other, she was surprised when Jack kissed her unexpectedly.

"What was that for?" she laughed.

"Everything," he said and laughed with her. "Just . . . everything."

ANITA STANSFIELD HAS MORE THAN fifty published books and is the recipient of many awards, including two Lifetime Achievement Awards. Her books go far beyond being enjoyable, memorable stories. Anita resonates particularly well with a broad range of devoted readers because of her sensitive and insightful examination of contemporary issues that are faced by many of those readers, even when her venue is a historical romance. Readers come away from her compelling stories equipped with new ideas about how to enrich their own lives, regardless of their circumstances.

Anita was born and raised in Provo, Utah. She is the mother of five and has a growing number of grandchildren. She also writes for the general trade market under the name Elizabeth D. Michaels.

For more information and a complete list of her publications, go to anitastansfield.blogspot.com or anitastansfield.com, where you can sign up to receive email updates. You can also follow her on Facebook and Twitter.